IRISH
GOLD

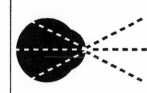

This Large Print Book carries the
Seal of Approval of N.A.V.H.

IRISH GOLD

Andrew M. Greeley

Thorndike Press • Thorndike, Maine

Published in 1995 by arrangement with St. Martin's Press, Inc.

Thorndike Large Print ® Basic Series.

The tree indicium is a trademark of Thorndike Press.

The text of this Large Print edition is unabridged. Other aspects of the book may vary from the original edition.

Set in 16 pt. News Plantin.

Printed in the United States on permanent paper.

Library of Congress Cataloging in Publication Data

Greeley, Andrew M., 1928–
   Irish gold / Andrew M. Greeley.
     p.   cm.
   ISBN 0-7862-0404-4 (lg. print : hc)
   1. Irish Americans — Travel — Ireland — Dublin — Fiction.
2. Man-woman relationships — Ireland — Dublin — Fiction.
3. Ireland — Politics and government — Fiction. 4. Violence —
Ireland — Dublin — Fiction. 5. Dublin (Ireland) — Fiction.
6. Large type books. I. Title.
[PS3557.R358I75 1995]
813'.54—dc20   94-45646

For Andrew, Neil, Kathryn, Kristine,
Nora, Brigit, *et al.*

The description of Ireland in the time of the Troubles in this book is historically accurate. However, the story of the Galway Brigade of the Irregulars, its achievements, leaders, and conflicts, is the work of my imagination. There were no real-life counterparts of either Daniel O'Kelly or William Ready.

Moreover, as far as I know, nothing like the Consort of St. George and St. Patrick or any of its members actually exists.

The death of Michael Collins continues to be a mystery. My attempt to explain it is a work of imagination, not a description of what actually happened but of what might have happened.

A chronology of the Troubles appears at the end of the book.

Lovers should treat one another like shy children.
— Ingmar Bergman

Young lovers think they have forever
Hormones, however, have social origins
Intent and consequences.

Private minutes of affection
Celebrated in ecstatic interludes of
    spring freedoms
Inevitably involve the families from
    which they come
And the family toward which they
    are going.
— Patrick O'Connor

The tragedy of his death went far beyond the manner of it or the place where it occurred, and far beyond the killing in combat of a young Irishman of notable appearance and physique. . . . he was a guerrilla genius and much more besides. At the age of thirty-one, and in a public life of barely five years, he was already a national and international figure. Greatness had touched him, leaving him on the threshold of a career that could well have brought him to heights to which no Irishman before him had attained. It was in such terms that the common people of Ireland thought of him, expecting that his gallantry, his leadership, and the gifts of organization and statesmanship he was displaying would surely be at their service for many years to come. . . . the most tragic element in Collins's death was that it occurred at all, for it was as unnecessary as the bitter and furious civil war which the compassionate realist strove so hard and risked so much to avoid.

— Leon O'Broin, *Michael Collins* (1980)

"Between 11:00 and 11:15 P.M. there was a knock on the door of my house. My housekeeper answered it. She called me and said I was wanted outside. A soldier and a civilian, who lived locally, were standing at the doorway. The soldier asked me to come outside as there was a soldier shot.

"It was a dark night and the soldier carried in his hand an old carbide lamp which was giving a very bad light. I walked out to the roadway where the convoy had stopped. There was a soldier lying flat with his head lying on the lap of a young officer. The young officer was crying and sobbing and did not speak.

"There was blood on the side of the dead man's face. I said an Act of Contrition and other prayers and made the Sign of the Cross. I told the officer to wait till I got the Holy Oils. I went to the house but when I returned the convoy had gone."

— *Testimony of a parish priest in West Cork*

North Channel

Atlantic Ocean

U L S T E R

Belfast

Irish Sea

Maamene
Maam Cross
Lough CORRIB
Moucheread
Golam head
Lettermullen
Costelloe
Carraroe
Galway
Salt hill

Dublin

the Curragh

River Shannon

Ennis

Limerick

St. George's Channel

Killarney
Mallow
Macroom CORK
Crookstown
Bandon
Cobh
Clonakilty
Skibbereen

N

0   25   50
miles

Ireland

PLH 1994

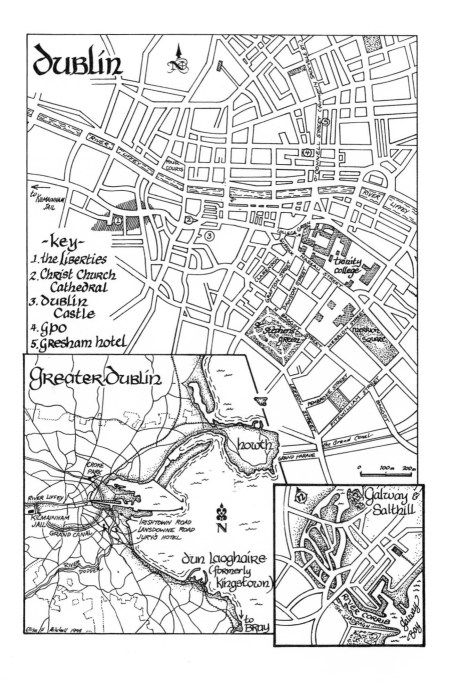

– 1 –

"The Irish," I insisted to the black-haired young woman whose face might have belonged to a pre-Christian Celtic goddess, "are different. They look like some of the rest of us and they speak a language that's remotely like ours. Many of them even have the same names as we do. But they're different — almost like aliens from another planet."

I've never met a pre-Christian Celtic goddess, but the girl looked like the images I formed in my head when I read the ancient sagas.

"*Pissantgobshite.*" She peered at me over her dark glass of Guinness, mildly offended but intrigued.

Not very goddesslike language, huh?

I had sworn off women, for excellent reasons I thought. But, as my brother George the priest had insisted, the hormones tend to be irresistible.

"Womanly charms," George had observed, "are not of enormous moment compared to intelligence and personality. However, especially for the tumescent young male, they must be reckoned as not completely trivial."

That's the way George talks.

I avoided the distraction of telling my Irish goddess that the words of her scatological response ran together like a phrase in the writings of her man Jimmy Joyce. I was homesick, baffled, and a little frightened. My body ached in a hundred places from the brawl on Baggot Street the day before. I was worried that Pa, my beloved grandfather, might have been a terrorist and a murderer when he was a young man. I wanted some sympathy.

Womanly sympathy.

Young womanly sympathy.

"That's an example of what I mean." I leaned forward so she could hear me over the noise of the student-filled pub — O'Neill's, on Suffolk Street across from St. Andrew's Church (C. of I., which means Anglican). "What did you say your name is?"

"I didn't." She frowned, a warning signal that I had interrupted her pursuit of world economics and that, if I didn't mind me manners, she would stalk away from the table.

"Mine's Dermot," I said brightly. "Dermot Coyne, Dermot *Michael* Coyne — son of the dark stranger, as you probably know."

"Fockingrichyank."

The child — she was twenty at the most — was strikingly beautiful. At least her cream-white face and breast-length black hair promised great beauty. The rest of her was encased in a gray sweatshirt with "Dublin Millennium" in dark blue letters, jeans, and a dark blue cloth jacket with a hood — not goddess clothes, exactly. Her face, slender and fine-boned, was the

14

sort that stares at you from the covers of women's magazines — except that the cover women don't usually have a haunting hint in their deep blue eyes of bogs and druids and old Irish poetry. The bottom half of her face was a sweeping, elegant curve which almost demanded that male fingers caress it with reassurance and affection. However, the center of the curve was a solid chin that warned trespassing, or potentially trespassing, male fingers that they had better not offend this young woman or they would be in deep trouble.

I'm a romantic, you say?

Why else would I loiter in O'Neill's pub around the corner from Trinity College with nothing to do except look for beautiful faces, the kind whose image will cling to your memory for the rest of your life?

The mists swirling outside the darkened pub, which smelled like Guinness's brewery on a humid day, seemed to have slipped inside and soaked the walls and floors and tables and the coats of the noisy young people with permanent moisture. My friend across the table was an oasis of light and warmth in a desert of wet and gloomy darkness. Blue-eyed, druid maiden light.

All right, I'm a terrible romantic. I'm worse than that, as you will see when I have finished telling my story. I'm a dumb romantic.

"That established my point." I continued the argument, unable to look away from her suspicious but radiant blue eyes. "Do you speak Irish?"

"Better than you speak English," she snapped. "And I'm trying to study" — she gestured with a slim elegant hand — "for my focking world economics quiz, which is why no one is sitting with me at this table."

"Ah, but someone is indeed: one Dermot Coyne. Now tell me, nameless one" — I smiled my most charming dimpled smile — "what obscene and scatological words exist in your language?"

She tilted her head back and her chin up, ready for a fight. " 'Tis a pure and gentle language."

"Ah, 'tis all of that." I leaned closer so that her inviting lips were only a foot from mine — and felt the pain in my ribs from last night's brawl. "I'm surprised that you didn't say it was a focking pure language."

Did I detect a hint of a smile? What would she look like if she took off her jacket?

As George would say, a not completely trivial issue.

"Now," I continued reasonably, "let me tell you about an event I observed when I was doing research on this alien race that claims some relation to my own harmless Irish-American people. In pursuit of this project I am attending a cultural exercise in an artistic center with which, O lovely nameless one, I am sure you are familiar — Croke Park."

16

The ends of her lips turned up a little more. I was a big Yank, probably rich like all Yanks, probably preparing to make a pass like all rich Yank males, but I was also ever so faintly amusing. My heart, which ought to have known better after my earlier failures in love, picked up its beat.

I must add for the record that I was not preparing to make a pass. I had enough troubles in life as it was without becoming involved with a woman. All I wanted at that point was a little maternal sympathy because of my recent and unfortunate encounters with the Special Branch, a euphemism for the local secret police. Nonetheless, at twenty-five an unattached male of our species will inevitably evaluate a young woman of the same species as a potential bed partner and perhaps even as a remote possibility for a mate — even if my mother is convinced that I am destined to be a typical Irish bachelor. Such an evaluation will be all the more intense if the young woman across the table from him in a smoke-filled Dublin pub possesses the most beautiful face he has ever seen, a face all the more wonderful because of its total innocence of makeup.

"Maybe you'll find a sweet little girl in Ireland and bring her home," Mom had said brightly during our last phone conversation.

"Like your mother?"

Mom laughed. "Well, she was little anyway."

I was beginning to fall in love, you say? Ah,

17

friend, I begin to fall in love almost every day and, having been badly burned twice, rarely get beyond the beginning. When I begin to fall in love, the issue is infatuation and flirtation, not the kind of love out of which permanent union might be fashioned. I'd known that kind of love too, and I didn't want any of it now, thank you very much.

This lass from the bogs was more appealing than most of the women who stir my heart, you say? And I had actually talked to her, which is a rare event when I begin to fall in love?

Too true.

The nameless one had already forced me to reevaluate my contention that all the beautiful female genes had migrated to America.

"You went to the All Ireland match at Croke Park, did you?" She tapped her notebook impatiently with a Bic pen. I didn't have much time to tell my story or her royal majesty would dismiss me to the nether regions of her empire.

Most Irish conversational dialogue, I had discovered, ends in question marks. I tried to adjust to the custom, with only modest success.

I will not try to write English the way the Irish speak it in this story. For that I strongly recommend the books of Roddy Doyle. Thus when you see the letters "th," you must realize that their language has (sometimes) no sound to correspond to those consonants. Moreover, the vowel "u" is often pronounced as if it were "oo," as in "Dooblin." For example, if the Gaelic womanly deity to whom I was talking should say "The only thing to do is to tell the truth when you're thinking about it," you must imagine her as sounding as if she said, "De only ting to do is tell da troot when you're tinking about it."

"Didn't I now?" I continued my tale of Croke Park. "And didn't Cork beat Mayo? And wasn't I sitting next to a nice old Mayo lady who prayed her rosary beads before the game, uh, match began? And didn't she put away her beads and shout encouragement to the players? I now recite a typical expression which I had the foresight to jot down in my notebook." I removed a spiral pad from my Savile Row jacket pocket. "Jesus, Mary, and Joseph, Slattery, for the love of God, will you get the load of shit out of your focking pants and kick the focking ball into the focking net, instead of standing there like a pissant amadon!"

I snapped the notebook shut, my case having been made. The nameless one laughed, a rich, generous, and devastating laugh. She probably had no idea how beautiful she was or that she was even beautiful — an innocent child from the bogs.

Time would prove that the first part of my estimate was accurate enough. The second remains even now problematic.

"At least for an alien race," she conceded, "aren't we colorful now?"

"About that, lovely nameless one, you will

19

get no argument from me."

"A song, Nuala," some large oaf with a thick Cork accent demanded. " 'Tis time for one of your songs!"

"Can't you see I'm studying me world economics?" my companion protested with a notable lack of sincerity.

"You're not studying," a woman shouted, "you're chatting up the *fockingrichyank*. Sing us a song."

"A song from Nuala," a chorus joined in, emphasizing their demand by pounding their mugs on the shabby and unsteady tables.

"Holy Saint Brigid." Nuala — for that must be her name — sighed loudly.

She winked at me, stood up, doffed her jacket, and stretched for a guitar under our table.

In this exercise her torso came enchantingly close to my face. It exceeded my wildest, or should I say my most obscene, expectations.

A matter of trivial importance for a young male, no doubt, but nonetheless, she was so elegantly lovely that a spasm of pleasure and pain raced through my nervous system and caused me to bite my lip.

Yet I almost stopped ogling when she began to sing — in Irish. It was surely a love song and just as surely, being Irish, a sad love song. Nuala's voice was sweet and precise, yet powerful. She filled the pub with her song and reduced the noise of her fellow students to a

20

whisper — though the steady traffic back and forth to the bar was not terminated. Just the same, they walked softly.

As I say, I did not suspend my astonishment at her wondrous breasts. Presumably no male in the pub did. The gentle, melancholy song made my astonishment all the more pleasant and poignant and frightening.

She glanced at me a couple of times while she was singing, nervously I thought.

Ah, if I brought this one home to Mother, there would be universal rejoicing in the family.

The rest of the kids in the pub cheered enthusiastically. I was so dazzled that I forgot to applaud. She noted my failure and favored me with a dirty look.

Ah, you don't mess with this one, not at all, at all.

They demanded another song. Feigning reluctance, which was calculated to fool no one, she sang a lullaby that made me want to be a baby again. I noticed that her mug of Guinness, like mine, was nearly empty and tiptoed over to the bar to refill them both. I felt two scorching blue eyes burn holes in my back.

Uh-oh. I think I made a mistake.

I made it back to the table just as the lullaby ended. Her eyes avoided mine. I was afraid she wouldn't come back to our table.

"Good luck with the play, Nuala," someone shouted.

21

"You'll be great," someone else chimed in.

She stood at the table, towering, it seemed, above me.

"Play?" I said cautiously.

"TCD Players." She scowled at me, ready to pick up her economics notes and storm out of the pub. "*Playboy* — and that's not a magazine with naked women either."

"And you'll be playing herself?"

"Herself?"

"Pegeen Mike. Who else?"

"I am."

" 'Ah,' " I began, " 'six yards of stuff for to make a yellow gown. A pair of lace boots with lengthy heels on them and brassy eyelets. A hat is suited for a wedding day. A fine-tooth comb. To be sent with three barrels of porter in Jimmy Farrell's creel cart on the evening of the coming fair to Mr. Michael James Flaherty. Best compliments of this season. Margaret Flaherty.' "

Nuala listened carefully to my recitation of the opening lines of *The Playboy*. "You do it better than I do," she admitted as she put her guitar back beneath the table with the same delightful passage of her torso by my face. "Sure, a male Pegeen in drag, that would create a scandal, wouldn't it now? Something that Nial Jordan would think up."

"Beautiful songs, Nuala."

"Och, the first one is an eejit. Lamenting an amadon that walked out on her."

22

The word "eejit" would normally be translated as "idiot" in American English, but something of the affectionate nature of the reproach is lost. I also note that for reasons of delicacy, I tend to omit in this story further use of the colorful language with which Nuala began our relationship, though I am firmly convinced that, worddrunk people that they are, the Irish are more skillful at obscenity and scatology than anyone else in the world. Again, if you want the full details, consult Roddy Doyle. Nuala was much more restrained than the citizens of "Barrytown" as portrayed in *The Commitments* or *The Snapper*, for example.

"There are," I said, cautiously moving the replenished pint in her direction, "three themes in Irish song — lament for a lost love, farewell to Ireland, and poor old Ireland."

"I don't want your focking jar." She pushed it away angrily.

"Nuala . . . short for Fionnuala, right? . . . I'm not trying to seduce you. Not that it wouldn't be a most interesting and rewarding exercise, but it's not, as we *richyanks* would say, where I'm at now. I'd like to be friends, if you don't mind."

She reached tentatively for the jar. "Would you be gay now?"

"Woman, if you knew the thoughts that were dancing in my head while you were singing, you wouldn't be asking that."

"Nothing wrong with being gay." She flushed

a light pink and turned her eyes away from mine.

I noted another difference between her face and that of a model on a magazine cover. The model's face is impassive, content with its own immobile beauty. Nuala's face was in constant motion, disclosing a rushing torrent of emotions — anger, interest, shyness, amusement. Either she was too unsophisticated to hide her emotions or she didn't give a damn about hiding them. Later, much later, I would understand that, like the good actress she was, Nuala could manufacture emotions at will — and then convince herself that she really felt them.

"Nuala, it is then?"

" 'Tis." She did not look from her Guinness, which she moved back and forth uneasily on the pockmarked table.

"And the name that goes with it?"

She hesitated, not sure she wanted to cross that boundary. "McGrail," she finally admitted, not at all sure she wasn't making a big mistake.

"That's better. Now that we're friends you can drink that jar, can't you?"

She looked up at me and grinned. "Sure, wasn't I perishing from the thirst after singing?"

I tried to place her accent. It wasn't like any of those I had learned to identify since I'd been in Ireland, yet somehow it was familiar, soft, light, sweet, and ever so faintly ironic.

"So you're studying music and drama, Fionnuala McGrail?"

"I am not," she said hotly. "Would I want to starve to death, and there being enough unemployed in this country as it is? Wouldn't I be a terrible eejit altogether if I wasn't doing accounting?"

I wasn't sure that her voice was good enough to be commercial. Probably not. Everyone in Ireland could sing ballads.

"Your voice is as lovely as you are, Nuala."

"Hasn't the man swallowed the blarney stone instead of kissing it?"

"I didn't mean to make you angry."

"Sure, Dermot Coyne, aren't you the terrible eejit not to realize that I like your flattery and that it scares me, and yourself" — she flushed again — "a big amadon of a *fockingrichyank*."

So, basically I attracted her and I scared her. Progress, too much progress altogether. For all her beauty and talent, she was only a teenager from . . . from where?

"And so how would you be earning the money to pay for your expensive London clothes?"

My heart sank. My answer to that question persuaded most young women that I was a total flake.

"I didn't know this was a student pub, or I wouldn't have come in with this suit," I said. "I didn't want to look like *a fockingrichyank*."

"Would I mind how you're dressed?"

Probably not, Nuala McGrail. But you'll probably mind how I get my money.

Moreover, even if you don't mind, I can't

25

burden you with my story about the Irish secret police. You're too young and too innocent and I may just love you too much.

– 2 –

The man was a cop and a bully. So I made up my mind that I would pay no attention to what he said, except maybe to do just the opposite.

"Would you mind having a word or two with me, Mr. Coyne?" The words, spoken the day before I encountered Nuala McGrail, were polite enough; the manner was designed to intimidate, a linebacker pretending to prepare for a blitz.

"I would mind, yes," I replied, shaking his paw off my arm.

"I'm Chief Superintendent Conlon," he said, recapturing my arm. "I'd really like a word or two with you. Special Branch."

"If I'm supposed to be impressed, I'm sorry. Somehow I can't work up that reaction."

He was a big man, not as tall as I am and not as solid either, but a hell of a lot more bulky. Moreover, he was skilled at using his bulk to intimidate, to create the illusion that in his black bowler with his black raincoat and his black umbrella and his thick black mustache, he was a powerful and determined man whom

26

it would be foolish to resist. In short, he was a bully.

Now, in my own defense (and I have a lot to defend in this story), I must say that ordinarily I am a peaceful and nonviolent person. I quit the football team at Fenwick because I was disgusted by the physical and personal violence of one of the assistant coaches — who was also a bully. I stayed on the wrestling team because one-on-one combat did not require undue violence and because the bullies always lost.

Only those who were weaklings had to be bullies, I thought. I refused to play football at Notre Dame, though I might have made the team. I would have flunked out of school anyway, probably a little sooner. I messed around with martial arts and learned a lot about self-control and resistance to pain from the Japanese master who taught me until I discovered that martial arts also attracted bullies who wanted to intimidate others despite their weakness.

I don't know where I get this aversion to bullies. Neither my father nor my older brothers ever bullied me. I was too amusing and too exasperating when I was a kid for them to want to, even if it was in their character.

I guess there must have been incidents in the schoolyard when I was a tiny punk that I have repressed. Anyway, the point is that Chief Superintendent Conlon, with his broad shoulders and his big belly and his heavy sigh, had chosen the wrong technique to deal with me.

People do. They figure I'm a big, happy-go-lucky goof with no steel in his spine. Usually, I have to admit, they're right. A suggestion that something, anything, might not be worth the argument is likely to win my lackadaisical assent. But try to intimidate me and something starts rumbling in the dark basement storerooms of my soul.

So sometimes I get myself into a whole of a lot of trouble needlessly. This was one of those times.

"You have a badge or card or something?" I asked the cop.

"I have." He sighed and produced a laminated card.

"Doesn't look very impressive to me."

"Just a word or two." He pushed his bulky self in my direction, nudging me in the direction of the Dubliner, a pub off the lobby of Jury's Hotel, where he had cornered me when I came in out of the Dublin rain.

When such a man nudges you with his bulk, you're supposed to agree to drift in the direction he wants you to go. If you do that, he has you.

I resisted. So he continued to shove. Mexican standoff.

"Special Branch of the Guards, is it?" I adopted the Irish ploy of communicating through questions. "That's kind of the secret police, isn't it? Like an Irish Gestapo?"

I admit that I don't sound very attractive in

28

this scene. After all, he was making a civil enough request, wasn't he? The point is that he was trying to push me around. I don't want you to admire me at this point, just understand that's how I react.

"We'd like to think of ourselves as the Irish FBI." He stopped pushing, baffled apparently by the failure of his usual sure-fire intimidation technique.

"That's what I mean, Fascists."

His big, flat face turned an ugly purple. He was about to lose his temper. I wouldn't have wanted to be in an interrogation room with him when he lost his temper.

"I wanted to talk to you about your grandfather, Liam O'Riada."

Why hadn't the stupid bastard said so in the first place?

"Bill Ready to us."

"Aye." He sighed.

"All right." I led him over to the Dubliner, the hotel bar, pretty effectively disguised as a typical Dublin pub (but cleaner), signaled for the waiter, and ordered a pint for him and a Ballygowan water for me. If he had learned his lesson from our preliminary exchange, there might not be a story to tell.

"My grandfather died a year ago," I said.

"Aye." The cop's big belly moved up and down against the table. "God be good to him."

I waited. It was up to him to take the next step.

"He never came back to Ireland, did he?" Conlon's big black eyes flashed as if he knew some terrible secret.

"I guess not." I tried to dismiss the subject. "Personally I never noticed."

"Left during the Troubles, didn't he, and never came back?"

"The Troubles" is the polite name for the era after the end of the Great War — 1916 to 1923. It includes the Easter Rising of 1916 ("A terrible beauty is born"), the Anglo-Irish War of 1919–1921 (the War of Independence, it is called in Ireland), and then the Irish Civil War, between 1921 and 1923, which occurred after the Brits left Ireland, and was fought between those who accepted the treaty setting up the Irish Free State and those who rejected it. For a couple of years, in other words, the Irish set about the task of killing friends and relatives and those who had been the best men at their weddings.

The rebels of 1916 were poets and dreamers. If the British had imprisoned them after they shelled their handful of outposts into submission, it would have been the end of the matter, since most of the Irish thought the rebels were a crowd of eejits. Typically the Brits overreacted, shot the lot of them, and made them heroes. Typically too they missed the dangerous men — the crafty politician Eamon DeValera and the brilliant guerrilla leader Michael Collins. In 1919, after the end of the Great War, Collins changed the strategy of previous Irish insurgencies. Instead of pitched battles, the Irish Volunteers (renamed the Irish Republican Army) fought a series of hit-and-run attacks that slowly destroyed British power in Ireland.

Britain, preoccupied with other postwar troubles, proposed a truce and then peace. Collins, though the leader of gunmen, realized, as many of the young hotheads did not, that there was no ammunition left to continue the fight and little support from the people for continued killing. Reluctantly he accepted the treaty the British proposed, arguing that, while it was not the republic which the IRA wanted, it was the best that could be had and the beginning of a republic. Despite the fact that Collins's faction won the election, the young radicals rejected the treaty and rebelled against the so-called Irish Free State government. Collins, the only man who might have been able to make peace, was killed near his home in Cork, and the bloody civil war continued until most of the leaders were killed and most of the ammunition consumed.

"I suppose so. I'm sure he had unpleasant memories of all the foolish killing."

"Aye." The superintendent rested his jug of Guinness on his belly.

My grandmother, Mary Anne, alias Nell Pat, had told me once that she and Bill did not dare go back because if they did they would be shot. She wouldn't tell me why and now she, great and good woman, was dead too.

I wasn't going to admit any of this to a Special Branch cop.

"And himself a hero of the Rising too, wasn't he?"

"He didn't talk much about it. He became an American."

"And was very successful at it too, wasn't he now?"

"Moderately."

"Not as successful as you, was he? Not so young anyway?" Conlon's black eyes flashed again as if he had dug out some great, dirty secret from my past.

"Depends on your standards."

"There are them that say you're asking questions about him. That wouldn't be true now, would it?"

Fair point to you, Chief Superintendent. I'd been digging up old newspapers and reading through histories of those dismal years of revolution started by poets and ended by gunmen. I'd met with a fat little professor at UCD (University College Dublin) named Seamus Nolan who had written a cautious book some twenty years ago about the Troubles. Nolan's responses were as suspiciously evasive as his book. So he had squealed to the Special Branch? Why bother? It had happened sixty-five years before, when Bill Ready was eighteen and Nell, the only love of his life, was a mere sixteen. All the principal characters of the story were dead, weren't they?

"So what if it is true? Is there a law in Ireland against reading newspapers and history books and talking to professors?"

"Not a law, in a manner of speaking." Conlon drained his jug. "A man could still get in trouble for asking questions that are perfectly legal to ask."

"I thought this was a civilized, democratic country."

"We don't kill our presidents, now, do we?"

Another fair point, I guess, but his making it increased my ire. "Let's stop this silly Irish game of indirection, Chief Superintendent Conlon. You're warning me off my casual inquiries about my grandfather and the Troubles."

He winced, as the Irish always do when you address them directly and spoil their elaborate circumlocutions. "I didn't say that, now did I?"

"What are you saying then?"

I must note here that my interest in my grandfather's story was casual. I had always adored the man and he seemed to like me, the youngest, more than any of the other grand-children. Surely Grandma Nell, poor woman, doted on me. She had told me many stories about the Rising and the Troubles. She hadn't told the stories to my mother or her brothers and sisters.

I'd ask about what Pa (as I called him, im-itating my mother) had done during the violence.

"That was long ago," she would tell me, with

a distant glow in her eye. "Pa has left it behind."

I was out of the country when he died. I didn't learn about his death till after the funeral. My mother's disappointment in me at that blunder forced me to call home more often. So I arrived in time for Grandma Nell's funeral.

I hadn't said good-bye to either of them, though I had loved them very much, almost as much as my own parents. Perhaps I was expiating by playing with the notion of writing a book about them and their early lives — I am kind of a dilettante writer, you see.

It was not, however, a serious project. Very few things in my life have been serious projects. If they hadn't tried to bully me out of it, I would have probably, irony of ironies, given this one up.

What difference did it make, two-thirds of a century later, why my grandfather and grandmother left Ireland fugitives, why they never went back, why they never communicated with any of their relatives left behind? They had been happy and successful in America and lived rewarding lives. If there was some kind of blot on his reputation in Ireland, so what? Wasn't he a respected and admired real estate developer in Chicago? Wasn't he a man whose reputation for integrity was impeccable? Who cared what octogenarian Micks and a couple of fusty historians thought about him?

"I'm saying" — the cop stared longingly at his empty mug — "that no good comes of stirring up old troubles."

"I thought that was what historians did."

"But, with all respect, Mr. Coyne, you're not a historian, are you now?"

"An amateur one."

"Aye," he said, nodding his head significantly as if I had made an important admission. "Wouldn't some things be better left to the professional historians, especially things that would upset a lot of important people?"

"And if I don't care about a lot of important people?"

"Well" — he heaved himself out of his chair — "sure, isn't it the job of the Guard to protect American tourists, especially if they are wealthy and from well-known families? And don't we do our best? But aren't there some things we can't prevent, if some tourists take foolish risks?"

The Civic Guard (Garda Siochana in Irish) are an unarmed national police force that replaced the old Royal Irish Constabulary after the establishment of the Free State. Guard (or Garda) is both the singular and the collective and Guards (Guardai) are the plural — as in "The publican called the Garda and didn't five focking Gardai show up a half hour later? One Garda would have been enough if he had come right away."

"I think I understand your message, Chief Superintendent Conlin." I stood up with him. "Let me illustrate how much of an Irish American I am by giving you a direct answer to those that sent you: Tell them I said that they should go fuck themselves."

Tough, huh? Really fierce, right?

The cop had hardly left Jury's, shaking his head in astonishment at rudeness, when I realized what a fool I had been. Riding up my suite in the new tower, I told myself I was crazy to let them — whoever they were — bully myself into a commitment that I did not want to make.

Nonetheless, I was stuck with my resolution; Come what may, I would learn why Liam O'Riada and Nell Pat Malone, God be good to their great, gentle souls, had fled their native land never to return.

– 3 –

Despite her forceful objections to leaving the pub with me, Nuala McGrail and I were walking down College Green (a street, no longer a real green) huddled under my umbrella, she with her student's bag over one shoulder and her battered guitar case over the other. She was tall, probably five foot eight, maybe six inches shorter than I, and there was a certain delightful intimacy between us already, two young people close together and isolated by the darkness and mists from the rest of the world.

"I can't tell you my life story in this noisy pub," I had insisted again.

"Well, I'll not be walking out of here with you, Dermot Coyne. They'll be thinking you've already seduced me."

"I'm not trying to seduce you, Nuala Anne McGrail."

"How did you know my middle name was Anne?" she demanded, frowning dangerously.

"Every Irish woman" — I tried to placate her — "claims the name of the mother of Jesus or his grandmother somewhere, if not as her first name at least as her middle name. My second guess would have been Moire."

"I'm really Marie Fionnuala Anne" — she picked up her pint of Guinness — "pronounced Moiré and spelled Marie — and I don't believe in Jesus or his mother or grandmother or God."

The "ua" in her name, by the way, is pronounced as the "ou" in "Lou."

"Why not? Too much evil in the world?"

"Just the opposite." Her eyes flashed, a streak of lightning racing across the bog on a dark night. "What kind of a God would it be that would waste his time on the likes of us? God, if there is a God, shouldn't give a good fock about us silly humans."

"That's an interesting position."

"And your middle name is John?"

37

"No. I told you once."

"You did not."

"I did so."

"Patrick?"

"Certainly not."

"Michael?"

"Right!"

"Dermot Michael Coyne? Well, it scans nicely."

"And, as I say, Dermot Michael Coyne does not have seduction on his mind, although I shall assert again that he won't deny that it would be an interesting experience to take off your clothes. He just wants to be friends."

"I'm not worried about seduction" — she shoved her glass aside — "or losing my clothes. I can take care of meself if it comes to that. I don't want to be friends with any Yank. I don't like Yanks, not at all, at all."

She didn't sound completely convinced, however.

"Then you're not interested in my occupation?"

Ah, but, you see, she was curious.

And where had I heard that delightful melody in her accent before?

"I don't give a fock what you do to earn all your money . . . and if I walk out of here with you, they'll be thinking I'm headed for a bed in the Shelbourne."

"Jury's, actually, and I'm thinking from the way they react to you, there's no doubt at all,

38

at all about the virtue of the fair Fionnuala."

"They're thinking I'm frigid," she responded tersely, "and maybe I am."

"I'll not debate that point," I said, "except to say that I find it inherently improbable. Let me suggest a ruse. I'll walk out of here and wait outside in the Dublin fog. You finish your world econ notes and join me in five minutes, and I'll walk you to wherever you're going and relate the fascinating story of the lives and loves of Dermot Michael Coyne."

She pondered the appeal of such a possibility and then laughed. "I don't know why I care about my reputation anyway. Let them think I'm in bed with a —"

"Fockingrichyank?"

She laughed again. Dear God, she was beautiful when she laughed.

"Go along with you." She dismissed me. "Maybe I'll see you outside and maybe I won't."

Impulsively and foolishly I leaned across the table and touched her lips with mine. They tasted so good, despite the flavor of Guinness, that I did it again.

She closed her eyes and swallowed. No resistance, no protest.

For a moment I was weak and dizzy, tottering on the edge of making a complete fool out of myself. I beat a hasty retreat before I could discover whether she was balanced precariously on the same edge.

She's only a kid, I thought as I picked my

way through the clouds of cigarette smoke towards the door, and I took her by surprise. That wasn't fair. I exploited her.

On the other hand, I told myself as I waited for her in front of St. Andrew's (Church of Ireland or C. of I. — not ours) in the Dublin gloom that reminded me of a cemetery on a stormy night, she didn't seem to dislike my kiss, even if I am a *fockingrichyank.*

Well, she's perfectly free not to seek shelter under my umbrella when she comes out of that dingy, unhealthy place.

Dublin was in one of her ugly moods that night. It perhaps shows that state of my libido that I picture the city as a handsome matron in her early forties, cultivated, well preserved, charming; for some reason she delights in tricking you by pretending to be unattractive on many occasions — particularly when she arranges for bad weather.

"An umbrella, miss?" I extended it over her head precisely five minutes later.

Without comment she ducked under it. "All right, let's hear your fascinating story."

Not a word about the stolen kiss. If I had been in trouble, I was already forgiven. Maybe I should try to steal another one.

I noticed that her jacket cuffs were frayed, her jeans were worn, the jacket hood pulled down over her ears had a hole in it, and her unpolished shoes were cracked.

Nuala was poor. Not a good omen for her

40

reaction to my story.

I have told the story many times, especially to young women. It provides a nice test for me to decide whether I should continue to fall in love with a young woman. Some are horrified by my story and think I'm feckless and irresponsible. Others think I was intolerably lucky and will be unlucky for the rest of my life. The former want to remake me; the latter want nothing to do with me. I had yet to find someone who understood.

"Well, to begin with, Nuala McGrail, I'm not much good at anything —"

"Except talking."

"I suppose. . . . I'm the youngest child of seven, you see."

"No crime in that. So am I."

"If you keep interrupting me, I'll never get to the good part."

"No promises."

The woman was an imp — a beautiful, innocent, impoverished imp with lovely breasts and sweet lips. What more could a lonely romantic ask for?

I decided to modify the authorized version of the story. "You see, Nuala McGrail, I don't do anything at all."

"Not at all, at all?" She turned to look up at me, skeptical, suspicious, perhaps a little scared.

"Not at all, at all."

"A great big, overgrown amadon like yourself?

41

And yourself not working at all, at all?"

Ah, I had exorcised the imp.

"That's right."

"And yourself living off your poor parents?"

"I didn't say that, now did I?"

"It's all right for us Irish to be indirect, but you Yanks must tell your stories straight-like."

Nuala's First Law.

"Well, I'm retired! I write a little bit on the odd occasion. Nothing more."

We had walked past the front gate of Trinity and into Grafton Street at the top of which was the statue of Molly Malone that Dublin had acquired as part of its millennium celebration and promptly dubbed the "tart with the cart" because of her décolletage.

(And the statue of Anna Livia, James Joyce's evocation of the Anna Liffey River, in front of the General Post Office — where it replaced Lord Nelson — was called "the floozy in the Jacuzzi" or the "whore in the sewer.")

"Retired? At twenty-four? Go along with you now."

Ah, she'd been guessing at my age. She is interested in me.

"Twenty-five actually. As I say, I've been pretty much a failure in my life. I'm the youngest child and the only one who hasn't been a credit to his parents. Two of my brothers and one of my sisters are doctors. My sister Linda is a hotshot lawyer. Another brother is a priest. My sisters are both married and mothers. I guess

42

I was spoiled and indulged as a kid because I've never been very ambitious."

No comment from the fair Nuala.

"I'm supposed to be pretty bright. At least the IQ scores say that I am. And I'm supposed to be creative, but my grades in school were on the low side of average. And as you say, I'm a great big overgrown amadon who should have been a star athlete. I quit the football team in high school because I had a fight with the coach."

"A fight with him, is it?"

She seemed impressed. Or was she hunching closer to me because the rain was coming down harder?

Grafton Street, a usually crowded pedestrian mall, was deserted because of the bad weather. We were walking toward St. Stephen's Green, away from Trinity. Was Nuala prolonging the walk because she wanted to hear my story or because she liked clinging to my arm as much as I liked it?

"He was a bully. If we played the way he wanted, we could have hurt people. . . . Anyway, I went to Notre Dame — that's the big Catholic university with the famous football team."

She patted my arm. Really.

"I'm not a complete onchock, Dermot Michael Coyne. I *have* heard of the Fighting Irish, though most of them don't look very Irish. Did you play football there?"

"I did not," I said, unconsciously slipping into

Irish idiom. "Though some people suggested that I should and my father would have been very proud of me if I had. To tell the truth, most of the fighting Irish are now fighting black Baptists, not that there's any disgrace in that."

"Not at all," she agreed fervently. "Nothing wrong with being a Prod."

"They probably shouldn't have let me in because my grades were so poor. But my test scores were sky high and I studied a little in the first semester of my senior year — that's the last year of secondary school — and my brothers and one of my sisters and my father had gone there and maybe they could change my mind about football and —"

"What position would you be playing now?"

"You've been watching Yank football on the telly and yourself hating Yanks?"

"Sure." She actually patted my arm a second time. "Isn't it a savage sport just right for the likes of them savage Yanks?"

"I was a defensive end."

"Isn't that the most savage of them all, like your man Richard Dent?"

A girl from the West of Ireland and herself a Chicago Bears fan.

"I wasn't that good. I probably wouldn't have made the Notre Dame team anyway. Not first string. I flunked out at the end of my sophomore year."

"Ah, sure, wasn't that terrible for your poor mother?"

44

I was sure of it now. Her accent was the same as Nell Pat Malone, Grandma Nell. Nuala Anne McGrail was from the Gaeltacht, an Irish speaker, the last of the druid maidens. One more point in her favor.

"Mom gave up worrying about her children after the fourth. If I did anything it was all right. As I say, I was spoiled rotten."

"And what were you doing with your time? Drinking and drugs, was it now?"

I patted her arm, turnabout surely being fair play. " 'Tis a wonderful prosecuting attorney you would be, Nuala Anne McGrail. I spent most of my time reading and walking around in a daze and dreaming and thinking. Such activities were a lot more fun than class. So I went off to Marquette for two years and didn't fail anything, but I didn't collect nearly enough credits to graduate so I gave college up as a bad job."

"And there wasn't any young woman in your life, was there not?"

A perfectly legitimate question, delivered in a completely neutral tone.

"Ah, weren't there scads of them, all willing to straighten out me life and make me put me nose to the grindstone?"

"That's no reason to marry anyone," she said firmly. "Sure, if they're not what you want before you marry them, they're not likely to become that afterward."

"And isn't yourself wise beyond your years,

45

Nuala Anne? Anyway, my family was faced with a problem. They had a perfectly healthy son who was not college material. They couldn't make a doctor or a lawyer or a priest out of him, not even an accountant." I patted her arm a second time. "What were they to do with him?"

"A terrible problem altogether." She sighed.

I had found a woman who wanted to listen to me, even if I couldn't tell her about my conversation with the chief superintendent yesterday or the thugs who assaulted me last night, in memory of whom my ribs ached as I held the umbrella over her head.

"So they did what any Chicago Irish family does if it has a little money and a son who is not good for anything at all, at all. They bought me a seat on the Mercantile Exchange and gave me some capital to play with — like sending the youngest son off to the army or the colonies a century or two ago. I traded in the Standard and Poors index — I don't suppose you know anything about the commodities futures market, do you, Nuala Anne McGrail?"

She pounded my arm in protest this time. "Do you think that I'm such an awful eejit? I told you I was studying accounting, didn't I now?"

"You know the difference between going long and selling short?"

"I'll walk away by myself in all this terrible rain if you ask me another question like that."

"Well, I did my best, honestly I did, but I'm afraid I wasn't very good."

"Sure, you shouldn't have tried it, should you now?"

"I didn't lose much money and I didn't make much money either. Some of my father's friends, doctors like himself, gave me a little bit of their business. I managed usually not to mess up their orders too badly. On my own deals I simply wasn't quick enough. I had to stop and think while the other traders my age acted on instinct."

"Poor dear man." She sighed, just like Grandma Nell used to sigh.

"Anyway, the last time the stock market decided to take a plunge, there I was, standing in the S and P pit, bemused and confused. Some of my friends were making tons of money and some of them were losing tons of money and I wasn't doing anything, because I had no idea what was happening. On Friday the market started to rally and everyone was buying like mad, hoping to ride up the index as it soared. One of my few clients called in a sell order — three hundred contracts —"

"He thought the rally wouldn't last and himself selling short?"

"And he was right of course. But somehow I got confused and bought three hundred cars —"

"You never did!" she shouted, stopping in her tracks, hand at her mouth in horror. "Ah, you poor thing!"

"That's what I thought on Saturday morning when I went down to the exchange to catch up on paperwork. I was down six hundred cars, the three hundred he wanted me to sell and the three hundred I had bought on my own. Millions of dollars that I didn't have, Nuala Anne."

I shivered at the recollection. It was a terrible weekend, saved only by the Bear victory that Sunday afternoon.

"So what happened?"

"So I went in on Monday morning, expecting the worst. I'd try to buy immediately before the market went up any more."

"And it fell?" She started to walk again, beginning to understand my story.

"Like a rock. I watched it go down all day and bought just before the closing bell."

"Glory be to God." She gasped. "And the holy saints Brigid, Patrick, and Columcille too! You must have made a fortune!"

"Just a little over three million dollars, not that I deserved any of it. I had made a dumb mistake and was very lucky. I know you don't believe in God or the holy saints you just invoked and probably not even in the holy guardian angels, for which God forgive you, says I. Anyway, I thought the last-named must have been working overtime for me. It was like winning a lottery, even though you hadn't bought a ticket."

"So then what did you do?"

48

"I sold my seat, returned the money and the capital to my father, paid my income tax, invested everything else in tax-free municipals, and retired."

"You never did!" she exclaimed.

"I did so! And don't I feel like a terrible eejit altogether. I've finally found a woman who understands what happened and knows what a real eejit I am."

She pounded my arm. "You are the biggest eejit in all creation, Dermot Michael Coyne," she announced. "The worst altogether."

Firmly she turned me around at the bottom of Grafton Street and directed me back towards the front gate of Trinity. We walked for a long time in silence.

"I know," I admitted sheepishly. Now it would come; she would urge me to go back to the trading pits just as other women had.

"I'm thinking you don't want to know why I think you're such a terrible eejit."

"I do too want to know."

"You're an eejit" — we stopped again, right across from the entrance to Trinity College — "for thinking that you're an eejit."

"I beg pardon?"

"And yourself a clever man all along."

"I'm an idiot, excuse me, an eejit for thinking I'm an eejit when I wasn't an eejit at all, at all?"

"Didn't I just say that?"

"Did you now?"

49

Damn! I was mimicking her again!

She didn't seem to mind. She was looking up at me, her face wet with rain and glowing. "Anyone can be lucky. Isn't it only the wise man who knows what to do with his luck?"

Well, there it was: the first woman to understand completely and approve.

"You don't disapprove?"

She jabbed a sharp finger into my chest. "And why would it matter whether I approve or not? And isn't the world a better place if it has a few men who can drift and dream and then maybe someday tell the rest of us about their dreams?"

Ah, Nuala, you're an impoverished and shy kid from the Gaeltacht, smart and talented maybe, but shy and inexperienced. Yet you speak with all the wisdom of the ages. I should take you in my arms and hug and kiss you because I'll never find another one quite like you.

I didn't do that, of course, worse luck for me. My life might have been much different if I had.

She admired and liked me. She had already let me kiss her once, no, twice, without protest. We probably would have fought often in the years ahead and then made up loving each other even more. I was wise enough, maybe, to accept my luck with money. I was not wise enough to accept my luck with love.

Why not? Why did I lose my nerve under

50

the streetlight in the rain in front of Trinity College, next to Molly Malone with the tart smell of the sea in my nostrils and the woeful moan of the foghorn in my ears?

Wasn't I telling you that I am a romantic? What more romantic situation could I find? Why did I blow the opportunity? Why did I lose my nerve?

I guess because I'm shy too. I talk a big game. Beautiful and intelligent women scare me.

Besides, I've had a lot of trouble with women.

So what I said, still talking my big game, was "Can I ask you a personal question, Nuala Anne McGrail?"

"Wouldn't that be depending on the question?"

Did she look just a little disappointed? Was she an incorrigible romantic too?

"You're from the County Galway, are you not?"

"I am." She seemed surprised that a Yank would be able to guess.

"From Connemara?"

"Now how would you know that?"

"Carraroe?"

"Glory be to God!" She jumped away from me.

I recaptured her arm and pulled her back underneath my umbrella. "Who doesn't exist."

"Or if He does, doesn't care about us. . . . But how would you be knowing that I'm from Carraroe?"

"Irish is your first language?" I took possession of her other arm, holding her captive.

"A focking museum piece, that's what I am."

Somehow she slipped away from me and directed me again towards Trinity.

"My grandmother, God be good to her, was from Carraroe, Nell Malone that was." I fumbled in my wallet for the pictures of her and Grandpa Bill and held them for her to see in the dim glow provided by a streetlight next to Molly Malone.

Nuala inspected the pictures carefully under my umbrella. "Och, a beautiful woman, wasn't she now?"

"She was that and much more. He was from Costelloe down the road. Bill Ready, Liam O'Riada you'd probably call him."

"Sure, there's no one there with that name anymore. And no Malones either."

"Here's the last picture of them I have, both in their eighties."

She didn't seem surprised that the big Yank amadon would carry his grandparents' picture like a father would carry a snapshot of his son.

"Grand-looking people, sure, aren't they just like the rest of us from out there? Brilliant!"

"Grand" and "brilliant" are the two most popular adjectives in Dublin's Fair City, the former being comparative and the latter superlative, especially when expressed as "focking brill!" or even "dead focking brill!"

"Here's a reprint of their wedding photo."

"Ah, and aren't you the spittin' image of himself?"

"That's what Grandma Nell said. It's probably why they both spoiled me rotten."

"Terrible rotten altogether. . . . Sure, aren't they children, beautiful children, in those wedding clothes?"

Ma was not as tall as Nuala, maybe only five foot three, and her hair was short and red, not long and black, and her figure was understated compared to that of my companion. But she had, even in her old age, blazing blue eyes, just like Nuala's. She was a dangerous woman, no doubt about that. Was Nuala equally dangerous?

Probably.

"Younger even than you are, Nuala Anne. They ran away during the Troubles and never came back."

"Eejit times and eejit people. Well, they had one another, didn't they?"

"And lots of children and grandchildren." I returned the pictures reverently to my wallet.

We walked by the statues of Burke and Goldsmith, the two sentinels at the Front Gate of Trinity.

The names had meant nothing to her. The scandals of seventy years ago did not matter to the young people of Connemara today. It was ancient history, as unimportant as Wolfe Tone and Brian Boru.

Nuala McGrail was considering me carefully.

I was a quare one all right, odd even for a Yank. But maybe not all that bad. We walked into the Front Court of the college.

"I'll be taking my bike and going home now," she said. "Thanks for the use of the umbrella."

She pulled a cheap plastic rain wrap out of her book bag and draped it around her head and shoulders. Then she began to unlock a solitary bicycle from a rack I had not noticed before.

"You can't ride home in this weather, Nuala," I protested.

"Don't I do it every day?" She walked her bike through the vestibule and out the Front Gate, obeying the college rules against riding a bicycle inside the gate.

"I'll get a cab."

"You will *not*."

"But —"

"No buts about it." She mounted the cycle and then paused to ponder me again. "I didn't like the way you looked at me while I was singing."

"Huh?"

"Like you were taking off my clothes."

"Woman, I was not!"

"You were too!"

"I know when I'm doing that and when I'm not. I was admiring you but respectfully. Mind you, I make no promises about what my imagination might do the next time it sees you."

She hesitated. "Little enough to admire."

"A lot to admire. You're a beautiful woman, Nuala Anne McGrail."

"I am no such thing and I won't let you say that I am." She kicked away the stand and prepared to ride off into the mists.

I grabbed her arm. "A man can see a woman as desirable, Nuala, and still treat her with respect."

"Focking sex object." She struggled to free her arm.

"Sexed person." I wouldn't release her. "Understand?"

She stopped struggling. "Clever-talking Yank. . . . You embarrassed me something terrible. I didn't like it at all, at all."

"I wouldn't want to embarrass you, Nuala. I'm sorry if I did. But you are gorgeous and I can't help admiring you."

"I am *not*." She wrenched her arm free. Then, as if penitent, she added, "Mind you, I liked having you look at me that way."

"I thought you said you didn't like it."

"Don't be an amadon! I *didn't* like it but I *liked* it, in a manner of speaking."

As I had said to her earlier the Irish aren't like the rest of us.

She started to pedal away.

"Wait a minute! Where do you live? What's your phone number?"

"I don't have a phone," she shouted over her shoulder. "And you have no business asking where I live."

"How will I find you?"

"Sure, won't you be looking into O'Neill's pub the odd time?"

And she disappeared in the mists and the rain.

— 4 —

Isolated in soggy gloom that cut me off from the rest of the world, I reveled in self-pity. Sure, hadn't I lost the last great Celtic goddess of the Western World?

It was still a game then — infatuation, flirtation, self-pity.

Then I realized, after enjoying my allusion to John M. Synge, that I could find out when and where they were performing *The Playboy* and track Nuala down that way — as she doubtless realized even before she slipped off, shy and embarrassed child, into the wet night.

Shy, embarrassed, and attracted to me.

She ought to know better.

How could she know better?

I had better protect her.

From what?

From myself.

Don't be an eejit.

Forget about her. Don't go back to O'Neill's and don't find out where they're performing *The Playboy.*

Well, that's just what I would do. Probably.

Not exactly a druid goddess, but a shy Catholic virgin. I suppose I couldn't complain. They made much better wives than your druid goddesses.

I glanced around uneasily. I thought I heard faint footsteps behind me on Dawson Street. It was a half-hour walk back to my suite in Jury's and not a cab in sight. If they wanted to attack me again, this would be the perfect night to do it. This time they'd send tougher thugs.

They had tried the night before, after my unpleasant conversation with the Special Branch cop. It was a lovely warm evening, the air fresh and soft, a three-quarter moon shining over Dublin Town and bathing the streets, still wet from the afternoon rain, a magic silver. On nights like that Dublin seems a faerie city, perhaps the set for a Walt Disney fairy-tale film. I drifted out of Jury's, aimless as usual. I was still angry at Chief Superintendent Conlon's clumsy attempt to bully me. I was a citizen of the United States of America, wasn't I? Ireland was part of the free world, wasn't it? And what the hell kind of professor was it that would report a couple of honest questions to the gnomes of the Special Branch?

I'd show them. I'd write the whole story, the true story about Bill and Nell Pat Ready, and publish it as an American best-seller.

Ah, not without ambition after all, you say?

Dermot Coyne wants to be a writer, does he now? And a famous writer at that?

I didn't want it so badly that I'd return to my suite after supper and work on it. If literary fame came as easily as commodity trading profits, well, maybe. But in a choice between a leisurely walk down Pembroke Road and Baggot Street to St. Stephen's Green and research for a book, the former would win any time.

Auto traffic was heavy on the street, not unusual at that time of night, and there was a steady stream of pedestrians. I was hardly alone. There are streets in Dublin, particularly north of the Liffey, you avoid at half ten of an autumn evening, but not Pembroke Road.

I noticed the three punks when they walked by going in the opposite direction just after I had crossed the Grand Canal, a glittering black velvet band in the moonlight.

There was nothing particularly remarkable about them, kids in their late teens, jeans and black jackets, long hair, sneers painted on their faces. Over in the "Liberties" section behind Christ Church Cathedral or on the north side of the Liffey east of the Catholic pro-cathedral, they would be scary. Not, however, on Upper Baggot Street at this hour of the night.

It takes longer to describe my reaction to them than the reaction itself lasted.

When I felt someone grab my arms from behind, I knew who it was.

I must have looked like a pushover — I usually

do. A big patsy maybe, but still a patsy. Definitely not a white Richard Dent, as Nuala Anne would suggest the next day. Anyway, the three of them piled on like they expected a pushover.

I let them drag me down the two flights of iron steps to a concrete areaway in front of the darkened windows of a basement tea shop. I thought about yelling but decided that they wouldn't have jumped me if there was anyone nearby. They had waited for what seemed just the right moment.

"We'll teach you a lesson, you focking bastard," one of them sneered as he buried his fist in my stomach.

He must have felt pretty safe because his two pals were holding my arms. As I say, the focking Yank bastard was a pushover.

So he was not prepared for the impact of my foot in his groin.

He screamed and doubled up in agony, spitting out curses. Then I broke loose from the punk that had pinned my left arm and slammed him into the concrete foundation of the stairway up to the ground floor. Next I turned and slugged the punk who was trying to kick me. He fell back against the opposite wall, banged his head against the concrete, and stood there, momentarily stunned.

The other one came at me from behind. "I'm going to cut off your balls, bastard!" He had a switchblade in his hand, a very long switchblade.

He dove towards my groin.

His knife slit my trouser leg as I jumped away from him. He wheeled around for another try, this time aiming at my face.

I stepped aside, grabbed his arm, and twisted it behind his back. He roared with injured fury as the knife popped out of his hand.

Looking back on the fight, I should have broken his arm. I don't have much taste, however, for alley fighting.

The other kid had his knife out and rushed at me wildly. I ducked his first swipe. He crashed into the wall of the tea shop, bounced off it, and rushed me again. I jumped up on a windowsill and tripped him.

He fell forward, crashed into a bench, leaped up quickly, and lunged once more.

One chop on his arm sent that switchblade flying too.

Bounding back in blasphemous outrage, the two of them jumped on me and pulled me down on the cold concrete. I noticed a pot of geraniums next to my head, a useful weapon if I needed it.

I bellowed like an injured bull, shook them off, and staggered to my feet. They jumped me again. I was hurting in a number of places and was now thoroughly angry at them.

So I shifted my shoulders abruptly and threw the two of them through the plate-glass window into the tea shop. The third punk, still moaning over the damage I had done to his reproductive organs, lurched towards me, drunkenly waving his switchblade.

I scooped up the pot of red flowers and bashed it against his head. He collapsed like he had been shot. I lifted him off the ground and tossed him after his friends into the wreckage of the tea shop. I hoped that the owners had insurance.

I dusted off my hands and, trying to ignore my aching ribs and sore shoulder, walked back up the steps to Baggot Street.

I looked around for Chief Superintendent Conlon with the thought that I might toss him through the plate glass too. He was nowhere to be seen.

Back in my room at Jury's I noted that no visible damage had been done save to my jeans, though my ribs and shoulder were hurting. I took a couple of Advils, hung up my clothes, dirty and wet from the concrete, and slumped into my chair.

Then the reaction came. I realized what had happened and began to shake.

Should I call Conlon and tell him where he could find his thugs? Call the American embassy and protest? Call the local Garda station and report an assault?

I decided to do nothing at all.

So they called me.

I picked up the phone. "Good evening."

It was not Conlon's voice, at least I didn't think so. "Tonight was a hint of what we can do if you don't let the dead sleep in peace."

"You haven't seen your punks yet. What I did to them is a hint of what I'll do to you, focker, if you don't leave me alone."

I hung up on him.

Big deal.

But why? What were they warning me about? Could it be worth so much trouble merely to stop me from poking around in my grandparents' history? That didn't seem to make any sense.

It took me a long time to unwind and sleep. The sound of the cleaning staff in the corridor woke me up in the morning. I ached all over.

And for the first time I was consciously scared.

Not so scared, however, that I was ready to give up my determination to trace the story of my grandparents during the Troubles.

Nevertheless, I stayed away from the Long Room of the library at Trinity where I had been poking around for a couple of days and did not visit again Professor Nolan who had probably blown the whistle on me.

Instead I called home.

"Why, Dermot darling, how nice of you to call. We were just wondering about you yesterday. Have you met any nice Irish girls?"

"There aren't any, Mom. All the beautiful ones like you and Grandma Nell are in America."

"Now, darling, you shouldn't say that. I'm sure there's some lovely girl there just waiting for an American like you."

"Scores of them. . . . Mom, did Pa and Ma

leave any papers or anything?"

"Well," Mom replied, "your grandfather was not one for writing much down. But your grandmother kept all kinds of paper, she'd never throw anything out, you remember. There must be five or six crates down in the basement. I don't know what we should do with them."

So Mom, being Mom and believing that if you wait long enough, all problems, including a problem son, will solve themselves, had done nothing.

"Mom, could you ask George to wrap them up and ship them to me at Jury's in Dublin, Federal Express? Today if he can. I'm trying to write a book about their early days here in Ireland."

"Why, darling, what a wonderful idea. I'm sure Father George will be glad to help. . . . Will the book take long?"

George thought me a little less useless than the rest of my siblings did. He even professed to believe that I had some talent as a writer.

"Not too long. I'll be home soon. Would you ask George to send the boxes Federal Express today?" I repeated my instructions, less Mom forget them in her concern about me finding a nice little Irish girl. "I'll mail him a check."

"Of course, dear. And keep your eye open for some nice, sensible Irish girl."

"There aren't any, Mom. There isn't a sensible woman in this whole island."

"Your grandmother came from Ireland, dear."

"That was a long time ago, Mom."

And she wasn't all that sensible.

Rather Nell Pat Malone Ready was passionate — she threw herself into things with a mix of determination and abandonment, Grace O'Malley storming down out of the mountains.

If I were like her, I would have then and there purchased two (first-class) tickets for Chicago, rounded up Nuala Anne McGrail, and brought her home to Mother.

No, Grandma Nell was not what you'd call sensible. Shrewd maybe, clever maybe, cute in the Irish meaning of that word, but sensible? No way.

Mom was as pretty as Grandma Nell and as sweet and loving but neither sensible nor shrewd. She didn't have to be.

I half expected another attack that day, or another phone call. Nothing happened. Maybe they thought my absence from the library was a message. Maybe they were amateurs. So I wandered out into the fog and, my ribs still aching, into O'Neill's, looking for a quick one — and maybe a sympathetic womanly shoulder.

And found Nuala. Not a druid maiden, as it turned out, but a virginal Catholic agnostic from the West of Ireland who sang and acted and did not object to my kissing her and rather liked snuggling close to me under my umbrella.

Later that night, dazzled by the young woman who had sped off in the fog, I walked up Dawson

Street towards the green, listening for footsteps behind me and fantasizing about holding Nuala in my arms.

Respectfully, of course.

Not that I would have any choice in the matter, except to be respectful.

I was almost at the bottom of Dawson Street when I thought I heard footsteps behind me in the dark. I stopped. They seemed to stop too. Maybe I was hearing my own echo.

My mind still on the luminous — and numinous — Nuala Anne McGrail, I foolishly cut across the green instead of skirting it. I would walk up Lesson Street to the canal and then back to Pembroke Road. The mists and fog were now so thick that I could only see a couple of feet ahead. The green seemed deserted. The footsteps now were right behind me and coming faster.

I ducked off the pathway and hid behind a bush next to the pond. This time I'd get the jump on them.

Two people emerged from the darkness. I yelled like a banshee and jumped. I grabbed both of them in a mighty bear hug and prepared to throw them into the pond.

Then I heard my prisoners whimper in fright and looked at their faces.

Two kids, a boy and a girl, younger even than Nuala. Young lovers walking arm and arm in the park.

I released them. "Don't ever sneak up on a

man in the fog," I warned them, trying to sound gruff.

The girl screamed and rushed off in the fog, still screaming. The boy — he seemed half my size — paused as if he were pondering a thorough thrashing of his assailant. Then he turned and ran after his love. "Eileen! Eileen," he shouted. "Wait for me!"

I hurried away before the Guards had a chance to sweep the green.

The next morning a headline in the *Irish Independent* announced, "Couple Assaulted in the Green by 'Bigfoot'!"

According to the story, the couple had told the Guards that some "terrible monster creature" had grabbed them in his arms — a bear or a gorilla or maybe even Bigfoot — and shouted at them in a foreign language. "He was certain to kill us both," Eileen McGovern had told the *Independent*. "And done horrible things to me before he chewed off my head, but sure didn't Henry chase him off."

Lucky Henry to be the recipient of such love.

The Guards had searched the green and found no trace of the assailant, except for large footprints near the pond. "They were very big prints," said Garda Sergeant Tomas O'Cuiv. "No ordinary human could have made them."

Size eleven, Sergeant? You must have too much of the drink taken.

The Guard sergeant also noted that the attack seemed to be similar to that of an unknown assailant who the previous night had thrown three young men through the plate-glass window of a tea shop on Lower Baggot Street.

"This Bigfoot person has been quite active this week," the Garda had said.

The story concluded with the observation that no zoos or circuses reported any missing animals.

Doubtless there would be more sightings of Bigfoot around the city and the country. I had started a crime wave.

The last Bigfoot of the Western World.

What would Nuala think if I told her?

First I would have to find her.

And kiss her again. Naturally.

I waited a few days and went back to the Berkeley Library at Trinity College, my eyes searching the face of every woman with long black hair to see if she was Nuala, and hunted up newspapers from 1922. When I returned to Jury's I found that the boxes had come from America, six large cartons stuffed with memorabilia. It occurred to me that the materials might be useful for an immigrant archive somewhere. I ought to put them in order or maybe hire someone to put them in order. I didn't sort through them myself, because I didn't know yet what I was looking for.

I was more certain than ever that Professor Nolan had turned me in. I half made up my mind, as the locals would say, to corner him in his office and offer to toss him through the first plate glass that was available.

– 5 –

NO LOST GOLD, R.I.C. SAYS
Chief Superintendent Roderick McShane
of the Royal Irish Constabulary, Galway
Barracks, gave assurances today that there
was no gold missing in the West of Ireland
following the arrest of Sir Roger Casement,
who is now awaiting trial for treason in
the Kilmanhaim Jail.

"Treasure hunters may amuse themselves
with such legends," the Chief Superintendent said. "However, the plain truth is
that we confiscated all the bullion that Sir
Roger attempted to smuggle into the country from an enemy submarine. Rebel leaders should not deceive themselves or others
into thinking that there are any funds available to finance their seditious plans."

The clipping, brown with age and crumbling
at the touch, was not dated. But the time had
to be late winter or very early spring of 1916.
Nell Malone was only eleven years old. Why
would she save this bit of a Galway newspaper
— and put it on the top of the little stack I
had found in her archives?

Was it the beginning of her story?

Sir Roger Casement, an agent of the secret Irish Republican Brotherhood, the IRB, later hanged by the English after they had released his "black diaries," which told tales of sexual perversion, had tried to smuggle German weapons and money into Ireland to support the "Rising" that the Irish Volunteers were planning for Easter 1916.

(Some distinctions: The shadowy secret society called the Irish Republican Brotherhood — condemned by the church — was the real power behind Irish revolutionary agitation. The Volunteers — later to become the Irish Republican Army — were the fighting force that was manipulated, without knowing it, by the secret society. Michael Collins would become the head of the Irish Republican Brotherhood in 1919, and it supported his peace treaty, but by then it had lost control of the IRA.)

An informant had tipped off the English of the attempt to land the cargo from a German submarine. The identity of the traitor had never been learned. There were always Irish informers ready to betray revolts.

In a country where there was so much poverty and suffering and so little hope, informing had become almost a cottage industry.

The next several clippings were accounts of the Easter Rising in Dublin in April of 1916 and the executions that followed. Knowing that their cause was hopeless without the German weapons and money, the leadership of the IRB had tried to cancel the planned rebellion. However, the Dublin branch, convinced that a gesture would stir the souls of the Irish people, went ahead with the plan. The Irish Volunteers and the Citizen Army seized the General Post Office — because it dominated Sackville (or O'Connell) Street, the main street of the city — and other strong points in Dublin on Easter Monday. After several days of artillery bombardment, the rebels surrendered. Most of the Irish people were horrified by the revolt and by the bloodshed in Dublin during the fighting for which they blamed the leaders of the Rising.

However, the English, in one of their many classic miscalculations about Ireland, promptly executed the leaders and turned them into martyrs. Willy Yeats's "terrible beauty" was born, and the final battle for freedom was launched with the now-overwhelming support of the Irish people.

THE WEST HAS RISEN!

June, 1916

The West has Risen! Irish Volunteer forces in the West have continued to fight despite the surrender of their colleagues in Dublin. A communiqué issued by Domhnall O'Ceallaigh, commandant of the Galway Brigade.

"We have no intention of surrendering," the communiqué said. "We shall continue the fight until the last soldier of British

70

imperialism is driven from the sacred soil of Ireland. In Dublin poets became fighters. In the West all we have is fighters. There is nothing else for us to do but to fight. We shall fight and we shall win."

Chief Superintendent Roderick McShane of the Royal Irish Constabulary dismissed the manifesto. "It represents nothing more than the drunken ravings of a handful of romantic dreamers. There is no rebellion in Galway or anywhere in the West."

Daniel O'Kelly, as his name would be spelled in English. Could I remember Ma or Pa ever mentioning his name?

I didn't think so. Yet his manifesto was important to her, or it wouldn't have been included in the stack.

McSHANE SHOT DEAD

December 1919

Bulletin! We have just learned that Chief Superintendent Roderick McShane of the Royal Irish Constabulary was shot dead this morning in the Claddagh while returning from Sunday Mass. R.I.C. officers suspect the work of the republican rebels.

Shot coming home from Mass? Catholics now were killing other Catholics. It would get worse. And in the Claddagh, the ancient thatched-roof section of Galway city, near the docks (and hence its name, which means "key"). It was always a wild place. What was an RIC officer doing there on Sunday morning?

The guerrilla war had begun.

The next several clippings, from 1919 to 1921, recounted the so-called Anglo-Irish war between the British army and its notorious mercenary Auxiliary Police and the hated "Black and Tans," and the Irish Volunteers, who were soon being called (by themselves) the Irish Republican Army. Britain was tired from the Great War and had no stomach for a long and perhaps useless campaign in Ireland. This time it looked like the Irish meant business.

The headlines didn't leave much doubt about that.

THREE MORE HOMES BURNED
April 1920

Constabulary officers said today that three more houses had been burned last night, all of them homes of landlords. The irregulars are running wild, destroying every home owned by the gentry. Many landlords are leaving for England. The countryside, particularly in North Galway and South Mayo, according to some, is as desolate as it was in the time of the "Little Famine" forty-five years ago.

AUXILIARIES SHOT DEAD
November 1920

72

The bodies of five members of the Auxiliary Force were found this morning outside the Harp and Shamrock public house in Oughterard. Townsfolk professed to know nothing of their deaths, but Constabulary officers suspect that the five dead men had been drinking in the pub when they were set upon by the flying squad of irregulars directed by "Commandant" Daniel O'Kelly.

The Harp and Shamrock had been badly damaged in the course of the night. The publican said that he did not know what had happened to it or whether the Auxiliaries or the irregulars had laid it waste.

The motorcar used by the auxiliaries has disappeared from the village. The latest report, on the phone this afternoon, from Lord Crowe's home, is that the Constabulary had yet to recover the vehicle.

Army reinforcements are reported on the move from Cork to Galway to put an end to Kelly's depredations.

AMBUSH IN CLARE
May 1921

According to reports received late yesterday, an army convoy was ambushed on the road between Limerick and Ennis. Several transports were destroyed as well as two Crosley tenders. There were no reports of army casualties. The rumors in Galway last night attributed the ambush to a joint attack by the Clare and Galway brigades of the irregulars, said to be operating under the leadership of Commandant Daniel O'Kelly.

TWO MEN HANGED
July 1921

The bodies of two men were found yesterday hanging from a gibbet at Maam Cross in Connemara. The identity of the victims was not learned immediately. However, there is reason to believe that their deaths are another brutal deed of Commandant Daniel O'Kelly of the Irish Republican Army flying squad that has been operating in Connemara.

IRA DESTROYS FISHING BOATS
August 1920

In its most daring assault yet, the flying squad of the Irish Republican Army's Galway Brigade stove in the hulls of five fishing boats in the Corrib River yesterday. It is believed that the fishermen had refused to pay the "tax" levied on them by Colonel Daniel O'Kelly, the leader of the Brigade.

R.I.C. officers admit they are powerless to prevent O'Kelly's brazen raids. "They are singing ballads about him in every pub in the West of Ireland," one of them remarked. "As long as the people not only tolerate but admire such crimes, we will be unable to stop them."

The IRA, now led by Michael Collins, one of the great military and political geniuses of the twentieth century, had learned the truth that Chairman Mao later articulated: The guerrilla must swim in the sea of the people.

Had Pa, Bill Ready, the genial, gentle hero of my youth, a man of story and song, a daily communicant till the day he died, burned English manor houses, shot Black and Tans, hanged suspected traitors, ambushed English convoys, stove in the hulls of fishing boats, and helped bring the British Lion finally to its knees when he was younger than I was the year I flunked out of Notre Dame?

Was he what today we would call a terrorist, and perhaps a brutal one at that?

Ma had hinted vaguely to me that Pa had been involved somehow in the Troubles. But as a killer? I could hardly believe it.

Yet why else would she have saved this little treasure trove of clippings?

Surely she was not ashamed of his involvement; she was never ashamed of anything her man did or said.

I tried to picture what it was like in Galway after the Great War, a time that had more in common with the remote past than it does with our era. There were no radios, no TV, no electricity, only a handful of telephones, a few motor vehicles — buses and an occasional rich man's auto. Newspaper stories were brief because, especially in provincial cities like Galway, there were no teams of reporters and the editor could do little more than report rumors. One moved by walking or by horse or perhaps by bicycle (invented in Belfast a couple of decades earlier). One communicated by word of mouth.

And if one was young and educated in a secondary school, one perhaps dreamed of doing great deeds for Irish freedom. In our more sophisticated day such dreams might seem like patriotic nonsense — though not to terrorists in many parts of the world.

Ma and Pa terrorists?

How could they have been?

Yet who was I to judge? What would I have done if I came upon a squad of Black and Tan rapists and murderers terrorizing a defenseless town?

The IRA invented guerrilla war, it is often said. It invented modern terrorism too, or at least perfected it.

Were Pa and Ma involved in such deadly inventions?

How could I deny it?

The Sinn Fein ("We Ourselves") party, running on a platform that promised an Irish republic, had won the 1918 election in Ireland. Its delegates had refused to go to Westminster but constituted themselves the Dáil Eireann in Dublin and proclaimed the independence of Ireland. Astonishingly, the British permitted them to meet. In late 1920, however, the issue was still very much in doubt. If the British were not able to defeat Michael Collins and the IRA, neither did the rebels have much hope of driving the British out of Ireland.

Worn out by the Great War, Britain had no stomach for a long campaign in Ireland. General Sir Neville McCready, the British commander, had candidly informed Prime Minister David Lloyd George that he saw no prospect of a military victory. McCready was the first general, but not the last, in this century to discover that a small band of men, if its members are brave enough and dedicated enough, can hamstring a large modern army.

Collins and the more moderate leaders of the IRA realized that they were running short on men and munitions and that they could not sustain their campaign at the same level much longer.

The two exhausted sides stumbled to the bargaining table in London during the winter and spring of 1921 to work on a peace treaty.

The treaty established the "Irish Free State," a kind of dominion within the British Empire. Britain would keep possession of two "treaty ports" in Ireland — Cobb and Kingstown. The province of Ulster, its precise boundaries undetermined, whose Protestants had sworn to fight against union with the rest of Ireland, was granted de facto existence as a part of the United

Kingdom, and an oath of allegiance to the British crown would be required of all officials of the Free State government.

Collins, Arthur Griffith, William Cosgrave, and Kevin O'Higgins, the leaders of the moderate wing of the revolutionaries, did not like the treaty. But they were sick of the conflict and the killing and knew that it was the best deal they could get. They signed the treaty (signatures that were death warrants for two of them) and persuaded the majority of the Dáil to ratify it.

As Collins (called "the Big Fella" because of his broad shoulders and his commanding presence) said, "It's not the total freedom we want, but we can turn it into total freedom."

De Valera, the president of the "Republic" (nicknamed "Long Fella" because of his height), disagreed, resigned as president, and rejected the treaty. So in early 1921 the two men and the factions they represented were at war with one another, although Collins had taken care of Dev's family when the latter was in jail because of his participation in the Easter Rising and indeed had arranged for his escape from prison.

Thus began the Irish Civil War in which the former allies in the Anglo-Irish War executed, assassinated, and murdered one another with reckless enthusiasm. Both sides called each other traitor and showed no mercy in their killings.

The "Big Fella" was one of the first to die

— he himself had predicted that he would not survive the conflict.

Years later, long after the Civil War ended, De Valera followed Collins's plan to turn the Free State slowly into an independent nation. Yet for all his long life "Dev" felt that he lived in the shadow of Collins.

I opened a book I had been reading and flipped to a full-page picture of Michael Collins — a broad-faced, square-shouldered Irishman with brown wavy hair and a smile that was almost a mischievous grin. I knew his kind well: the life of any party, witty, handsome, and intelligent beneath the fast talk, not altogether unlike my brother George.

The picture was taken at the beginning of the Anglo-Irish War. Collins must have been about twenty-five. At the end he was said to be thin and worn and close to despair because of the horror of former comrades killing one another.

He who takes the sword . . .

A very old, and much handled, clipping from the *Cork Examiner* in Ma's pile of clippings gave the first account of his death.

GENERAL COLLINS SLAIN

August 1922

Bulletin. According to reports just received in Cork, General Michael Collins, Acting Minister of Defense for the Irish Free State, is believed to have been killed in an ambush between Skibbereen and Crookston in Bealnablath. It would appear that General Collins was the only casualty of a brief skirmish between his convoy and a band of Irregulars. Born in Sam's Cross in West Cork, General Collins was thirty-one years old.

Killed in his own country where he thought he would be safe, killed in an expedition into the front lines where the chairman of the Provisional Government, minister of defense, and commander in chief of the Free State Army (and the soul of the Free State government) ought not to have been, killed at the head of a column fighting a skirmish. Killed under mysterious circumstances.

A loss for Ireland and for the world.

I knew the whole story because I had read the books about him before the Special Branch warned me off my research about the Civil War in the West and Liam O'Riada's participation in it.

It was not clear exactly what happened. Apparently most of those who waited in ambush had left the scene because the convoy was late in arriving. Only a handful of men in a rear guard opened fire on the armored car, touring car, and Crosley tenders as they turned into the gloomy little vale. Collins died after the shooting had apparently stopped, killed by a single bullet to the head.

Nor is it certain who organized the ambush and why. Some stories say that the Irregulars feared an attempt to capture De Valera, who was nearby, though the convoy was on an inspection and not a military mission and Dev was not likely to forget then that Collins had organized his escape from a London jail. Later when he learned of Collins's death, he lamented that the last man who could stop the Civil War was dead.

Erskine Childers, an English officer fighting with the Irish (later executed by the Free State), who had become a leader in the "Irregulars" (as the antitreaty forces were called by the Free State government), was only ten miles away and knew nothing of either the convoy or the ambush.

While the IRA (as the Irregulars called themselves) felt that Collins was a traitor, they were not eager to claim credit for his death. They professed to know nothing about the attack.

Moreover, the fact that Collins was killed *after* the skirmish was over has led some to claim that he was shot by a member of his own convoy who had a grudge against him — or perhaps who wanted to replace him.

The most common belief today is that the affair was an accident of war — a chance meeting between two small units in the mountains of West Cork, a short, ugly firefight, a final shot fired at a high officer (with red collar tabs on his green uniform) by a retreating rifleman, most likely a Kerry man called Dennis "Sonny" Neill who had been a sharpshooter in the British army during World War I — and a daily communicant at that. No one, however, especially if one is Irish, willingly gives up a conspiracy theory.

My hand was trembling as I picked up the last of Ma's clippings. Had Ma saved the clipping because Pa killed Michael Collins? Surely he had killed others if he was part of Daniel O'Kelly's flying squad. He would not have known that the officer with the red tabs was Collins. And what would the Galway flying squad be doing in West Cork on August 22, 1922?

I can remember Ma on the subject of Collins. "Well, my dear, he was a great man, now wasn't he? And don't let anyone tell you anything different. He might have been wrong about the treaty, but wasn't his death a terrible loss to all of us? Sure, didn't a lot of them on the other side weep when they heard the news that he'd been killed, and right in his own county too?"

Would she have spoken so easily if she knew Pa had killed him, however unintentionally? Was that the reason they could never return to Ireland?

I recalled the rest of the history of the Civil War as I stared out the window at the rain falling on Jury's outdoor swimming pool. I should go down and swim in it. Keep my resolution about exercising, even if it rained.

De Valera learned what happened when the

guerrillas lose the sea of the people in which to swim. Most of the Irish people were satisfied with the Free State. Irish Americans, who had furnished the money to support the revolution, lost interest after the treaty was signed. What difference did the two "treaty ports" make? And if the Protestants in the six counties wanted to remain part of England, well, it was only fair to let them do so, wasn't it?

So after two years of the Civil War, the Long Fella ordered the Irregulars to "dump" their arms and run for seats in the Dáil. After serving a year in jail, he managed to find a way to take the oath of allegiance to the British crown when he was elected to the Dáil in 1927. His own conscience thus salved, he moved from being the leader of a rebellion against the Free State to the opposition leader in the Dáil. In 1932 he won the election and became president of the Executive Council (prime minister) himself (and "Taoiseach" in 1937 under a new constitution). The "pro-treaty" party and the "anti-treaty" party have alternated in power ever since. Eventually Dev would outlaw the IRA — the handful of intransigents who would not accept his decision to switch from the bullet to the ballot.

They have not gone away.

I paused to figure out which party was running things now. It was Dev's party, the anti-Free State party. Ireland moved almost overnight from settling differences by civil war to settling them by elections. A reasonable enough change. But why . . .

I finally looked at the last, no, it was the second-to-the-last clipping.

O'CEALLAIGH SLAIN

September 1922

The body of Domhnall O'Ceallaigh, commander of the Galway Brigade of the irregulars, was found late yesterday at Maam Cross, the site of his numerous executions of suspected traitors. His body was riddled with bullets. The Garda Siochana have no suspects in the killing, though they theorize that it was the result of another internal quarrel among the remnants of the irregulars.

In recent months O'Ceallaigh is reported to have lost most of his supporters and has narrowly escaped capture by the Gardai Siochana on several occasions. Commandant O'Ceallaigh was thirty years old.

When informed of the Commandant's death, we are told that Lieutenant General Richard Mulcahy, Commander in Chief of the National Army, remarked in Dublin, "He was a brave man and in many ways a great Irish patriot. It is unfortunate that he did not understand everything that is required of a patriot. However, that fact does not distract from his very real accomplishments as an army commander."

It is rumored that Commandant O'Ceal-laigh's adjutant, Captain Liam O'Riada, has succeeded him as Commanding Officer of the now depleted Brigade.

So Pa did fight with Daniel O'Kelly! And replaced him as guerrilla commander. But, wait a minute, this was in late 1922, about the time that Pa and Ma were married and left Ireland, never to return.

There was probably nothing left of the brigade to disband. But couldn't he have joined Dev and become legal? Or was the price the Free State might have put on his head too high for that ever to happen? Was there no room in the New Ireland, forgiving as it might finally have been willing to be, for the killer of Michael Collins?

I thought about that for a minute or two. The old animosities were not forgotten. After all, despite the official figures of eight hundred dead in the Civil War (more than in the Anglo-Irish War), perhaps as many as four thousand people had died. There was much reason to hate. But the animosities were less important for those who remained in Ireland and tried to make the new nation work as a peaceful and democratic country than for those who migrated to the United States in the early 1920s and kept their hates alive.

Childers's son became president of Ireland and Cosgrave's son served as Taoiseach under him.

They might not have been friends, but they didn't try to kill one another. Quite the contrary, they probably went out of their way to be civil to one another in sessions of the Dáil.

Ma and Pa didn't seem to hate anyone, however. Nor to pay much attention to Irish news or politics. Pa became an Organization Democrat and a Cubs fan. I sat on his knee and watched the '69 Cubs blow the pennant, to the deep dismay of both of us. Whatever had happened, they cut all their ties, even ties of interest with Ireland.

Why would that bother anyone more than seventy years later? The mystery of who killed Michael Collins and Daniel O'Kelly might be a fascinating historical detective story, but who cared anymore — beyond perhaps a few argumentative folks in the pubs who too much of the drink had taken?

It didn't make much sense.

I glanced at my map of County Galway. Maam Cross was not all that far from Carraroe, just up the road, so to speak. Was Nuala part of the group that was watching me?

Then I realized that my suspicion was silly. No one would know that I might wander into O'Neill's pub on a rainy autumn afternoon.

Though if they found out afterward of my interest in her, they might. . . .

It wasn't likely but it was a possibility.

The last clipping was dated 1932 — the year Mom was born. It was a picture with a caption.

COUNCIL PRESIDENT DEDICATES MEMORIAL IN OUGHTERARD

Mr. De Valera, the President of the Executive Council, is shown at the dedication of a statue of Commandant Daniel O'Kelly in Oughterard. Commandant O'Kelly was a hero of the Anglo-Irish War. He and his flying squad of the Galway Brigade of the Irish Volunteers saved the town after a night of drunken depredations by the British Auxiliary Forces, the hated Black and Tans.

Was there a subtle irony in Ma's inclusion of that picture? Was she saying that the gombeen man Kelly was a hero again and her husband still a fugitive?

What did it all mean? What did it matter even if I found out what it meant?

It was, nonetheless, a fascinating mystery puzzle that I had to solve.

I went down to the lobby and made Xerox copies of Ma's file. The old newsprint wouldn't last much longer. Then I returned to the room, put the copies in a thin file folder in my luggage, and left the originals inside the Margery Forester biography of Michael Collins on one of the end tables in the parlor of my suite. Later I'd reread the newspaper article on Collins and compare it with the biography. Then I'd put the stack of clippings back in Ma's archives, which now lined one wall of my suite.

Was Pa, who told me stories and sang songs for me as far back as I could remember, the man who killed Michael Collins? Or maybe the killer of Daniel O'Kelly?

Or maybe both?

– 6 –

I did go to watch her in *The Playboy*, even though I swore to myself that I would not do so.

Mind you, I had wandered about the classic squares and playing fields of TCD looking for her among the swarms of students, now mostly Irish and Catholic, who walked briskly to and from classes — as if they didn't know that there would be no jobs for most of them when they graduated.

The Players bulletin board in the vestibule between Front Gate and Front Court announced that the Players were presenting John M. Synge's "once-controversial play," in 103 Front Court at half eight on Friday, Saturday, and Sunday. Marie Fionnuala McGrail would play Pegeen Mike.

So that's how she spelled her name.

I fiddled with Grandma Nell's archives on Friday and Saturday night and decided on Sunday afternoon that I'd ride out to Houth on the DART and watch the tide go out. Or come in. Or whatever.

And stay there till after the play was over.

I went out on the train all right and marveled at the green sea in the golden autumn sunset, a splash of red and purple like the expensive mass vestments the pastor of Saint Mark's back home occasionally exhumed from his treasure chest of pre-Vatican Council relics.

Then I rode right back into Dublin and hiked over to Trinity College.

The "theater" was small and half empty at that — a few young people on an inexpensive date, some elderly folks with nothing else to do, a couple of "Yank" tourists — I could recognize them by now — and some fusty-looking faculty types.

I think you are all in for a surprise, I muttered to myself.

My image of *Playboy* was formed by the film Siobhan McKenna made twenty years ago, staged on the strand at Inch in Dingle Bay. The College Players didn't have the wonderful Kerry scenery to work with. Moreover, the setting of the inside of a public house in the West of Ireland at the turn of the century was pretty much left to the audience's imagination.

They didn't have Siobhan McKenna either, God be good to her.

But they had Nuala, my Nuala.

Sensibly she didn't try to be the late Ms. McKenna. She played Pegeen Mike her own way

— a tomboy with headlong energy, a fierce temper, and a fiercer wit.

The rest of the cast seemed to think they were lucky to be on the same stage with her.

At first I was put off by the fact that Siobhan McKenna, my fair Nuala was not. How dare this slip of a girl from Carraroe play Pegeen Mike as if Synge's heroine was an energetic teenage hoyden?

As the play continued, however, utterly dominated by Nuala Anne McGrail's passion, I began to see her point. She was engaging in an intelligent and original interpretation of the story. Synge might not have liked it (though perhaps he would have liked Nuala), but it was a challenging reading of the play.

The audience loved it, aware, I suspect, that this "wee lass" up on the stage was one of their own. When she delivered her last sad lines, there were a few dry eyes in the place but not many.

" 'Oh, my grief, I've lost him surely. I've lost the only playboy of the Western World.' "

I must be honest: Mine was not one of the dry eyes.

I walked up to the front of the hall and cornered one of the young women ushers. "Would you ever be giving this bunch of weeds to herself?"

Note that I was talking their language again, this time quite unselfconsciously.

"Is it a dozen roses now?" the apple-cheeked child enthused, glancing at my height. "Ah, sure, wouldn't she be happy to accept them herself?"

"Ah, it wouldn't be right for me to intrude in her privacy, would it now?"

I scrawled "from one Pegeen Mike to a much better one" on the blank card attached to the bouquet and shoved it into the kid's hand.

"Should I tell her who it's from?" she asked dubiously.

"Won't she be knowing as soon as she sees them? But couldn't you say it was from a tall Yank? And won't she sniff and say, well, he's not the worst of them?"

"Isn't that a compliment in our country?"

She looked at the roses so wistfully that I wished I had brought a second dozen for my go-between.

I hurried out of the building, lest herself come running madly after me. She could sing and she could act and she was studying accounting.

She was also a detective, I would learn later, a puzzle solver, a young Irish Ms. Marple maybe, someone who knew the answer to the puzzle long before anyone else. Looking back on our adventure, I now realize that I played Watson to her Holmes most of the time. She was so clever that I didn't realize my role until the very end.

I don't like being Watson to anyone.

It was raining again in Dublin's fair city, a slow, gentle rain, "soft," the locals would call it. I thought that I might just as well be in Gary, Indiana.

Feeling infinitely sorry for myself, a great Irish pastime, especially when it's raining, I wandered down Grafton Street to St. Stephen's Green, listening out of one ear for footballs behind me and thinking of the possibility of another Bigfoot caper.

I was glad to get back to my suite in Jury's. Out of my bedroom window, when it wasn't raining, the Dublin Mountains loomed in the distance. From the windows of my parlor I could see Christ Church and the Liberties. The suite wasn't home, but it was as close to home as I had been in a long time.

I had chosen Jury's because it had both a pool and an exercise room and the suite because if I took it for a month there was a big discount and, I argued to soothe my conscience, I needed a room in which to work on my computer. My suite with its light floral wall covering and green furniture was comfortable and reassuring, if a bit lonely, and I could cook my own snacks in it. The hotel, glass atriums and fountains, throbbed with life — American tourists, Irish businessmen, and young men and women awkward in formal attire for dinners at night. Life pulsed through Jury's and managed to miss me, which was the way I wanted it.

Till I met my Pegeen Mike.

After a very small taste of Bushmill's Single Malt, I sighed almost as heavily as if I were a native and began the melancholy task of systematically searching through my grandmother's

92

memorabilia. She was a convinced paper saver — newspaper clippings about her husband, marriage announcements of her children and grandchildren, baptismal photos of her great-grandchildren, crayon drawings by the children and the grandchildren — half of which, I fear, were manic fantasies by her favorite ("because he's the spitting image of himself"), a certain Dermot, or as she preferred, Diramuid Coyne.

"Ma, you'll spoil him rotten," my own mother used to protest with notable lack of sincerity.

"Ah, he's such a winsome one, poor little thing," Ma — as I called her too — would respond, "wouldn't anyone just adore him?"

They all adored me, all right, my parents, my siblings, my aunts and uncles, my cousins. Maybe they did spoil me. Or maybe the ambition genes had run thin by the time I came along. Or maybe my parents, while greeting me as a happy surprise, didn't have the energy left to inculcate the work ethic in me.

I could do no wrong, not even when I did things wrong, like flunk out of Notre Dame or quit the Fenwick football team. They'd line up, led by "Ma," to provide excuses.

And they had a week of parties to celebrate my success at the Merc — it was a "grand achievement, altogether grand," Ma said, as if pure dumb luck was any achievement at all.

Six months later "Pa" was dead and herself another four months after her husband.

My eyes filled with tears as I sorted through

her archives. I told myself that there was no reason to weep. Ma had led a full, happy, and passionate life, struggling from dire poverty to comfortable affluence, raising seven children, and living to see her great-grandchildren: "Ah, sure, Derm, me boy, 'tis no great feat at all, at all. You only have to marry young and live long."

Why was I crying for Ma?

Because I missed her. And because I missed her at the end, when, they told me, she kept asking for me — and characteristically she made excuses for my not being there.

At the bottom of the second box I found a stack of tiny paper-covered notebooks, neatly piled and wrapped in rubber bands, maybe thirty of them. I opened the first one. It was written in Irish and in a tiny script whose letters I could not decipher. I could, however, make out numbers on the first page: 14, 05, 19. I glanced through the other pages. Dates on all of them. A diary! Ma's diary. In May of 1919, she would have been fourteen years old!

Ma had not made entries every day. She had apparently written things down when she thought she had something worth recording.

Ma kept a diary! She never told me! She probably never told anyone, except "himself," and a secret told him was as safe as one told to a lion in front of the Art Institute.

I considered the little booklets and permitted the first hint of an idea to form in the back of my head. Might there not be in these old books, the early ones discolored with age, an explanation for why they never went back, the reason why — I could hear her voice whispering in my ear when I was maybe eight — "Sure, if we went back, my poor little gosson, would they not shoot the both of us?"

I shivered again, in memory of an eight-year-old gosson's shivering.

Moreover, might there not be in these books a publishable memoir, or at least a rich document for the Chicago Historical Society?

It occurred to me then that I probably ought to call home. Mom and Dad would be watching the Chicago Bears in the family room, probably with George the Priest present to second-guess Mike Ditka, since the Bears were playing at Green Bay. Why not call them?

(Did I keep track of the Bears' schedule even though I had been wandering the world? Of course I did! What kind of a fan wouldn't?)

Fortunately for me it was half time and the Bears were ahead — or the conversation would have been short and my temporary antidote for homesickness denied me.

"Mom, did you know that Ma kept a diary?"

"I'm sure she didn't, darling. She didn't keep secrets from us."

"She did, Mom. From the fourteenth of May 1919 to" — I flipped open the final book "to three weeks before she died."

"Well, what did she say?" Mom was mildly

interested, but unperturbed — Mom was rarely if ever perturbed, a serene child of a wild and passionate woman.

"I don't know. It's all in Irish."

"*Really?* I didn't know she remembered the language! Ah, Dermot, she was a grand lady!"

"I know."

"Maybe it's just as well we can't read it. She wouldn't want us prying in her secrets."

"Then she would have destroyed them, wouldn't she?"

"I suppose so. . . . Have you met that special Irish girl yet?"

For some crazy reason I told her I had — perhaps because of the hint of longing in my mother's voice: She believed firmly that if her last child would only meet a "nice young woman," he would settle down, come home, and use his many talents wisely and well, all most unlikely eventualities.

"What's her name?" Mom demanded happily.

"Nuala Anne McGrail — the first name is short for Fionnuala. She's a student at TCD, Trinity College, that is, studying to be an accountant but she acts and sings."

Why was I letting all this spill out? There was as little chance of my ever bringing Nuala home to Mom as there was of Boris Yeltsin joining the Young Republicans.

"Is she pretty?"

"Outstanding!"

God forgive me for what I was doing.

Then Dad came on and analyzed for me the Bears' mistakes during the first half. He was followed by Prester George, as I called him.

"A girl?" he demanded incredulously.

"It's not serious, George. Never will be."

"She look like Ma?"

George, you will perceive, is a very clever young cleric.

"Not at all."

Ma was short and compact with flashing green eyes (which I inherit from her along with Pa's blond hair and height) and red hair in her youth. "My wee Gypsy lass," Pa used to needle her, a description that always caused her to pretend she was furious with him.

In fact, I can't remember her ever really being angry at her husband.

"Yeah?" Prester George said skeptically.

"Tall, black-haired, blue-eyed, willowy, foul-mouthed."

"Sounds like just your type."

If I had told George that she was from the Carraroe Gaeltacht, he would have been overjoyed — "the model fits the data," he would crow.

I'm fond of George, admire him and respect him as a matter of fact. But I don't like to be the subject of his pop psychological hypotheses.

"It's not important, George. I've only spoken to her once."

"Sometimes that's all that's required," he said

97

carefully. George was acutely aware of my troubles with women and careful not to tread on too many raw memories.

"She called me a pissant Yank gobshite."

"Sounds very perceptive." He laughed.

I changed the subject to Notre Dame's team, for which I still root as a matter of right, even if they did bounce me out.

When I had said good-bye to them, I returned to feeling sorry for myself. It was delightful.

What, you might well ask, is the trouble with Dermot Coyne? Is he short on hormones? Here's a gifted, intelligent, and gorgeous young woman, contentious enough to be interesting, vulnerable enough to be appealing, and interested enough in him (she didn't protest the kiss, did she?) to perhaps be open to pursuit.

So why doesn't said Dermot Coyne begin the preliminaries of pursuit? Is he not of such an age that a woman like the fair Nuala Anne should produce all kinds of physical reactions in him? To say nothing of obscene (though respectful) fantasies?

Hasn't he admitted the reactions and the fantasies already, poor dear man?

Why didn't the eejit go backstage with his dozen red roses and present them to the aforementioned young woman, perhaps the first flowers anyone has given her in her young life?

Surely that would earn him the right to another kiss, would it not? Perhaps a brief hug of gratitude?

You've got to understand that while I've been lucky in the S and P pit at the Merc, I have had an unlucky history in love. I'd already been seriously in love twice in my life, I mean really seriously. One of those relationships ended in tragedy, the other in catastrophe, though perhaps the catastrophe was comedic.

No, in retrospect, it was surely a comedy, even if the laugh was on me.

I stacked Ma's diaries and returned them to the crate in which they had come, making sure that they were as neatly arranged as she had left them. Ma was not, as I've said before, obsessive-compulsive. But she did keep things neat.

The phone rang. Who the hell was disturbing my peace here in Jury's on a cold foggy Dublin night?

"Dermot Coyne," I said.

Silence.

"Well?" I said impatiently, though my heart beat rapidly and my mouth suddenly dried up.

"You enjoyed the play tonight, did you now?" The voice was hoarse, deliberately disguised, not the same disguise as the last time.

"And if I did?"

"Nothing wrong with that at all, at all, is there? So long as you continue to be a good boy and don't ask any more questions you shouldn't be asking, if you take my meaning?"

"Fuck you," I shouted, and slammed down the phone.

Instantly I regretted that I had not added a

crack about Bigfoot.

Like "never fock around with Bigfoot, you fockers!"

As I have said before, when they tried to bully me, they turned on all my jets.

So what if they had followed me to the play. Big focking deal!

— 7 —

She was born Kelly Anne Morrisey.

In her early teens that became Kellianne. Later it was simply Keli. To me she had always been Kel.

She was my first love.

I can't remember a time when I didn't know her. Or didn't love her.

Her father and mine had been classmates in medical school. Her mother and my mother had graduated from Trinity High School in River Forest the same year. She was born a month before me, the last of seven and a surprise, a mistake perhaps that became an adored child.

I had sensed from the beginning — one so far back that I can't remember when the feeling came — that I had lucked out on parents compared to her. Mom and Dad are unfailingly refined and gentle folk. I cannot remember either of them ever being drunk. Her father is a loudmouth braggart even if he is a highly successful urologist. Her mother is a tasteless and overweight bitch, three words that no one could imagine predicating of my mother.

However, Dr. and Mrs. Morrisey were part of the environment into which I was born and in which I was raised. They were as much an element of my personal scenery as St. Mark's parish, Oak Park Country Club, Lake Geneva, and my brother who wanted to be a priest. Only when I was a teen did I realize not only that I didn't like them but that I had never liked them. Later I would discover that my parents didn't like them either.

"If we ever need proof," George said, his quick, wry grin indicating that he was about to be perceptive and harsh, "that our parents are both saints, we only have to consider that they put up with those two drunks for thirty-five years."

George doesn't look or act much like my brother. He's five eight, black-haired instead of blond, with a sharply etched face, thick eyebrows, and an animated grin. He is quick, intense, forceful. Epigrams and quotes spin off from his lips like bullets from an automatic weapon. When he is talking or thinking or both (which is almost all the time), he strides up and down like a bantamweight boxer before a fight.

"Drunks?"

"You miss things, don't you, Derm? They're

both alcoholics. Of course."

"I never thought of it that way."

"You wouldn't," he said partly in exasperation, partly in admiration.

He was right about the elder Morriseys: They were indeed both alcoholics. Their heavy drinking had been as much part of the world in which I grew up as their daughter's pale blond hair, light blue eyes, and pretty, pretty face. Just as I had assumed that "Kel" would be pretty, so I had always taken for granted that her parents drank a lot and acted kind of silly.

I cannot remember a time when Kel and I were not inseparable friends. Nor can I remember the time when we first kissed, though she probably kissed me. She certainly initiated the kisses in the early years of grammar school and resumed them again in seventh grade when we boys were no longer ashamed of kissing girls but began to brag about our conquests — I never bragged about kissing her, however.

Kel and I were always together. We made sand castles on the beach at Lake Geneva and splashed each other with water, we walked the side roads and picked wild raspberries, we watched television together, we did our homework together, we threw snowballs at one another sometimes but usually at others, pretending that they had thrown the first snowballs at us.

Every morning in St. Mark's schoolyard my eyes, pretending to be uninterested, would seek her out — and meet hers looking for me. We'd both giggle and turn away, not wanting to admit to anyone else how much we meant to one another.

At parties and dances in high school, I was never at ease till I had spotted Kel — an easy enough task because her effervescent laughter usually told me where to look.

More skillfully perhaps, she kept an eye out for me.

"You came at ten after nine," she said accusingly after one such party. "Late."

"Keeping tabs on me?"

"You bet." She hugged me. "Where would I be without you?"

Did she love me more than I loved her? Or was it easier for a young woman to display her love?

I don't know. Maybe both.

In our teen years the kisses turned passionate, and that was my doing, though she did not protest. Our parents had mixed emotions about the two of us. Our affection for one another was "cute," and they thought we'd make an "adorable" marriage. But they worried about whether we were becoming "too involved," by which they meant that they were afraid that adolescent passion might interfere with our careers.

As I've already suggested, my family was not terribly worried about my career — a little concerned maybe at least for the record. Kel's family, however, was always apprehensive about her future.

All my brothers and sisters had become "successful," so I was kind of a wild card, gifted surely but not necessary to prove the family's worth.

Tom Morrisey, however, was a disappointed man because none of his children had become M.D.'s like himself.

"It's the highest profession a man can have," he said once to my father.

"Only if he likes it," my dad replied — one of his cautious little bits of wisdom that Tom never heard.

The problem was not that the Morrisey kids didn't try to be doctors. Alas, they either failed to get into medical school or flunked out, a disgrace far worse than my failure at the Golden Dome.

"They're not cut out for it," my father would say. "They inherited their father's looks and their mother's brains."

"Jim, that's terrible," Mom would remonstrate with him in the tone of pious insincerity which she used to demonstrate that she was in complete agreement with one of my father's more outrageous comments.

Kel, the last and most golden child, was different. She was number one in everything from kindergarten on — highest marks in the class, class officer, valedictorian, student council president, merit scholar semifinalist, prom queen, captain of the volleyball team. . . . You name an honor, she won it.

She had all the natural talent I had and more. Moreover, she worked at success.

"The difference between you and little Kelly Anne," my mother said once, "is that she uses her talents and you don't."

"She's a girl," I protested with notable lack of logic.

"Ah, you noticed that, did you now?" Ma grinned impishly. "Sure, you've always acted like she's one of the guys."

"She's that too," I said stubbornly. "She's not stuck up like the other girls."

"The poor child is a nervous wreck," Ma continued, shaking her head sadly. "And her parents pushing her all the time."

I hadn't noticed that. Quite the contrary, it seemed to me that Kel wanted to succeed even more than they longed for her achievements and that she worked hard at everything — harder than was required, given her natural abilities — because she liked working hard.

She pushed me harder than my parents ever would. I was more afraid of her reaction to my B's and C's than I was afraid of Mom's and Dad's. Her fury when I quit the football team was worse than theirs.

"You're stubborn and proud and lazy," she told me bluntly, in the front seat of her Mustang convertible after a date the Friday night I had walked out of the locker room never to return.

"But you still love me."

"Certainly I still love you." She nuzzled close to me. "But I want to be proud of you too."

"What about the A's I'm getting?" I touched one of her pert young breasts.

She did not pull away from me. She seemed to like to be fondled even more than I liked to fondle her. Our love play was an endlessly interesting sport, one in which I often sensed nervously that I could have gone much farther than I did.

"You'd better keep on getting them." She sighed contentedly. "I'd be awfully lonely at Notre Dame without you."

I dutifully pulled up my average, made it to Notre Dame by the skin of my teeth, and discovered that her father had other plans for her — Yale.

We were an oddly matched pair: Kel was always exuberant, an enthusiastic master of the revels as well as academic and athletic leader. I was the big amadon (a word that was affectionate, more or less, when Ma used it) who tagged along behind her.

She led the songs in the bus on the high school club picnics, consoled the lonely and unhappy kids in our crowd, organized the double dates, planned the dances, took charge whenever someone was needed to take charge, and even when, strictly speaking, no take-charge person was required. I arranged the chairs and cleaned up afterward.

I did win a prize or two — poetry and story contests, but who needs a scribbler when they have a prom queen who is also a merit scholarship winner and a volleyball ace who did not quit in midseason?

A mild spasm of pride did run briefly through the parish and the school when my prizes were announced, but such awards didn't get you into Notre Dame.

"Sure," Ma announced to the family, "merit scholars are a dime a dozen, but poets are rare birds."

"Rare birds indeed," said Pa, whose strategy for dealing with his wife's vigorous assertions was to echo her last two words and then add the decisive "indeed," usually with a happy grin that said, in effect, "Sure, the woman is a terror, now isn't she?"

Afterward I often wondered whether Kel and I would have become romantically involved if we had not been friends for so long before the hormones were dumped into our bloodstreams. We were locked into a relationship that we might not have chosen if we had been strangers at fourteen. As it was, adolescent passion trapped us before we had a chance to think, not that either of us minded in those days.

There was a dark side to Kel's sunny, dynamic personality. She drank one or two more cans of beer than she should have and experimented with both marijuana and cocaine, much to my horror.

When I begged her to stop the drugs and cut down the beer, she did so promptly, apologized for causing me to worry, and begged me to forgive her.

"I don't want to lose you, Derm," she said, tears in her eyes. "I don't know how I'd survive without you."

I'd tell her she didn't need me at all and she'd hug me and bury her head in my chest and say, "Yes I do, Derm. I really do."

Not so much that when Yale accepted her and "Doctor" — as Tom Morrisey was always called in his family — commanded that she go there instead of Notre Dame she was able to refuse.

These are all afterthoughts. In those days I thought Kel was the perfect girl and I was the luckiest guy in the world.

Was I brokenhearted when she told me that she "had" to go to Yale?

To tell the truth, as I look back on it, I was not. I consoled her in her tears and argued that maybe absence really did make the heart grow fonder. Looking back on that conversation, I wonder if I was not experiencing somewhere deep down inside myself a bit of relief.

I wouldn't admit it then, however. I was besotted with her, dazzled by her wit and energy, captivated by her beauty, astonished by her love for me, enraptured by her superb young body.

Yet she was not quite beautiful, not the way Nuala is beautiful. She was pretty and mildly voluptuous, a young man's fantasy of a woman he'd like to see naked rather than a mature man's image of ideal beauty.

I never did see her completely undressed, although I did have the opportunity.

Some of our friends were certain that we had slept together. We were too close to one another, they said, to have resisted the demands of our bodies. I won't pretend that the idea had not occurred to me. Yet I would never have suggested it to her. How do you proposition your best friend? I wondered.

She offered herself to me the day before the senior prom.

"Do you want to make love with me after the prom, Derm?" she asked with her usual direct candor. "Maybe we ought to be lovers this summer so we will remember each other when we go away to college at the end of August."

What kind of a young man would say no to such a request?

One that was frightened by the prospect, I suppose.

"I think we're too young, Kel. I respect you too much to do that to you now. And I don't need sex to remember you."

She sighed — disappointed, I suppose. "You're right, as always. But, just the same, I'm yours whenever you want me."

"A breathtaking offer, Kel." I wrapped my arms around her. "I won't forget it."

She hanged herself on Father's Day. Wearing her prom dress. In front of a video camera. After she had shouted her hatred for her parents into the camera. Just before she kicked the chair she shouted, "I'm sorry, Derm. I love you!"

I found out about the tape later. Denise Reid, her "best friend," called me hysterically about four o'clock on that softly pleasant late spring afternoon.

"Something terrible has happened at Kel's house, Derm. They say . . . they say she's killed herself." The girl's voice choked with horror.

I sprinted the two blocks that separated our homes. An ambulance and two police cars were parked in front, a silent crowd of perhaps fifty people waited outside. I pushed my way through them and up to the door. A cop stopped me.

"You can't go in there, son. Sorry."

"Let me talk to her mother or father," I begged, panting for breath. "I'm Dermot Coyne."

The cop glanced at me and guessed that I was the boyfriend.

"I'll get one of them." He nodded.

Doctor appeared at the door a moment later, smelling strongly of bourbon. "Arrest him, Officer," he shouted. "He killed my little girl! He murdered my little doctor!"

The crowd behind me murmured uneasily.

"How did he do that, sir?" The cop seemed to understand that he was dealing with a man out of control.

110

"He knew she was going to do it and he didn't tell us. He's responsible!"

"I — I didn't know, Dr. Morrisey," I stammered. "Honestly I didn't. . . . She isn't dead, is she?"

"He wanted her to go to Notre Dame with him. She was too good for that school and for him. That's why he killed her! He's a goddamn killer!"

Out of the corner of my eye I saw a young woman writing rapidly in a notebook. A reporter — all this would be in the papers and on TV. I was too sick with grief to care. I did not want to believe that my friend Kel was dead. Yet I was beginning to realize that she was.

Life seemed very empty, an open tomb without a bottom.

"You'd better go back in the house, Doctor," the officer said softly. "We'll take care of it for you." Then to me: "It would be a good idea, son, to go home. We'll come over and talk to you later. Don't worry."

The walk home was a stroll to the end of the earth.

My face, twisted with grief, filled the screen on the ten o'clock news that night. "Parents blame boyfriend in death of prom queen!" the *Tribune* said the next morning. Tom and his wife, Dot, became hysterical when I entered the wake on Monday evening, flanked by my parents, Ma and Pa, George (who had been ordained that year), and my sister Linda, a lawyer who warned one of the lawyers (male) in the Morrisey clan that, grief or not, his parents were asking for a defamation suit. Doctor started to shout obscenities at all of us. My father turned abruptly on his heel and walked towards the door. A hush fell on the crowd, as if someone else had just died. We all followed Dad out in the warm spring night, Ma and Pa acting as the Legion of the Rear Guard, just in case there was a fight Ma might miss.

As I left the funeral home with my grim-faced entourage all around me, I felt thankful at least that I didn't have to look at her in the casket.

Her friends told me that she looked *totally* gorgeous. I refused to believe them.

"They need a scapegoat to blame," George muttered through clenched teeth. "They can't accept their own responsibility."

"Hush, darling." Ma cut him off. "Everyone knows that."

"Knows that indeed," her husband agreed.

I sat in the last pew of St. Mark's Church for the Mass of the Resurrection and stood outside the chapel of Queen of Heaven Cemetery. Mom and Dad were with me, the rest of the family stayed away, even Ma and Pa, though the former wanted to come, just in case there was a fight.

Some of the elderly nuns at Trinity had told the girls who had rushed to them for consolation that, unless Kel had made a perfect act of contrition the instant before she died, she would have gone straight to hell. The pastor of St. Mark's, who hated all teenagers, had avoided the issue completely in his homily, a tribute to her mother and father that barely mentioned Kel.

Later George, furious at both the nuns and the priest, demanded of me, "You loved her, Derm?"

"I sure did."

"Do you think God loved her any less?"

"Certainly not."

"Then we can trust Him to take care of her, poor little thing that she is, as Ma would say, can't we?"

"I guess."

George was right, but all I could do then was wonder why God would permit such great vitality to be snuffed out. I still wonder that when I think about Kel. Or when she appears to me in my dreams.

If I had agreed to make love with her that spring, might she still be alive?

George himself, not knowing about her suggestion, argued that Kel had been trapped in a momentary firestorm of despair. "If she had made it another week, she would have been all right. But at your age in life you think you're going to have to exist in the lower depths forever."

That was the night after her burial. They had played the videotape on the five o'clock news — with the phony excuse that it might help parents to cope with depressed children in the future. I had turned on the TV to learn the Cubs score and saw Kel in her prom dress shouting at me. I watched, my hand on the remote control, frozen in place.

"Nothing in my life is worth anything," she cried, "except my love for Dermot. I'm no one. I am worthless. Everything I've ever done was to please my parents. I hate myself. I hate them. They're drunken bastards. I hate all the prizes and trophies and awards. You can have them, Mom and Dad, but you can't have me anymore. There's no reason for me to go on living. None! I'm useless. At least now I'm doing something I want to do. Dermot, I love you! I'm sorry!"

Then an anchorwoman appeared and urged parents to listen to the feelings of their teenage children.

I vomited on our big-screen TV.

There was a nasty media controversy about how the station got the tape and the ethics of playing it. The controversy provided an excuse for playing the tape again and again. No one showed the actual hanging, though the *Tribune* did report that Kel's last words were her plea to me for forgiveness.

"Her love for you will be enough to win her admission to heaven." George jabbed a finger at me. "Totally unselfish love is a ticket to paradise."

I hope so. Dot and Tom moved to California before the week was out, without a word to my parents, who, I think, were immensely relieved. We never heard from them again. I kept myself busy talking other young women in our crowd out of trying to follow Kel and reassuring the guys that they ought not to feel guilty.

I suppose I had some guilt feelings then, though I was too preoccupied to notice them. Mostly I was lonely. I missed her. There was a vacancy in my life that would never be filled.

"Why does God let these things happen?" I demanded of George.

"Maybe because He can't stop them." George shrugged. "One thing you can count on, however, is that God hurts for her as much as you do. More, in fact."

"God hurts?"

"Forget the Greek philosophy, punk." He jabbed his finger at me. "The God of Isaias and the God of Jesus is vulnerable, a shy and injured child like poor Denise to whom you've been so kind. We have to take care of God just as we do all the injured, fragile people we know."

"Shy children?"

"Sure. Remember the Bergman film? Ingrid Thulin says that lovers must treat one another like shy children. Fair enough, so long as we realize that God is included in the list of lovers."

"I have to take care of God like a vulnerable woman?"

"Now you got it!" He beamed. "And when you take care of vulnerable women, you take

115

care of God. Denise is God and God is Denise."

"Sounds like heresy."

"Solid Catholic mysticism."

Prester George is probably right. He usually is. Was God Kel? And Kel God? I guess I messed up with that vulnerable combination. Or maybe I didn't. Maybe I did the best I could, which is all any lover can expect of you.

Isn't it?

For a long time I kind of drifted along, carrying a burden of loss about which I could talk to no one. Why, I wondered, did she have to die? What had gone wrong? What had we all missed? Would I ever see her dancing eyes and her bubbling laughter again?

Dear God, how I missed her.

I probably would have flunked out of Notre Dame anyway.

No, that's not true. If Kel had been around to goad me, I would have pulled down the A's that I should have earned. And I would have played football for Lou Holtz — second string.

Maybe third string.

The emptiness is still there. My attempt after I left Marquette to fill it began and ended in folly.

Sometimes, even last autumn in Dublin, I would wake up in the morning, convinced that Kel was still alive and I would see her after breakfast.

I still looked for her face in the crowds on

116

Dawson and Grafton streets. Sometimes I even imagined that I saw her, her light blue eyes eagerly searching the street looking for me.

I encountered Nuala Anne McGrail, noted West of Ireland agnostic, coming out of St. Teresa's Church on Clarendon Street. It was three days after I had fled her, leaving my dozen roses behind. I had not been sleeping well, despite an hour every day in the pool at Jury's. Ma's archives had depressed me more than anything else in life except Kel's death.

I discovered that I missed Ma too, almost as much as I missed Kel.

Moreover, my dreams were tormented agonies that refought the Troubles in the West of Ireland. I failed to protect Oughterard from the Black and Tans. I was the Irregular who fired the single rifle shot that killed Michael Collins. I riddled the body of Daniel O'Kelly. I killed Ma and Pa as they tried to escape Ireland.

I would wake up several times during the night in a hot sweat, although the window was open and the temperature was cool. You don't sweat in Ireland during the autumn.

Each morning I would tell myself as I struggled out of bed that I ought to return to River

Forest and watch the World Series. I didn't belong in Dublin. The mysteries I had determined to solve were insoluble — and not worth solving.

I'd take my walk, often stopping in a church for part of Mass — or the Eucharist, as Prester George says I ought to call it these days — eat my breakfast, and decide that I would stay at least another day and hope something would occur.

Then I had the call from the cultural attaché at the American embassy — an invitation to a dinner at Lord Longwood-Jones's home on Merrion Square. I told myself that I ought to stay in Dublin at least for that event, especially since I wondered why His Lordship would be interested in meeting me.

I knew who Lord Martin Longwood-Jones and his wife, Lady Elizabeth, were, of course. You read the *Irish Times* for a week and you knew who they were. He was the president of the Irish-British Friendship League and she a patron of classical gardens. They seemed to be involved in every upright and honorable civic and cultural program in the city.

Goo-goos, to use the Chicago term.

So Lord L.-J. had read all the English-language literary magazines and liked my two stories. So he had remarked on them to the cultural attaché. So a junior officer at the embassy told the cultural attaché that I was in Ireland.

It also sounded fishy to me. Was this to be

another version of being warned off dangerous history, more cultivated, more elaborate, more delicate?

I neglected to mention that on my many walks through Dublin, I continued to stroll in the vicinity of Trinity College. My eyes searched the face of every young woman I passed in the street, hoping she might be Nuala. I no longer saw Kel's short blond hair everywhere in the crowd; now I saw the long black hair of the girl from Carraroe.

In the grotesque calculus I had worked out for myself, it would be wrong to seek her out but acceptable to encounter her by chance.

God — or someone — took me at my word and, being a comedian, arranged for me to encounter her in the Carmelite church — quite possibly the ugliest church in the world. I saw her, in fact, coming back from Communion.

It was a clear brisk morning, one of those days during which you think it might not be so bad to live in Ireland after all. Dawn had broken up the remnants of night as I drifted into St. Teresa's from Johnson Court, the little alley (with a shopping arcade) connecting Grafton Street to Clarendon Street. However, it was still dark in the church, illumined only by candles and lights in the sanctuary and a weird blue light from one of the windows that made the church look like a mausoleum.

The young priest who presided over the seven-thirty Eucharist was of the same age and style as Prester George. He preached an incisive and academic homily, to which I did not much listen since, to tell the truth, I was looking around the darkened church for a young woman who might be Nuala — even if I had her word for it that she didn't believe in God.

I saw long black hair on a blue jacket ahead of me and to the left, a combination that appeared thousands of times a day in Dublin. I told myself that I was falling in love with a girl I hardly knew and acting like a lovesick teenager.

An accurate diagnosis, as far as that goes. Unfortunately for me, it was much later that I came to realize that the diagnosis didn't go far enough.

On the way back from Communion, however, I managed to sneak a quick look at the white face above the jacket. The young woman's eyes were devoutly averted, but if it wasn't Nuala Anne McGrail, it was someone sufficiently like her that I wanted to meet the strange woman anyway.

I should have been praying after receiving the Sacrament. However, my mind was more on Nuala than on God. She was taller than I had thought. Five eight and a half or five nine. Statuesque. She did not slump, however, to hide her height. Rather she carried herself with elegant, almost regal, grace as she walked back from the altar, a countess in jeans and cloth jacket.

A countess in jeans with a lithe, willowy body, long black hair, pale white skin, and a smooth jaw that ended in a pert and determined chin.

I fear that my imagination went farther in its entertainments. As George had said when I asked him about ogling young women in church. "It's the way the species has been designed, punk. Their beauty reflects God's beauty so I imagine She doesn't mind."

If God was as attractive as Nuala, I thought to myself, trying to break away from my desires, She must be wonderfully alluring.

I waited outside the church, the early morning sun making Dublin town seem like a set for a musical, while the putative Nuala remained in intense prayer. At the Johnson Court entrance I saw a log encased in glass. It was not, however, as I first suspected, a relic of the True Cross but only evidence of rotting timbers to encourage contributions to the fund to repair the church.

"Sure, if it isn't Pegeen Mike herself," I observed as she walked out in the bright sunlight, her book bag slung over her back.

Squinting for a moment to adjust her eyes, she recognized me and began to babble.

"Ah, sure, weren't you an eejit for wasting time on our terrible play? And an amadon for spending your money on those roses? And didn't I make a terrible mess of it that night?"

I put my hand over her mouth to stifle the babble. "Listen to me, Nuala Anne McGrail from Carraroe in the County Galway. You were sensational. Wasn't the *Irish Times* itself saying you were a very talented young woman? I'll have no more of your Irish self-deprecation, which as you know yourself is only half serious. Is that clear?"

She didn't struggle to escape the grip of my hand. Rather, eyes wide, she nodded her head.

"If I said you were terrible and that the play was awful, I'd be lucky if I escaped with my life, now wouldn't I?"

I felt her mouth move in a grin. Her eyes danced in amusement. She nodded vigorously.

"Now, the first thing you're going to do when I let you talk is thank me for the roses. Understand?"

She nodded again.

"All right."

"Thank you very much for the beautiful roses, Dermot Michael Coyne," she said dutifully. "If I wasn't such an eejit, I would have thanked you for them first. Everyone said that me *fockingrichyank*" — she grinned mischievously — "must be sweet."

"And you said?"

"I just stuck my nose up in the air and said that, sure, he wasn't the worst of them."

"Very proper." I took her arm. "Now let me buy you breakfast."

She yanked it away from me. "I'll buy me own breakfast, if you don't mind."

The imp had instantly become a fury. I wasn't

going to fight it. "Well, then, will you join me for breakfast?"

She pondered that invitation suspiciously. "Where?"

"You name it."

"Bewley's?" She gestured at the café a few steps across Johnson Court.

"Why not? Do you have your bike?"

She gestured at the sign in the small front yard of St. Teresa's forbidding bicycles. "Don't the priests forbid us to leave them here?"

"You sound like an anticlerical."

"I *am* not," she insisted. "I just don't like priests."

I recaptured her arm and walked into the café. Bewley's is a wonderful tea shop where you can buy some of the best scones and drink some of the best tea and coffee in Ireland. It's not a place where you can buy nutritious meals like we Americans pursue, but the Irish are not much into nutrition, probably because they cannot afford to be. It's also a great place to watch parents and kids play. Ireland is the greatest country in the world to be a kid, because it's a culture steeped in play and the presence of kids gives adults a chance to act like kids again.

"And yourself telling me that you don't believe in God?"

"I never said I believed in Him, did I?" She frowned grimly.

"But you go to Mass every day, don't you now?"

"What if I do?"

"If you don't believe in God, why go to Mass everyday?"

"Haven't me mother and I been going to Mass every day since as far back as I can remember?"

"Your mother isn't around to check up on you now, fair Nuala."

"God is." She bowed her head stubbornly, not willing to give me an inch.

"But didn't you tell me that you don't believe in God?"

"What if I'm wrong?"

"Huh?"

She stopped and turned towards me, her face assuming an expression of feral shrewdness that I would see many more times in the weeks that were to come, the face of an impoverished housewife bargaining over the price of a pound of bacon or a half pound of butter.

"If there is no God, sure, it doesn't do any harm at all to go to Mass, does it now? And doesn't it get me out of me bed every morning? And if there is a God, well, He knows that I'm at least maintaining diplomatic relations with Him, doesn't He?"

"Her."

"Huh?"

"My brother George, who is a priest, says that God is as much womanly as manly."

"More. I mean if She exists, if you take my meaning."

124

"Why don't you go to Mass in the college chapel?"

I was sure I knew the answer. Nuala was hiding her piety from her friends, just as she tried to hide it from me by her anticlerical outburst.

"Why would I be wanting to pray in a Prod church?" she snapped, eyes glowing triumphantly as she fended off my question.

"I give up, Nuala! Let's go in and have breakfast."

"Mind you." She would not yield me the last word. "There's nothing really wrong with being a Prod if that's what you are."

It was hot in Bewley's, and dense with cigarette smoke as always. The lights behind the yellow stained-glass windows, however, made the place seem cheerful. We both took off jackets, mine the blue and gold of Marquette U. Nuala was wearing with her jeans a dark blue sweater that had seen better days at least a decade ago — a hand-me-down from an older sister. It did considerably more justice to her wonderful breasts than the Dublin Millennium sweatshirt had.

We purchased our tea and scones and my orange juice from the buffet and paid a sad-faced young Asian woman in native dress over her Bewley's uniform. I watched Nuala dole out her coins with the care of a poor person who doesn't have enough coins to risk making a mistake.

"Good morning, Shirley," Nuala said to the Asian. " 'Tis a wonderful morning, isn't it now?"

"Ah, it is, Nuala." The woman smiled brightly. "You have a good day now."

"As best I can with this big amadon in tow." She nodded in my direction. The Asian girl giggled.

"Do you know everyone in this part of Dublin?"

"She's in one of my classes, poor thing."

We found ourselves a table in an alcove in the front corner of the basement floor, protected on three sides by walls with rose-colored covering.

"You should drink orange juice in the morning, young woman," I told her firmly. "It's good for you."

"Is it now?"

" 'Tis, especially since you have better teeth than any Irish person I've ever met. You should take care of them."

"Should I now?"

"You should."

She looked like she was about to sail off into another argument and then thought better of it. "Maybe I will."

"Can I get you some now?"

"Didn't I say I'd buy me own breakfast?"

"A glass of orange juice isn't breakfast."

She pondered that and then laughed. "Ah, sure, what a terrible witch I'm being. Make

126

it a large glass, if you don't mind."

I smiled happily as I went back to the buffet. I also bought another large pot of tea and a plateful of scones.

"What are you doing with the extra scones?" she demanded suspiciously.

"I like them, woman, if you don't mind. And if you try to take a single one of them away from me, won't I be chopping off your hand?"

She laughed again. And impudently grabbed for one of my scones.

I grabbed the hand and kissed it.

I told you I was a romantic.

She blushed furiously. "You're a desperate man, Dermot Michael Coyne. A desperate man altogether. Now if you don't mind, I'll eat me pilfered scone."

"You might want to run the risk of pilfering another. But drink your orange juice."

"Yes, sir."

While she gulped down the juice with considerable enthusiasm, I studied her carefully. Nuala's clothes were not much above the poverty level, but her face, once more devoid of makeup, was freshly scrubbed, and her sweater and jeans were clean. Moreover, there was a slight aroma of inexpensive scent about her. Nuala's mother had brought her up right.

"I'm glad you have not acquired the terrible Irish habit of smoking all the time, Nuala."

"Och, isn't it a terrible habit altogether and so much better things to do with your money?

Still, you can't blame them." She glanced around the room. "There's little enough in most of their lives."

"Tell me about your life, Nuala."

"What's there to tell?" She put down the empty juice glass and deftly pulled the entire plate of scones to her side of the small table. "And if you want more scones, won't you have to be going back to the buffet and buying some for yourself?"

I filled her teacup. The kid was hungry. Dear God, how poor she must really be.

"Tell me about your family and Carraroe."

"Not much to tell. We have a couple of acres of poor farmland, a few cows, and a small tea shop at which some of the tour buses stop. There were seven of us, all married but me, and I'm never going to marry, not at all, at all. A brother and a sister live in London, and a brother in San Francisco and another in Boston, a brother in Montreal and a sister in Christ Church, that's in New Zealand."

"And where are you going to live when you graduate from university?"

"In Carraroe," she said stubbornly. "I won't leave me poor parents alone. I'm sure I can get a job in Galway city."

How many jobs were there for accountants anywhere in Ireland? I wondered.

"Your brothers and sisters come back often, don't they?"

"Too often altogether, if you ask me." She

128

layered clotted cream and raspberry jam on yet another scone. "And themselves showing off their rich Yank ways and staying at the fancy hotels in Salt Hill with their spoiled brats."

She seemed on the verge of tears.

"You don't like them much?"

"I love them all something terrible."

"Do you now?"

"Haven't I said so? That's why I'm never going to marry. You have children and you break your heart and sometimes your back too raising them and educating them and then they go away and leave you alone."

She was frowning again, a bitter and angry frown.

"Are your parents angry at your brothers and sisters for leaving?"

"They are not!" she exclaimed. "Aren't they terrible proud that all of the eejits are doing so well? And don't they miss them just the same? All the West of Ireland exports is people and sweaters."

"Handsome and gifted people."

"Isn't that the truth now?"

"Some of them looking quite lovely in sweaters."

She blushed again and turned away her eyes. "Go 'long with you."

"You're really planning not to emigrate?"

"Ah." She grinned wickedly. "I was saying that, wasn't I? But can you really believe me? Weren't you saying yourself that I'm a pretty good actress? Might I not be pretending? How do you know that I'm not looking for some *fockingrichyank* to seduce so I can escape this soggy and impoverished island?"

She leaned back in her chair, still grinning. How would I handle that scenario?

"I think, Nuala Anne McGrail," I said, slowly and cautiously, "that if you set out to seduce someone, you'd probably accomplish it pretty effectively."

Her grin faded. "You think so, do you?"

"I do, woman."

Her grin returned, a little less cocksure this time. "We'll just have to wait and see, won't we now?"

"I'd be delighted to."

"Of course, you've been engaged once already, haven't you?"

I gulped down a large swallow of tea. "How did you know that?"

"Was she the one who died, or was it someone else?"

"It was someone else . . . and how do you know about either of them?"

"I just know, Dermot. I don't know how I know." She shook her head sadly. "I'm by way of being a wee bit of a witch."

That's why she would turn out to be a first-rate detective. She "just knew" things. I don't know whether it was the shrewdness of Europe's last Stone Age people by which they put together as quickly as a computer isolated facts that others noticed but did not really see or whether she was really one of the faerie folk. Or some combination.

"Are you now?"

"Haven't I said that I am? . . . Does it scare you?"

I thought about it. "Just makes you more fascinating."

"Do you want to tell me about your engagement?"

That was direct enough, astonishingly direct for an Irish person.

Yes, I did want to talk about it. Womanly sympathy, you can't beat it, Pa always used to say.

"It's a crazy story, Nul. Probably a comedy. I met this girl, Christina, in a bar on Rush Street — that's our big singles' bar district — the summer after I gave up on college. She was Irish on her father's side and Italian on her mother's side. There's nothing wrong with that in Chicago anymore. One of my brothers and one of my sisters are married to Italians. It seems to be a good combination. Anyway, we hit it off well and began to date regularly. I hadn't dated much since . . . since I graduated from high school."

I wasn't about to tell my West of Ireland witch that Tina took me home to her apartment the night we met and that we made love, she with considerably more skill and experience than I.

"She was two years older than me and had an excellent job in the finance department of the First Chicago, that's a bank —"

"Shouldn't a man be careful of them accountant women?"

We both laughed. I felt like I was on a psychiatrist's couch.

We didn't move in with one another, but we sustained a torrid sexual relationship. The best part of it was that I forgot about Kel. Or thought I did.

"Her family liked me and my family liked her, except Ma and George the priest, both of whom had some doubts that she'd value my, uh, dreamy side."

"If she didn't, wasn't she a terrible fool?"

Dear God, this lovely child is already defending me.

Tina was small and slender, not exactly voluptuous but, to put it mildly, extremely sexy. We were both infatuated; we talked about sports and business and of course about sex, but not about much else.

"The following Christmas we were engaged with the wedding set for June. Her mother and her Italian grandmother took over the arrangements, which was fine with my family since we'd pretty much had it with weddings."

I was, if the truth be told, swept along on a tide of loneliness and lust, not convinced that George was wrong but unwilling to admit the possibility that the issue was worth considering.

"I finally met her Italian grandfather, the *padrino*, the head of the clan. They have no monopoly on such people, we Micks have them too. But this guy, a frail, apparently kindly old man, who had built up the family electronics industry from scratch, had more power than most of our patriarchs have."

"Not more than our matriarchs," she said quietly.

I didn't like the bastard but I didn't see that he made much difference. Not till he asked what I did for a living.

"He found out that I worked at the Merc and hit the ceiling. I was nothing more than a gambler. An Irish gambler. He would not have a granddaughter of his marrying an Irish gambler, and probably a crooked and drunken one."

The explosion took Tina and her family by surprise, but they didn't disagree. "He really has your best interests at heart," she said to me mildly after that first eruption of the *padrino*'s volcano.

"It didn't seem credible that in the 1980s a grandfather could veto a marriage. A couple days later her father, who was the executive vice-president of the family firm and the man who really ran it because her uncle, the *padrino*'s son, was a lovely guy but with no sense for business, called me to offer me a job at the company. Vice-president at $80,000 a year with no particular responsibilities described.”

“Brigid, Patrick, and Columcille!”

“I declined.”

“You certainly should have declined.” Her face was crimson again, not with embarrassment but with anger.

“My family, George again excepted, thought it was a very generous offer. They would not have to worry about me any more. Ever again. Tina was overjoyed. How could I possibly not accept such largesse? I still said no.”

“Tough focker.”

“Me or the *padrino?*”

“Both of you, but you especially.”

“I didn’t think it was serious. I really couldn’t believe that the job was a *sine qua non;* no one acts that way any more. Well, I was pretty dumb. As I would find out later, I wasn’t the only one who encountered such a stone wall. Most of the guys that were offered jobs as a condition of marriage, all of them that I talked to in fact, accepted the condition enthusiastically. They couldn’t understand why I turned down such a grand opportunity.”

“ ’Cause you had balls.” She reached for the scone plate. It was empty.

“More likely just a stubborn streak. I’ll get some more scones.”

“And maybe some of them cute croissant things, if you don’t mind?”

“I don’t mind.”

"And . . ." She smiled shyly. "Would you ever think of bringing some more of that orange juice?"

"Ah, sure, woman, 'tis yourself that has a grand appetite, isn't it?"

"A terrible appetite altogether when someone is telling me a love story."

"I'm not sure it's a love story."

Tina and I had furious arguments. I was selfish and ungrateful. Besides, Grandpa was right. Most traders faded from the floor. There was nothing in my record as a trader that suggested I would ever be very successful. Why didn't I want the job? I guess because I didn't want to be under anyone's thumb that way, not ever.

"To continue," I said when I returned, this time with a tray. "I never quite caught on to the fact that Tina and her family were deadly serious. I knew she was unhappy about my stubborn refusal to take the job, but I couldn't imagine that she might call the marriage off because of it."

"Did she ever say she would call it off?" The fair Nuala was wolfing down a croissant, also lathered with cream and raspberry preserves.

"Two weeks before the wedding. We had a monumental row. She told me that she wasn't sure she wanted to marry me if I was such an ungrateful and irresponsible person. Everything was prepared, the church, the country club; we had made our pre-Cana conference, filled out all the forms; her family had mailed the invitations, over a thousand of them; our pictures were in the papers. I felt confident that it was too late for her to turn back. I was wrong."

The fight took place after a particularly spectacular session in her bed, designed, I later decided, to overwhelm my reluctance to become part of her family.

"My father is not under anyone's thumb, is he?" she demanded hotly. "How would you be different?"

"I'm not sure he really is his own man," I replied. "Anyway, he likes his job and I wouldn't like it."

Those ill-chosen words launched our brawl. She hit me and I left her apartment.

"So then what happened?" Nuala's interest did not interfere with her draining the orange juice glass.

"I didn't talk to her for a few days. Let the dust settle, I thought, and then we can have a reconciliation. The day I was going to call her, the cancellation announcements started showing up in the mail."

"Blackmail?" She stopped eating.

"I think so. As she said to me when we got together a couple of days later to try to see if we could work it out, it was the only way she had to make me understand that she was serious. It wasn't Grandfather, she said, not really. She had always worried about my financial future; Grandfather merely made it explicit for her."

"Oh." Nuala continued to stare at me.

"She was willing to send out another set of invitations now that I understood the situation. I told her I'd think about it. That was the next-to-last time we spoke to one another."

"Poor dear man." Her eyes filled up with tears.

"That was in June. The following October I made my three million. Tina called to congratulate me. So did her father. So too did the *padrino*. I was very gracious in my expression of thanks for their kind words. So it was kind of a comedy."

"I don't think so." She found a tissue in her book bag and dabbed at her eyes. "Course, you were still missing the poor girl that died, weren't you now? And so you weren't being very careful in your choice of substitutes, were you!"

That's what you call a gotcha. And how could I be angry at her, with tears slipping down her cheeks?

"You couldn't be more accurate, Nul. That's precisely what I was doing. George said so after the breakup. I wasn't willing to accept it then."

She nodded. "Do you want to tell me about the girl that died?"

"Later, if I may. This is more self-revelation than I've ever experienced before. You are indeed a bit of a witch, Nul, but a very kindly and lovely witch."

"Go 'long with you. . . ."

I thought of a question I wanted to ask her.

137

"Do you know the town of Oughterard, Nuala?"

"And isn't it right up the road from Carraroe?"

"Through Maam Cross?"

"Haven't you been looking at the map?"

"You've been there then?"

"Hundreds of times, I suppose. Didn't my brother marry a girl from there and herself with a nose stuck so high in the air she couldn't see the horse shite on the road?"

"You know the statue at the crossroads?"

She frowned, trying to remember.

"Daniel O'Kelly?"

"Who was he?"

"Commandant of the Galway Brigade of the IRA back in the Troubles."

She dismissed him and all his kind with a brisk wave of her hand. "Focking eejits."

"Perhaps. Yet there was a band of Auxiliaries, Black and Tans, tearing up the town back in 1919, beating up the men, molesting the women, destroying property. O'Kelly and his crowd saved the place."

"Killed all the Brits?"

"Yes."

"Savages. . . . I remember the statue now. Ugly focking thing."

"If you were a young woman in the town then, you might have welcomed Daniel O'Kelly and his bunch."

She thought about that. "Maybe I would. Those were different times. Still, wouldn't the

Brits have given us home rule anyway after the war? What was the point in all the shite of the Rising and the Troubles?"

Thus is the patriotic past written off with one devastating swipe. They must teach revisionist history at TCD.

"Surely you've heard the name of Michael Collins?"

"Wasn't he one of those eejits who opposed the treaty and was gunned down by his best friends?"

"You're probably thinking of Cathal Brugha. Michael Collins was chairman of the Provisional Government, the commanding officer of the Free State army. He was shot probably by a sniper in Cork, his home county."

She shrugged indifferently. "They were all eejits."

"Collins died at thirty-one. He was the man who finally drove the English out of Ireland."

"Weren't they leaving anyway?"

"He was one of the great geniuses of the twentieth century, Nul. His death was a terrible loss to Ireland and the world."

"Worse luck for him then, and himself dying in a foolish fight."

"My grandfather — Liam O'Riada he was called, Bill Ready to us, Pa or Grandpa Bill to me — was part of the Galway Brigade. I don't know what happened but he and Ma — Grandma Nell — left right after O'Kelly was killed and never came back to Ireland. She told me once that if they came back they'd both be shot."

"Poor things. Maybe I would have been on their side in those days." She shook her head as if trying to understand human folly.

"They were sweet, gentle people, Nul. Daily churchgoers like yourself."

"Well" — she tilted her jaw at me — "you can believe that I'm not tied up with them eejits in the IRA today. Maybe they were necessary then, but not anymore. And meself a daily Mass person too."

She was uninterested in Irish nationalism, past and present, and had apparently never heard of Daniel O'Kelly, William Ready, or the Galway Brigade. My suspicions that she might be on the other side — whatever the other side might be — were foolish.

Or were they? The Connemara district has always been a hotbed of nationalism and republicanism. The people from the Gaeltacht were not likely to be revolutionaries, but they were not opposed to them either. What about Nuala's grandparents? Where were they and what were they doing during the Troubles?

Questions to be asked later. She didn't seem so much to resent my interest in the past as to dismiss it as irrelevant.

"Eucharist."

"Huh?"

"Prester George says we should call it Eucharist."

"The focking Mass" — she chuckled — "is the focking Mass no matter what you call it. And tell that to George the priest for me."

"I sure will. He'll love it."

"Will he now? Doesn't he sound like an interesting priest? . . . Glory be to God, will you look at the time! I'll be missing me ancient Irish literature class and I'll never learn whether Diramuid gets Granne." She stood up hastily. "And let me tell you that one was no better than she had to be, not at all, at all."

"I'll walk you over to class."

"You will *not*." She struggled into her jacket. I assisted her.

"I will *so*."

She slung the book bag over her back. "*Well*, 'tis a free country and a man can walk down any street he wants, can't he now?"

"He sure can."

"And thank you very much" — she seemed suddenly very vulnerable — "for the supplement to me breakfast."

"We'll do it again?"

"Sure." She pulled the stocking cap down on her head. "Don't I have to learn more of your story, especially" — she hesitated — "about the poor girl who died?"

Suddenly I had an idea, as ideas go a pretty good one.

"Nuala," I said as we emerged in the sunshine, "I need a favor."

"Do you now?"

141

"Wasn't I just saying so? I need a date. For a dinner. At Lord Longwood-Jones's house in Merrion Square. The cultural attaché at the American embassy set it up. They want me to bring a date."

The last sentence was a bold lie.

"In Merrion Square? Dinner jacket and all that shite?"

"They do that every night. White tie."

"Holy saints preserve us! And you'd be taking the chit of a lass from the West of Ireland whose only dinner jacket occasion was her sister's wedding? You're daft, man, totally daft!"

"You'll never be out of place anywhere, Nuala."

"Go 'long with you. I know my place."

"Your place is anywhere you want to go."

"*No!* I won't hear any more about it."

Yet I was sure she would, that in fact she wanted to go, for reasons of curiosity if nothing else. I had to reassure her and persuade her. My first attempt was a failure.

"You're a beautiful young woman, Nuala. They'll love you."

She stopped walking and turned away from me, as if she were about to walk the other way down Grafton Street towards the green. "I'm *not* beautiful. I won't to listen to such horse shite."

I grabbed her arm. "You are too."

"I am *not*. And —"

I put my hand over her mouth again. She didn't struggle.

"I thought I told you I'd not tolerate your self-deprecation. I meant it, woman, do you understand?"

A couple of old fellas smiled at us as they walked by. Lovers' quarrel, they probably figured.

I must have been a little rougher than I intended. Nuala's eyes showed fear. Mild fear. Well, good enough for her.

"I said, do you understand me?"

She nodded quickly.

"That's better." I removed my hand from her mouth, hooked her arm around mine, and began to walk north on Grafton towards Trinity College.

"Fockingbrute," she murmured, but she was laughing at me. "Enjoys pushing defenseless women around."

"I'll put up with none of your shite, woman."

She nudged my ribs. "I'm terrified, and yourself finally talking like an Irishman."

"We're agreed that you're beautiful?"

"Ah, sure, won't I get myself battered and right here on Grafton Street if I dare disagree?"

"I'll accept that as a characteristic Irish affirmation of assent."

She laughed again. "Ah, but aren't you the dominating male now?"

"Not with one of your Irish matriarchs."

"Anyway" — she turned grim again — "what

143

good is beauty? It just fades away."

"It changes as we get older." I was quoting George the priest. "But we direct its change by who and what we are. My grandmother Nell was a beautiful woman at eighty. You'll always be beautiful, Nuala."

"I will not." She said it gently, as if afraid of my assault.

"How old is your mother?"

"Sixty. I was the last of the brood."

"And she's not beautiful?"

"I *never* said that at all, at all, did I?" she shouted at me. "She's the most beautiful woman I know."

"And you don't look like her? Isn't everyone saying that Nuala is the spitting image of her ma?"

"How would you know that?"

"Maybe I'm a bit of a witch too, Nuala Anne McGrail."

She leaned against me, laughing again. "I'm no match for you this morning, Dermot Michael Coyne, and that's the truth, no match at all."

I could have put my arm around her. I could have patted her gorgeous rump, a gesture I had been contemplating all morning. I lost my nerve. Instead I turned the corner to Nassau Street.

"So it's all settled, woman. You'll join me for dinner at Lord Longwood-Jones's house.

"Won't I be disgracing you?" She nodded to

a group of students that we passed. "Good morning to you."

"Good morning, Nuala."

The kids took a careful look at me: *fockingrichyank.*

"That should be up to me to judge, shouldn't it?" I pursued my argument.

"I'm thinking that you don't know them folks well enough or me well enough to be able to judge."

"And I'm thinking that I'm old enough to make me own decisions."

Nuala sighed, that wonderful West of Ireland sigh that suggests the onslaught of a serious attack of asthma. "Well, I don't have anything to wear."

I don't pretend to understand much about women, but I do know enough to recognize agreement when I hear it. "I bet you can find something."

"Good morning, Nuala."

"And the best of the day to yourselves."

"Are you running for office?"

"They all know me because I sing in the pub."

"A likely story. . . . I take it that you'll be my date."

"You don't give a woman a chance to decide. Sure, if I say no, won't you be coming after me with brute force, you big amadon?"

She was enjoying the game again.

"I would if I knew where you lived."

"And I'll not tell you that, will I?"

"Then I'll steal you away from church in the morning."

We were now opposite the entrance to Trinity College.

"When is this white tie dinner?"

"Friday night at half eight."

"Glory be to God, man, that's only two days away."

"I guess."

"Why didn't you give me more warning?"

"How did I know I was going to meet you at church this morning?"

"You're a focking eejit!" Nonetheless she was amused by me.

"His Lordship said he would send a car to pick me, uh, us, up. What time should we come by your place?"

"You shouldn't. Won't I be meeting you at Jury's at a quarter past eight?"

"Will you now?"

"Haven't I just said I would?"

I took possession of a long strand of jet-black hair and caressed it like it was fine fabric. "It's a date."

She stared at the sidewalk. "I'm sure I'll be disgracing you, Dermot Michael Coyne."

"Bet on it?"

"I'm not a gambling woman." Faint grin.

I tilted her chin upward and kissed her forehead. "I'm not a gambling man either."

"And yourself a commodity trader."

146

"Former commodity trader. . . . A quarter past eight, Nuala. And you be there, Nuala Anne McGrail."

"Haven't I said I would?"

— 9 —

I floated back to Jury's in a happy daze, so happy that I didn't notice the subtle change in my suite.

Humming a tune to myself — the lullaby that Nuala had sung at the pub, to tell the truth — I put on my swimming trunks and terry robe and rode down to the heated pool.

I was inordinately proud of myself. Hadn't I won this gorgeous young woman over to my side? Wasn't it true that she liked me? Didn't she enjoy my company? Wasn't she going on a date with me, one that scared her? Didn't she enjoy the quasi-embrace right there in the middle of Grafton Street? Hadn't she been proud of me when we passed the Nuala-worshipers on the walk to Trinity? Hadn't I been sensational in reassuring this shy child, this vulnerable image of what George insisted was a vulnerable God?

It took a quarter hour for me to swim off my euphoria and realize that if there were any ministering to a shy child at our breakfast, Mary

Nuala Anne McGrail had been the minister and I the child. I had been so proud of my behavior at the beginning and the end of our encounter that I had forgotten the middle of it. Looking back on our adventures with the perspective of time, I realize that the morning would be a paradigm of our whole relationship.

"You haven't grieved yet," George had said after my breakup with Christina, his finger in its usual jabbing position near my chest. "You won't talk about it to anyone, not even me. You've got all that grief tied up inside you. That's why you stumbled into this relationship, which now you admit was a mistake. . . ."

"At least you didn't say I told you so."

"I just did. . . . Anyway, punk, did you share any of your grief with Christina?"

A damned impertinent personal question. Yeah, but that's George.

"I tried to talk about it once. She didn't want to hear about Kel. She said it was too gross to talk about."

"Kind of unfeeling, huh?"

"That's the way she was. She didn't like to talk about the ugly aspects of life."

"So you just bottled up the grief?"

"You could say that."

"Well, if you can't talk about it to the family and won't talk about it to a shrink, you'd better find a girl who is ready to listen and understand."

"Yes, George."

"And, if she doesn't want to listen and understand, don't go out with her more than once."

"Yes, George."

"And find that girl!"

"Yes, George."

Nuala had listened sympathetically to my crazy story about Christina. She would listen even more sympathetically when I worked up the courage to tell her about Kel. I hesitated to tell her because the grief, once out of the bottle, might explode. I did not want to break down in the presence of a woman. I would not do so.

Even in the pool, deliciously warm under the bright Dublin sun (which probably would not survive till noontime), I felt my eyes sting at the thought of finally talking to someone about Kel.

Maybe I wouldn't have to talk about it. Maybe I could just give her the story to read.

Then I became very embarrassed. The child, contentious, sensitive, foul-mouthed, innocent, had pried open my soul with ease. She had no right to do that.

And how had she known about Christina and Kel? A witch, she said?

Then I became suspicious. It didn't seem likely that the history of freedom fighters, to use a more modern word, of Connemara would be unknown to a bright schoolchild. Surely the teachers must have talked about it. And was it possible that a young woman could grow up in Ireland, even in the pacifist Ireland of the 1980s, and know almost nothing about Michael Collins?

What was she trying to pull on me?

Still, she was beautiful and I had a date with her on the day after tomorrow and I would tell her my story and maybe weep in her arms and rest my head on her elegant breasts.

That thought made me feel good again. I returned to my room, refreshed from my swim and humming the lullaby again.

I showered, still humming, and then dressed in a jogging suit because I needed more exercise to run off the various energies that breakfast with Nuala Anne had released.

I sat at the table in my parlor where I had set up the Compaq 425C that I had lugged around Europe with me, turned on the machine, and hammered out a dozen paragraphs about Nuala in the journal I was keeping. It was more than a journal entry, however. It was the beginning of a short story, the end of which was still uncertain.

Would this one have a happy ending?

Well, the first beginnings of sexual arousal had at least produced a burst of literary creativity. Maybe that was a good sign.

I came to the part of the story in which I would recount her reaction to Michael Collins. Was he thirty-one years old or thirty-two when he died? I reached for the biography, which I had left on the end table next to my makeshift workstation.

It wasn't there.

Mechanically I glanced around the room. I was sure I had left the Collins book, with Ma's file of clippings, on the end table. I had planned to compare the article from the *Cork Examiner* about his death with the later account in the book and had never quite got around to it — like other things I had planned during a life of procrastination.

For a moment I sat frozen on the hard-back chair that was my work chair. Slob or not, I rarely mislaid things. Had someone taken the book and the file of clippings?

Impossible! Why would anyone bother? The book was a paperback, worth no more than a couple of Irish punts (which is what they call a pound). What good would the clippings be for anyone?

I bounded out of the chair and ransacked my suite. No trace of the book or clippings. I dove into my luggage to look for the copies I had made. Sure enough, they were still there.

I stood in the middle of the parlor, baffled.

Why would anyone take a harmless book and a stack of old newspaper clippings? Could they possibly believe that I hadn't read them? Or that, having read them, I would forget the story at which they seemed to point?

What the hell was going on?

Had they taken anything else from Ma's papers?

I examined the crates very carefully. As far as I could see, nothing had been removed. Someone, however, had gone through the materials. I couldn't quite put my finger on how I knew they had searched through the papers. They'd done a careful job, leaving only a few traces of their activity — a manila file turned upside down, a rubber band stretched in the wrong direction.

Or maybe I was imagining it all? Maybe my suspicious romanticism was turning into paranoia. Maybe. Then again, maybe not.

How did they know I'd be out of my room for a long breakfast conversation? Had I been set up?

No one could be sure that I would wander into St. Teresa's Church and see Nuala, could they?

Not unless they knew I dropped in there often at the end of my walk down to the Liffey.

I had never seen her at Mass there before, had I?

The light in the church was dim. She might have been there on other days too.

Maybe.

I felt like a heel for suspecting her.

Still, they, whoever they were, might know that a lonely young man would be a pushover for a pretty girl.

Ma's little diary books were still there. I sensed that someone had examined them and then returned them to almost the same place in the box where I had left them. Perhaps the searchers couldn't read Irish and didn't know that the diaries might be important or even that they were diaries. I'd have copies made that afternoon, just in case.

I collapsed into an easy chair, my heart pounding, partly in anger and partly in fear. The search had actually happened. I was not imagining it. A warning from a cop, possibly a bent cop, an attack on a dark stretch of street, a threatening phone call, and now a search of my room. These were the kind of things that happened in mystery novels, not in real life.

And, oh yes, a beautiful young woman. Except novelists didn't think up young women as improbable Nuala McGrail.

Who had taken the book and clippings? The maid who normally did my room? A skittish little teenager with a Kerry accent who jumped with fright whenever I spoke to her?

Not likely. She had a hard enough time making a bed right. She would not have been up to the challenge of a careful and thorough search of a single drawer in a dresser, much less five crates of papers.

Someone else then. I would demand to know who had been in my room.

Would that do any good? Whoever the searchers were, they had surely covered their tracks well, either with bribes or threats or government identity cards. Why not ignore them? That would surprise them and perhaps give me an ever so slight advantage over them.

The phone rang.

"Dermot Coyne."

"Is that you, Mr. Coyne?" A womanly voice, precise, sophisticated, sultry. Not Dublin, not even Anglo-Irish. Oxford.

"I think it is."

Pleasant little laugh. Amused at the peasant from America.

"Angela Smith here. Smythe with a 'y' and and an 'e.' From the British embassy."

"Good morning, Ms. Smythe."

"I wonder if I could persuade you to come round for lunch with me tomorrow. There's one or two matters our people here would like me to discuss with you."

"Oh?"

A cop doesn't scare the dumb Yank, so you try a woman whose sex appeal oozes through the telephone line. Well, that's direct enough.

"Nothing very serious or important, I assure you. If you'd rather put it off till next week . . . ?"

"What if I'd rather not have lunch with you at all?"

"That's entirely up to you, of course." She laughed lightly, implying that she was no threat to me. "We *would* rather like to talk to you."

"All right."

"Shall we say at half one. Julio's? It's in the mews behind the Bank of Ireland building right

154

off Pembroke Street."

"I know where it is."

"Her Majesty's government will look forward to buying you one of the best meals available in Dublin."

"You must thank herself for me."

"Who?" She sounded confused.

Good enough for you, Dermot Michael Coyne.

"Her Majesty. And Mr. Major too."

"Oh, yes. Quite. Till tomorrow then."

I reclined again in my easy chair. That was pretty quick work. They searched my files an hour or two ago at the most. Already they have a temptress on the phone to me.

Damn efficient, these Brits.

I put on gym socks and running shoes and set off on my jog.

I was most of the way down the Grand Canal towards the ocean when I finally asked myself the obvious question: Why would the Brits be all that interested in the death of Michael Collins?

Dermot Michael Coyne, longtime solitary bachelor, now had dates on two successive days with one woman already proven to be beautiful (even by her own grudging admission) and another who certainly sounded sexy on the phone.

Poor dear man.

– 10 –

Angela Smythe was all that the voice promised and maybe a little more. She was not perhaps a British woman operative out of a James Bond film, but she was someone with whom 007 (in his various manifestations, of which Sean Connery is my favorite) would not be ashamed to be seen. She smiled at me as I entered the restaurant — walls painted white and a huge skylight that, together with bright lights, created the impression of a sunlight glare more appropriate for Marseilles than Dublin — and I decided that the gumshoe business might be more fun than I had thought it would be.

"Mr. Coyne, isn't it?" She extended her hand.

She knew damn well who it was. Had she searched my room? Would she have been so clumsy as to have taken Ma's file and left a certain clue that she'd been there?

Only if she and her superiors wanted to leave a clue.

"I think so." I shook hands with her. "I answer to the name of Dermot, Ms. Smythe."

"Angela." A quick, bright smile, with a hint of smoldering fires.

She was a few years older than I, medium height, trim, and neatly shaped in a beige jersey

156

dress. Short brown hair, skillful makeup designed to create the wholesome English country girl impression, nicely formed face with full lips that seemed always to be playing with a smile.

If I hadn't met Nuala, this one would have swept me off my feet. As it was, she disconcerted me enough that I bumbled my way through the preliminaries of the conversation, yes, I would like some sherry, and of course white wine with the fish. No, I didn't want to order for myself. I'd trust the wisdom of Her Majesty's government in the matter. Yes, Dublin was a beautiful city on a day like this. Yes, I thought London was lovely. No, it was not my favorite city in the world. A place on the shore of Lake Michigan was still my favorite.

Richard M. Daley, Mayor.

The only point I scored.

Angela Smythe was certainly not a shy child; rather she was smooth, practiced, sophisticated. No crude young woman from the bogs of Connemara she.

"Oxford or Cambridge?" I asked.

"Oxford of course. Harvard for you?"

"Notre Dame, then Marquette."

"Marquette?"

"Jesuit University in Milwaukee?"

"Milwaukee?"

"A city in Wisconsin."

I thought I saw a faint upward twist of her lips, a hint of a contemptuous smile. "I intend to visit America someday soon. It must be a fascinating country."

"Big."

"Yes, indeed."

The waiter arrived with the Galway smoked salmon that, along with brown bread, was a staple for me at every meal in Ireland. This time, however, I didn't even have to order it.

When he had left, she deftly steered the conversation to the subject of her assignment.

"I suppose you wonder why Her Majesty's Government is buying you lunch?" She lifted a perfectly groomed eyebrow.

"To promote international goodwill?"

"That, of course. However, my colleagues have asked me to share with you some of our government's thinking on the Irish question. They believe it is important that you understand all the implications of the present situation."

"Decent of Her Majesty."

"Quite." Her smile was mechanical this time. Maybe I'd better be a good boy.

"Not all Americans realize how intent the British government is on finding a solution to the problems in Northern Ireland. Obviously we must put an end to the violence. The recent Anglo-Irish proposals for peace represent the best hope in this century. You'll note that the Irish Republican Army has not rejected them."

"I see." I scooped up a piece of salmon and dropped it on a slice of brown bread. If she was offended by my (deliberately) bad table manners, she didn't betray her distaste.

What kind of a diplomat doesn't know where Milwaukee is?

Harvard indeed!

"We have been successful in diminishing discrimination against Catholics, which pleases me" — quick smile — "because I'm Catholic myself."

A Catholic Brit, nice touch.

"The unemployment rate is still high, higher even than here."

"Almost as high as among American blacks."

"Not quite." I finished off the last bit of my makeshift salmon sandwich.

"Moreover, Whitehall understands and has made clear that there must be some political role for Catholics in the North. Indeed we have made a number of attempts in that direction in the last several years."

"Which the Prots won't buy."

"It is a very difficult situation."

"Genocide creates very difficult situations."

"Genocide?" She frowned at me. "Isn't that a strong term?"

"Let me be blunt, Angela. I'm not real Irish so you don't have to be indirect with me. I'm not a rabid Irish nationalist. I'm not a rabid anything. I have no sympathy for the IRA. Moreover, I sense that the real Irish here in the republic often wished that the six counties might be towed out into the Atlantic and either be annexed to Greenland or used for target practice by Her Majesty's Navy. I understand the sentiment. I don't contribute to NORAID. I'm not one of those Yanks who supports violence thousands of miles from my own home. . . ."

"That's nice to know," she said curtly, now quite upset with me.

"*But*, I know and you do too that the Ulster Protestants were settled by an earlier Elizabeth and your man Cromwell and other such worthies with the explicit intention of eliminating the wild Irish just as the wild Indians were to be eliminated in America and the wild Tasmanians in Australia. You also know that Cromwell sold fifty thousand Irish women and children into slavery in the West Indies."

"It was your ancestors who eliminated the Indians."

"We call them Native Americans now." I smeared butter thickly on yet another slice of brown bread. May as well get a good lunch out of Her Majesty. "Those who killed them were not my ancestors. Mine were surviving persecution and starvation on this island."

"All that was a long time ago."

"There's a statute of limitations on genocide?"

The waiter showed up with our poached grouper. Angela bit her lip and cooled down. I congratulated myself on making her lose her temper. Maybe she was Irish in her remote origins too. There weren't many Catholic Brits who were not Irish somewhere in their past.

"I really don't want to argue with you, Dermot. My colleagues and I hardly want to defend the actions of past British governments here in

Ireland. They are, candidly, quite indefensible. I might disagree with your vocabulary, but I do not disagree with the general position it represents. The problem, however, is not the past; the problem is the future."

"Which is shaped by the past." I sipped the wine she had chosen. First rate.

"Not determined by it. . . . Are you familiar with the present Anglo-Irish initiative?"

"I read the papers here."

"May I explain it to you?"

"Sure."

She sipped the wine too and beamed her approval. "A nice year."

"Sure is. The California Chardonnays that year were not up to their usual standards."

Fake? Certainly. But I liked being 007 for a few minutes.

"Quite." She sipped it again, perhaps trying to recall what she might have read about California Chardonnay. "In the agreement both governments made major concessions, of symbolic and substantive importance. The Irish government explicitly agreed that it would never constrain Ulster to become part of the republic unless the Protestant majority agreed to such a merger."

"You mean the six counties, the other three counties of historic Ulster having been gerrymandered out because Catholics would have possessed a majority in Ulster too."

"The past, Dermot," she said primly.

161

"Yeah. Well, it was good of Taoiseach Garret FitzGerald to agree a few years ago that he'd never try to force the six counties back into union since he didn't have the military might to do so or the stomach for fighting with a million Prots. Your man Albert Reynolds, now that he's Taoiseach, doesn't have the military to do it either."

She bit her lip again. I had better stop being a bastard.

"Quite true, yet it was an important symbolic concession for Ireland to make. Frankly, Her Majesty's government went much further than that. Several years ago when we agreed to establish the Anglo-Irish Secretariat in Northern Ireland, we acknowledged that the Government of Ireland had the right to a legitimate and formal interest in the problems of the North. In sum, the two governments now agree that there would be no forced union between the two Irelands but no denial of the right of the Irish government to be concerned about what happens in Ulster. You must admit that the agreement represents progress."

"And Mr. Major has not backed away from it despite the fact that the Prots reject the agreement."

"Nor is he likely to back away from it. . . . I have had the honor of having served on the Secretariat in Ulster. I must tell you, Dermot, that the civil servants of the two countries have made considerable progress, undramatic perhaps, but we are developing a tradition of co-operation between the two countries that shows great promise."

"Lucky guys to have you around."

"Is that a chauvinist remark?" she demanded furiously.

"No, ma'am." I tried my most charming dimpled smile. "It's a statement of fact. An able and dedicated woman must make that bunker up there a more pleasant place."

"It's not really a bunker." She calmed down a bit. "Only a former secondary school. It is rather bleak, I admit. Yet we . . . forgive me for sounding like a starry-eyed idealist instead of a civil servant. . . . I think we have a fair chance of ending a thousand years of conflict and suffering."

She was, however, a starry-eyed idealist, the kind that might appeal to a Yank who had a few vague ideals of his own.

"All possible success." I raised the wine glass in a toast to her. "And I think you are an idealist and that it becomes you."

"Thank you." She blushed. "But then you understand how important the current initiative is and how fragile are its chances?"

"Why is it fragile? John Major has so involved his future in the initiative that he is no more going to back down than the Pope will become a Mormon. The government here has nothing to lose by supporting it. The Catholics in the North are in favor of it, except for the gunmen.

163

The Prots are against it, but some of their younger leaders and a lot of their people are beginning to talk 'deal.' Where's the problem?"

And, more important, how do I fit into this Irish civics lesson?

She was trying to catch up with my devastating attack on the grouper, now persuaded that she had won me over. "Your assessment of the situation here in the republic is not perfectly accurate, Dermot. Perhaps nine-tenths of its citizens do not approve of the terrorists. The same proportion, as you said, do not put the North high on their agenda of priorities. Yet they are not totally unsympathetic to the goal of a united Ireland; and, however friendly they may be to individuals from my country, they don't trust the British government. . . . Before you make the ritualistic comment, Dermot, that they have reason not to trust my government, let me say I agree with you."

"So if there was some major problem, the government here might pull the plug on you folks up at the bunker and on the peace initiative in which Albert Reynolds and John Major have invested so much?"

"Precisely." She sighed with relief, having made her case — one with which I agreed and which I had understood before the free lunch.

"Like what?"

"A more spectacular repetition of the Gibraltar incident where our SAS gunned down three unarmed terrorists. I make no case for either side

164

in that incident, Dermot." She reached out and touched my hand. "Believe me, I have little affection for the SAS. I thought I was in love with one of them once and then discovered that they are beasts."

"Like all gunmen."

"Indeed so. Suppose that the SAS should gun down a group of innocents by mistake. The agreement would become a dead letter."

"It could happen," I said slowly. "Not very likely, but it could happen."

"You hardly can blame my colleagues and me for being careful."

"Not at all. . . . But how do I fit in?"

She shook her head, as if puzzled herself. "I'm afraid I can't answer that question specifically. Candidly I don't know. I was merely informed that you were engaging in some kind of behavior that seemed innocent to you but that could have serious implications for our efforts."

"Did you search my rooms at Jury's yesterday?"

"Certainly not!" She threw down her fork. "I'm a diplomat, not a spook!"

"Someone did."

"I have no knowledge of it." A tinge of angry color blazed on her cheeks. "My invitation to you was based on no such search."

I thought about it. Maybe it was only a coincidence. "I've no previous experience with my rooms being ransacked. So I don't know whether they were good or bad at it. They didn't make a mess, but there were a few traces."

"Perhaps deliberately." She was watching me intently.

"Perhaps. All they took was a book about Michael Collins and a stack of clippings from my grandmother's archives."

She shook her head again. "How bizarre!"

"You know who Collins was."

"Vaguely. Wasn't he one of the anti-Free State terrorists?"

"Just the opposite. He was commander of the Free State army. He signed the Anglo-Irish Treaty of 1921, and it turned out to be his death warrant."

"I'm afraid I don't know much about that era."

"Neither does anyone else. Now, Angela Smythe, pretty and intense idealist, let me tell you what I have done to stir up this concern in at least two governments. My maternal grandparents" — I took out their pictures — "left Ireland in 1922, never to return. They died last year. Ma, my grandmother, told me that if they came back they would be shot. All I have done" — I put the photos on the table, took her chin firmly in my hand, and tilted it up so our eyes locked (pretty gray eyes — and vulnerable after all; she too was a shy child) — "and this, believe me, is the honest truth, all I have done is to try to find out why they couldn't come back."

She licked her lower lip, but did not try to

pull out of my grasp. "Is it important to you to answer that question?"

"Not particularly."

"Then perhaps you should drop it. . . . Your grandparents had long and happy lives?"

"Indeed yes."

"I don't know why such an investigation would cause a problem. Truthfully I don't. But my colleagues must be convinced that it would or they would not have asked me to have lunch with you."

I fear that my thumb was caressing her chin. She was a very appealing woman, and she'd been hurt and she was afraid of me. "Can I propose a deal?"

"Of course." She smiled. "I make no promises."

"If they'd sent you in the first place instead of a pushy Irish cop, I'd probably have forgotten about the whole thing. I'm a terrible loafer, Angela Smythe with the haunting gray eyes, terrible altogether, as they say in this country. My proposal is that I'll agree to forget the whole thing if someone in some government will explain to me, in strictest confidence, what the mystery is."

"Why these people" — she pointed at my pictures — "such sweet, handsome people, could not return to Ireland after they migrated?"

"That's right. And they were sweet people. They were never involved in IRA fund-raising or anything like that. Yet they left Ireland behind, definitively."

"May I propose a counter deal to you, Dermot Coyne." She captured my chin, a fair enough turnabout.

"If you promise to let me take you to lunch the next time."

"Agreed. . . . I'll do everything I can to find the explanation you want. I promise that. On my honor." She brushed her fingers against my lips, oblivious to the waiter who was proffering the dessert menu.

"And?"

"And if I can't find out or can't tell you if I do find out, but can assure you that it is essential that you not know, will you keep your promise?"

"We'll have tea, and sherry trifle with double cream and a bottle of your best dessert wine," I told the waiter. "And yes, Angela Smythe, I will if you agree that the dessert wine is on me."

She laughed happily. "I'm sure Her Majesty would approve."

We left an hour later, the last couple to desert the restaurant, both of us slightly tipsy. In the alley outside the mews, Angela Smythe glanced in either direction, threw her arms around me, and, standing on tiptoe, kissed me.

"I want to establish" — she paused in her ferocious assault — "that this is personal and

168

not part of my assignment for Her Majesty's government."

"I'll take your word for it." I dug my fingers into her rear end, lifted her off the cobblestones, and responded to her kiss in kind. Her lips tasted of wine and tea and fish sauce as I broke through them into her mouth. We locked ourselves in a furious embrace that seemed to last for a couple of eternities.

I think I was the one who stopped.

"Oh, my," she said weakly. "Neither of us did that, did we?"

"Certainly not," I agreed, shaken by the burst of passion.

"The second bottle of wine."

"Definitely."

I commandeered her right shoulder and caressed her firmly, breast, belly, flank, thigh, and then up the other side.

"Dermot." She shivered and leaned against me. "Please. . . ."

It could as well have meant "please don't stop" as "please do stop." I rested my hand a little longer on her breast, solid and appealing to my fingers under her dress.

It would be so easy to take her back to my hotel room.

I captured her other breast. She sighed deeply but made no attempt to escape.

"Don't . . . I beg of you, don't!"

I tightened my grip on her for a moment, then I heard footsteps at the other end of the alley and released her from my prison.

"Definitely the dessert wine." My own voice was unsteady.

We walked quickly back to Pembroke Road.

"I'm sorry," I murmured.

"Don't be." She laughed uneasily. "I liked it. But we shouldn't —"

"I know."

"I'm walking back towards the embassy," she said, more calmly this time. "We'd better not stay together."

"I agree."

We both laughed, our animal natures suppressed and our rational confidence restored.

"I'm sorry," I said again.

"Oh, Dermot." She smiled gently. "I did start it, you know. And got back what I richly deserved in the circumstances. Don't blame yourself, please."

"One more lightly affectionate kiss." I brushed her lips hastily.

"Perfect way to end. . . ." Her gray eyes caught mine. "I'll be back to you about our arrangement. You can reach me at the embassy any day. For either governmental or" — her voice wavered again — "personal reasons."

"I'll keep that in mind."

– 11 –

"Sure, don't you look exactly like himself." The old man on the bench next to me sighed loudly. "The spittin' image, isn't it now?"

I had been sitting on the bench across from Sussex Terrace, just down from the Grand Parade watching the ducks and the seabirds and trying to figure out my problems with women. The old fella had sat down so quietly next to me that I became aware of his presence only when he spoke to me.

"Who?"

"Whom," he corrected me with a dry cackle. "You must forgive a retired schoolteacher, must you not?"

"All right, whom?"

"Wouldn't it be Liam O'Riada?"

I had been staring gloomily at the dull gray waters of the Grand Canal, telling myself that I was not drunk. Perhaps I had the drink taken, in the happy phrase of this ingenious people, but, no, I was not drunk.

Nor had I made a fool of myself because of the drink taken with Angela Smythe. It was merely a mild exchange of interested affection, nothing more than that.

Nuala was responsible. If she hadn't stirred

171

up my emotions yesterday, I would not have been so open to womanly attractions. Yes, it was all Nuala's fault.

The truth is that I am not a practiced drinker and that with the "creature," as the Irish call it, I am one of your short hitters.

I bunt at best.

So two sherries and the better part of two bottles of wine put me out of the ball game pretty quickly. Oh, yes, it was the dessert wine that really did me in.

Hadn't I said that already?

I had been pondering the Grand Canal and trying to make sense out of what had happened at Julio's. I thought I had struck a pretty good deal with Angela, though I could not quite remember all the details. I regretted my passionate embrace with her as a drunken pass; and I also regretted that I had not carried her off, figuratively speaking, for a romp in my bed at Jury's. Love on a gloomy afternoon in Dublin.

Nothing seemed to make very much sense.

As I have said before, I'm not much good as a man of action. I have to think things out before I make a decision.

When I have finally thought them out, often the decision has already been made for me by events.

The Grand Canal, as you know if you've ever been to Dublin, is not all that grand, just a tiny ribbon of dirty water wending its way through Dublin, hardly as wide as the Little

Calumet River picking its way through Gary, Indiana, which Dublin looked like as the mists and the rain and the smell of dead fish moved in again from the sea.

Was the dead fish smell worse than the soap factory smell from Hammond and the oil refinery smell from Whiting?

Hard question to answer.

Then the old fella accosted me.

"I look like my grandfather?"

"Wasn't I just saying so? Though he was even younger than you when I last saw him, wasn't he?"

"You knew him?"

"And your grandmother too. Wasn't she the most beautiful colleen in the whole County Galway in those days?"

I closed my eyes and shook my head. Was this another part of the crazy game in which I had been caught up? Or was it a drunken dream?

"They're both dead now," I said. "God be good to them."

"Ah, aren't almost all of us dead? But they were great times, weren't they?"

"Were they?"

" 'Tis a pity they never came back. Sure, they never came to Dublin and only to Cork the morning they caught the boat and just in time, let me tell you."

If I could clear the alcohol out of my bloodstream, I might be able to question this visitor

173

from the past. "How did you know I would be sitting here?"

"Weren't they telling me that you were after walking along the Grand Canal often? And didn't I say to meself that if I sat here long enough, you'd come by?"

"Who are *they?*"

"Themselves." He waved his hand vaguely.

I tried to focus on this old man. He was tall and thin, perhaps at one time as solid and strong as Pa. His suit, overcoat, tie, and hat were black, but clean, well pressed, and fashionable. His face was lined with creases and wrinkles but retained traces of past distinction. His gnarled hands, perhaps crippled with arthritis, gripped an expensive-looking black thorn stick. His blue eyes, pale blue behind thick glasses, seemed to be gazing at a distant scene. A Jesuit-educated schoolteacher, I told myself, probably a lifelong bachelor who had always regretted that he had not become a priest.

He reminded me of pictures of Eamon De Valera when that tall, ramrod-stiff old man, almost completely blind, had been president of Ireland, one of the last survivors of the Easter Rising.

"What did they say about me?"

"Didn't they say you were trying to puzzle out why Nell and Liam had to run away?"

"Did they now?"

He waved vaguely again, as if his consciousness was fading. "Terrible things happened in

174

those days. . . . The gold and all, if you take my meaning?"

"The gold? What gold?"

"Roger Casement's gold, who else's?" He pounded his thorn stick against the canal bank as if any fool should know whose gold.

"I see."

"The only man who knew where it was is long since dead, do you understand?"

"O'Kelly?"

"Now you've got it, boy." He patted my arm briskly. "Sure, you're a chip off the old block. Terrible thing that happened to him and Nell."

"Ma and Pa had happy lives in America." Somehow I wanted to reassure this old man who seemed to be living in a world of his own dreams. Or nightmares.

"Weren't they entitled to be happy? Hadn't they both fought for Ireland? Wasn't I saying that losing Liam was almost as bad as losing Michael Collins, and some called himself a traitor too, didn't they?"

I sighed loudly, figuring that such a response was sufficiently noncommittal to keep the old man going.

"Didn't I always say that it was good for Liam and Nell that they left but bad for the rest of us?"

"I'm sure you did."

He matched my sigh. "Mind you, it was not right what was done to him, not at all, at all."

"He never talked about it."

"And the little woman was as brave as ever lived in the County Galway, wasn't she? Ah, wasn't I half in love with her myself?"

"That showed good taste."

"Didn't it ever, sonny." He laughed dryly and patted my arm. "Sure, who wouldn't have been half in love with her?"

"She was a grand woman, wasn't she?"

"And wasn't she as brave as any man, braver in fact?"

"Braver in fact." I adopted Pa's technique of repeating the last few words.

"All of that. . . . Well, wasn't I telling them that you wouldn't be her grandson if you let them talk you out of finding out the truth?"

Well! "But what is the truth, sir?"

"Ah, that's a long story, isn't it now, sonny? Don't let them stop you."

"Who?"

"The politicians, who else? Weren't they the ones who betrayed the republic then and are still betraying it now?"

The damned Irish are always indirect and opaque, I thought. And when they approach senility they don't even understand themselves.

"Why do they care whether I find out the truth or not? Is it the gold?"

"Sure, who wouldn't want to find the gold? It would be worth millions and millions now, wouldn't it? Ah, but they'll never find it, will they, not till Judgment Day when Sir Roger comes back to tell."

"And Daniel O'Kelly."

"Aye, that one too." The old man closed his eyes. " 'Twas exciting to be young in them days, sonny. Young people today don't know what youth really means. They don't care about the republic, one and indivisible." He opened his eyes for a moment, and they were glowing. Then he closed them again. " 'Cept maybe those fellas up north, and most of them being eejits too."

"Eejits too."

Dead silence. Had he fallen asleep?

"How did Michael Collins die?"

His eyes jerked open. He sat up, startled. "You shouldn't be asking that question, should you now?"

"How can I find out the truth about Liam and Nell unless I know the answer to that question?"

He shook his head in dejection. "Them were great days, but they were terrible too. Maybe we shouldn't have any memories, sonny, not at all."

"I must find out how he died."

" 'Tis a long story and myself an old man who doesn't remember all that well."

I put my hand on his chest. "Who wanted to kill Nell and Liam?"

"Wasn't it the same ones that betrayed the republic?"

"Will they try to kill me?"

His eyes opened wide and fixed on me. "Not unless you find out what they did."

177

I felt my flesh crawl. So it *was* a dangerous game. "But are not they all dead?"

"Don't they have children and grandchildren, just like Liam and Nell? And haven't they profited from what happened even until now? Does betrayal ever die?"

He struggled to his feet, leaning heavily on his thorn stick.

"Do you know why they wanted to kill Liam and Nell?"

"They wanted them out of Ireland forever. Your folks wanted to live. They knew there was no hope of fighting the traitors. So they kept their secret."

"What secret?" I yelled.

The old fella tottered away.

I grabbed him. "What secret?"

"Don't let them stop you, little Liam," he murmured. "Don't let them stop you. 'Tis time the truth be told before they betray the republic again."

"What truth, for the love of God?"

He clung to my arm. "Big Liam, as we called him, Big Liam and Little Nell, they couldn't tell the truth. But times are different now. You can. Tell the whole truth."

He pulled away from me and pitched slowly away from the canal bank toward the street.

Was he a plant? I wondered. For the same side as Angela Smythe and Superintendent Conlon? Or for the other side? Was there another side, in addition to this feeble old man with

dim memories and an ancient love for Nell Malone?

Whatever the truth was, it was not merely,
if I were to believe the old fella, part of the
dead past, but part of the living and dangerous
present.

I would need another long talk with Angela
Smythe, to whom I had made a promise about
which I now had doubts, even if I couldn't quite
remember what it was.

Not, however, till after my date with Nuala
Anne McGrail. Usually I was lucky if I had
one woman on my mind. That was bad enough.
I had no idea how to cope with two sets of
desires.

If the old fella was for real, if he was not
a plant, if he was not a clever actor, if he was
not part of a game someone was playing with
me . . . then it seemed that there was a decisive
question at the heart of the matter, the question
that had made the old man jump:

Who killed Michael Collins?

– 12 –

Though overcome with ill-health, Collins
still persisted in going to Cork. Officially
it was for the purpose of inspecting the
army garrisons; on the night before his

departure had conversation with Mr. Moylett, and during the course of it he expressed his real intention. "I'm going to try to bring the boys around. If not, I shall have to get rough with them." The old loyalties still persisted, accentuated by his ill health and gloomy foreboding of the future.

He said to [Liam] Cosgrave: "Do you think I shall live through this? Not likely!" — "this" apparently meaning the civil war. He made a gloomy joke to his typist and she repeated it to Joe O'Reilly. So it went on. Under the weight and the personal responsibility attached to the civil war and torn by loyalties, his great strength was breaking. He was finding it difficult to concentrate, and was in the constant grip of a restlessness as he had never known before.

On the morning of his departure, a friend advised him that it was foolish to go, to which Collins replied that his own fellow-countrymen would not kill him.

O'Reilly awoke at six o'clock in the morning and the last he was ever to see of the man he had served so faithfully was of Collins waiting for the armored car to arrive.

He wore a small green kit bag over his back, his head was bent in gloomy meditation, and O'Reilly thought he had never been so tragically dejected. Collins, thinking himself unobserved, let himself fall slack in the loneliness and silence of the summer morning.

Collins went to the Curragh and there inspected the army units. From the Curragh he proceeded to Limerick. From there he set out for Mallow in County Cork. It was the beginning of the end of the last journey of his life.

— Rex Taylor
Michael Collins (1961), pp. 196–197

– 13 –

"George, what do you know about Michael Collins?"

"The astronaut?"

"The Irish revolutionary."

"Not a damn thing, Punk. You pulled me away from the eighth graders to ask me that?"

"Would you find out all you can about him, particularly about his death?"

"It's important?"

"Very important."

"Can't you find out over there?"

"No." I was phoning George from a public booth on Pembroke Street, the way they do in the Robert Ludlum stories. 007 indeed.

I thought of Angela again and was momentarily distracted from my conversation.

"It's been a long time since you've been so excited about anything, Punk. Is there a girl involved?"

"Not at all." I smiled at the pun I was planning. "Only a Holy Grail."

"Huh?"

I had stumbled back to Jury's and into the swimming pool for the second time that day. I worked the alcohol and the hormones out of my bloodstream, told myself I was an eejit for being neither fish nor fowl with Angela, and decided that I would take no further action till I heard from her.

Then I realized that George could find out a lot for me without stirring up the "other side," whoever and whichever the other side might be.

Also George had contacts.

"That friend of yours who works for the government?"

"Who?"

"Tony."

"The gumshoe?"

"Spook. Find out from him if (a) there's any secrets at his place about the death of Michael Collins and (b) whether there's any alert on those secrets now."

"Tony owes me. If he can find out anything without stirring up the other spooks, he will."

"And don't tell anyone what you're doing, especially not Mom and Dad."

"Are you in any danger, Punk?"

"No way."

Which may or may not have been the truth.

"You received Ma's papers okay?"

"Fine."

"I made copies of some of the stuff that seemed important, just in case."

"Always the prudent priest."

"Except in my choice of brothers."

I ambled back to Jury's deep in thought. Well, trying to be deep in thought. The alcohol was out of my bloodstream. The hormones, however, were another matter.

I'm not much of a lover, I told myself. So how come I turned her on so quickly? Or did I? Was it all part of an act?

Had she been abused by her friend in the SAS? Did I think I could heal her from that? Coyne, you gotta be kidding!

My agreement with her was not unreasonable. Maybe, all things considered, I should let sleeping dogs lie. Even if the old fella was right that the traitors were still a threat to the republic, what difference did it make to me?

I'd call Angela in a day or two, after the party at Longwood-Jones's, to find out what she had learned. Then I'd fly home. My call to George had just been a precaution.

Did she really find me attractive? Or was she just an accomplished woman 007? On Her

Majesty's Secret Service?

I stopped dead across the street from Jury's. How did I know she worked for the Brits? I had seen no proof that she was an English diplomat. Maybe that was part of this crazy game whose rules I didn't know.

Then why tell me to call her at the embassy?

I waited for the light to change and crossed the street.

She probably was what she claimed to be. However, I had been dumb not to ask to see her credentials.

Sean Connery would never make that mistake.

And he would have taken the woman to bed immediately.

I sighed over the inconvenient fact that reality is not as easy as an adventure film.

Tomorrow I would have to deal with the ineffable Nuala Anne McGrail, who, I told myself, might be the cause of all my problems.

I tried to blame Nuala for everything and found that it didn't work.

Whatever she might be, she was not an enemy.

A threat, a danger, perhaps. An opportunity, well, maybe. But not an enemy.

I imagined again the feel of Angela's breasts against my demanding fingers. Then I thought about the same embrace with Nuala. No doubt about which set of breasts I preferred.

If the latter woman wanted to resist me, I might have found myself on the flat of my back on the cobblestones.

I grinned happily to myself and then phoned the American embassy and told the cultural attaché that I would be bringing a guest to the dinner at His Lordship's.

He said that he had assumed I would.

I wondered what *that* meant.

However, my dreams that night were about Angela, not Nuala. And about Kel Morrisey. And about a red-haired woman with flashing, passionate eyes named Nell Pat Malone.

Braver than all the men.

– 14 –

"Ms. McGrail is waiting for you in the lobby, Mr. Coyne," the soft Dublin voice of the concierge informed me.

"Is she now?"

"Yes, sir." I caught a hint of a grin and a twinkling eye in the woman's voice. "She certainly is."

"Then I'd better be right down, hadn't I now?"

"I would strongly recommend it, sir."

I applied a final tug to my white tie, glanced in the mirror, decided that I looked ridiculous, and, heart pounding fiercely, left my suite and rode down the elevator.

When I turned the corner from the corridor

into the lobby, I saw Nuala standing near the door of the gift shop in the confident pose of a young woman who came into the lobby of a luxury hotel every day of her life, a faintly amused smile on her face and utterly indifferent to the admiring attention she was attracting.

She might have been twenty-five, an experienced and poised woman of the world.

I confess that I stopped dead in my tracks. Where had I found this radiant young countess?

She was dressed quite simply — an off-the-shoulder white gown, fitted tightly at the waist, a black cape, a single silver pendant around her neck. Her hair was piled high on her head, increasing the regal effect, and there was ever so slight a trace of makeup adding color to her face.

How had Nuala, perhaps with the help of friends, contrived to create such a mesmerizing effect?

They watched TV, didn't they? They went to films, didn't they? And even in the West of Ireland, you could buy *Vogue*, couldn't you?

"Good evening, Ms. McGrail," I whispered softly. "You look lovely tonight, as always."

" 'Tis himself now." Her accent had changed from Gaeltacht to Dublin. "And looking like a member of the House of Lords in all his finery."

I kissed her, permitting my lips to linger on hers. She tolerated their presence and maybe, just maybe, responded with a touch of pleasure.

"The Court of Saint James wouldn't be good enough for you, Nuala."

"If I weren't in my ladylike mode" — she cocked an eyebrow at me — "I might have a scatological comment on that remark."

"Countesslike, I'd say."

"Actually I'm trying for the grand duchess effect."

"It has been achieved, Your Grace."

Her confidence suddenly vanished and her lovely white shoulders slumped. "I don't want to disgrace you, Dermot Michael."

"That you will surely not do." I gently straightened the shoulders back into place.

"Is there too much boob?" Her hand fluttered to her throat.

"Not for a formal dinner, Nuala," I assured her. "Any more might be a bit risqué and any less might be a bit prudish."

"You're sure now?"

"Indeed yes." I kissed her again.

"You'll be ruining me lipstick," she protested but not seriously.

"You did find something to wear, didn't you?"

"It's all borrowed." She laughed, her confidence restored. "Except for the dreadful obscene underwear, which embarrassed me altogether when I bought it, and I'm not sure this terrible thing will function right all night long."

I extended my arm around her waist and pointed her towards the door. "I bet you loved every second of it."

"I didn't say that I didn't, did I?"

And we both laughed happily, two young people who just then approved very much of one another.

A liveried gentleman appeared at the door. "Mr. Coyne, His Lordship sent me over to pick you up. My name is Arthur."

"Good evening, Arthur. This is Ms. McGrail."

"Good evening, Ms. McGrail."

"Good evening, Arthur." A grand duchess at least.

The car was, need I say, a Rolls. Nuala caught my eye and rolled hers.

Arthur discreetly closed the window between the front and the back of the car, leaving me alone with this sweet-smelling bog flower, this ravishing druid princess, this Celtic goddess with wondrous breasts, this mythic heroine returned from the past.

I wanted to put my arm around her, but my nerve failed me.

As Arthur eased into the heavy traffic on Pembroke Street, she poked my arm.

"I never did ask why you're so important as to merit an invitation to a dinner at Lord Longwood's." Her well-educated Dublin accent was still well nigh perfect. When Nuala took on a role, she did it to perfection.

"Well." I squirmed uncomfortably. "He devours all the literary journals from both sides of the Atlantic. So he happened to read my two short stories that have been published and he told the American cultural attaché that he liked them. In fact, he thought I must be Irish because, as you know, Nuala Anne, only the Irish can write good short stories."

"He *never* did!"

"Ah, but he did. Anyway, the attaché happened to mention that he'd run into me at a concert, and His Lordship insisted that I drop over for a bite."

Dead silence from my young friend. New data were being processed.

"And yourself never telling me that you were a published writer."

"Two little stories, Nuala."

"Tell Arthur to take us back to Jury's."

"Why?" I felt my throat tighten in panic.

"I'm not going to walk into that dinner without having read your stories first."

Don't fool around with the grand duchess. No way.

"Is that all?" I reached in my jacket pocket. "I brought them both along."

"Ah, wonderful Dermot." She patted my arm approvingly. "He thinks of everything."

"I try."

I also tried to take her hand. She withdrew it firmly. I turned on the reading light behind her head.

She read the ordination and first Mass story first. I heard her snicker.

"Do you like it?"

189

" 'Tis hilarious, Dermot Michael. The young priest is your brother George?"

"Not exactly. The story is not completely autobiographical."

She began the second story and my stomach tightened.

When she had turned the first page, she reached for my hand and held it tightly. I made no attempt to escape.

"Dear God, Dermot. So this is the girl who died?"

"More or less."

"I want to cry, but if I do I'll ruin me makeup."

"The show must go on."

"So I'll cry tomorrow . . . and pray for you, poor dear Dermot Michael." She squeezed my hand. "No wonder you look so glum now and then."

"Do I?"

"Like you're far away thinking of someone else."

"Sorry." Tears were stinging at the back of my eyes. I wanted her consolation and yet I didn't want it.

"Sure, it's not your fault, is it now?"

"Did you say you'd pray for me? I thought you didn't believe in God?"

"I only said" — she pulled her hand away in exasperation — "if there is a God, I don't see why He'd waste His time with eejits like us. But there's no harm in praying to whom it may concern, is there now?"

"To whom it may concern?"

"Sure, like the mail that comes addressed to 'occupant.' "

I laughed and she laughed and her hand edged its way back into mine.

"Poor dear thing, she must have been terribly unhappy."

"Yet she never showed it."

"Kept it all locked up inside?"

The car had slipped down FitzWilliam Street and was approaching Merrion Square.

"Never a hint."

She sighed loudly. "Well, I'll never do that. . . . I'm glad you let me read these." She returned the two stories to me.

"I didn't have much choice, now did I?"

"Brigid, Patrick, and Columcille, Dermot, we're almost there!"

" 'Tis true."

"Kiss me just once before the play begins?"

"Gladly."

I embraced and kissed her, solidly and effectively. She clung to me, her heart pounding.

"I won't disgrace you, Dermot Michael. Truly I won't."

"There's always the possibility, milady, that I might disgrace you."

"You wouldn't dare!" She continued to cling to me. It was a most pleasant experience. She smelled and tasted delicious.

"We're here now, sir," Arthur informed us.

"Thank you, Arthur." I moved to open the door of the Rolls.

A firm white hand restrained me. "Let him open it, you eejit. Don't you know anything at all, at all?"

"Yes, ma'am."

"You don't want to hurt the poor man's feelings, do you now?"

"No, ma'am."

"Or embarrass me" — she chuckled — "and meself being such a grand lady."

"No, ma'am. Yes, ma'am."

Arthur opened the door and tipped his hat to Her Ladyship as I conducted her out of the car.

"Thank you, Arthur."

"You're quite welcome, ma'am. I'll be waiting for you when you are ready to return."

We walked up the door stoop. Nuala grabbed my hand again.

"All the world's a stage," she said.

"And all the people players," I added, lifting the door knocker.

"Wish me luck, Michael Dermot Coyne."

"A long life of it, Mary Nuala Anne McGrail."

The door opened and bathed the two of us in a rectangle of light. Curtain going up.

– 15 –

"Martin Longwood-Jones." A brisk, silver-haired man, perhaps five feet eight inches tall, shook my hand vigorously. "You're most welcome to our little house, Mr. Coyne and Miss . . ."

"Nuala McGrail, Martin."

I was not about to call anyone Lord, except the real article, and She wasn't around. Longwood-Jones was quick, intense, slim — perhaps an athlete when he was young and still in excellent trim. His brown eyes, however, seemed sad, as if he had seen much suffering and learned much wisdom from it; a younger Hulme Cronyn, perhaps.

"We are delighted that you are able to join us, Miss McGrail."

She absorbed the Anglo-Irishman in her smile. "Sure, I wouldn't want to miss seeing the inside of the most famous Georgian house in Dublin, would I, milord?"

The little witch had deliberately reverted to her Carraroe diction. Longwood-Jones was charmed.

Who would not have been?

His Lordship was friendly and affable, hardly, it seemed, the kind of man who would be part of a plot to drive me away from my quest. However, his invitation to dinner came soon after Superintendent Conlon had warned me off. Coincidence? Maybe.

I was too fascinated by Nuala's advent into elite Anglo-Irish society to think much about the quest and the threats against it.

When we walked into the Georgian parlor, authentic in every detail and, for my bungalow-belt tastes, overstuffed, overdraped, overcrowded, and overdone, every eye in the room turned to my Hibernic Diana.

Small wonder.

She played it perfectly, quiet and reserved at first, though always smiling, her diction Dublin again with just a trace of the reels of the West, her regal self-confidence untouched, her blue eyes twinkling with amusement.

My lovely date stole the show. Naturally.

In fact, she performed so superbly that I was displeased with her. Nuala was a great actress, so impressive that I wondered if one could ever believe her. She shifted into the role of the aristocratic young woman with ease that hinted that she could deceive almost anyone at almost any time.

Was Nuala able to distinguish reality, I wondered, from the various stages on which she performed?

Martin Longwood-Jones was about fifty; his wife, Lady Elizabeth, the only other woman in the room with an off-the-shoulder dress, was about ten years younger, a slightly plump and tasty dish, quite aware of her full-blown sex appeal but not at all threatened by my Nuala.

The American attaché, John McGlynn, was thin, nervous, and bald, an Irish American in his middle thirties, from Boston to judge by his accent, an anxious bureaucrat. His wife, Norine, Bostonian too, seemed faded and worn and perhaps out of place.

The minister of culture of the republic of Ireland, Brendan Keane, was a genial, smooth-talking, black Irish politician, like a ward heeler from Chicago with a university education and refinement. Was there a hint, I wondered, of shiftiness in his eyes, or was I reading into them images of slick and seedy Chicago Irish politicians of "the good old days"?

His wife, Fionna, was much younger, only a few years older than me, slim and hard-faced with darting eyes. She did not like Nuala at all.

I should say at all, at all.

So Nuala set out to win her over by asking about her children and listening with rapt attention to minute descriptions of their behavior.

Clever little bitch, she succeeded. By the time we left, she and Fionna Keane were as thick as thieves.

Need I say that not a single obscene, scatological, or blasphemous word passed her lips?

Her initial strategy was to listen and observe, shrewd blue eyes taking in everything without appearing to. She said little and always with a warm smile and a twist of wit. She continued to dominate the parlor as we sipped discreetly at our sherry.

Well, the others were discreet. So distracted was I by Nuala that I drank two glasses rather quickly and noticed what I had done only when my head started to spin.

"Now what do you do, Miss McGrail?" the minister asked politely during the lull in the conversation.

"A little bit of acting and singing, Mr. Minister."

"Really?" Longwood-Jones was intrigued. "With the Irish harp?"

"When I can find one, milord."

"What would it require to persuade you to sing for us after supper?"

Nuala glanced at me, an elaborate pretense that she had to go through the formality of asking me, though what I said really wouldn't matter at all. "Ah, it would be a great effort to persuade me, milord, and I'm sure it wouldn't be worth it. But you wouldn't have to ask a second time!"

"Good! That's settled then! Incidentally, did you see the performance of *Playboy* at Trinity? I was in London regrettably and missed it, but I'm told the Pegeen was superb."

Perfectly straight face on herself. "I was able to see a little bit of it, milord."

"And the Pegeen?"

Not a side glance from her to me. "It was

196

a privilege to watch her, milord, wasn't it, Dermot?"

"It was all of that."

We were then conducted into the dining room. Lighted by scores of candles, reflected on shimmering china and silver, the room, small by modern standards, was, I assumed, a perfect re-creation of a Georgian dining room. With liveried servants, a violinist playing near the table, an array of different sizes and shapes of Waterford goblets, two attractive women with naked shoulders and partially bared breasts, the room invited me into a world of two centuries ago, a world of Handel, elaborate manners, relaxed amusements, and chairs that were not designed for the body of a defensive end.

My head was still whirling from the sherry. Nuala was across the table from me, Lady Elizabeth next to me. I was drunk from alcohol and erotic beauty and fantasy. For me it almost was Dublin in the time of Grattan and the Ascendancy, that highwater mark of Anglo-Irish Protestant rule before the revolution of 1798 (the Year of the French) and the forced merger of the Irish parliament with its English counterpart.

The Longwood-Joneses did not refer to the historical accuracy of their re-creation. That would have been tasteless; and, whatever else they might be, they were paragons of taste.

"Your young woman is lovely," Lady Elizabeth whispered to me. "And so sweet!"

"She has a mind of her own, that one."

"Would you have it any other way?" She smiled up at me.

"Certainly not! But I wouldn't have Irish blood in me if I didn't complain about it."

She laughed. "I think the Anglo-Irish males have the same disease. Actually, it's rather attractive in them."

Lady Elizabeth and her husband had as much right to be considered Irish as I did, and maybe more. They were citizens of the republic and active in its civic affairs, even if they did have a town house in London too.

Yet somewhere in the back of my head there lingered the thought that when their ancestors were building Trinity College, the Custom House, the Four Courts, the Parliament Building (now the Bank of Ireland), and the Georgian mansions, mine were barely surviving in the thatched huts of the West.

After we were seated for supper, the minister returned to the subject of Nuala. "You're not Dublin born, are you, Ms. McGrail? There's the melody of the West in your voice?"

" 'Tis the melody of your own district, Mr. Minister."

"Clifden?" He frowned as he tried to place her.

"Carraroe."

"Irish speaker?" He seemed surprised.

She spoke a few words of Irish. It sounded like she was singing a song or saying a poem.

Keane replied in kind.

"A walking museum piece, Mr. Minister." She said it without the bitterness with which she had spoken the same phrase to me. The light irony in her voice, however, was, if anything, more powerful.

"Well worth preserving, I'd say." John McGlynn tried to enter the conversation.

"Ah, 'tis a difficult task." Nuala's eyes danced mischievously. "We're a different people altogether, a throwback to prehistoric times, the last Stone Age race, as a British poet laureate once called us. We look like some of the rest of the Irish and speak a variety of English that's remotely like yours. Many of us even have the same names as you do. But we're different — almost like aliens from another planet."

The imp had stolen my early gambit to her in O'Neill's and put it to her own use — with only a quick shift of an eye towards me, and that mischievous.

"All the more reason to preserve the Irish-speaking culture, my dear."

"There's more of us here, Mr. Minister, in Dublin than in the Gaeltacht. Probably more of us in Boston than in Carraroe."

"We are making progress against the unemployment rate." The minister frowned, not pleased with this deft reference to Ireland's social and economic problems. "I hope you're not planning to join those in Boston."

"Ah, they wouldn't have me in the States."

She shrugged her marvelous shoulders and laughed. "This one" — she nodded in my direction, acknowledging my existence — "says they already have enough shanty Irish in America."

I never said that, absolutely never. The bitch was a menace. So that's what Dr. Frankenstein felt like.

And Henry Higgins.

The conversation turned to the Irish economy. I watched as Nuala studied the various knives and forks that surrounded her plate. She was careful to use only the instrument that she saw in Lady Elizabeth's fingers. I myself concentrated on Lady Elizabeth, though my interest was, for which God forgive me, focused on her cleavage, and that as a distraction (I told myself) from Nuala.

Martin Longwood-Jones was a lucky man. I suspected from the quick glances between the two of them that he knew he was.

Her Ladyship, I was certain, had noticed my attention and rather enjoyed it. Certainly she did not hesitate to turn often in my direction to give me a full view of herself, which from my height was full indeed.

I had downed two glasses of the white wine, so I was disposed to enjoy the view.

Nuala didn't know yet I was a short hitter, so I presumed that she wasn't counting my drinks.

An erroneous presumption, as it turned out.

"What do you think of Mr. Coyne's short stories, Ms. McGrail?" Martin Longwood-Jones drew her back into the conversation. "Do you agree with my judgement that there is a strong West of Ireland element in his imagery?"

She sighed. "Ah, milord, isn't your man a bit young and a bit inexperienced to have matured yet as a writer? And perhaps just a bit too casual?" Her eyes were dancing with devilment. "I should have thought that we would withhold our judgments until he produces a larger body of work."

"I'm working on a third story," I said, flustered and blushing.

Lady Elizabeth laughed at me, tolerantly amused at an appealing little boy. "Surely, my dear, you can make a tentative judgment about the two stories that have already been published."

"Well . . ." Nuala drew out her response as if she were pondering it carefully. "Doesn't the poor dear man reveal great promise as a writer? The story about the ordination was wonderful. Frank O'Connor and Sean O'Faolain would have been proud to have written it. The story about the suicide, grim sad tale that it is, might be more Slavic than Irish, though I'm sure, milord, that we'd both agree that it's very well written."

All right, the woman was a fraud and an imp and part banshee to boot, but she was right about my stories. So how could I stay angry at her for long?

"I quite agree, milord." John McGlynn propelled himself into the conversation. "The mix of Irish and American cultural themes in both stories is most skillful. Our young friend here is not the first Irish-American writer to have attempted this blend, but he does it as well as anyone."

"Tell me more," I murmured.

They all ignored me. The Grand Duchess Fionnaula, white-wine glass in her hand, was still holding court.

"The third story" — she waved an elegant hand — "is the most interesting of all. I think we'll all agree that the women of Dublin are an excellent subject for fictional treatment. Our author is not the first one to write about late-adolescent fixation on the breasts of Dublin women, but there is enough gentle self-ridicule in the story for us to realize that his narrator is a comic figure struggling towards a maturity he will certainly attain. Some day."

There was no third story, neither published nor written. Not yet.

General laughter.

"I think, if you don't mind, Martin, I'll go home now."

"I can hardly wait till the story is published." Lady Elizabeth smiled benignly at me.

"He sounds like a male chauvinist," the minister's wife snapped.

"Ah, no, Fionna," Nuala corrected her. "The poor dear man — I mean the narrator, not the author, about whom the less said the better — the poor dear man couldn't be less of a chauvinist. That's what makes the story so poignant. And so hopeful."

"I haven't finished it yet."

I was not going to spoil her performance by saying that my date was guessing and that she hadn't read a single word of the story.

Guessing very accurately.

"So, Dermot," Brendan Keane said, taking charge of the conversation as the plates from the fish course were removed to be replaced by the meat course — and the white wine by the claret. "You are staying with us in Dublin to absorb some of the culture of your ancestors?"

"Unlike my narrator, Mr. Minister" — I tried to recapture some of my dignity — "I have not come to Dublin to ogle Dublin women —"

"Not only that," Nuala agreed piously.

More general laughter. A man married to her would be subject to a lifetime of general laughter whenever he ventured forth into public conversation with her by his side

". . . as I was about to say, as pleasant a pastime as that might be. But it would be hard to be specific about what I am doing. Drifting, listening, thinking, absorbing, collecting impressions and images, sights and sounds, lights and shadows. This is one of the most fascinating periods in the whole history of Irish culture. The old ways are dying, but what is being born, with a third of your young people receiving some kind of tertiary education, is no less Irish for all the change. Men like Friel, Sheridan, Roddy Doyle, Heaney, Jordan, Bono, to say nothing of the young poets, storytellers, and dramatists through whom one must fight one's way on the street . . ."

I was babbling, of course, but Nuala seemed impressed.

"How very interesting," Martin murmured. "Many authors work the way you do."

"It's not" — I was making it up as I went along — "goal-oriented work. You don't know when you're starting and when it's time to stop. Eventually you just stop. And then, hopefully begin to write."

"Your parents were born here?" Brendan Keane asked casually, a little too casually for my liking.

Well, we were going to arrive at that subject eventually.

"No, sir. On my father's side the Coynes, Mayo folk, God help us, came over at the time of the Little Famine, 1875. My mother's parents, my grandparents, left in 1923."

"At the end of the Civil War — ours, that is, not yours?"

"I'm not sure that there was a connection between their departure and the end of the Troubles, Mr. Minister. My grandfather, William Ready, was involved with the Galway Brigade of the Irregulars, but I know nothing more about that."

There was a moment of silence. Everyone seemed to be listening closely.

"Before the treaty?" Keane was watching me very closely.

"After the treaty, sir. Not long after because he then married my grandmother and migrated to America, never to return."

"Really?" Lord Longwood-Jones seemed surprised.

"He fought with a man named Daniel Kelly, or Daniel O'Kelly, if you wish."

"I don't quite remember the name."

"There's a statue of him at the crossroads in Oughterard in your district, Mr. Minister."

He frowned, as if trying to remember. "Oh, yes, a battle with the Black and Tans, wasn't it? So long, long ago. I'm sure that most of the young people in Oughterard don't know the story, do they, Miss McGrail?"

"I never heard it, Mr. Minister. Young people have other matters on their mind. The patriot game doesn't mean much to us. Maybe it should."

"I don't think so," he said softly. "They fought long ago so we wouldn't have to play the game."

I found myself liking the man. He was sleek and a little too "cute" (in the Irish sense of the word, which means "clever"), but he was perceptive and perhaps even wise.

"My grandmother told me that they would be shot if they ever came back."

Brendan Keane turned over a fork thoughtfully, the consummate politician searching for the consummate political reply. "There were amnesties for every one as the years went on, Dermot. Meaning no disrespect to your grandparents, I've always felt that there was a bit of romance for an Irish-American immigrant of that era if he could hint that there was a price on his head."

"He never spoke about it, Mr. Minister. And Ma, my grandmother, mentioned it to me only once."

The minister continued to play with his fork. "It's odd that much of the political shape of Ireland today was formed in those years, and yet the conflicts are so distant as to be forgotten. I am, as you know, a member of the antitreaty party. By that definition, the opposition are traitors to the Irish Republic. Yet I can assure you that no one has thought in those terms since 1930 at the latest. I don't want to say that we forgave and forgot. It's merely that we have acted like we had ever since. . . . I'm sure your grandfather would have been quite safe if he had returned."

"An alien paradoxical people," Nuala observed. "Long memories and yet short memories."

"Precisely, my dear. We don't quite forget,

but we see no point in remembering too much either."

"As a member of a party descended from the anti-Free State forces, the Irregulars on whose side my grandfather fought, what would you say today about the traitor Michael Collins?"

Again dead silence.

"I don't think there would be any hesitation about the judgment" — he continued to speak casually — "that he was a genius of the first magnitude. His death was a terrible loss for Ireland. If he had lived he would have been Taoiseach and probably Uachtairan — that's president — and a major world figure. He was the only man on the other side who had the determination and the political astuteness De Valera possessed and a lot more flare. We would have had a different history and a much more interesting one."

"Yet he almost certainly had a death instinct," Lord Longwood-Jones suggested.

"Definitely."

"Kit Kiernan was quite worried about him," Nuala remarked. "His sweetheart, you know. Poor dear woman."

Someone had been doing her homework, without telling me, of course.

"You have a special interest in him, Dermot," Lady Liz (as I had learned she was called) asked.

"Not particularly, Liz. But to an outsider trying to understand Ireland, he seems a striking figure, a giant, even if the present government did not celebrate the centennial of his birth back in 1991."

The minister laughed. "We did not let the event go completely unnoticed. We did hail his great work in the Black and Tan war, and the other party celebrated his wisdom in bringing peace to Ireland."

A waiter refilled my wineglass with claret, the best I had ever tasted. I should watch myself. The last time I had too much of the drink taken I had behaved badly; and tonight I was in the company of a much more alluring woman — a shy child with a tart tongue.

"Are you planning to write about those times, Dermot?" Martin asked.

"I don't think so. I have enough images from the present to keep me going for years."

"At the rate of a story every eighteen months," Nuala observed.

More general laughter.

The candlelight gleamed on her bare shoulders and the tops of her breasts. The dancing lights in her eyes were spinning a Kerry reel.

Irresistible.

You have captured me, young woman. At least for the night in this fantasy dining room. In the cold light of tomorrow morning, dark and rainy I expect, I might want to reconsider the matter. Now, however, I'm yours if you want me.

You're acting, all right, but it is still the real Nuala we're seeing, at least one element of her complex self. There are other versions of the real Nuala. I like them too.

You would make a challenging wife, difficult, contentious, passionate, and sensitive.

You would also nurture the shy child in me and permit me to protect the shy child in you.

I'd be a fool to let you get away.

Still, you scare the hell out of me. And you're too young to marry. And I'm not ready for marriage yet.

She saw me staring at her and bit her lip to suppress a smile. She knew she had spun a web of enchantment about me and was amused by my adoration. Her eyes flicked to Lady Elizabeth at my right and rolled ever so slightly, just to let me know that she had noticed my fascination with that woman's shoulders and chest, didn't really mind, but wouldn't let me forget it either.

Did this crowd think we were close to being engaged? Or living together?

Probably.

God help a man of hers who was a writer if he didn't write. If a man marries her he'll never have a moment's peace.

Or a moment of boredom.

Just like Grandpa Bill.

As much as I had loved Ma, I had often thought that I wanted no woman like her running my life.

The minister continued to look thoughtful. "The trick of it, I suppose, is to learn from the past, even drink in its romance and drama, and at the same time not to be tied to its causes and slogans."

"As the lads are," I said, using the term often applied to the IRA gunmen.

"Precisely. In some sense they can claim lineage with the antitreaty forces. Unlike Michael Collins and unlike Dev after 1923, they don't know when to stop."

"And like my father's commandant, Daniel O'Kelly?"

"You know the history better than I do."

Everyone was looking at me — the Yank being expected to explain his attitude on the violence in the six counties. How many times had I been forced to do that?

"Whatever my grandfather's position was, and he never spoke about it — which is sort of strange, isn't it? — I am not in sympathy with the present IRA. I don't believe in violence and the murder of the innocent. However, I agree with Mr. Cruise O'Brien that they use the symbols of 1916; they, not any of us around this table, are the legitimate descendants of Michael Collins during the Black and Tan War and of Dev during the Civil War. Moreover, I don't think that England would have been forced into the current Anglo-Irish peace initiative if it had not been for the lads and their killing the last twenty years."

"Tragically, I think you're right. Don't you agree, milord?"

"Indeed yes. Until the Ulster Unionists accept political equality for Catholics in the North, the killing will continue."

"It's not our war here," Fionna Keane said stubbornly.

No one disagreed with her.

"But it's a paradox, isn't it, Dermot," my date observed, "that the North is grist for the mill of a storyteller?"

"Only, my dear, when he's at ease enough with it to write about it. I'm not sure I'll ever quite understand Ireland well enough to write about anything more than Dublin's fair city where the girls are so pretty!"

More general laughter, this time on my side.

The trifle they served for dessert was at least a mortal sin. Many more lengths in the pool for the Yank tomorrow.

"You'll have to drench it in double cream for himself," Nuala warned.

Her remark, which produced more general laughter, as by this time everything she said did, at least spared me the embarrassment of asking for a second helping of the double cream.

To my surprise, the Longwood-Joneses did not honor the old aristocratic custom of the men and women separating after the meal. We were to adjourn back to the parlor, still overstuffed as now I was, for port (no cigars, indeed no smoking of any kind) and Ms. McGrail's song.

"Still, Dermot," His Lordship said to me as we were leaving the table, "it would be interesting to explore your grandparents' tale, wouldn't it, an opening to the paradox of how a peaceful people can be so violent and how a people with long memories can so easily forget?"

"I suppose so, Martin. I suppose so."

No commitments either way. Let them guess what I would do.

The Celtic harp was brought out. Sitting on the edge of an antique chaise that was probably insured for seventy or eighty thousand pounds, Nuala tuned the strings, glanced at me triumphantly, and began.

> *"In Dublin's fair city,*
> *Where the girls are so pretty*
> *I first set my eyes*
> *On sweet Molly Malone.*
> *She wheeled her wheelbarrow*
> *Through streets broad and narrow,*
> *Crying cockles and mussels*
> *Alive, alive oh!*
>
> *"Alive, alive oh!*
> *Alive, alive oh!*
> *Crying cockles and mussels*
> *Alive, alive oh!*
>
> *"She was a fishmonger,*
> *But sure 'twas no wonder,*
> *For so was her father and mother before.*
> *And they both wheeled their barrow*

Through streets broad and narrow
Crying cockles and mussels
Alive, alive oh!

"Alive, alive oh!
Alive, alive oh!
Crying cockles and mussels
Alive, alive oh!

"She died of a fever
And no one could relieve her,
And that was the end of sweet
  Molly Malone,
But her ghost wheels her barrow
Through streets broad and narrow,
Crying cockles and mussels
Alive, alive oh!

"Alive, alive oh!
Alive, alive oh!
Crying cockles and mussels
Alive, alive oh!"

I'd heard the song often and sung it lustily.
It never meant as much as it did to me at that
moment. I didn't want sweet Molly Malone.

But I did want sweet, perhaps bittersweet,
Nuala McGrail.

– 16 –

"I don't want to talk about it. Leave me alone."

Nuala was curled up in a knot against the side of the Rolls, her head turned away from me.

"You were wonderful. They adored you." I reached out tentatively to touch her shoulder. She twisted away like there was electric current in my fingers.

"They did *not*. They saw right through me. They knew I was a focking fraud!"

"You weren't a fraud, Nuala. You were simply being yourself, one of the many varieties of Nuala!"

"I wanted to shout shite, shite, at all of them, the focking snobs!"

"Would you use such language in the presence of your mother!"

"Brigid, Patrick, and Columcille, I would not!"

"And she's a snob!"

"I never said that, did I?"

"You're not being logical, Nuala."

"Fock logic!"

That said it all. She did not want to be consoled.

So I'd better shut up. It was a reaction from

the strain to trying to be the Grand Duchess Nuala, one of her *personas* doubtless, but not one that had been let out of the box all that often.

"And yourself a pissant drunk!"

"I am not drunk!" I protested. "I have some of the drink taken maybe, but I'm not drunk."

"If I hadn't held your arm on the door stoop," she mumbled, "wouldn't you have fallen down it?"

"I would *not!*"

"You would *so!*"

She was trying to pick a fight with me. Well, she'd have to learn early in our relationship that such a tactic didn't work. Not even when I had a bit too much of the drink taken.

She hunched into a tighter knot. No tears yet, so she probably wasn't going to cry.

"Where do you live, Nuala? Arthur has to take you home?"

"I *won't* tell you! I'll walk from Jury's!"

"You will not!" I grabbed her and turned around, so I could see her face in the dim light of the car. "Now listen to me, young woman. You can indulge in your self-hatred and enjoy it as much as you want, and I won't argue with you about it. But I'm not about to let you walk home by yourself after a date with me." I shook her once or twice for good measure. "Do you understand that?"

She wouldn't look at me, but she did nod her head.

215

"Arthur can take me home after he drops you off."

I shook her again. "Arthur is not your date and I am."

"Isn't it so poor that I'm ashamed of it?"

"I'm not ashamed of you, Nuala Anne Mc-Grail, even when you act like a focking asshole!"

At that she sniggered. "All right, if you must know. It's on Chapel Lane off Irishtown Road."

"Where all the yuppies live?"

"The focking yuppies live on the west side of Irishtown, along the Dodder River. We poor folk live on the east side." Then she twisted away and returned to her sulking.

I gave the address to Arthur through the voice tube.

"Nine drinks," she muttered. "Nine and a half counting that half glass of cognac at the end. If you had taken the full glass, wouldn't you have fallen down the steps and my arm not strong enough to hold you up? Wouldn't you have disgraced me?"

"You were counting, were you?"

"I wanted to see if you were an alcoholic!"

"I am not an alcoholic!" I was beginning to be angry. "I hardly drink at all. The wines were so good tonight and the company so exciting that I drank more than usual. And, as you yourself admit, I stopped in time."

"And all the time staring at that woman's boobs, embarrassing me altogether!"

"Weren't they meant to be stared at? Isn't

216

that the point in strapless gowns?"

"You were too obvious." She sniffed. "I'm thinking you were half ready to chew on her tits."

"More than half ready. Yours too as far as that goes. But I remained in the bounds of good taste, Nuala."

"Georgian good taste." She wouldn't give an inch.

"They were much more lewd than we are. If I were a Georgian male with as much of the drink in me as you say I have, you wouldn't be safe in this car. I'd have your dress off and that obscene lingerie thing too, which incidentally seemed to do its work pretty well."

"Pissant drunk," she muttered. "Besides, you'd be afraid to try."

Now, there was a challenge for you. Also a truth not to be denied.

"Probably you're right, Nuala. Also too respectful of you to try."

"Focking gobshite!"

I gave up, not that I minded the argument, which I thought I had won.

Then she changed completely. "I'm sorry, Dermot Michael." She turned and leaned her head against my chest. "I'm a terrible bitch altogether and I had a wonderful time. Thank you for inviting me."

"Here we are, sir," Arthur said dubiously before I could respond to her transformation. "A

217

bit rundown, I'm afraid."

"Ms. McGrail is a student, Arthur."

"Yes, sir."

"I'll walk up to the door with you, young woman." I put my arm firmly around her. "Don't embarrass me or Arthur by making a scene."

"If you think you can come into the apartment and screw me" — she shoved me away with a laugh — "you're wrong. Aren't there two other girls sharing with me?"

"All of them waiting for the whole story of your triumph, which you will narrate for them in elaborate detail."

"Humph. . . ." She giggled, now a little silly, perhaps from exhaustion.

Oh, yes, Dermot Coyne won the argument, much good it would do him.

"Thank you very much, Arthur," she said to the driver. "It's a beautiful car and you drive it well."

"May there always be a beautiful car for you to ride in, miss."

She was willing enough to permit me to escort her to the door of the shabby little two-story house — workers' quarters from the Victorian era.

"And if it was rape I had on me mind, woman, four other girls wouldn't stop me, do you understand?"

She actually laughed at me. "We'd kill you, one way or another."

Then at the door, she hugged me and kissed me. "I *am* a focking asshole, Dermot Michael Coyne," she said. "I'm sorry. Didn't I have a wonderful time? Thank you."

I stood there for a minute, the soft Dublin mists bathing my face, the smell of the sea again on the air. I was still in a daze. The evening had been too much for me, too much altogether, as a matter of fact.

How many subtle Irish signals — and not so subtle ones — had been hurled at my head that I had missed because I was besotted by good wine and beautiful women?

Well, as Nuala might have said, fock 'em all!

The best part of the night, I told myself fervently as I walked back to the Rolls, was the last moment.

It had been a wonderful kiss, mostly innocent of lust, but filled with tender affection.

– 17 –

"Miss Angela Smythe, please. Dermot Coyne calling."

"I'm afraid, Mr. Coyne," the woman said in a very proper British voice, "there's no one on the embassy staff by that name."

"Are you sure?"

"Quite sure, Mr. Coyne."

219

"She was attached to the Anglo-Irish Secretariat."

"Then she wouldn't be stationed here, Mr. Coyne."

"Uh, thank you very much."

"You're quite welcome, I'm sure."

What the hell?

I replaced the phone slowly. What the hell?

I had not asked to see her credentials. What a dumb mistake. Sean Connery would have thought of that immediately.

No, that was dumb, too. She would have had credentials.

Sean Connery would have phoned a schoolmate of his at the embassy to make sure there was such a person on the staff.

He would have realized at lunch that a member of the Secretariat would not have worked out of the Dublin embassy but out of the Foreign Office in London.

Dumb gobshite.

Yet why would she say that I could reach her any time at the embassy?

I pondered that question.

If I had been smart enough to call the embassy right after she had phoned me, the same superior British voice probably would have said, "I'll put you through to her, Mr. Coyne."

Maybe not. Maybe Angela Smythe was working for someone else and felt pretty confident that, dummy and gobshite that I was, I would not check on her.

Then why did she undercut her position by telling me that I could talk to her at the embassy and by not calling me back to confirm our agreement?

While I was trying to figure out an answer to that question, the phone rang again.

"Hi, punk! You engaged to that beautiful girl with the foul mouth yet?"

"When I told her that you said we should call the Mass the Eucharist, she said that the focking Mass was the focking Mass and that I should tell you so!"

"Hey, she sounds wonderful! Ma would have loved her!"

Note that Ma's approval was more important than my mother's. No, that's not quite right. Mom's approval of the "nice girl" was taken for granted, assuming that she was a nice girl, which was not a hard part to play, although Christina didn't quite measure up to it.

"They would have been thick as thieves, that's for sure."

"I'm calling because I have a collection of books and articles about Michael Collins that I'll Federal Express over to you."

"Great."

"And I talked to my friend."

"Yeah?"

"Call me back on a public line, will you?"

"You bet."

It was Tuesday afternoon, dark, dismal, and damp, and I was dreaming about golden autumns in the Midwest and noisy football weekends at Notre Dame. I had not heard a word from either Angela Smythe or Nuala Anne McGrail. Nor had I sought the latter out at O'Neill's or Bewley's or St. Teresa's.

My hangover, for which God forgive, on Saturday had been terrible. When I recovered sufficiently to reflect on the evening in Merrion Square, I was not sure that I wanted to meet that woman ever again, affectionate kiss or not. Beautiful and challenging she was, but intimacy with her would involve hard work that would never end.

So on that Tuesday afternoon, Angela Smythe — with a "y" and an "e" — seemed a much safer bet. I was in a mood for safe bets just then.

So I discovered she might not have been so safe a bet after all.

I rushed out to the public phone across Pembroke Street and fiddled with a shilling to get the operator and then tried very patiently to give her my international credit card number. After much transatlantic confusion, which direct dialing avoided, I finally got through to the Prester.

"George?"

"Yeah, Punk. You know, it's all kind of strange."

"Tell me about it."

"My friend who works for the government was suspicious about me. How did I know about this Collins case? I told him that he owed me lots of favors and that this was one of them and that I wasn't working for a foreign government. I figured you didn't want me to tell him about your interest."

"No way."

"Well, it comes to this. They have a note on their computer which says that the official story about how Michael Collins died is not to be believed. There's also a 'blue flag,' which in their terms means an indication that the issue is still live, which means sensitive, and a 'black flag,' which means that they know something about another government's intelligence that they are not strictly speaking supposed to know. My friend says that he doesn't have the clearances to go through those files. We could really search for higher clout —"

"Do it."

"Maybe we can and maybe we can't. . . . Is the girl involved?"

"No."

"Ma and Pa?"

"Maybe. I'm not sure yet."

"I don't want you take any chances, Punk."

"I won't. Don't worry about me."

"Punk, do me a favor. Check in every day, huh?"

I hesitated. "Sure. . . . Oh, yeah, one more question. The agency for which your friend works wouldn't be likely to be bugging the Irish intelligence, would they?"

"Maybe for gunrunners. Not much else."

"So if they had some information, it would be most likely about an operation the Brits are running, huh?"

"That sounds reasonable."

"I don't care whether they know about my interest. Maybe your friend can pass up the information that the issue could warm up again."

"He won't want to hear that."

"Use your own judgment."

"Take care, Punk."

"You bet."

I strode back to the hotel at top speed, a whiff of the chase in my nostrils. Then, before I went down to the pool, I calmed down. I knew now that I wasn't losing my mind. There was something strange going on, something that someone, probably the Brits, wanted to keep secret that was important even today. I didn't care about their precious secret. All I wanted — and by now it had become as close to an obsession to me as anything had ever been in my life — was to learn more about the story of Ma and Pa. I would continue to search out that story without giving any hints to those who might be watching of what I was about. I could do this because the secret was surely in Ma's diaries — which she had surely left because she wanted me to find out the truth.

The other side would think that I had abandoned the search. Gradually they would lose interest.

When I discovered the truth in my own mind, I would decide what came next. Probably nothing.

The only problem was how to continue my search for the truth without the other side knowing what I was up to.

In the pool I saw an answer to that problem too. It was ingenious, I told myself, and it had its own element of danger, though of a different kind.

Sean Connery wouldn't do it. He would bash heads and seduce women.

I wasn't Sean Connery. While I could bash heads if needs be — and I had demonstrated that — there were other and more subtle ways of learning the truth.

I knew something that they didn't know. Well, probably didn't know. They were not the only ones with a secret.

What would happen if I should learn their secret and discover that it was something that I didn't really want to know?

Well, that's a chance you take, isn't it, when you set out in pursuit of the truth?

I'd sleep on my scheme, which had been bumping around in the back of my head for more than a week. Tomorrow I would act on it.

Maybe.

Back in my room, showered, and consuming my afternoon tea — sandwiches and scones with clotted cream and jam — I ran through my scheme again. Where were the dangers?

There weren't any. No one would know what I'd found out until I knew all the other side's secrets.

That seemed a reasonable assumption then. Now in retrospect, it was foolish and naive.

– 18 –

I overslept the next morning. When the sun, which had made one of its occasional appearances in Dublin, woke me up, I remembered that there was something I was supposed to be doing that morning.

What was it?

My idea, my scheme, my master plan, bounced back from my unconscious like an energetic child frolicking in the morning sunlight.

I thought about it again. Should I?

I struggled out of bed. I still had some time to make a decision. I dashed hastily through my shower, donned jeans, a sweatshirt, and my Marquette jacket, stuck a small package that I had prepared the night before into my pocket, and dashed down Pembroke Road and Baggot Street to the green and then over to Grafton Street and Bewley's Café.

In search, need I say, of Nuala Anne McGrail. I found her way over in a corner in the basement with a single scone and a cup of tea. The rest of the room was deserted in the brief lull between the breakfast crowd and midmorning rush. She was poring over a textbook and furiously scribbling notes on a pad of paper.

I dashed upstairs, purchased a huge order of scones, toast, bacon, orange juice and tea, crowded it all on a tray, and hurried back to her table.

She was wearing a green sweatshirt with the words "Galway Races" emblazoned on it in gold. She look tired and disconsolate, as if she had been up late several nights in a row.

"May I be after sitting here?" I asked, putting on my best Irish brogue.

"I don't give a fock." She didn't look up.

I sat down across from her and pushed a glass towards her. "Drink your orange juice, woman. I'll not be telling you again that it's good for you."

"Brigid, Patrick, and Columcille!" She looked up, pleased and astonished. " 'Tis yourself!"

"I think so and meself carrying a nutritious breakfast. Now close your book, woman, and eat your breakfast, and talk to me."

Dutifully she closed her book. "I'm thinking that it's a terrible surprise you'd ever want to set eyes on meself again and me being such a terrible pissant bitch on Friday night."

"Ah, you were terrible, that's true enough, isn't it?"

She smiled wanly. "Though I didn't as much

227

of the drink take as certain other parties did, did I?"

"I don't know. I wasn't counting as certain other parties were."

She touched my arm. "I was a real shite. I'm sorry. If I'm ever with you again when the creature is available, I won't be counting the jars."

"And the Pope will become a Mormon!"

We both laughed.

Then she sobered up. "I'm truly an awful person, Dermot Michael."

"Woman, how many times must I tell you I won't tolerate such self-hatred? You were exhausted after an exhilarating and difficult evening. You also learned that you can walk into any room in the world and be at ease and talk to any group in the world and charm them. That could be a disconcerting insight about oneself."

She was silent as she pondered that conclusion. I noticed again how tired she seemed. Worried too. Was there someone sick in her family?

Then she spoke haltingly. "Is that really true, Dermot Michael?"

" 'Tis."

"I know I can fit in wherever I am. I've been able to do that all my life. I'm not so sure though that there's any real 'me' there. I'm one person with me ma, another with me roommates, still another at O'Neill's. At that party I was a fantasy person I always dreamed of being, the Grand Duchess Nuala, and wasn't she a terror now? I change me masks to fit the crowd and there's no core in me at all, at all. I'm too cute by half."

Hadn't I myself thought the same thing about her?

"You're a very shy child with lots of masks, some of which are funny faces." I kissed her cheek lightly, very lightly.

That did it. She threw back her head and laughed. "Go 'long with you now!"

"Eat your breakfast, woman."

"Haven't I started already?" She spread a thick glob of marmalade on a croissant and began to wolf it down.

"Did you write to Lady Elizabeth?"

"Do you think I'm a focking eejit?" She grinned, her mouth full of food. "Do you think me ma didn't teach me any manners at all, at all? Did you write?"

"I have a note on my desk to write."

"Eejit!"

"I sent her roses the next morning, and yourself thinking my ma didn't teach me any manners!"

We laughed again.

"I made terrible fun of you."

"Did I seem to mind?"

"You did not." She gulped at the orange juice. Had she eaten nothing at all since Friday night?

"You were wrong on one point. The Dublin story is not about Dublin women in general, but about one woman in particular, and she's not sweet Molly Malone either."

"Didn't I know that?" She sniffed. "Sure, I wasn't going to let those bloody West Brits think I was sleeping with you, was I now?"

I didn't quite see how that would follow, but I thought I'd better not ask. "God forbid, especially since I'm not, worse luck for me. . . . Feeling better?"

"Nothing like two glasses of orange juice to make the young gobshite lass from County Galway feel better. . . . Now tell me about the girl that killed herself."

I felt the blood drain from my face. I did want to talk about Kel. Not today, however, later maybe. Like next week.

"That's what we Yanks would call a fast pitch, Nuala Anne."

"I want to hear about her, Dermot Michael. You loved her very much, didn't you?"

I pondered that question. "It's strange, Nul, but I'm not sure that I did. Well, yes, surely I did love Kel — Kelly Anne to be exact — enormously. We'd been friends for as long as I could remember. We were bonded together. I don't know whether I was in love with her. Probably not. Our friendship was much deeper than falling in love and yet . . . it's hard to describe. I can't say less erotic, because there was a lot of passion in it. I'm not making much sense, I'm afraid."

"If she had lived" — Nuala's wondrous blue eyes brimmed with sympathy — "would you have married her?"

"I don't think so. In my realistic moments I imagine that we would have decided after a year or two of college that we were destined only to be good friends. The trouble is" — my eyes were stinging — "we never had a chance to decide that. The conversation never took place because she was dead."

"You blame yourself?" She sipped some tea, put the cup down, and took my hand.

"Yes. No. I don't know. Sometimes. A kid my age at the time couldn't have been expected to perceive what was happening to her. It's taken me seven years to comprehend that."

She was stroking my fingers gently. How could one so young understand so much?

"She wasn't like a sister. I have two of those and it's not the same. She really wasn't a lover. She was a special friend." The tears were flowing now. I couldn't control them. I didn't want to control them. "A friend whose face I searched for whenever I came to a place where she might be. I still look for her . . . even in the streets of Dublin. . . . I always will."

She laid her hand against my cheek and smiled affectionately. I broke down and began to sob. I glanced around: No one nearby to see me. I could enjoy the sympathy.

"You never wept for her before." She stroked my blond curls. "Did you, Dermot Michael Coyne?"

Overcome with grief I could only nod.

" 'Tis terrible hard for men to grieve."

She let me cry myself out in silence.

Then when I was finished she gave me a pack of clean tissues from her book bag. "You'll never forget her, Dermot," she said. "Never. And you never should."

That was all that needed to be said.

The spirit of Kelly Anne Morrisey had not been exorcised. There would still be grief. There would always be some grief. But her spirit was now beginning to be a benign one. I could finally believe that George was right when he insisted that nothing that was good or true or loving was ever lost from the mind of God. Somehow, some way, someday, Kel and I would meet again.

"Do you carry her picture?" Those intent blue eyes probed my soul as I wiped my eyes.

"No, not really. I have her graduation picture back in the hotel. But I never did put it in my wallet."

"You should, you know. Besides, I want to see her."

"All right."

"What do you think of the story, I mean the true story, not the fiction?"

She hesitated. "The poor thing, that's all I can say. Will that do?"

"No other judgments about her?"

"Who am I to judge? . . . Now drink your tea and eat your scones, Dermot Michael Coyne."

The therapy session was over.

What about my plan to solve the mystery of the death of Michael Collins? It was a crazy idea from start to finish. In comparison with the grief I had expressed and the sensitivity and sympathy I had experienced, my puzzles and riddles and clever schemes were insignificant.

We chatted as we polished off our breakfasts. Someday soon I would take her to Jury's for a real breakfast. She looked so preoccupied. Was there something else on her mind besides me and my repressed grief?

"I don't want to seem to play the turnabout game, Nul. Is there something wrong in your life?"

"I'm fine, Dermot. Just a little tired from studying too hard."

She was not, however, looking at me.

"What's wrong?"

"It's not important."

"Can I judge that?"

"I should tell you that it's none of your *fockingrichyank business.*" She smiled wanly.

"But you haven't?"

"Not yet."

"So?"

She poured tea for both of us. "I have to go back home. I think I can get meself into UCG — University College Galway — next term. Wasn't it good enough for me brothers and sisters? Who do I think I am?"

"Why did you come here?"

"Weren't me ma and da proud of me winning

233

the scholarship prize? Weren't they all puffed up and proud that their youngest could go to Trinity?"

"Why can't you?"

"I don't want to tell you."

"But you will."

She paused and sipped some tea. "You like Earl Grey, do you now?"

"I do. And don't change the subject."

"I don't want to tell you, because you'll want to help me and I can't let you do that."

"No money."

She tipped her head slightly. "I'm redundant at my job, selling sweaters at Brown Thomas. The tourist season is over and they kept me on as long as they could."

"Your friends can't find you anything?"

"I'm too focking proud to ask. There are no jobs in Dublin. They'd want to loan me money. The posh folk. 'Won't you come down to my home in South County Dublin for holiday, Nuala?' " She imitated a posh type from Dublin 4. "I won't take charity from anyone, do you hear that, Dermot Michael Coyne?"

"I hear it."

"Good enough for you." Her face was as hard as stone, pure Protestant ethic, or maybe Gaeltach integrity.

As my brother George always says, you should never fight the Holy Spirit.

I reached into my Marquette jacket, pulled out a small manila envelope, and removed the first book of Ma's diary. "Look at this, Nul."

She opened the yellowed book carefully. "Sure, it's the old script, the way me gram used to write."

"You can read it?"

"I can indeed. . . . 'tis your gram?"

" 'Tis."

"May 1919." She examined the document carefully. "How old was she then?"

"Fourteen, going on fifteen."

"She has a crush on a boy. Liam Ready, is that your grandpa?"

"Yes."

"How old was he?"

"Seventeen."

"Glory be to God, he's a member of the IRA! On the run! He's hiding in her house! She's adored him for years! Now she thinks he's beginning to notice her! She's ecstatic, the poor dear thing!"

"It's not hard to translate, then?"

"I told you I was a museum piece, didn't I? No, it's plain old modern Irish Gaelic — though the script is hard enough to read. A few turns of the phrase are different than the way we speak it now, but just like how me own gram spoke."

"Could you translate it all for me, Nul?"

"Translate it, is it now? Well, I don't see why not. It would take some time, but it's not a very big book, is it?"

"There are about thirty of them."

"Glory be to God, her whole life story, is it?"

" 'Tis."

Nuala examined the tattered notebook. "She's an interesting young woman, I'll say that for her. . . . Her whole life?"

"Till a couple of weeks before she died."

"It might be worth publishing, and herself a fascinating woman even on the first page. But, sure, don't you need a better translator than I would be?"

"Eventually maybe, but you could at least get it started and tell me whether it's worth doing all of it."

"You'd trust me to take all these notebooks back to Galway?"

"Not at all. I'll hire you to translate it right here in Dublin . . . and before you shout at me about charity, I want to point out that I brought this notebook along before I knew you needed a job. How many hours of work can you put in a day?"

"Three at least, some days four." She was trying to think of an excuse to turn me down and none was coming.

"Can you do word processing?"

"I'm not a bloody eejit, am I?"

"You are not."

"I don't have a computer, except in my class, and I can use that only for schoolwork."

"You can use the one in my suite at Jury's."

Nuala was tempted, oh, how she was tempted.

236

Manna was falling from heaven. Her eyes faded back and forth from hesitation to eagerness.

"They'll think I'm your whore."

"They will not. I'll tell the manager of the hotel exactly what you are. Being Irish, he'll have the housekeeping staff snoop a little to make sure."

"Will you now?"

"I will. It's an honest offer, Nul. Purely a business arrangement."

"I know *that*."

She considered me shrewdly, weighing the costs and the benefits like any good accountant should. "It's a business relationship, is it now?"

"Only that. How much did they pay you at Brown's?"

"Twenty punts a week."

Twenty-five dollars! Was that the difference between starvation and survival for a young woman college student in Dublin?

"I'll make inquiries as to what the rates are for beginning translators — I bet they're more than twice that — and I won't pay you one focking penny more! Understand?"

She continued to weigh the risks and the pay-offs, a shrewd, shrewd trader. She was the one who belonged in the Standard and Poors pit at the Merc. "Only business in the suite?"

"Nuala! You don't know me very well, if you think I'd make a pass at you there. I won't promise what might happen elsewhere, but not while you're working for me."

237

"I won't make any passes either." She did not smile at that remark. I assumed that she was touching a feminist base.

"Glory be to God, I hope not!"

She smiled thinly.

She was merely making a feminist point, wasn't she? I hoped so.

"You can eat your evening meal in the room while you're working. I'm not even likely to be there much. I'll be doing my exercise. I'll tell you one thing, woman: I'll not distract someone who's costing me so much money."

"I think you probably will distract me, Dermot Michael Coyne." She had made up her mind. "But I can take care of meself if I have to — and if I want to."

"You'll do it?"

"Haven't I said I will?" Then her smile broke through, a Dublin sun at last driving off a storm. "Oh, Dermot! How wonderful!"

She hugged me, very briefly.

It might be quite distracting indeed. The distractions would be complicated because our relationship, only a couple of weeks old, was already pretty complicated.

The distractions, however, I told myself, would not be unpleasant ones.

Not at all, at all. But it would still be strictly a business arrangement. I was not ready yet to fall into the kind of love that would lead me to the altar.

So has every cowardly Irish bachelor defended

himself down through the ages.

Looking back at my relationship with Marie Fionnuala Anne McGrail, I think that incident was the turning point. I had subtly changed my role. I was no longer a potential suitor looking for a mate, permanent or temporary. I was now a protector. I had to take care of her, respect her, provide for her.

– 19 –

"Your brother called." Nuala did not look up from the PC monitor.

"George?" I flopped in a chair on the other side of the parlor, exhausted from an hour-and-a-half swim in the darkness of a Dublin autumn afternoon.

"*Father* George," she reproved me.

"Did he say I should call back?"

"He did." She continued to type, slowly and carefully. "He said that you should use an outside line because it was personal and he didn't want me to listen in."

"He didn't!"

"He did too. He's a very nice priest. Like the young priest at home. Very nice. He didn't even mind that terrible story you told him about me."

"What awful story?"

"That I said the focking Mass was the focking Mass. I never use language like that."

"*Nuala!*"

"Well." She turned around and looked at me over her glasses. "Not in my present mask."

"You not only said those very words" — I sighed as loudly as she would — "You told me that I should tell him you said it."

"I didn't mean you should *tell* him."

"I thought you didn't like priests."

"Isn't he your brother and himself a nice young priest?"

Even in her responsible professional woman mask, Nuala Anne McGrail was exasperating, all the more so because she enjoyed exasperating me.

She had showed up for work that afternoon looking every inch the mature businesswoman — dark blue suit, white blouse, low-heeled shoes, dark stockings, hair severely tied in a bun, and glasses. She carried a large, businesslike shoulder purse, a new Irish-English dictionary, and an artificial leather notebook.

"Glasses, Nuala?"

"Magnifying glasses so I can read your gram's small print."

"And so you can look like a dowdy secretary."

"It's me new mask. Do you like it?"

"Very professional. Focking professional, I'd say."

"I don't use that language when I'm being a professional. I wish you wouldn't either."

Her lips turned up in her imp grin. That wasn't excluded apparently by the new persona.

She had not wanted to take two weeks' advance pay. I insisted that it was appropriate for someone who was a professional translator. She argued a little but not convincingly.

I didn't want her to starve to death.

Of course she wouldn't starve to death. But you see, I had become her protector. I could still have lewd thoughts about her. Yet now I was responsible for her.

I also decided that now I'd have to stay in Dublin. I wouldn't be able to return to Chicago to watch Notre Dame try for an unbeaten season — not that I had ever seriously considered such a plan.

Couldn't I have left her in Dublin with my computer and the diaries?

Sure.

By then I was so bemused and befuddled by my lovely protégée that I was not thinking straight. She would keep me in that condition, not without some intent I think, till I finally flew home.

I wondered how much money she had spent on clothes to create her new image. Probably not too much. The clothes were inexpensive and became stylish because of the person who wore them and the way she wore them.

Maybe she still had a discount at Brown's.

I introduced her to the manager, the concierge, the director of the towers, and the housekeeper on my floor. Nuala was servile in her respect for these dignitaries. They couldn't possibly doubt that she was exactly what I said she was, a translator of some old documents. She confirmed this by murmuring a few bashful words in her first language to the manager, who responded in kind, with a broad smile of approval.

"No doubt that the young woman is an Irish speaker, Mr. Coyne. She's flawless."

"I'm glad to hear that."

Nonetheless, they would check on her and me to make sure that I was telling the truth, not that they would do anything about it if I wasn't.

Nuala inspected my suite with a critical eye, noting carefully the artificial plants, the two TV sets, and the two impressionistic paintings, one of a vase of flowers and the other of sailboats on Dublin Bay.

"It's a bit posh," I admitted, embarrassed as I always was by my affluence.

"I'm a materialist, Dermot Michael." She sighed loudly. "Not too much of a one, mind you. I don't want to be wealthy. Me ma and da are poor and they're the happiest people in the world. All I want is to be a little less poor."

"Maybe you should find yourself a *focking-richyank*."

"Maybe I should." She tilted her head defiantly. "One that doesn't think these rooms are something to be ashamed of."

"Ouch."

"Wasn't I only joking?" She touched my hand. "Don't put on your angry look."

"I promise." I laughed.

"Now show me how your computer works."

"Yes, ma'am."

I showed her how to turn on my Compaq, argued with her about the relative merits of Microsoft Word and WordPerfect (the only religious war in the Western World outside of the Six Counties and Bosnia) and instructed her in the use of MS Word.

"Ready to go?"

"You can fire me anytime you want if I'm no good," she said dubiously.

"Break your neck, possibly; fire you, no way. Now I'm going swimming."

"To Sandymount on a day like this?"

"No indeed. In Jury's heated pool. Right down there."

She joined me at the window overlooking the pool, glasses in hand. "Glory be to God, a pool! Did you say it was heated?"

"For Americans, about eighty-two or eighty-three Fahrenheit, I think. We like our pools warm."

"Me ma and I used to swim in the ocean every day. Sure, it was refreshing."

"In winter?"

"Faith, it's cold all the time, fifty degrees Fahrenheit."

"You can use this pool if you want, Nuala. I'm sure the manager wouldn't object."

"I'd *never* do that." She scurried back to her workstation and began to pour over Ma's diary.

"It's up to you . . . oh, yes. Ring room service for your tea. I'll want some too when I come back. Tea is not the meal you're entitled to when you work here, by the way."

"I'm thinking you want to make me fat."

"Not a chance, Nul, not a chance."

I went into the bedroom, closed the door, and put on my swim trunks and terry robe for my daily trip to the pool.

Nuala was hard at work when I emerged.

"Don't try to do too much the first day."

"Room service, you said?" She peered at me over her glasses, a look to which I perceived that I would have to become accustomed.

"Yes. You pick up the phone, push the buttons, and tell them that you'd like to have tea and whatever else you want. I'll have scones and sandwiches, but no sherry, lest someone be counting."

"And the Pope not a Mormon yet."

"Now get to work."

"Yes, sir." She turned back to the screen, then looked again in my direction. "Just ring room service and tell them what I want."

"Just like in the films, Nuala."

"Just like in the films." Her face lit up in a smile of admiration and gratitude that almost broke my heart.

"I'm going swimming," I said lamely.

"Don't catch cold," she called after me, words that Ma and Mom called after me almost every day when I left the house from September 15 to June 15.

The poor kid, you're the rich Yank savior who treats her with respect, what else would she do? She's a shy child. You'll have to protect her from herself. If she was a little bit more experienced, she'd know better than to fall in love with you.

Fortunately, your own heart is armor plated and you are not falling in love with her.

Suppose she translates a couple of weeks and then you go home, leaving her copies of the diaries and your computer to finish the work. Then what? Will she get over you?

Probably. No, certainly.

Will you get over her?

Most likely. Do you want to get over her?

Maybe and maybe not.

Nuala as a companion for a half century? You could do a lot worse. I don't want a domineering woman running my life.

My mile-long swim completed, I went back to my suite and learned of George's phone call.

"The tea's just come," she informed me. "Help yourself."

"Room service was cooperative?"

I did help myself. Obviously the professional Nuala didn't pour tea.

"It wasn't like the films at all, at all. Wasn't

245

the young woman who brought it up from the County Galway? We had a nice little talk. . . . I'll pour the tea."

"You don't have to."

"Me ma raised me proper." She hurried over to the table. "And you should get out of those wet clothes or you'll catch a cold. Cream or sugar?"

"A cold is a viral infection, Nul. It is not caused by wet clothes on a chilly evening."

"A lot you know about it." She sniffed.

Exactly what Ma would have said, God be good to her.

"How is the translation coming?"

"All right. When you're dressed proper, I'll show you the screen."

"I'm not sure who's the boss in this company."

She ignored that crack. "You should finish the story, Dermot Michael. It's good."

"Glory be to God, woman!" I exclaimed. "Are you reading all my documents?"

"Only the ones that have my name as a file label. I see Nuala.doc in your short story subdirectory, how can I not be reading it?"

That seemed a not unreasonable argument. "You liked it?"

"Haven't I said that I did?" She nibbled cautiously at a scone, joining the ranks of the women of the world who worry about their weight. "Sure, would I not like to be that Celtic goddess you describe and yourself with such lascivious thoughts about her?"

"Am I blushing, Nuala Anne McGrail?"

She poured more tea for me. " 'Tis not for me to say," she said primly. "But 'tis a good story. You should finish it. Sure." She glanced up from her tea pouring for a quick glance at me. "Sure, if the story was about me, I suppose I'd be terrible flattered that a man like your narrator found me that interesting, but since it's not about me at all, at all, 'tis not for me to say."

"Right."

"You take your tea and go put some warm clothes on and I'll show you what I've done."

"Do I have a choice?"

"Not at all, at all."

The water is getting deeper, I thought to myself as I dressed in a jogging suit. It's pleasantly warm water, however.

I went back to see the first segment of Ma's diary with a rapidly beating heart.

For any number of reasons.

– 20 –

May 14, 1919

Liam Tomas came home yesterday. For the first time he noticed me as someone distinct from the chickens and the sheep. I was so thrilled by what he said to me that I'm thinking to meself now is the time to start writing that diary you've been thinking about for so long. 'Tis the proper time to start the story of your love affair with Liam Tomas O'Riada, even if it never does become a love affair.

I hope it does become a love story. I love him so much. He is so sweet and so kind and so good and so handsome. I want to spend all my life with him. Deal, my cousin, says that I'm too young to know anything about love. You're only fourteen, she says. Liam Tomas O'Riada doesn't even know you exist.

Liam Tomas is a great big bull of a man with a gentle heart and a sweet voice and long blond hair and red face and doesn't he look like a Viking pirate or an ancient Celtic king or maybe holy Saint Columcille himself?

And doesn't me da say that it's a miracle that the Galway Brigade is able to keep the British army on the run and themselves only twenty men with twelve rifles?

No one in Connemara will betray them and the Black and Tans killing and raping and burning houses and hanging people whenever they feel like it!

Liam Tomas's smart too and works hard and me da says he'll make a big success out of his life if he gets only half a chance and there's some peace in this country. And he likes children and sings so wonderfully in church and says the rosary every day.

And Ma says that I shouldn't make a fool out of myself. But I lit a candle after Mass this morning with the penny I got for making butter for the Widow O'Malley and I prayed to the Mother of Jesus that She make Liam love me.

If it be your Son's holy will, I added, like the nuns say we should add whenever you pray a prayer of petition.

But then I said to Herself, sure, I'll make him a better wife than anyone else in the world so why wouldn't it be your Son's holy will and Yourself being only fifteen or sixteen when you were betrothed to Saint Joseph, as the young priest was telling us.

Anyway I think my prayer was heard because he smiled when he saw me and himself so tired from fighting in the terrible war that's going on all around us to make Ireland a free nation, brave and proud alongside all the other free nations in the world.

The only world I know is here in Carraroe, though I go to Galway sometimes with me da when he goes to market. I'm real shy in Galway because it's such a big strange place and so many strange people and myself as bold as brass here in Carraroe with the bay on one side and the lough on the other and the stone fences along the curving roads and the town looking so lovely when the sun is out on the freshly whitewashed cottages. Me granda, who had been everywhere, said it's one of the most beautiful places in all the world, but I couldn't tell about that because

249

it's the only place I know.

Didn't Ma give me his tea to bring out to him and himself standing guard down the road, so wide awake and brave with his Lee-Enfield over his shoulder? She knows I'm sweet on him and she doesn't seem to mind.

It was a warm spring night without any moon and the sky like a great crystal globe hanging above us and not a sound in the fields or the bogs but only the surf whispering secrets away to the ocean strand.

"There's only one road into Carraroe," that big amadon Daniel O'Kelly says to Liam Tomas, "and the enemy won't dare come down it on a dark night. Liam, do you think you can stay awake and keep guard on it just in case?"

I could have killed him for being so rude and the other men all laughing.

"I can, sir," Liam says, all proud and brave.

"Well, then, look to it, man." And he takes another swig out of his jar.

I don't like Daniel O'Kelly, God forgive me for it.

So an hour or so later, Ma gives me the tea to bring out to him.

"Here's your tea, Liam Tomas," I says, shylike and my heart beating something fierce.

"Ah, Nell Pat," he says, touching my hair, "haven't you the most lovely red hair in the whole of Connemara?"

I thought I'd die with delight. But of course

I wouldn't dare let on. So I says real snippy, "Much time you should be having for red hair and yourself supposed to be fighting for the freedom of Ireland."

" 'Tis for the red-haired colleens and the right to admire them as free men that we're all fighting, Nell Pat."

" 'Tis terrible dangerous, is it now, Liam Tomas?" I said, melting all over inside for the love of him.

"The truth of it is" — he scratched his great blond head — "the truth of it is that it's mostly dull with lots of waiting and lots of hard work and lots of walking in the rain at night. Then when the fight is about to begin you're terrible scared for a half hour or so and then the shooting begins and, before you know it, it's all over. And some of your lads are dead and a lot of their lads. You're glad you're still alive and you mourn your own lads and you feel sorry for their lads."

"But they're Brits or Irish traitors," says I, thinking to meself that I wouldn't mind killing all the enemies of our poor island.

"But they're not all bad fellows, Nell Pat, and they have wives and sweethearts and mothers whose hearts will be broken. Sure" — and didn't I see tears in his eyes? — "I hated them at first. Then I realized they were as scared as I was before the shooting started and as lonesome for those that loved them. Then I couldn't hate them any more. God knows" — he sighed

— "we have to keep fighting, but I'm thinking that I'll be glad when it's all over and we don't have to kill lads that are just like us, just like your brother Tim and just like me."

I wanted to cry too, but I didn't want him to think I was a silly little girl and himself being so candid with me.

"You and Tim are not going to die, are you, Liam Tomas?" I said.

"Please God we don't." He sighed again, and himself so tired he could hardly talk. "But 'tis all in the hands of God, isn't it? Tim says you go to Mass every day to pray for us. You won't stop, will you now?"

"Never," says I. "Not till old Ireland is free."

"This time we'll win." He looked very somber and proud. "We'll finish what they started in '98 and '48 and '67. We have old John Bull on the run at last and before we're finished he be run right out of Ireland for once and for all."

Wasn't my heart on fire with pride and love when he says that?

"I wish I was a man and I could fight with you," I says, real fierce.

"Ah, no, Nell Pat Malone," says he, with his big hand on my head. "Someone must keep the faith alive for the next generation. All men are good for is winning wars. 'Tis the women that win the peace."

I could have died I was so happy. "We will win, won't we, Liam?"

"We will finally win, Nell." His hand kind of slipped around my neck. "If I die tomorrow night, I'll die happy knowing that my nieces and nephews if not my own children will live in a free Ireland."

And wasn't I thinking that I'd be glad to be the mother of a child of his even if he did die tomorrow night?

The nuns would say that thought was a great terrible sin. I don't care. There's a war all around us. Young people should love one another and have children. Doesn't me own Ma say that about Tim and Moire and themselves getting married so young?

I'm sure God wouldn't mind if I had a child for Liam Tomas.

Naturally I didn't say *that* to him. What I did say was "Why do you think we're going to win this time?"

" 'Tis our leaders, Nell. Has ever any country in the world had so many great leaders at one time — Old Arthur Griffith and himself not even a Catholic. And Dev, the Long Fella, and Kevin O'Higgins and Cathal Brugha and Rory O'Connor and, sure, you know our own commandant, Daniel O'Kelly."

"Aye," says I, and myself not liking Daniel O'Kelly all that much, though my brother Tim adores him.

He's a big tall man, almost as tall as me Liam, but slim and, well, almost dainty like a girl with a long thin face and a quick smile and a big head of wavy black hair and sharp blue eyes that sear at your soul. I don't think he's handsome at all, at all, but I'm probably the only girl in Connemara who doesn't think so. He's a great one with all the lads, laughing and joking and telling stories and singing songs and making the humorous comment and drinking all the night long and playing football with them and himself the best there is at the game. They say he'd be all-Ireland if it wasn't for the war.

I think I'd never buy a horse or cow from him because you'd be taken in by his talk and never look at the animal. Me da says that the O'Kelly family has been dirt poor for hundreds of years and that they've always had great ambitions to be wealthy but were behind the door when industry and luck was passed out. You can't blame him for enjoying being commandant, says me da, 'tis the first respect anyone has shown an O'Kelly since long before the famine.

"And then there's the greatest of them all," says me Liam, "the Big Fella."

"The Big Fella?"

"Mick Collins. Like the young priest says, isn't he a man sent by God to free poor old Ireland? Isn't he a better man, and himself a daily communicant too like yourself, than all the other heroes of Ireland put together?"

"Have you met him, Liam?" I asked, filled with awe for this Mick Collins.

"I have not. Sure, doesn't he have better things to do in Dublin than to wander out here to the far West of Ireland? Still, our commandant says that he wouldn't be surprised if one of these days Mick doesn't appear out of nowhere — that's the way he does it, you know — to see how we do it out here in Galway. He doesn't miss a trick, that one."

"Sure, I'd die of fright if I ever met your Mick Collins."

"No, you wouldn't, Nell Pat." And his hand still on the back of my neck. "No, you wouldn't. Don't those who have met him say that he's unassuming and like someone you might have met at Mass last Sunday or played hurley with last Friday?"

"What a grand man he must be!"

"The man sent by God to free Ireland."

Well, then that old flannel mouth Daniel O'Kelly calls from the house that he wants the brigade for a staff meeting. Brigade indeed and them only a dozen kids not much older than myself.

They left early this morning, long before sunrise. No one said where they were going but they looked so wonderful grim and brave that I wanted to sing "A Nation Once Again" as they marched out.

I think Liam Tomas waved at me. Well, at least he waved at someone.

I've said so many rosaries for them today that I've lost track of the number. Holy Mother of God, take care of him for me.

Nuala was weeping, head buried in her hands. I was close to tears too.

"Isn't she a brave and glorious woman, Dermot? No wonder you loved her so much."

"She was all of that," I agreed, a small choke in my voice. "The passion never died, Nuala, not till the last day of her life. Mom told me that Ma said that Pa was in the room with her when she was dying, 'To take me home with him at last,' she said, 'and himself young and strong like he was that spring night in Galway when he first touched my hair.'"

"Do you believe that, Dermot?" She dabbed at her tear-stained face.

"I believe that your friend Father George is right when he says that no love is ever lost in the mind and heart of God."

She nodded slowly. "Do you think you'll ever see them again?"

That's what it's all about, isn't it, when push comes to shove?

"I do, Nuala Anne McGrail. I do. I don't know how it happens and I can't prove it, but I do believe it."

"I don't quite yet," she said solemnly, "but I don't not believe it either. I tell myself after reading this woman, almost hearing her voice in my ear, that the person she is can never die."

"You'd better go home now, Nuala. I don't want the provost of Trinity College, or whatever you call your dean, blaming me for interfering with the studies of one of his prize students. Don't take the book along, because you'll work on it."

Reluctantly she closed it and laid it at a neat right angle to the Compaq. "You're beginning to know me too well. . . . I did peek ahead a little. She does meet the Big Fella."

"Mick Collins."

"Himself. And he tells her that there is some kind of secret British plot to steal their victory."

"Wow! Nuala, maybe you shouldn't talk to anyone about this until we're finished."

"Wasn't I thinking the same thing meself?" she said, buttoning up the thin trench coat that completed her professional ensemble. " 'Tis between you and me and herself."

"Right."

"Uh, Dermot, could I be asking you something?"

"Wouldn't you ask it anyway if I said no?"

"Those pictures you have in your wallet of themselves. Would you ever let me look at them here on the table while I'm translating for you?"

"Certainly."

"You're thinking I'm a sentimental fool?"

"If you are, there are two of us in this room.

Now go home with you, woman."

"You can call your brother from the room now."

She closed the door softly. I thought of something else.

"Nuala!"

She stopped halfway down the corridor. "And yourself just after chasing me out!"

"I'll ask the manager about you using the pool. It's up to you whether you choose to."

"Sure, where could I put on my swim suit?"

"There isn't a bathroom adjoining your office?"

"There is."

"And a terry robe there too?"

"There is."

"Even slippers?"

"Even slippers."

"Well?"

"I'll think about it."

The elevator opened its door and she ducked into it.

A secret English plot to steal victory from the Irish? Surely Lloyd George and Winston Churchill did their best to mess up the treaty. They were old pros at the political process. O'Higgins and Collins were novices compared to them. Griffith was older but in poor health. Dev, as they called Eamon De Valera, the Long Fella, was one of the great political operators of the twentieth century, but he had yet to learn how to blend stubbornness with flexibility. It's a wonder that the Irish delegation came away with anything, much less "dominion status," which, as Collins foretold (and as Dev did not believe), would be the path to freedom. Those who denounced the treaty thought it was a betrayal. Collins and those who signed it and won its ratification from a dubious Dáil thought it was a compromise from which they would eventually win all they could expect — Ulster not being theirs for the taking, no matter what happened.

Collins was right. In the end he and O'Higgins won, even if they paid for their victory with their lives. They had outsmarted Lloyd George and Churchill.

So what was the secret that Mick Collins had told Ma seventy years ago?

Churchill was no lover of the Irish. During the Second World War he repeatedly accused De Valera and Ireland of cooperating with the Germans while he knew damn well that Irish intelligence was cooperating with his own intelligence services.

These thoughts were racing through my head as I waited patiently for George at the Telefon Eireann booth on Pembroke Road near the family planning clinic.

"George? Dermot."

"That is some young woman you have answering your phone, Punk."

"Tell me about it."

"If you don't bring her home you'll have to

259

answer to me as well as Mom."

"We'll see."

"How old is she?"

"Twenty . . . almost."

"She sounded like she was thirty-five, so poised and sophisticated."

"That's the mask she wears when she translates for me."

"She's a lot like Ma, isn't she?"

"Crazier — and judging by what we're finding in her diary, Ma was pretty crazy at that age."

"I can believe it."

"Do you have something for me?"

"Do I ever. Tony talked to some of his friends and they were very interested in your interests. They want to help."

"Huh?"

"They really do want to help — offer support, they say."

"Why would his part of the government want to help me?"

"Beats me, and I wouldn't trust them as far as I can throw the whole town of Langley, Virginia. I trust Tony, however. And what they propose seems safe."

"Okay. What do they want?"

"A man named Patrick, not Pat, not Paddy, but Patrick, will call you tomorrow or the next day. He will say that Anthony, not Tony, sent him. He will propose a meeting place to you, 'a safe place' was Tony's exact words. He will meet you there and talk. You will listen, maybe argue with him, but don't ask any questions. After the talk you can draw your own conclusions. He may initiate later contact. They, uh, promise protection, as best they can provide it for you and your associates, should you have any."

"I don't get it."

"You're not supposed to get it, Punk, but it sounds very, very interesting. Keep me posted. Every day. Remember."

"I sure will."

"And, oh yes, Patrick isn't exactly part of the, uh, Company."

"What is he then?"

"Don't ask."

Nuala showed up a half hour early the next day with her book bag over her shoulder as well as her notebook and dictionary. She was wearing a gray suit and a blue blouse.

"Gray is it today?"

"This exhausts my professional wardrobe. Do you like it?"

"One of your many admirable attributes, young woman, is that you have excellent taste."

"Go 'long with you now. I can look at the fashion magazines like everyone else. And isn't everyone saying that I have terrible taste in boys?"

"I don't believe anyone has said that. And why the book bag? It doesn't quite fit the image."

"Sure, I wasn't going to bring me swimming

things in a suitcase, was I now?"

"That's why you came a half hour early?"

" 'Tis. I'll do me exercise on me own time, not yours."

"Fine with me."

I thought about offering to join her and decided that I should wait a few days before trying that. Also I wanted to stay near a phone for Patrick's call.

"I just put on me suit and the robe and the slippers and ride down on the elevator and walk across the lobby?"

"Just like you were some *fockingrichyank* tourist."

"Which language we don't use in this office, do we now?" She slipped into the bathroom and closed the door.

"Yes, ma'am," I shouted after her.

She emerged a few moments later, wrapped in a terry robe and huddled within her own arms so the robe couldn't come open. I glanced up from my *Herald-Tribune*. "Don't catch cold, Nuala Anne."

She laughed, granting me for the moment the last word.

I put the paper aside and walked to the window. It was dark already, but in the glow of the lights around the pool I would get a distant look at Nuala in a swim suit, a possibility that seemed decidedly attractive.

A few minutes later, a young woman still shrouded in an ample robe emerged from the inside of the pool area and bent over to feel the pool water. Even from the fourth floor I could sense the surprise on her face. It really was warm. Quickly she tossed aside her robe and eased herself into the pool.

Moire Nuala Anne McGrail in a bikini was well worth admiring, even from four stories up. "Wow," I said to myself. "Wow!"

Her crawl, as I might have expected, was better than mine, smooth, strong, and determined. Naturally.

Shaken, I would have said visibly shaken, I went back to my paper. Then I tossed the paper aside, turned on the Compaq, and returned to my short story that was in the Nuala.doc file.

On the first page I typed in bold caps, 30-point type:

ABSOLUTELY

CONFIDENTIAL —

THIS MEANS YOU,

NUALA ANNE!

Then I indulged myself in a rhapsodic piece about a woman swimmer, not totally uninfluenced by Seamus Heaney's swimming otter poem in which the otter at the desert museum in Tucson reminds him of his wife back home in Ireland.

Would she honor my restriction?

Hard to tell and it didn't much matter. If she did read it, she was smart enough to realize that it was a love letter, albeit a clinically descriptive one.

She'd also know I was stealing just a bit from Seamus.

Hell, steal from the best!

The phone rang.

"Dermot Coyne."

"Hi, Dermot. This is Patrick. I'm a friend of Anthony's."

"Nice to hear from you, Patrick. Any friend of Anthony's is a friend of mine."

He laughed. "I'm glad to hear that. . . . You know where Bray is?"

"Sure."

"Do you think you could find your way out there on public transportation?"

"Why not? Don't they have sonnets in the car ads?"

Patrick chuckled. So I knew the DART (Dublin Area Rapid Transit).

"You get off the station in Bray and turn to your right and walk along the tracks till you come to the street with the Martello Tower, the street where Joyce's family lived for a while when he was growing up — not the one in Black Rock, mind you. Turn right again, cross the tracks, and walk towards the harbor. On the harbor road you turn right again and you'll come to a place called the Harbor Bar, white

264

with red trim. I'll be sitting in the corner by the window. Do you think I could buy you a pint or two out there at half six?"

"Absolutely."

"And, Dermot, no Savile Row and no jogging suit, right?"

"I should look like a bit of a bum?"

"By your standards, yes."

"Okay."

"And, Dermot, one more thing: Come alone, got it?"

"That's the way I planned it!"

"Great! I'll see you. Bye, Dermot."

The voice, I reflected as I hung up, was pure Midwest. Not Chicago exactly. Certainly not St. Louis. Maybe Minneapolis. Maybe Milwaukee, about which Angela Smythe of regretful memory did not know.

A Midwesterner, probably Irish and with a sense of humor.

I heard Nuala opening the door, so I quickly saved the Nuala.doc file and turned off the computer.

"Change your clothes, woman, or you'll catch your death of cold."

She burst out laughing. "You sound authentic, Dermot Michael."

"Weren't the best of models provided me for years?"

She collapsed into the same chair I had occupied yesterday. " 'Tis at least venially sinful, possibly mortal." She sighed contentedly. "I'll

265

have to ask me priest the next time I go to confession. Or *Father* George if I answer the phone when he calls."

"It beats the North Atlantic, huh?"

"Ah, does it ever!" She leaned forward, clutching the robe so it would not open and reveal any of herself in the bikini. "Sure, the heated pool is probably the greatest contribution of you *fockingrichyanks* to human culture."

"Did you try the whirlpool?"

"I did *not*." She wrapped herself tightly in her virtue and her robe. "That's certainly a mortal sin."

"I'm humiliated by your crawl, Nul. It's a lot better than mine."

She straightened up in righteous rage. "You came down and watched me, did you now?"

"Woman, I did *not*." I gestured at the window. "Would I be invading your privacy?"

She bit her lip, blushed, and laughed. "You're a desperate man, Dermot Michael Coyne, son of the dark stranger, desperate altogether."

"It wasn't only the crawl I admired, Nuala."

"Humph!" She rose to change her clothes.

"You wear that immoral swim suit when you swim in the North Atlantic? With your ma?"

"Why shouldn't I?" she demanded haughtily. "And, just to give your prurient adolescent fantasy something to worry about, Dermot Michael Coyne, sometimes I swim in the North Atlantic without anything on at all, at all."

In high dudgeon, mostly feigned, she sailed

into the bathroom and slammed the door.

Ah, the games our reproductive urges force us to play.

I went to my bedroom and dressed for my swim. When I came out, Nuala was already at the computer.

"Fast shower?"

"I can take a shower here?"

"You can."

"I've never taken a shower in all my life."

"Be sure you wear your swim suit when you do."

She threw her Irish dictionary at me, gently so it landed on the couch.

I left quietly.

After my swim I dressed in an old jacket and jeans. "I'll be going out, woman. I'm not sure when I'll be back, but I will keep count of the number of jars I take."

"At last I can work in peace, can't I now?" She was frowning over the diary, either displeased with what she was reading or searching for the right word.

"See you tomorrow."

"Don't get fluttered."

"I'll try not to."

— NUALA'S VOICE —

Well, Nell Pat,

I'll tell you one thing, anyway. You and his mother did a good job in raising that lad and fair play to you both, says I. One of me teachers said that you can predict a man's attitude towards women if you know his relationship with his mother and vice versa. He has the blarney and all that but I've never met a young man who is so respectful. He scares me the way he soaks me up with his eyes, but I'm not afraid of him at all, at all. He wouldn't do anything to me unless I encouraged him.

Now, Nell Pat, that's the problem, isn't it? Don't I have the worst crush I've ever had in all me life and meself hardly knowing him? My legs turn to water whenever I see him and my heart thumps away like it's gone crazy.

It's just a crush, I know. Nothing more. I'm too young to marry anyone, much less a young man who has been badly hurt a couple of times already and meself not the one to heal him unless he's willing to heal himself.

Maybe in five years.

But I have the crush now, not five years from now. I've never known anyone quite like him. And you got me into this, you know you did.

Why? Couldn't you just have left me alone? I'm not like you and he's not like your man.

And he isn't much of a detective, is he now? A dreamer and a poet and a storyteller and that's all wonderful. But if he hadn't hired me, he would have messed up this quest of his before he started.

He's not going to like it when he finds how

many of his mistakes I'm going to have to cover up, not at all, at all. His male ego is pretty weak to begin with, and there being no reason for that either.

Ah, Nell Pat, for all of that, am I not already half in love with him? And himself being so sweet and gentle?

– 22 –

Patrick looked like Mick Collins, a handsome, curly-haired Irishman with a quick smile and flashing blue eyes.

"Hi, Dermot." He shook hands vigorously. "Welcome to the Harbor Bar."

For a moment I was spooked. Mick Collins was dead. As far as anyone knew, he died without children. This couldn't be a descendant of his, could it?

Like all Irish pubs, this one was dense with cigarette smoke, as thick as the fog outside, which obscured the rest of Bray, a seaside resort for the Victorian era and now a commuter suburb for the posh folk in Dublin 4, as Nuala would have called them.

In the Harbor Bar, like many a serious Irish bar, the conversations were in whispered tones, as if we were in a funeral parlor with the corpse present or a library with the head librarian just

269

around the corner. The Harbor Bar was a bar not for serious drinking — the patrons could nurse a pint all night long — but for serious talk.

I recovered quickly from my shock at how much Patrick looked like Michael Collins. The world was filled with genial, witty Irishmen with charming smiles — even if this man was broad-shouldered and powerfully built, just like the Big Fella.

"Hi, Patrick. The Harbor Bar isn't what I expected. It's not a dive, just a respectable bar."

He glanced around. "For rich yachtsmen in the summer. Note all the sailing paraphernalia scattered about and the overturned barrels in front for drinking outside during the season. They're not around now. These folks are mostly locals. They nurse their drinks pretty carefully, the women keeping accurate count of the number of jars their menfolk have consumed."

"I've noticed the habit."

We both laughed. "You'll have a pint?"

"One at the most."

"Let me get them. My company likes its salesmen to pick up the tab. Helps the image."

The DART station at Lansdowne Road was a quaint old place, constructed as a stop for the Dublin horse show in the last century — the Dublin–Kingstown (as Dun Laoghaire was called in those days) railroad being the second

270

oldest in the world. Fare on the DART for the half-hour ride to Bray was 98 pence, as good a mass transit bargain as you can find anywhere in the world.

On my ride along the picturesque coast of Dublin Bay — it looks a little like Naples when the sun is out, which in my stay was a rare event — I thought about Nuala. I absolutely could not afford to become seriously involved with her, I told myself firmly.

Patrick and I sipped our drinks and talked about Ireland. I listened carefully, searching for the hints I was supposed to hear from him. If there were any in the first fifteen minutes, I missed them.

"There are those that think the whole thing was a mistake, you know?"

"The Rising, the War, the Troubles?"

"Right. If the Brits had given the Irish home rule in the 1800s, or even before the Great War, this whole island would still be a happy part of the United Kingdom and the Ulster problem wouldn't exist."

"That's altogether possible."

"Moreover," he continued, hand on his pint, "with the boundaries of Europe coming down, a United States of the British Isles makes a lot more sense than two separate nations."

"Perhaps it does."

"From the point of view of history, the existence of a separate Irish nation, truncated from its northern counties, may be seen as an ab-

271

erration, a nationalist blip in an internationalist trend."

"Could be."

He sounded like a glib professor whose specialty was the long view of historical processes, a geopolitician from Georgetown maybe.

Which might be exactly what he was.

"Mind you, it wasn't the plan of the Irish leaders. At first the ordinary folk thought that they were quite mad. The Brits drove the people into the arms of the IRA in the end. Still, until 1916 most of the Irish could have lived quite comfortably with a dual monarchy of the Austro-Hungarian variety. Some people think they can still live with it."

"Return Ireland to British rule!"

"Not rule in the old sense of the word, heaven knows, but a federation — a federal parliament in Westminster and regional parliaments in Dublin, Cardiff, Edinburgh, and maybe Belfast. It would make a lot more sense."

"Maybe."

"The root of the present problem was the termination of the independent Irish parliament with the Act of Union in 1800. In time that could have evolved, especially with Catholic political emancipation, into a functioning Irish parliament bound to England by loyalty to the crown and common interests."

"A lot of 'ifs.' "

"Sure, Dermot, we're just speculating." He smiled genially. "Aren't we? The point some

272

people make is that with the emergence of a united Europe, we have a framework now for reconsidering the relationship between the two British Isles. When that happens it becomes clear that the present nationalist pretense at separate countries masks a de facto unity of problems and concerns and interests. In a united Europe, a new union between Britain and Ireland becomes almost inevitable — and the beauty of it is that it solves the Ulster problem overnight."

"I suppose it might."

"The Irish people, who as you well know don't hate English people at all, would accept reunion enthusiastically, especially if it promised to solve a lot of the current economic problems. The Republic of Ireland, let's face it, is not economically viable and never will be. But as a part of a larger British Union, let's call it that, this island would prosper."

"Like it did in 1849."

Patrick ignored my reference to the Great Famine. "This whole idea assumes that the English have learned from their past mistakes."

"They often haven't."

"Isn't the Anglo-Irish peace initiative a sign that times are changing? . . . Unfortunately, most of the contemporary Irish political leaders are irrevocably committed to the symbols of 1916, even though they don't take them seriously. No one has the courage to step forward and say, look, we had to be independent for a while so that we could come to understand interdependency. Let's now rejoin Britain as full partners."

He was thinking the unthinkable and making it sound reasonable and inevitable.

"The economic problems here are not going to get any better. In a few years, by the end of the century at the most, a new generation of political leaders in this country, and in the North too, will begin to say let's end this foolish independence and return to interdependence. The promise of better economic conditions will bury the memories of 1916, which don't mean much to young people anyway."

"That sounds very reasonable."

"There was too much war-weariness in Britain in 1919 and 1920 and too much legitimate anger and frustration in Ireland for common sense to develop a new relationship. In the next century, it is very likely that those years will be forgotten and leaders and people on both sides will understand the opportunities in reaffiliation as more or less equal partners."

"More or less?"

"Great Britain is the larger island and the larger and richer component of any union. Obviously it would be the senior partner."

Did Patrick believe any of this stuff that he was arguing so plausibly? Or was he trying to tell me that there were people who did believe it?

"Obviously."

"Nonetheless, all the economic advantages would be to the Irish partner, wouldn't they?"

"I presume so."

"I'll fetch us both another pint. No woman keeping track."

"I'll be asked."

"So will I."

We both laughed. Was Patrick married to an Irish woman? Or an Irish American? Not that the difference mattered as far as counting the "jars" was concerned.

"Where was I?" He placed the Guinness on the Formica table in front of me. "Oh yes, the advantages of union. The most serious obstacle to reunion will be that British leaders and people will not want to believe in the long run such a renewed partnership would be of benefit to the senior as well as the junior partner. The English are, ah, a little weary of the Irish just now."

"Are they?" This was all bullshit.

"However, there are responsible people on both sides who see this as the wave of the future, who indeed have always seen it as the wave of the future. They're prepared to wait till the appropriate time and then go public with a plan for political and economic union that will be irresistible to both potential partners."

"Ah?"

"The trick of it will be to persuade both peoples that the plan is not a return to a past relationship, but an opening up of a whole new

275

relationship in the framework of a united Europe and that it would solve at one stroke the Ulster question."

"If the lads and the Prots would buy it."

"They might not have much choice, you know. The world is growing weary of their nasty little seventeenth-century religious war."

"They have a long record of not caring what the world thinks."

"Too true. The paradox is that the worse the conflict up there is, the closer we come to the day when these responsible people will be able to advance their plan."

"I understand."

So maybe these "responsible people" were not above making the situation in the Six Counties worse. I had better not ask that. The rules of the game said that I should listen and not ask.

"As you may imagine" — Patrick spread out his lean and graceful hands — "these responsible people are not necessarily representatives of their respective governments, though I think I may say that they are not without contacts in those governments."

"I could well believe that."

"I must insist" — his eyes were blank, his sharply sculpted face emotionless as he spoke — "that these people have enormous respect for Ireland and a determination to see that the imperialism does not reappear, though in truth imperialism doesn't work any more, as our friends in the former Soviet Union are presently discovering. No one intends, I repeat, to deprive the Irish of their freedom. The dream is rather to sustain that freedom in a new relationship with England while at the same time improving the economic conditions on this island."

"Naturally."

"In fact," he said, his eyebrows contracting, "but for a few mischances, this new relationship could have been established in the middle 1920s. Many experienced men and women on both sides of the Irish Sea did not expect the Free State experiment to work. They assumed that the resulting chaos would lead to a demand from the Irish themselves that the island be reoccupied by British troops. It was a near thing for a while, but eventually the Free State leaders, much to the surprise of many intelligent Irish as well as English observers, were able to put their house in order. As you yourself can certainly see, however, the Free State/Republic of Ireland experiment has hardly been successful. It would have perhaps been much better if it had failed early. Then this new relationship of which I have spoken could have developed in the first part of this century instead of in the first part of the next."

"A near thing."

"The young revolutionaries were really not capable of government — surely that is obvious to anyone who has read history. If De Valera had been able to hold out in the West for another year or two at the most, the Free State would have collapsed, much to the benefit of Ireland, I might add."

I'd have to sort this out later, but I could now see where Patrick was headed. I didn't much like it. "Yes, I understand."

"I might say that these men and women — to use a term with which you might be interested — friends of my friends, were quite involved in the recent Anglo-Irish Agreement. While it is publicly praised as the beginning of a solution to the Ulster problem, it is in fact the beginning of a British Union Civil Service."

"How clever of the friends of your friends."

Where I came from the term referred to the Outfit, the Mob, the "Boys on the West Side."

"Yes, wasn't it?" he agreed amiably. "I thought you might be interested to learn of this body of thought — rational, sensible, and fully aware of the past mistakes, the historical trends, and the present possibilities."

"Oh, yes."

He finished his Guinness. Why would Langley — or whoever — want me to know about these ideas? Patrick was a charming man, but I shouldn't trust him any more than I had trusted Angela Smythe with a "y" and an "e."

"So it has been very nice discussing it with you. I'll stay in touch, more or less."

"Patrick." I rose from the table with him. "It's the biggest pile of shite in all the world."

He laughed cheerfully. "Why?"

278

"It ignores seven hundred years of history and the conviction of the Brits that they are better than the Irish."

We ambled towards the door.

"Does it now?" He grinned at me.

"Haven't I said that it does?"

We both laughed together.

"Well, did I ever say it wasn't shite?"

"You did not."

"Shite, Dermot, is where you find it."

As I rode the DART back to downtown Dublin — service every fifteen minutes even at half ten — I tried to analyze my conversation with Patrick. A lot of the pieces of the puzzle began to fit together. I saw the general outline but not the complete picture. I didn't much like what I saw.

The theme was the same as it had always been: The Irish are not capable of taking care of themselves so the English will take care of them.

As I said to Patrick, shite!

But why should the CIA — or whoever Patrick represented — give a damn?

Irish-American voters? Maybe. But were we that important?

I abandoned my analysis as we rode by the darkened villas and the semidetached homes and the golf courses of South County Dublin and the three yacht clubs at Dun Laoghaire. Instead I thought of Nuala and hoped she'd still be in my rooms when I returned.

The lights were out in my suite. A neat print-out waited next to the computer with a cover page note:

Dear Boss,

This is the second passage. It's quite astonishing. God help me, but I identify with her, wild little woman that she is.

I did not go beyond your warning note in "Nuala.doc" but I was sore tempted.

Thank you for the opportunity to swim. And for everything.

Love,
N.

– 23 –

March 9, 1920

I met himself yesterday. The Big Fella. Mick Collins. And himself telling me about traitors trying to steal away our victory.

At first I was unimpressed. Well, at first I didn't believe it was him. *Then* I was unimpressed. Then I realized that everything my Liam says about him is true.

At first you think here is just one more of

your smooth-talking, good-looking, charming gombeen men from Cork with wavy hair and twinkling brown eyes. Then you see a look in those eyes, a turn of his head that tells you that he's someone special, as great a hero as Ireland has ever had — and himself all the time winning your heart with his smile.

I was taking the laundry back from the stream to the house at the end of the day, with the summer sun still high in the sky, when this fella comes strolling along the road in a tweed suit, cap pulled down over his face, black thorn stick in his hand.

"God and Mary be with you," he says to me in Irish.

"God and Mary and Patrick be with you," I says back to him.

"Could I be giving you a hand with your baskets?"

"I'm thinking that it would be a right kindly favor."

"Might I ask the name of the young woman whose red hair makes the sun look dim?"

"Like all Cork men," says I, "you swallowed the Blarney Stone, and isn't my name Nell Pat Malone?"

"Ah, so it's for Pat Malone's house I'm destined this night. It must not be far on?"

" 'Tis not . . . and I didn't hear your name when you told me."

He laughed like I said something terrible funny. "It's Micheal O'Coileain," he says, pronouncing it the Irish way.

"And I'm Kathleen Ni Houlihan," says I, just as bold as I could be.

He laughs again. "Well, Ireland could not find a better symbol than you, young lass."

"You're not Mick Collins of the Irish Volunteers, not the Big Fella?"

"I'm sorry to disappoint you, Nell Pat Malone." He laughed yet again, but his eyes were taking me in, watching me every move. "But I'm afraid I'm that poor fella."

When I say that he watched me, I don't mean that he was looking at me hair and me face and me body, though he didn't miss those either. He was making up his mind about me as a person. For just a wee moment I felt that not only were all my clothes off but my whole soul was bare.

It was scary. It was also very nice.

"Glory be to God!" I shouted out. "I'll run ahead and tell me da and me ma!"

He grabs my hand with a grip of steel. "Ah, Nell Pat Malone, you'll be doing no such thing. The last thing we want is to have unfriendly eyes see your da and ma making a fuss about a poor weary traveler."

I blushed for shame. What an eejit I was.

"I'm only a beginner in this secret service thing, Mr. Collins," I says, terrible ashamed of meself.

He laughed again, always laughing and such a warm and appealing laugh. "There's none of us that are very good at it, Nell Pat Malone, and won't it be a grand thing when the killing is over and we give it all up?"

"It will," I agreed with him, "and isn't that what my Liam says?"

"Your Liam?"

"Captain Liam Tomas O'Riada, adjutant to Commandant Daniel O'Kelly of the Galway Brigade."

"And he's *your* Liam, is he now? Faith, and here I am thinking that maybe I've been meeting the love of me life and I hear she's already spoken for."

Pure Cork Blarney and best ignored altogether.

"Ah, sure, Mr. Collins," says I, my face burning again. "I misspoke. He's my Liam, but I don't think he knows it yet."

This time he laughs, louder than before. "Ah, you're a strong woman, Nell Pat, and isn't Captain Liam Tomas O'Riada a lucky man and himself not knowing it? *Maybe* not knowing it. And don't you be calling me Mr. Collins, heaven save us all. When I help a young woman carry laundry back to her cottage, shouldn't she be calling me Mick?"

"I never could!"

"You don't believe in obeying orders?" He winks at me.

So doesn't my face catch fire again? And doesn't Jim Tom O'Kelly, all two and a half years old of him, save me and himself running across the road like an eejit without looking in either direction and charging right into the Big Fella?

And doesn't he sweep the gosson off the ground and swing him to the air and Jim Tom laughing like the great terrible eejit he is?

"A fine young Irishmen." Mick Collins puts him down on the road, pats his little rump, and sends him home to his ma. "It's for the likes of him that we're fighting, isn't it now? And for their future?"

"As free citizens," I chime in, "in a free republic!"

"Ay," says he, "a free republic if we can stop the enemy and their allies in this country from stealing it away from us with their secret societies."

"Like the Irish Republican Brotherhood," says I, still bold and meself knowing that he's the head of the IRB.

He doesn't laugh this time. "Aye, Nell Pat, they've lifted an idea from us. Let them win the war, they say, and think they're independent, we'll still run Ireland."

I don't know what to say to that at all, at all, so I return to Jim Tom.

"You like the wee ones, Mick?" says I, and proud of myself I am that I call the general by his first name.

"I do," he says sadly.

"You have none of your own, then?"

"Ah, no. Neither child nor wife. Not yet anyway."

"But you have a sweetheart, don't you now?"

Wasn't I the terrible bold one?

"Well," he says, winking at me, "there is a lass in Granard over in County Longford named Kitty Kiernan that I'm thinking of as me Kitty, just like yourself and your Liam Tomas. The trouble of it is that me best friend Harry Boland thinks she's *his* Kitty Kiernan too. You see the problem, are you not?"

"I do indeed. But who does she favor?"

"You give a man no peace, do you, Nell Pat Malone?" And he winks again. "If you'd be asking Harry, he'd say she favored him. Most of them that know the both of us would say the same thing. But if you'd ask Kitty herself, well, now I think she'd say that Mick Collins is such an awful amadon that she'd better take care of him for the rest of his life."

"I'm thinking she's a very lucky woman."

"And I'm thinking Liam Tomas is a very lucky man."

And I hardly have time to blush again because aren't we at the cottage?

So we walk in, and Mick puts down the laundry basket and Ma and Da and Tim and Liam are all waiting for us. Liam looks terrible angry at this stranger who is walking down the road chatting with me. So maybe I'm his Nell after all.

"This is Mick Collins," I says, real casuallike.

"I met him on the road. He has business with you and the commandant, Liam, and, Ma, himself perishing with the hunger after a long walk on the road."

Well, didn't that make them all open up their eyes wide?

So that gombeen man Daniel O'Kelly shows up when it's dark and he and my friend Mick go down by the strand and talk for a long time.

Liam was not on guard duty, so doesn't he take me by the hand and lead me out for a walk along the lough? Pa frowned at us, but Ma nodded her head, knowing that we are young and Liam could be dead tomorrow, as could I if a stray bullet from one of the Tans should find me.

It was not really dark, a kind of summer twilight. When Liam took my hand, I gave it to him without a word.

"You're prettier every time I see you, Nell Pat," he said, "and myself not seeing you nearly enough."

"You look all tired and worn, Liam," says I. " 'Tis terrible hard work, isn't it?"

"If a man were working in a field for himself and his family it would be harder work and more purpose in it too. But this is something we have to do."

"We're winning, aren't we, Liam?"

"I don't know, Nell. We don't have many bullets for our guns or any money to buy the bullets. The general is wondering if our commandant knows where the gold that Roger Casement brought over from Germany is."

"Does he know, Liam?"

We were on the lough strand now, the lights of the bay flickering on the water and the moon peeking up over the rocks and peaceful quiet of heaven above us.

"If he does, he'll tell the general, won't he now?"

I didn't think that Liam really believed the truth of what he was saying. So maybe he has begun to see through the wee gombeen man. Yet they all still worship him, me brother Tim worse than the rest.

We walked along quietly, himself holding me hand for dear life.

"I miss you something terrible, Nell Pat," himself says to me. "I go out of me mind thinking about you."

Well, didn't I think I'd die for joy? But, sure, you can't admit right off that you feel that way, can you now? Even if it's a time of war?

"Little enough you have to do," I says with a sniff and a toss of me head, "if that's all you can think about, Liam Tomas O'Riada."

So doesn't he take me in his arms and kiss me?

As long as I can remember I've been hoping he'd do that. But he catches me by surprise and wasn't I resisting him at first?

287

"What kind of a woman do you think I am, Liam Tomas?"

"Me woman," he says, real fiercelike.

Then I'm collapsing altogether. I let him kiss me as long as he wants. Then, just to let him know I have a mind of me own too, I kissed him a little longer.

'Twas glorious altogether.

I could have stayed there the rest of the night with him, but he said we had to go back. He and Ma and Mick and I went to Mass this morning before the general left to go back to Dublin. I thought that maybe we had committed a terrible sin last night, and then I decided that God wouldn't mind because he was loving us as much as we love one another.

The young priest said Mass. He recognized Liam, and himself being no fool at all, at all, he probably recognized Mick Collins too. But nary a word from him.

We all lighted candles after Mass and Mick said to me, "If you find time in all your prayers for Liam Tomas, would you, Nell Pat Malone, say a wee prayer for meself?"

"And for Kitty Kiernan too."

The Big Fella laughs and kisses me on the forehead, and isn't Liam dying to do the same thing and Ma watching all the time, so he can't do it?

So that's how I met Michael Collins and was kissed for the first time on the very same day.

And as I write this I'm thinking that Daniel O'Kelly probably told me friend Mick that he didn't know where the gold was. I wonder if Mick believed him. If he did, he shouldn't have.

Daniel is still around, smiling at everyone and leering at me, which I don't like at all, at all. He's leaving tonight to travel north on some secret mission.

I'm thinking two things.

First, Captain Liam O'Riada can have me any time he wants.

And second: I know how to find out where the gold is hidden.

– 24 –

"I want to read you some of these letters," Nuala announced.

She had brought *In Great Haste*, the letters between Michael Collins and Catherine "Kit" Kiernan.

"I'm not illiterate," I pleaded.

"You listen just the same."

That settled that.

"This one is from October 1921. The poor man is dead tired."

As she read the letters to me, she became Michael Collins and Kitty Kiernan. It was a remarkable performance as she brought back to

289

life a young couple torn between war and love, a woman who could not understand the complexities of war and peace, and a man, increasingly enchanted by her, who could not find enough time to love her the way he wanted and she needed.

"October 12, 1921

"Kit dear,

"Have just returned from the Brompton Oratory. I was late for Mass a little, but the car hadn't come and I didn't know the way very well. Lit a candle for you, a very big one. I did the same yesterday morning.

"I was so glad you liked that note written in the Gresham. That was the most spontaneous on my part and came from a very great longing. We must, I think, make that arrangement more binding, but just as you desire. I feel somehow that it will work out and work out well.

"Slan leat,
"M."

"I think he's in love," I observed.
"You *think* he's in love? But wasn't he a religious man now?"
"He was."

"Kit, my dear Kit,

"Am hastily scribbling a note before going out to Mass. I know there will be no chance afterwards, for I already see ominous signs of work here. I wonder if you're sleeping soundly at this moment or are just awake and thinking of me. It's 7:50.

"How do you feel about it all this morning? Did you really enjoy yesterday? I do wish I had been nicer to you, but perhaps I wasn't too bad after all.

"I've just said my rosary for you.

"Slan leat for the day;

"With my fondest love,
"Micheal"

"So she went to London."
"She did."
"Were they lovers?"
"Not at all." Nuala tossed her head scornfully. "This one makes me cry."

"My dear Micheal,

"With me nothing seems to matter except that love between the two of us. In my opinion what else matters? And there the tragedy lies. I must try and be more matter of fact and sensible in the future and I'll see how it works with you. As you know

291

by now, no matter what happens or what you could give me, I want your love more than anything else. . . . God gave us the biggest thing of all in life. . . . You are the first who made me believe in love.

"*Yours with love,*
"*Kit*"

Nuala was in tears when she finished, for a moment totally identified with Kitty.

"The poor man, doesn't he love her? But he's so tired and she doesn't understand that. So tired."

"*Kitty dearest,*

"Am back, but I'm so tired that I can scarcely remain awake. This is a line just to tell you so and to say I am thinking very much of you today, also to say that no matter how short my note is, I am writing it.

"May God bless you always and may I see you again soon.

"*Your own,*
"*Micheal*"

"Isn't that sweet?" she demanded.

"Yeah, but she doesn't understand what's at issue."

"Not at all, poor woman. How could she? Doesn't this letter show that?"

And she was Kitty Kiernan again.

"They're sleeping together by now." I insisted.

"You keep your dirty male thoughts to yourself," she reprimanded me. "They are *not* . . . not that I'd blame her if they were. But, sure, isn't he happy and proud in this one?"

"My dearest Kitty,

"I am as happy a man as there is in Ireland today. My thoughts just now are all with you and you have every kind wish and feeling of mine. Have just taken over Dublin Castle, and am writing this note while awaiting a meeting of my Provisional Government. What do you think of that? Otherwise I see all sorts of difficulties ahead, but never mind. Please come up tomorrow night — send a wire. Failing that, Wednesday. There is nobody like you, I find, and I wish I'd been nicer to you. Twas my fault.

"Fondest love, dear Kit,

"Your own,
"Micheal"

Nuala wept in my arms, a position in which

I was delighted to find her despite my resolutions to protect her. With the simple and poignant love letters of the couple now long dead rushing through my head, how could I possibly feel desire for her?

Alas, it was easy.

<h1 style="text-align:center">— 25 —</h1>

"Are you satisfied?" Nuala demanded as I was reversing the videotape *Shadow of Bealnablath*, an RTE (Irish Television) miniseries about the death of Michael Collins.

"No way. You?"

She pondered thoughtfully. "Not really, Dermot Michael. Isn't it a bit too neat, too neat by half?"

"By three-quarters."

It was late evening in my suite at Jury's, the end of what was for me a reasonably busy day.

When I came in from my swim, Nuala, eyes glowing, was waiting with a book she had picked up at Fred Hanna's bookstore — *The Day Micheal Collins Died* — and a video and audio tape she had somehow borrowed from RTE.

I glanced at the book. She had highlighted in yellow the key passages.

The book repeated what had now become the

almost official line: Collins had died from a dum-dum bullet fired by Kerryman Dennis "Sonny" Neill, who did not know for several hours whom he had shot.

The evidence seemed to me, even at first glance, to be circumstantial — the theory fit the data, but the data did not make the theory certain.

"We'll watch the tapes later," I told her. "As soon as I'm dressed we're off to the Lord Mayor's mansion for a reception."

"We're *never* going there," she insisted.

"We are so. The mayor of Chicago and his wife are in town. They're neighbors of my family at Grand Beach — that's a summer resort across the lake in Michigan. I'm invited and I must see them."

"Sure, aren't they too high and mighty for the likes of me?"

I wasn't about to tell her that George had almost certainly tipped off the mayor's office about my presence in Dublin and arranged for the invitation. He wanted a report from the city's first family about Nuala.

Clever fellow, that priest brother of mine.

"They are not, Nuala Anne; they're South Side Irish and nice people. Herself is from a Galway family."

"I'm not dressed to meet a lord mayor."

"Yes, you are."

"You'd be sure about that?"

"Would I say it if I wasn't?"

I went into the bedroom to dress for the reception, my best gray suit and a tie with the Irish tricolor and the American stars and stripes crossed on it.

In case there was any doubt.

Nuala was waiting for me when I came out, coat on and looking dubious. "Do I curtsy for them?"

"Glory be to God, Nuala! Not unless you want to embarrass them something terrible. I beat himself at golf, herself mops up on me at the tennis court. They're friends."

She was torn between curiosity about the Lord Mayor of Chicago, as she persisted in calling him despite my insistence that he was only a mayor, and shyness.

Nuala could face down the Anglo-Irish aristocrats on their own turf without much trouble. Yet the Bridgeport Irish turned her shy.

Maybe that was the real Nuala, a very shy child.

Her image at the reception in the Round Room in Mansion House on Dawson Street was certainly that of a shy child — sweet, pretty, bashful. The Daleys liked her instantly, as of course they would.

Good reports to Father George.

"Father George" — the mayor smiled at me, that remarkable smile which seems aimed only at you — "said we should check up on you. You look fine."

"As best as I can be when I've fallen into

the hands of a Galway woman," I replied. "Mrs. Daley" — I turned to Nuala — "is from a Galway family. We all know that the real Ireland begins only at the Shannon."

They both laughed. Nuala smiled sweetly but did not reply.

"What part of Galway?" Mrs. Daley asked. "I've never been there, but maybe next trip."

"Connemara," she murmured softly, the only word she said during the whole meeting.

She charmed them completely — as I knew she would.

"They're grand people altogether," she informed me afterward as we walked towards the green. "Such nice smiles."

"They'll report on you to George."

"Whatever will they say?" She seemed troubled.

Not so troubled that she didn't slip a couple of shillings into the hand of a young traveler — the politically correct name for a tinker or an Irish "Gypsy," as these poor folk are also called — who was begging on the street.

"That you are a lovely, sweet, shy young woman who will undoubtedly take good care of me."

"Sure isn't that the truth?" She grinned wickedly.

"Having talked to you on the phone, George won't be so sure. On the other hand, he knows the Daleys are pretty good judges of people, so he'll half believe it. I won't disillusion him."

"Brute." She pushed me lightly, inordinately satisfied with herself.

George would in fact size her up perfectly and report to the family that I had indeed met a nice girl — and one who was more than a match for me.

"We're not going that way," I said as she turned left for the walk back to Jury's.

"Where are we going?" She stopped and considered me suspiciously.

"I'm taking you to dinner."

"Where?"

"It's impolite to ask."

Sudden panic. "Will I look all right?"

"Probably not, but I'll have to put up with you!"

She poked me again, but even more affectionately.

We walked west along the green and crossed in front of the new shopping center across from the Gaiety Theater.

"I have to send a Brigid cross off to a niece in America for her birthday. Do you mind walking into that place?"

"Sure, haven't I told you that I'm a materialist and meself afraid to go in there before now?"

Afraid of a mall?

"You'll note on the left," I said as we entered the glass-topped building, "the ruination of Ireland: lingerie that even whores wouldn't wear a couple of decades ago and now devout and holy matrons buy and put on."

"Sinful," she said insincerely as she carefully took in the window display, "altogether."

"You'll note that young woman showing her embarrassed husband a scandalous bit of white lace and himself shocked something terrible. I tell you, Nuala Anne, it will be the ruination of the Irish race."

"Ah, it will, won't it now? But sure, won't the poor man enjoy taking it off her?"

"Not as much as she will enjoy having it taken off. 'Tis the women that are the divils."

"Aren't they now?"

"Sure, the bishops should do something about sinful places like this, shouldn't they?"

"I'm sure they will. They don't have anything else to do, do they?"

The two of us giggling still, we walked into a jewelry shop, where Nuala took charge of buying the Brigid cross for my niece, Brigid Maeve Ready.

I had little to say in the matter. Nor did I dare ask about the price until the bill was handed to me.

"Places like this will make a terrible materialist out of me." She sighed, not feeling any guilt at all.

On the way out, she darted into the lingerie shop. Flustered, I trailed after her.

"Now, wouldn't this be a nice thing to have?" She held up a red and silver garment that was not totally transparent, but might just as well have been.

"Nuala. . . ."

"Sure, I can buy it meself," she insisted. "I don't have one like this and a woman can never tell when she'll need this sort of thing, can she now?"

She paid for the teddy — I think that's what it's called — in cash, tucked the tiny package under her arm, and, head high, walked out of the shop, myself still in attendance.

In the game we were playing I was now pretty much the loser.

"Do you think, Dermot Michael," she said as, back on the street, we were passing the Chicago Pizza Factory, "that I'll look nice in this obscene thing?"

"I don't want to imagine, Nuala Anne."

She laughed noisily, knowing full well that I already had. "Are we going in there in honor of Chicago?"

"We are not, woman."

She gave money to another little traveler.

I breathed a sigh of relief when I finally conducted her into White's on the green, one of the best restaurants in Dublin. Nuala looked around dubiously, searching for the lay of the land so she would know how to act. She decided for the grand lady image, not quite the duchess, mind you, but still someone who had eaten in better restaurants than this thousands of times.

"You'll order for me, won't you, Dermot Michael?" she begged me. "Sure, I can't even read the menu."

I could and did — garlic mushrooms and then smoked sea trout. A single glass of white wine for each of us.

She demolished the sea trout.

"Could I ever have another glass of wine, Dermot Michael?"

"I suppose so." I sighed, as if I were not totally delighted by my charming dinner companion.

At least she hadn't made me pay for the lingerie.

"You're a strange man, Mr. Coyne." She inspected me over the wineglass. "A strange man altogether."

"Am I now?" I found my face turning hot.

"Now, don't get that hurt look in your eyes. I'm not being critical. . . . I don't know all that many men, but I'm sure that most of them aren't like you. You're kind and sweet and good" — her eyes seemed to be misting — "and respectful and those silver-green eyes of yours see everything and want to heal everything." She reached for a tissue. "And now I'm going to cry about how wonderful you are."

She reached for my hand, touched it, and then quickly withdrew it.

"Thank you, Nuala." My own voice was hoarse.

Two sentimental Micks — and on a glass and a half of wine each. We went back to Jury's,

301

read the book by Meda Ryan, and watched the tape directed and narrated by Colum Connolly.

There was certainly prima facie evidence of a cover-up — no autopsy, no inquest, no determination of the kind of wound or wounds. No wonder conspiracy theories had flourished for so long. Had he been shot by his own men, by Emmet Dalton, fearing either a war against the Protestants in the North or a too-easy peace with the Irregulars?

This theory no longer seemed likely because some of the IRA men who fought in the chance ambush had told the truth before they died, after lying about what had happened for years.

Or *had* they told the truth?

How could one be sure?

How could they have been sure?

It seemed that after their retreat from Cork, a group of IRA officers had met for a strategy conference at Bealnablath. De Valera had been there in the morning but had left, aware that Collins was in the area and taking a terrible chance of ambush. He said that he hoped he would not be shot because he was a strong man and a strong man could make peace. Weak men would continue the war.

The Long Fella was right. Thousands would die in a war that Collins might have ended that week.

The Collins convoy moved through Bealnablath in the morning on the way down from Crookstown (where he had met with a "neutral" officer in search of peace) to Bandon and Clonakilty, where he would visit his brother at the family home — and talk to another "neutral."

The motorcyclist who led the convoy stopped an IRA man on the road (they didn't wear uniforms, of course) and asked the way to Newcestown. The man recognized Collins and reported back to the pub where the meeting was in progress that Collins was on the road to Bandon and might well come back the same route later in the day.

The officers debated an ambush. They had no desire to kill Collins, but they resented the invasion of Cork by the National Army and felt they ought to fight.

Were they aware that if there was an ambush, they might kill him?

It was wartime and men might not think of such things. They might also believe in his invulnerability, as he himself apparently did.

So they set the ambush and planted a remote-controlled land mine. They waited most of the day and then, assuming the convoy was returning to Cork by another route, most of them drifted away. There were only four men in the laneway above the road (and the various groups of Kerrymen drifting along the hill on the other side, unknown to anyone else) as the light faded. Two of them went down to remove the mine so that no countrymen would be hurt the next morning.

303

Then the convoy appeared. The two, having just disconnected the mine, rushed back up to the laneway and began to shoot. The troops returned the fire.

Nobody was shooting very accurately. As the troops turned up the laneway, the four Irregulars retreated, still firing. Some of those who had left earlier rushed back to the scene of the fire-fight. Gunfire crackled vigorously for a few minutes, but no one on either side was hit.

There was a lull in the shooting. The National Army forces relaxed. Collins came out from behind the cover provided by his car. The shooting started again.

It was one of these bullets, fired during the retreat, that killed Collins, according to both the film and the book. The rifleman was "Sonny" Neill, a sometime soldier in the English army who was reputed to be a crack shot and who by mistake had loaded dum-dum bullets (stolen from the Black and Tans) into his weapon. He had no idea whom he had hit because of the distance, the fading light, and the hedges that lined the laneway. Only hours later did the Irregulars learn they had killed Collins. Some of them openly wept.

There were four different groups in that gloomy valley: the National Army; the remnants of the ambush; those who had left the ambush and rushed back to join the shooting; and the two groups of Kerrymen who were retreating along the ridge opposite where the four ambushers were.

Anyone could have fired the fatal shot.

The matter was complicated by the nature of the wound — a massive injury in the back of his neck that might have been caused by a ricochet, or by a Mauser fired from behind, or by an exiting bullet fired from the laneway or a dum-dum bullet fired from the other hill.

There was some grisly conversation on the radio tape between Meda Ryan and Colum Connolly about the nature of the wound and the direction from which it was fired.

The Collins family's plea (on the videotape) that it no longer mattered who killed him seemed reasonable enough, as did their refusal to permit an exhumation to discover whether the fatal wound was an exit or an entry wound — unless you were obsessed with conspiracy theories, as I was. The dum-dum bullet might easily have been a solution invented to explain the mystery.

Sonny Neill might have fired the fatal shot, but so might any of the other men who were present in the fading August light.

IRA intelligence thought almost immediately that Sonny Neill was the killer, as he apparently did too. But was the dum-dum an explanation they devised to convince themselves, while hiding the secret from everyone else for a half century?

No one was alive who could answer that question.

The mystery remained.

The RTE program was skillful and moving. It began with a reenactment of the ambush at Bealnablath, then told the story of Collins's brief life and his remarkable achievements, then finally tried to solve the mystery of his death. It included pictures of Kitty, as did the Ryan book, and quotes from their correspondence. She was a beauty, no doubt about that — and with a charming smile.

No wonder Mick fell in love with her despite her poor health and her inability to understand the demands of public life, particularly his public life.

She was not, I noted to myself, as beautiful as Nuala.

Few were.

That worthy young woman watched the video — on a machine she had borrowed from the hotel management (which now ate out of her hand) and rolled triumphantly into the parlor — with considerable display of emotion. She sat on the couch, foot tucked under her, tissue in one hand, fingers of the other tightly clenched.

When I offered a comment, I was told sternly to "shush." However, she reacted with sighs, gasps, exclamations of protest, and sobs.

When a filmwriter who had failed to do a screenplay on Michael Collins contended that he had been unfaithful to Kitty in London with a woman named Hazel Laverty (wife of an artist and a native of Chicago) and received sacrilegious communions, I thought that my friend would go through the TV screen to tear out his eyes. Fortunately for all concerned, Colum Connolly offered evidence in refutation.

When the tape was finished and she asked my opinion, she was a basket case — a lovely one, I might add.

"It's like John Kennedy's death, Nuala. We may never know the truth. The IRA thought they were responsible but didn't want to claim credit because he was so popular with the people. But that doesn't mean that they were telling the truth or that they even knew the truth. They fit an explanation to the facts they had. So did Meda Ryan and Colum Connolly. I suppose they're probably right. Yet —"

"Yet you want to see what your gram says in her diary before you're sure that you don't have to worry about it. I'll peek ahead if you want me to. Isn't it hard though because she writes so small?"

"Don't do that, Nuala. There's no terrible rush. I want to treat her story fairly. Read it the way she wrote it."

She nodded. "I agree."

"That makes it unanimous. Now, young woman, you'd better be getting back to Chapel Row before the sun comes up. Take a taxi and bill it to my account. You can come back in the morning and recover your bike from wherever your friends downstairs let you park it."

"Aye," she said, standing up slowly. "We're

all terrible fragile, aren't we, Dermot Michael?"

"Indeed we are. It comes from being creatures."

"Doesn't it now?"

— 26 —

The next day Nuala arrived in the blue suit with a light blue sweater. She probably had a light gray sweater to match the gray suit — a four-day rotation, like baseball pitchers. But since she worked for only four days a week, that was probably deemed enough.

No jeans and sweatshirt in Jury's Towers. Not yet.

I was waiting for her in my swim trunks and robe. "Would you mind if I swim with you today, Nuala? I must go to the reception at the Royal Gallery at half five."

"Sure, it's your pool, isn't it now? Besides, you won't be satisfied till you gape at me in my bikini and meself too fat and too tall."

I pretended to swat at her rear end. "I said no more self-hatred, didn't I, woman?"

She didn't duck as I thought she would, so my hand came into contact with solid butt, very solid.

She was amused by my embarrassment. "And yourself such a terrible brute." She giggled. "I'm thinking you're Bigfoot."

"Maybe I am now. Hurry up and get ready, I haven't all day to wait for you."

Bigfoot. Would I have to tell my story to her sometime soon?

I decided that it would be better not to burden her with the whole complicated mess unless it became absolutely necessary. I hoped it never would. If Ma really knew where the gold was, we might be well on our way to solving the mystery — if the gold was linked to the death of Collins, which it might well have been.

Did I not notice at all, at all the last word in Nuala's letter to me?

Sure I did. However, I persuaded myself that she didn't mean it the way it sounded. It was merely the way she'd end a letter to anyone.

Right?

Nuala emerged from the bathroom, her robe tied tightly around her and her arms hugging it even more tightly.

"I can hear the woman talking in my ear as I type her words into your machine," she said. " 'Tis almost like she is in the room talking to me. It's the strangest thing."

"Literally?" We were standing by the elevators.

"Not quite. . . . Would you be thinking I'm daft altogether?"

"I am not, woman. You're one of the least daft women I've ever known — in that sense anyway."

She poked my arm. "I don't want to know what ways you think I am daft. . . . I feel like she's very close to me, protecting me from harm, maybe lighting a candle somewhere for me and watching me all the time."

"And not her favorite grandson?"

"Oh, she watches over him all the time."

"She told you this?" I stepped back to let her out of the elevator.

"Not so I could say I heard her very words, but, oh, Dermot, you'll know I'm daft, I just feel it as powerfully as I've ever felt anything."

"Will she protect you from me, Nuala Anne McGrail?"

"Haven't I said I can do that without any help?" She poked me again. "Come 'long with you now, let's do this swimming thing so you can get rid of all your fantasies."

"Won't it make my fantasies worse?"

"On the basis of the part of your story you let me read, I doubt that they could be worse." Despite her crisp words, she smiled at me affectionately. Maybe she did mean the last word of the letter.

What would I do about that?

"Shall we try the whirlpool?" I asked as we entered the pool area.

" 'Twould be a terrible sin." She looked at the spa suspiciously.

"You don't have to."

"I'm not terrible good at resisting temptation."

"It's easy." I tossed aside my robe. "You just climb into the whirlpool and push the button." I sank into the warm waters. " 'Tis nothing like it on a cold autumn night in Dublin."

"Umm." She took off her robe and my heart stopped beating. I wasn't sure it would ever start beating again.

As I would have predicted, Nuala Anne McGrail would peel off a robe over her minimal swim suit with the practiced ease of someone who had done it in front of men a thousand times instead of someone who was doing it for the first time.

In a floral print ensemble that would have been considered prudish on Cococabana Beach, she was everything I expected and a good deal more.

"Come on," I urged her. "It won't hurt you."

She dipped her foot, a good-size and not dainty foot, into the water. "Brigid, Patrick, and Columcille! Are you planning to boil me alive?"

I extended my hand and helped her into the swirling waters. "You get used to it after a few seconds."

She sank into the pool and sighed. "Wasn't I saying it was a grave sin!"

"Against a God you don't believe in?"

"Would I be wanting to make Her angry if She really did exist?" She threw back her head and closed her eyes, at peace for the moment with the world and everyone in it.

I noted that she took up a lot of the whirlpool

— a tall, strong woman, shapely indeed, breath-takingly so, but not petite by any stretch of the imagination. Slender indeed she was but also solid, to say nothing of generously proportioned. Her long trim legs were taut with strong muscles. There was a lot to Nuala, much of it available for my inspection.

She had told me that she had played hurley with the boys when she was a "young one." When those sturdy young arms swung a club, they could be very dangerous.

The Diana metaphor didn't fit. No, she was Sionna or Bionna or one of those athletic Celtic goddesses with whom you mess at grave risk.

"Stop thinking those thoughts about me." She kicked my foot.

"Your eyes are closed. How do you know what I'm thinking?"

"Be quiet." She sank deeper into the pool. "Don't I want to relax?"

"Yes, ma'am. . . . Actually, I'm wondering what sport you'd be playing at the college?"

She blushed. "A bit of Irish football, women's team of course. So all you were thinking was that I looked like an athlete?"

"Actually I was thinking how you'd swing a hurley stick."

She opened her eyes and grinned. "I still have one in me rooms, in case I need to fight anyone off. Don't forget that, Dermot Michael."

"I won't."

She took my hand in hers. If I was really

the heroic protector I claimed to be, I would have gently withdrawn mine.

I told myself better in her hand than on her breast — where it wanted to be. I tried my best not to look at the outline of her nipples, firm against the top of her bikini, and to restrain my fantasy about how they would taste in my mouth.

I thought of how much I hated college and that helped.

Nuala sighed. What was she imagining Ma was whispering in her ear about me? Had she imagined that Ma was telling her to end her letter to me with that one awesome and dangerous word?

"Well" — she sighed again, eyes still closed — "they tell me sex is hard to beat, but this must be more relaxing."

A signal to a potential lover that she was a virgin?

Did she imagine Ma whispering that too?

What if she wasn't imagining?

Nuala surely had some psychic sensitivities, no doubt about that. She'd sensed or guessed or whatever that I had lost to death a woman I loved. Ma had been that way too.

"She's just a good guesser," my mother would say to me. "She likes to pretend that she's a bit of a witch."

Two witches from the same town in the West of Ireland — could they become thick as thieves although one was dead?

Despite the heat of the pool, I shivered.

Ma was always terribly worried that I "wouldn't make the right marriage."

She would say that Kel was "a lovely girl, but, faith, I don't think she really appreciates what's worth appreciating about you, Dermot Michael."

She'd pronounce "appreciate" with the hard "c" the Irish use in the word.

Christina was "that little eyetalian thing."

What would she think of my young friend from Carraroe?

There wasn't much doubt about that. Not at all, at all.

Would Ma come back from the grave to meddle in my love life?

If she could, she damn well would.

I shivered again.

"*Well?*" Nuala opened her eyes and glared at me.

"Well, what?"

Had the little bitch been reading my mind?

"No comment on the nearly naked woman?"

"I didn't want to seem vulgar and stare."

"Humph!"

"You're the most beautiful woman I've ever met, Nuala Anne McGrail, more beautiful than anyone I had ever hoped to meet. But I didn't want to seem to stare at you disrespectfully like you were a sex object."

"You've never looked at me disrespectfully, Dermot Michael Coyne. Lasciviously maybe, but

314

not disrespectfully. To tell you the truth" —
she smiled affectionately and made my heart stop
again — "I don't think you could turn a woman
into a sex object if you wanted to."

It was my turn to blush. "I hope that's true."

"I'm embarrassed by the way you look at me."
She closed her eyes again. "But it's a nice embarrassment."

After we had enough of the whirlpool, Nuala
and I jumped out, dashed to the inside section
of the pool, and swam out under the dividing
wall into the outside section. It was raining now,
which added to the fun. We raced and frolicked
and fought and wrestled and played in the water
as young lovers probably have since humans discovered that you could do more with water than
drink it.

She was a faster swimmer than I and a stronger
wrestler, until I used one of my martial arts
holds to immobilize her.

Then in the darkness, with no one or the
hotel staff able to see us or interested in seeing
us, I kissed her, perhaps the same way Pa had
kissed Ma seventy years before.

Our bodies, wet and mostly unclad, pressed
together, overruling our sense and judgment.
Her breasts pressed against my chest. I caressed
her back and butt and kissed her time after
time, smothering her eyes and her lips and throat
with my affection.

Finally we stopped. Badly shaken, I helped
her out of the pool and into her terry robe.

"I've never been kissed that way before," she said calmly. " 'Tis an interesting experience altogether, isn't it?"

"I promised no passes in my room," I replied. "The pool is not in my room."

"Ah, sure." She sighed. "Would you say that was a pass? Faith, it wouldn't fit my definition of one."

I didn't want to know what her definition was.

Silently, our minds jumbled with wild thoughts (my mind anyway), we went back to my suite and dressed in our proper clothes (in separate bathrooms, I hasten to add). Nuala, her long hair lank on her blue sweater, was pounding on the Compaq as I left for the reception at the National Gallery.

If I was so stirred up by her and she seemed to be willing enough, why did not I try to bed her, either as a passing relationship or, given who and what she was, a permanent one?

What was a matter with me?

Some of it, I think, was virtue. She was young and naive and innocent — or so I thought then anyway — and probably a victim of a late-adolescent crush on me.

Part of it, most of it I have to admit now, was fear.

When I came back there was another printout with another note on the table next to the picture of Ma and Pa taken shortly before they left Carraroe.

I lingered on the picture — two handsome kids, arms around one another. The original had been taken by "the schoolteacher fella," Ma had often said. She'd had it colored. Did Carraroe in the background really look like a setting for *The Quiet Man*?

Could Ma really be dead?

Could she influence Nuala and me even if she were dead?

I turned to Nuala's note.

> *She found out where the gold is.*
> *N.*

– 27 –

September 1920

Well, I know where the gold is.

I don't know what I can do about it. I don't dast tell Liam Tomas that I spied on the commandant. He'd be terrible angry at that. If I told him that the gold General Collins needed to buy bullets to free poor old Ireland was hidden within eyesight of our village, he'd ask Daniel O'Kelly about it, since my Liam Tomas is a direct and open man, too open for his own good, I often think. Then there'd be a fight. A man who will hide gold from Ireland will kill to protect that gold. If he knew I was following him and spying on him with Granda's binoculars from the Boer War, he might kill me — and do terrible things to me before he killed me.

So it will have to be my secret until it's safe to tell, if it's ever safe to tell.

Anyway, I'm sure that Daniel O'Kelly, for all his big talk and all the admiration his men have for him, is a thief and a traitor. I'll wait till the day that I'm able to tell Liam and he'll believe me.

After O'Kelly woke up and had his tea, your man packed his kit and prepared to leave. He didn't carry a Lee-Enfield, none of the IRA men do that in daylight. But he did have a big Mauser pistol under his coat.

"This is the gun that did for Roderick Mc-Clory." He pulled it out and waved the awful thing at me.

"And himself coming home from Mass."

I was serving him his tea because Ma and Da had gone over to Spiddal for a wake and Tim was back with the Brigade, wherever that might be, and Moire weeping for him.

I think she's pregnant, God bless her.

"He was a traitor, Nell Pat Malone, in the service of English imperialism. He deserved to die."

"And himself with a wife and two little gossons."

"It's a war."

"You shot him in the back."

He shrugged his shoulders and grinned wickedly at me. "If he had a chance he would have shot me. We're doing it for Ireland."

"You love killing," I shot back at him. "You kill for the fun of it. I can see the light in your eyes when you talk about it. You'd rather shoot a man in the back than have a woman."

"A lot you'd know" — he sneered at me — "about being had by a man."

"I know enough about it to know that you'd kill a woman just as easy as you'd kill a man."

"You're a very provoking child, Nell Pat Malone." He stood up from his table. "I think a man needs to teach you a lesson since your father won't and Liam O'Riada can't."

My heart was pounding something awful and my throat was dry. He meant it. And afterward he'd throw me body into the bay and spread the word that a Tan or an RIC constable did it.

"You come near me" — I backed away from him — "and I'll smash your skull with this poker and shed not a tear for you."

When my ma and da had left for the wake and told me to give the commandant his tea, I got the big poker from outside the house and put it right next to the fireplace. I never let it out of my sight or my reach for a moment.

"You wouldn't hit me with that." He came closer to me, his hand on the gun stuffed in his belt. "And meself the commandant of the Brigade?"

319

"If you even touch that gun, I'll swing this."

And all the time I was praying to the Holy Mother of God to give me the courage to bash the dirty gombeen man's skull in if I had to.

We stood there glaring at one another, himself with his hand on the butt of his gun and meself with the terrible poker thing high in the air over me head.

Then he laughed and turned away from me. "Someday I'll tame you, my little hellcat friend."

"You take your kit and get out of this house or I'll brain you anyhow," I shouted at him, knowing now that he was a coward who could be frightened by a terrified little colleen.

He laughed again, picked up his kit, and sauntered out of the house like he was the high king of Ireland himself.

Trembling like an oak leaf falling off the tree in autumn, I watched him go down the path to the road.

Then I put the poker back against the fireplace and began to clean up.

I made up my mind that I would do what I had half thought I might do.

I found Da's old hunting knife, which he never uses anymore, and slipped it, still in its pouch, into me drawers, hurried out of the house, saddled up Dotty, me pony, and rode after him.

Then I remembered the dusty old binoculars on the shelf in the front room.

I pointed Dotty back towards the house and ran in to bring them along. When I was a wee lass, I used to borrow them (without telling Ma or Da) to watch the ships out on Galway Bay.

I reckoned that I had a couple of hours to follow the commandant if I wanted to be home before me parents returned about midnight, even later if the wake was an interesting one.

Dotty and I slipped along, real quietlike, maybe two hundred yards behind him, far enough back so that he wouldn't notice us and close enough so that I could follow him every five minutes or so with my binoculars.

He went up towards Maam Cross and then turned off to the left on a side road. It was getting darker so I was beginning to worry about Ma and Da coming home before me. But in the dark he couldn't see so far behind him and I was able to come closer, and all the time me crazy imagination thinking that the rock fences and the bare mountains and the harsh bogs of Connemara are laying in wait to trap me. I'm afraid of the dark, you see, when I'm alone.

He looked back a couple of times, to see if he was being followed. I was scared to death twice that he saw me, but he just turned around and kept on walking.

It shows you what fools men are. If I were General Mick Collins, I would have had someone follow Daniel O'Kelly. I would have suspected that he was the kind of man who would steal a million pounds in gold and also the kind who would want to go up and look at it after he had sworn he didn't have it.

Like a little boy gloats over the marbles he's stolen from his friends.

Well, doesn't he turn up a cattle path on the side of the mountain of Mamene? I hid behind an oak tree and watched him in the moonlight, a tiny figure even in me binoculars as he walked up the mountain.

I knew that there was an old shrine at the top called the Little Cell of Patrick, a cave cut out of the side of the mountain where 'tis said St. Patrick himself spent a night and himself sleeping on the hard rock.

The young priest told me once that it had been a pagan shrine even before St. Patrick and that before the famine they'd have great patterns up there on festival days, with the singing and the dancing and the telling of songs and terrible gang fights with clubs and the drinking of poteen. "Seven tents of poteen," he said, rolling his pretty brown eyes. "It was once even more important a shrine than Cro-Patrick up in the Archdiocese of Tuam. Someday," he goes on, "when Ireland is free, we'll rebuild the shrine and have pilgrimages again."

[Translator's note: By "pattern" she means the patronal feast of a saint. The shrine has recently been restored by me cousin, who is a Jesuit and teaches at Maynooth, and they have pilgrimages again. No poteen or gang fights. Not yet anyway.]

"Without the poteen," I says.

The young priest laughs. "The very words I was about to say, Nell Pat Malone."

So shivering now with fun of following your man, I watch him go into a little crevice, just below the ruins of the shrine, and come out again.

That's where the money is, says I. Up there behind the shrine of poor old St. Patrick. I'll come back here someday and make sure I can remember the right crevice.

I don't think I'd ever go near the gold itself. All that money scares me. People would do terrible things to one another for a million English pounds.

"Come on, Dotty," I says to herself. "You and I shouldn't be here at all, at all."

We got home only a few minutes before Da and Ma. I was pretty certain that after a wake Da would not check on Dotty. I hugged her, she nuzzled me, and I came into the house to write all this down.

I'm afraid to sleep because I know I'll see Daniel O'Kelly coming after me with that terrible gun in his hand and a dirty smile on his ugly face.

— NUALA'S VOICE —

Oh, Nell Pat!
Nothing like that has happened to me in all my life. It was scary and wonderful and I loved every second of it. I wish I knew more about

men and sex. Some of the onchucks in my classes claim they do, but I think they're as ignorant as I am.

Was it just a pleasant little romp in the swimming pool, or did it mean something? Or was it both? He didn't talk about it afterward so maybe it really wasn't a kind of offer of love.

I don't know what goes on in his head. He's such a complicated man — good and sweet and kind, but unpredictable and sometimes so dumb. My crush on him is driving me half mad. Maybe I should quit working for him and go home to Galway.

I know you don't like that idea, but I'm afraid. Not of him but of meself.

He's such an eejit. He has no idea what to do about this quest of his. The answers are as plain as they can be and he doesn't see them. I'll have to take charge, not that I haven't done it already.

I'm not going to hide it either. I won't flaunt it in his face, poor dear man. But I'm not going to pretend that I'm someone I'm not either. If he wants a dumb and docile woman, he's come to the wrong person.

Not that there's much sign he wants me or anyone else. Mostly it's all business. Except sometimes it isn't.

But, Nell Pat, I love him so much.

– 28 –

"Astonishing!"

"Me or the whirlpool or your gram?"

"All three." I patted her bare shoulder. "And I will refuse to choose among them. But I meant her."

"Can't you see that slip of a girl riding her pony down the back country road in the moonlight? Wasn't my heart in my mouth for her and myself knowing she lived a long life in Chicago?"

"And threatening that amadon with a poker! I didn't doubt it for a moment. That was Ma!"

"You know what I'm thinking? I'm thinking she left those diaries hoping you would have them translated. Wouldn't she be wanting someone to know about the gold?"

We were in the whirlpool on Monday afternoon. I had not seen Nuala through the weekend. She seemed relaxed and at ease with me.

Which assumption shows how little I understand women of the species — hell, the species itself, male or female.

In any case, she sat next to me in the spa, our bare shoulders only a couple of inches apart, and did not seem shy or anxious. We might

325

have been brother and sister or a couple long married, but not lovers or two people about to begin a love affair.

That was fine with me, I told myself.

"Could be, Nuala. I hadn't thought of that possibility. She was a great one for tricks and games. This might all be a game. . . . Do you still think you hear her?"

She stirred the water in the spa with her foot, as I have said, a very substantial foot.

"You'll know I'm daft."

"We're both daft."

"Aren't we now? You've noticed that in the first translation I used good English? I said 'myself' and not 'meself' and eliminated most of the mannerisms that make us an alien people by your standards?"

"I *never* said that."

"Stop talking like me. . . . Anyway, I couldn't do that after the first day. I had to translate it so that it sounded like she would have sounded if she was speaking in English. I, uh, well, I felt she wouldn't let me do it any other way. It's like she's inside of me or I'm inside of her."

"You know her personality and character pretty well by now, like a novelist who creates a character has to let the character speak on his own."

She nodded. "That's probably it. Maybe because I am an actress sometimes or, as you think, all the time, maybe I can imagine that I'm her and play the role of Nell Pat Malone. Yet, oh,

326

Dermot, it's so scary afterward! When I'm translating away it doesn't seem strange at all. Then I turn off the computer and I look around, half expecting to see her standing behind me and her red hair blazing and the smile on her face approving what I've done. I think I see her walking down the streets or kneeling behind me in church and I dream about her at night. Sure, don't I tell meself that it's me stupid West of Ireland imagination? But" — she shook her head as if to clear the images away — "doesn't she just laugh at me?"

"She would. Are you so scared that you want to stop for a few days?"

"Oh" — she clutched my arm — "glory be to God, Dermot. I wouldn't dare do that, would I now? Wouldn't she be furious at me altogether if I did that?"

"Let's do our swim before you scare me to death."

The swim was strictly exercise, no more playful clowning around by about-to-be lovers.

Fine, I reassured myself. Maybe later when I have cleared up this mess, I'll be able to think about the possibilities between me and Nuala. She is awfully young and we really do come from very different cultures.

That's what I told myself repeatedly. I don't think that even then I fully believed it. But I believed it enough to keep my hands off her.

Back in my suite, Nuala continued her work and I returned to my collection of books about

327

the Irish Civil War — and to thoughts about what I ought to do next.

Nuala answered my questions before I asked her about them.

"You wouldn't mind me making a small suggestion?"

"Of course not . . . so long as it's small, which I doubt."

"Maybe" — she took a deep breath — "we should drive out to Galway and visit Carraroe? Maybe by way of Cork and the vale where Michael Collins was killed? We could visit the sites of the incidents that Nell Pat was describing in her story. We might even climb up to Mamene and search for the gold. A million pounds of bullion would be worth twenty million now."

"Who does it belong to, Nuala?"

"By rights I suppose it belongs to the people of Ireland. Couldn't you educate a lot of kids with it? Or take a lot of men off the dole?"

"It's an interesting idea," I said judiciously. "I'll have to think about it."

Why hadn't I thought of it before she did?

I might also meet Nuala's family. No, that wasn't true. I would have no choice but to meet them. Perhaps they would remember stories about the Galway Brigade they heard growing up. Or maybe they would know someone who was alive in those days and could fill in a few of the details about what had happened during the Troubles.

What if the gold was there?

I'd worry about that when it happened.

Nuala assumed that she would come with me.

Why should she come? I didn't need her to explore the mountain where the gold might be hidden, did I?

Would there be any danger?

The other side would keep an eye on me if I went to Cork and Galway. They might not like it. I had no right to expose Nuala to any danger. It wasn't her fight. She had, however, identified so closely with Ma that she would not want to be left behind in Dublin.

I would have to tell her the whole story. She would have to know about the potential danger. She was sufficiently crazy to want to imitate Nell Pat Malone and risk the danger.

I couldn't let her risk being hurt, could I?

" 'Tis none of my business." She did not turn around from the Compaq.

"What's none of your business, Nuala Anne?"

"Well" — the housewife-at-the-fish-market tone crept into her voice — "I have no right to be asking, do I now, but would you be publishing this story when we're finished with it?"

"I'll have to see how it goes. If it's all as fascinating as the first few entries, it might well interest readers. Certainly my family, the nieces and nephews especially, would like it."

"What would you be calling it?"

I thought about that. "We might call it simply *Nell Pat.*"

"Faith, wouldn't she be liking that?"

"Translated by Nuala Anne McGrail and edited by Dermot Michael Coyne."

"You'd *never* do that!"

She was delighted at the prospect of her name on the cover of a book. She's really only a kid, I reminded myself, a shy child. You must not hurt her.

"I would *so!*"

The phone rang. Before I could reach for the one by my chair, she had picked up the extension on the desk.

"Mr. Coyne's office. . . . Ah, 'tis yourself, is it now, your reverence? Sure, he's not doing anything at all. Your man is not a good worker, and yourself knowing that already without me telling you. He just lollygags around all day in the whirlpool, which is a terrible sinful contraption if you ask me and I know you didn't. . . . You want to talk to him? Well, I'll see if he can be disturbed, you know what he's like. . . . 'Tis your brother the priest, Mr. Coyne!"

"Stop harassing my help," I said to George.

"She's too good for you, Punk," my priestly brother informed me. "Without even meeting her, I can tell that."

"She's a fine woman," I agreed. "The only trouble is that she lies a little. You can hang up now, Nuala."

She tossed her long hair, still wet from the pool, in disdain, but hung up very gently.

"Everyone well at home, George?"

"They all want to meet herself, but other than that they're fine. Why don't you wander out to do some shopping or something and give me a ring?"

"I think I could do that. Size forty sweater, is it now?"

"Great," he said. "I have some good news. At least I think it's good news."

I excused myself to Nuala, who merely nodded her head, and left the room.

"You impressed Patrick," George began our transatlantic conversation. "His group wants to support you."

"Why?"

"Punk, you're smart enough to know one of the answers to that question."

"Don't tell me the government is concerned about Irish-American voters?"

"You damn well better believe they are. Moreover, and I quote Tony, no, I don't quote him. I translate his bureaucratic evasions into standard English. They don't like amateur groups floating around on the fringes of the intelligence communities of allied nations. No telling what harm might be done by shadow-world types who have access to our data."

"And?"

"And I guess in the games they play with one another, they wouldn't mind a 'gotcha' with their counterparts."

I thought about it. Probably they were telling

George the truth, but not the whole truth.

"What is their price for this support?"

"No strings attached as far as I can tell. They simply say they'll keep an eye on you to see that nothing goes wrong."

"Goes wrong?"

"That you don't get hurt."

"I'm not going to get hurt."

"They propose to see that you don't."

"And if I don't want their protection?"

"I understand that you will receive it anyhow."

"So why did they want you to call me?"

"So you would know that they'd be around. I am merely to inform you and report back to Tony that I have. He assures me, personally, that they are not playing tricks this time."

"What's your guess, George? You know more about this stuff than I do."

"My guess is that there is someone in the British government that they want very badly to embarrass right out of power, and they see this as a chance to do it."

"Charming."

"We need intelligence operations in this sad old world of ours. We may not need the kind we have. But this caper sounds pretty straight."

"And I'll be protected by them whether I want to be or not?"

"That seems to be the size of it. You and your group, which I would assume means the young lady."

"I don't think I want the feds stumbling around her."

"Punk, I'll be candid: The choice is to get the hell out of Ireland, with or without her. Given your tastes, I assume she is gorgeous —"

"She as ugly as sin. . . . I told you I'm not bringing her home."

"Suit yourself." He sounded unimpressed by my denials. "Oh, yes, I was also told by Tony to say that Patrick might be in touch with you again."

"Great, just great."

Nevertheless, I felt better after the call. I didn't trust our feds all that much, but I trusted them more than Chief Superintendent Conlon.

So maybe it was safe to ride out to Cork and Galway.

As I walked through the gloom of a light rain and a thick mist, appropriate for the opening scene of a horror film, I reflected on the points of which I could be sure.

1. There was a fortune of gold in the mountains of Connemara.
2. A shadowy, extragovernmental group had been plotting, perhaps for decades, to reunite England and Ireland. For some reason the CIA, as I presumed, wanted that group busted up.
3. The death of Michael Collins was

333

probably connected with either my first point or my second point or both.

4. The reason my grandparents had fled, perhaps suddenly and most likely under the threat of death, was connected with one or all of the three previous factors.

However, no one knew that I had Ma's diaries, which might hold the key to a door where I might find an explanation of how everything fit together. Finally, they did not know that I knew where the gold was — or at least where it had been in 1920.

I wandered through the streets for a long time, permitting these ideas and the images and pictures behind them to ferment in my imagination. I had the feeling that perhaps I knew more than I realized I knew and that suddenly I would know what I didn't know and understand it all.

But the pattern, whatever it was, continued to lurk just beneath the threshold of my consciousness. Once or twice I thought I saw it, like a ship at the Dublin docks wrapped in the mists, and then it disappeared.

I gave it up and walked rapidly back to Jury's and Nuala's most recent translation.

As I did a foghorn wailed mournfully, lamenting, I thought.

I can hardly believe that this actually hap-

pened. I know it for both the living and the
dead.

If there was a difference.

Nuala's cover note again said nothing about
love.

I was a little disappointed.

What a woman!

N.

– 29 –

November 15, 1920

I'll never sleep at night again. I'll always feel
that man's hands on me. I'll always see those
two other men when O'Kelly pointed the gun
at their heads. It was so horrible I don't want
to write about it.

Yet I must write about it because I now have
proof that your brave man Daniel O'Kelly is
an agent for the Brits, not the kind of proof
that Liam Tomas, the eejit, would believe but
proof enough.

A fortnight ago, me Aunt Mary, whose husband Joe keeps the public house at the cross
in Oughterard, sent a note to me ma to ask
if they could have the loan of me for a week

and their young woman going off to visit her mother in Sligo.

I like Aunt Mary and Uncle Joe so I was happy to go up there, especially since some of the men of the flying column are hiding in the farms outside of Oughterard and meself not setting eyes on Liam Tomas for almost a month.

Well, worse luck for me, Liam Tomas wouldn't come into town because he was under orders not to show his face until the IRA moved to its next plan of action. My friend Mick Collins has the Brits on the run all right, though people are saying that they have him on the run too because the IRA are running out of ammunition.

I wish the war would be over and Ireland would be free and the Brits go home and Liam Tomas and I could be together for always.

Wishing won't make it so. I pray too and light candles every morning at Mass. Maybe that will help.

Yesterday was a grand summer day, a few clouds and blue sky, and we perishing with the heat in the pub and Uncle Joe gone to market in Galway. Late in the afternoon, the whole world still and peaceful and only a few men in the pub, I heard a motor car pull up outside. There's not many motor cars in this part of County Galway these days with everyone worried about the lads and the Tans. So I peeked out the window and, glory be to God, wasn't it the Tans themselves, in their black trousers and their tan coats, looking like they owned the whole of Ireland?

" 'Tis the Tans," I whispered to Aunt Mary, who is only ten years older than I am and easily frightened.

"The Holy Saints preserve us," she shrieked. "They'll murder the lot of us."

"We must keep calm." I hugged her. "Tell Joe Pete to sneak out the back way and go out in the woods by the lake and tell the lads that we're being invaded."

Daniel O'Kelly has told them not to attack until they receive the new plan of action, unless there's a provocation. I said to myself, sure, if the Black and Tans invading Oughterard is not a provocation, nothing is.

And themselves shooting down innocent civilians all over Ireland, even Catholic seminarians, and burning others alive.

They didn't come in to the pub right away. Instead they walked across the street to Maeve McManus's little tobacco shop, swaggering like they were the Black Watch or the Highland Guards instead of a bunch of mercenaries and criminals and soldiers of fortune.

I was pretty sure from watching them that they had already the drink taken. It was going to be a long night in Oughterard, let me tell you.

One of them takes out a pistol and smashes Maeve's window with its butt. Then they go into the shop and the next moment out comes poor old Maeve and herself falling flat on her face in the dust and laying there like she's afraid to move. I reach down in me drawers and make sure I can pull out me knife quickly if I have to.

Then they throw little Tommy, Maeve's grandson who helps her out, into the dust too and one of them comes out and kicks Tommy two or three times, and himself only a little gosson about ten years old.

By this time I'm praying something fierce to the Mother of God to send the lads in a hurry.

The Tans strolled down the street, smashing windows, beating storekeepers, stealing whatever they wanted.

"Mother of God, protect us!" Aunt Mary screams as they smash our window. Then they push into the pub.

The first thing I notice is that all but one of them, and himself a sergeant or something important, are young fellas, no older than our lads out in the hills and the hedges. I don't have much time to think about it, but I do wonder what war does to young men to make them join the Tans after it's over. Uncle Joe says that maybe it's the only job they can find.

"Bring us your best whiskey," shouts the sergeant, "and none of that Irish piss either."

They all laugh and sit around two of the big tables. As meek and quiet as turtledoves, don't Mary and I bring them two bottles of scotch, the last two bottles we have?

"Would you look at this?" One of them grabs

for me. "Two Irish cunts, isn't that nice now?"

I dodge him this time and meself wondering what will happen when they have more of the drink taken.

Mary is already crying.

"Where are your men?" another shouts at me. "Out in the hedges with them Irregular bastards?"

"Me Uncle Joe has gone to Galway for the market," I says, trying to sound real bold and confident, but I'm petrified altogether.

"Isn't that nice for us?" And they all laugh.

"Would you look at the tits on that one?" The sergeant points at me. "She should be fun, what do you think, men?"

They laugh again. They're still just talking but I'm thinking that if they keep on talking that way, they'll talk themselves into something.

All the time I'm praying as hard as I can.

"The older cunt has a neat little ass." A blond boy sneers, trying to pinch poor Mary. "What do you say, shall we bugger her?"

They all howl at that and Mary is sobbing now.

There's no mercy in any of them. I keep telling myself that today. They showed no mercy; no mercy would be shown to them.

They continued to drink and to smash the pub, breaking glasses and bottles, spilling stout and whiskey on the floor, and wrecking the bar and shattering the mirror of which Uncle Joe was so proud into a million pieces. Mary's near hysterical now. She won't listen to me when I tell her that we can't lose our nerve.

I'm making sure I can pull me knife out real quick when I have to.

I'm also noticing that the sergeant fella is looking at his watch a lot. They're expecting someone else. Regular British army? There's not many of them around here, afraid as they are of the lads ambushing them. RIC? They're even more afraid of being executed by the IRA if they collaborate with the Tans.

My heart sinks at that thought. Haven't they sacked a few towns already to teach the wild Irish a lesson?

"Well, Sarge," says the young blond one. "What do you say? We've messed this town up pretty well. Why don't we have some fun with these two cunts? It's a shame to waste them on the Irish who wouldn't know what to do with a woman if they had one naked and on the flat of her back and her legs pulled apart."

"Or" — another one sneers — "on her belly with her ass in the air!"

Mary starts begging them not to hurt her and meself reaching for me knife.

"You boys have done a good day's work," he says to them. "What harm would there be in a little romp?" He glances at his watch. "But make it quick."

Two of them grab each of us. Mary is screaming and I'm shoving and kicking and reaching for me knife.

"Do it outside," says the sergeant. "Let the people who are peeking out of their doors see what His Majesty's troops do to Irish cunts."

They drag us outdoors, and meself squinting in the bright sunlight and still kicking and fighting as best I can. I can't get at me knife.

They tear off Aunt Mary's skirt and throw her on the ground. She's screaming like a frightened seal.

One of them, the young blond boy, holds me while the other rips me blouse and pulls off the top of me shift. The boy that's holding me tries to grab my breast with one hand, so I finally pull out me knife and shove it in the other's stomach, real hard. He lets out a yell of surprise and grabs at the knife.

"She's stuck Harry," yells the sergeant. "Kill the cunt."

Then I hear shots and I think I'm murdered and meself not even saying an Act of Contrition.

The face of the man I stuck with the knife explodes into a mass of bone and blood and little bits of flesh and his blood spurting all over me skin and skirt. The boy behind me sort of sighs and lets go. I look around and see great globs of blood on his tan uniform.

I'm vomiting all over the place and meself not even noticing it. I try to draw a deep breath and gunpowder fumes choke me and I vomit again, worse this time.

Then I feel Liam Tomas's arm around me

and him whispering soft words.

"It took you long enough to come," says I, and meself vomiting yet again.

He wraps me tattered clothes around me real gentlelike and says, "Glory be to God, woman, you're a desperate one with the knife."

He meant it well, poor dear man, but what he said made me vomit once more and with nothing left to come up.

In a few minutes, I managed to pull meself together so I could take notice of what's happening.

Three of the Tans are dead, the two that had been playing with me and one of those who was trying to get on top of poor Mary, who is clinging to Maeve McManus and sobbing something desperate. The sergeant and the other Tan are tied up with three Lee-Enfields pointing at them. Liam Tomas has routed them with only three other of the lads.

"What will we do with them, Liam?" says me brother Tim, and himself real nervous because, I'm thinking, this is the first time he's ever shot a man up close.

"We'll wait till the commandant comes," says me man, real calmlike, and "then we'll have a court martial. They were caught in the act of abusing civilians. That's punishable by death."

I can see that both the Tans are terrified. The look in their eyes says that they know they're going to die, but they're still hoping for some miracle.

Then who comes ambling down the road, whistling a music hall song, but your man Daniel O'Kelly himself?

"Well," he says with his big smile, which I've always thought was fake, "I can see that you men have used commendable initiative in my absence. Well done, Captain O'Riada."

"Thank you, sir." Liam salutes him like he's in a parade in Sackville Street in Dublin, and meself never seeing a parade in Sackville Street and never even being in Dublin.

[Translator's note: Nell Pat later crossed out "Sackville" and wrote over it "O'Connell." However, she must have done that after she migrated to America because the name of the street was still Sackville at the time she wrote this diary entry. I looked it up. I also learned, however, that most Dubliners were already calling it O'Connell for twenty years because the Dublin Corporation had changed its name but Dublin Castle had reversed the decision. But the news apparently had not got out to the West. I looked that up too. No extra charge.]

I've been noticing that the sergeant looks relieved to see the commandant appear and that O'Kelly is avoiding the Tans' eyes.

So that's who he was waiting for! Daniel O'Kelly is in with the Tans! They came here to meet him. They couldn't keep their hands off the town or off us and spoiled the rendezvous.

"What should we do with these two, Captain?" O'Kelly asks himself.

"We should have a proper court martial, sir. They're guilty of crimes committed during war that are punishable by death."

"You're quite right, Captain." He pulls out his big Mauser and waves it at the sergeant, tormenting him with it. "Absolutely correct, in theory. However, we're not in a theoretical situation, if you take me meaning. The flying squad will have to fly" — he points the gun between the man's eyes — "because the Regulars will be up here in no time when they hear what's happened, unless GHQ orders us to stop them. So I think summary judgment is the indicated action, don't you?"

"Yes, sir," says Liam, kind of uncertainlike.

"But, O'Kelly, you can't —" the sergeant cries out.

O'Kelly grins and pulls the trigger. The Tan drops to the ground like a calf that's been hit in the head.

"Oh yes, I can." He turns the gun towards the other man. "Wouldn't you say, Corporal, that I can?"

He shoots him too.

The look on his face tells me that he enjoyed it more than he would making love to a woman.

"All right, men." He puts his gun back in his pocket. "We'd better clear out of here." He raises his voice. "You townpeople, you didn't hear anything, you didn't see anything. The constables will ask a few questions and leave you alone." The doors around the square open up a wee bit. "If you hear that the Regulars are coming, get out of town and hide in the hedges or on the farms or even on the lake. They'll burn some of the town but they won't chase after you because they're afraid of us."

"Sir," says Liam, real polite, "may I have permission to bring Nell Pat back to her family?"

O'Kelly glances at me, like he's surprised to see me and meself standing there, still shivering and holding the pieces of my clothes together. "Sure, you shouldn't be up here, Nell Pat." He leers at me. "You'll be getting yourself in serious trouble someday if you're not careful, won't you now? Permission denied, Captain. There's a war on and we're under orders to prepare for a new campaign. Unless I miss my guess, today's work will bring the Regulars out in force, which provides us with an excellent opportunity, wouldn't you say?"

"Yes, sir," says Liam, his eyes filled with agony.

"I can take care of meself just fine," I scream at the two of them, "and yourselves such fine examples of Irish manhood!"

"But, Nell —" my Liam pleads.

"Follow your frigging commandant," I shout at him, and using a word I've never spoken before in my life, though I've thought it a lot of times. "I don't care if I never see you again."

Later, when I'm riding home on me pony in the moonlight, I pray to the Mother of God to obtain forgiveness for what I said. What a

345

terrible thing it would be if those are the last words he hears from me and I never do see him again!

So I sob in Ma's arms and try to sleep and I can't. So I get out of me bed and write down these lines.

Tomorrow morning I will light a candle at Mass for the man I killed yesterday. Wasn't the look of death on his face before he was shot?

I'll pray for the repose of his soul every day for the rest of my life.

Now I have to look around and find meself another knife.

– 30 –

"Aren't these the final letters between Mick and Kitty?" herself informed me the next day.

"Are they now?"

"Haven't I said that they are . . . and stop imitating the way I talk."

"Can't help meself!"

"Gobshite bastard," she said, totally rejecting my plea. "Now listen to this one. . . ."

"Would you be wanting to read them to me now?"

She made as if to sock my jaw; the blow became a quick caress at the last minute.

My heart jumped a couple of times. Dear God,

she was beautiful!

"Would you ever fock off?" She adjusted the book and began to read. "He wrote this one in early April. You can tell the strain has taken its toll.

"My dearest Kitty,

"Things are rapidly becoming as bad as they can be and the country has before it what may be the worst period yet. A few madmen can do anything. Indeed they are just getting on the pressure gradually — they go on from cutting a tire to cutting a railway line, then to fire at a barrack, then to fire at a lorry and so on. But God knows I do not want to be worrying you.

"Are you going to Nobber for Easter? Or are you going anywhere? I am most awfully anxious to see you and quickly and this week is going to be a bad week with me by the look of things. I am anxious about you. I wonder if you're writing even today — Yes? No?

"May God bless you.

"Fondest love,
"Micheal."

"He wrote to someone else that he had signed his death warrant when he signed the treaty," I said. "He knew what would happen."

"The poor dear woman could only dream of a quiet life with him after the Troubles were over. Sure, there would never have been any peace if he had lived. But she didn't understand that. This next one is in July, just a month before he died.

"*My own darling Micheal,*

"I went to bed last night about 9 o'clock and, of course, I couldn't sleep, so I was talking to you and my heart ached with longing to have you with me. I was 'madly, passionately, in love with you,' to use your own words, and I understand those feelings now, and I feel that I'm blushing now because I tell you. But sure you know and we both know and remember Greystones and all the other wonderful times.

"Then I went through all the stages of the future until I came to the kind of matter-of-fact stage when we are so used to each other that it would be uncomfortable, cold and something gone wrong, if one or other of us were not there. We mightn't admit it, but it would be a natural sort of feeling. We would wake up in the middle of the night and not be able to sleep peacefully, because there was that something, something not exactly explainable. Now, sure, I wasn't building castles in the air with those dreams. Is that not what will happen? And I forgot to tell you that I decided last night that it was the matter of fact stage I like best, I think.

"I think I am really continuing last night's little romance today. Of course I couldn't tell you here all the nice things I said last night to you, all the love and everything I gave you or will give you, and I found myself promising you faithfully that I'd never have a real row, nor fall out with you at all (now don't laugh, because I'm real serious), if you are not too rough and don't hurt me when we are just playing, just fooling, and a few other little ifs.

"I hope to see you soon. It's three weeks yesterday. A very, very long time, but God is good.

"All my love,

"Your own,
"Kit."

"She was an incorrigible romantic," I said.
"So are you." Nuala was fighting back tears. "This is the last letter she ever received from him. He wrote it on August 8. It's so sad.

"My own dearest Kitty,

"Yesterday I wrote you a note — I think

the most hurried I have ever written to you — most hurried from every point of view and God knows today is not much better. At the time of writing yesterday I was on the point of setting out for a long journey and I did not get back until very late last night. I was in Maryleborough, the Curragh and so on. It was woefully cold and I was petrified when we arrived back at the Barracks. But I went to bed straight and am feeling very well this morning.

"We have had a hard few days here — the scenes at Mass yesterday for the nine soldiers killed in Kerry were really heartbreaking. The poor women weeping and almost shrieking (some of them) for their dead sons. Sisters and one wife were there too and a few small children. It makes one feel I tell you.

"There has been no letter from you. Perhaps you did not get back on Monday — even if a letter would come at such speed — which I'm afraid it wouldn't. But you will write, won't you?

"When are you coming up again? You said next week. And it's next week now. It is, you know. And when are you coming?

"Kitty, don't be cross with me for the way I go around. I can't help it and if I were to do anything else it wouldn't be me and I really couldn't stand it. And somehow I feel the way I go on is better. And please, please do not worry.

"Fondest love,
"Micheal."

Nuala and I sat in momentary silence.
"How she must have treasured that letter."
Nuala nodded, dabbed at her eyes, and tried to sound like a composed TV commentator. "The last letter he received from her was written on the fifteenth of August, the day before Arthur Griffith's funeral and a week before Michael's own death. It's beautiful.

"My own dear Micheal,

"I had a great time with you last night in imagination. It was quite real while it lasted.

"First I'd been making heaps of jam all the evening and was ever so tired. Then about 11, when they had all gone, I had a nice hot bath and after it I felt so clean and fresh (and looked quite nice I think) and found myself wishing that we could only meet when I'd be after a bath and looking nice. A bit too idealistic and far-fetched perhaps.

"Then I went to my room. I was feeling a bit lonely but energetic, so I thought

I'd have a bit of a dress rehearsal for you. I just pictured you there. First, I put on a pink and mauve silk pair of pyjamas and asked you how you liked them? Then next a pink pair — and then a nightie. I decided with you that the nightie was the nicest of all. Then I gave you a hug and felt you'd want to hug me etc. All the very loveliest thoughts were on my mind and then I felt cold and thought how daft I was and then I got into bed still thinking of you and wishing, wishing for heaps of things.

"I can't describe what a night I had almost as good as if you were there. I had the whole top of the house to myself and I could run from mirror to mirror and from room to room.

"I'll try to dream of you again tonight. It will hard to better last night's though.

"All my love,
"Kit

"Hugs and X."

"Not a bad memory to carry with you into paradise, Nuala."

"Is there a paradise, Dermot Michael?"

"Woman, there is."

"Will we meet them there?" Tears were cascading down her cheeks.

"Kit and Mick? Why not?"

"Will they approve of what we're doing now?"

"I sure hope so, Nuala Anne. I sure hope so."

– 31 –

Like Ma the day of the Oughterard massacre, I couldn't sleep. The vivid images conjured up by her diary rushed around in my head. She was a sweet and gentle woman when I knew her — passionate, sure, and sometimes a little crazy. But the wild young girl with a knife in her hand . . . could that have been my Gramma Nell?

Yes, it could very well be her; the only one in Galway who realized that Daniel O'Kelly was a traitor, that could be Ma too.

"Ma doesn't miss much, that's for sure," my own mother would say to me when I was a gosson. "And I don't think she's afraid of anything in the world except perhaps hurting Pa's feelings."

What effect did that wild and vivid story have on Nuala? If it is keeping me awake, what will it do to a sensitive girl who by now thinks she *is* Nell Pat Malone?

She might start carrying a knife too!

I laughed at that picture.

I told myself repeatedly that Nuala was a child, only a year and a half older than Kel when she died. Because she was so good-looking and so smart and so talented and, well, yes, so sensitive to my pain, it was easy to fool oneself into thinking she was at least twenty-five.

She had the right to time of her own in which to grow up, discover herself, develop her talents, create her own world.

Didn't she?

A marriage now would be a terrible mistake for Nuala. It would foreclose the rich possibilities that lay open before her, even if she couldn't see them clearly.

Having thus reassured myself, I dozed and then fell into a deeper but troubled sleep.

I was awakened by a knock at the door, soft and quiet. I lay there in bed, wondering if I had imagined it. No, there it was again.

I wasn't quite sure what time it was or even where I was. I staggered out of bed and, still in my shorts, stumbled to the parlor and over to the door of the suite.

"Yes?" I said thickly, realizing now that I was in a hotel room, but not sure yet where or why.

"Angela."

A woman's voice. At this time of night. What time of night was it anyway? Did I know any woman named Angela?

Had I arranged an assignation with an Angela? How could I have worked up the courage to do that?

I opened the door a crack, recognized Angela Smythe, with a "y" and an "e," and remembered in a burst of illumination where I was and who Angela was.

"May I come in, Dermot?" she said breathlessly.

How could I refuse?

I opened the door and let her in. I remembered that I was in my shorts and felt momentarily embarrassed.

"You look beautiful," she said. "I don't have long, Dermot." She hugged me and continued to cling to me. "I'm leaving on a new assignment, the States actually. I had to see you."

"Are you in trouble, Angela?" I held her close and felt her breasts firmly against my chest and her heart pounding wildly.

"Trouble? Oh, no. Not really. My colleagues here were unhappy with me, but they could hardly complain to the Foreign Office, given the nature of the case. They suggested I ask for a transfer."

"Your name is not Angela Smythe?"

"Of course not. Don't ask what it really is. Everything else I told you was the truth."

"So?"

"I didn't call you again and I canceled Angela at the embassy because I found that I could not keep my part of the agreement. Do you understand what I'm saying, Dermot?"

"I think so."

I also understood that she wanted to make love with me.

"I beg you to be careful. My colleagues are harmless, perhaps even on your side now. They were as shocked as I was to learn about the Consort."

"Consort?"

"Of St. George and St. Patrick. They're the dangerous ones, or some of them. Be careful of them. And don't ruin everything if you do find out the whole truth. There is so much at stake, Dermot. The agreement is only a first step, but it's all we have."

I was a tiny fraction of a millimeter away from taking her to bed. I was entitled to a little pleasure, wasn't I? How could it hurt anyone? She wanted love, needed it probably. So did I.

So why didn't I take advantage of a situation for which many men would long?

I'm not sure. Maybe the presence of the diary on the table behind me and Nuala's insistence that Ma was lurking in the room stopped me.

Ma would not have approved. Definitely not.

"I appreciate the warning, Angela . . . and the integrity of your visit. I'll keep in mind everything you said" — I gently disengaged from her — "and if you don't mind, I'll look you up in Washington when I go home, which will be soon."

She got the message — and took it with style. "Yes, please do, Dermot. I'll be in the trade section of the embassy. If you merely walk into the office, I'm sure you'll be able to find me."

"Good-bye, Angela."

"Good-bye, Dermot." She kissed me quickly. "Please be careful."

Back in bed and now wide awake, I was filled with regret, not a sense of virtue.

I was what Ma would have called in an irate moment a "galoot." I had done nothing with my life or my talents. I had failed Kel. I had messed up in school. I was a bumbler at the Exchange and had made my wealth by a stupid mistake. Now I was messing in a foolish and possibly dangerous quest and letting down a couple of women, who were even more beautiful than Kel.

Eejit!

Consort? What's a consort? I asked myself. A queen's husband?

More likely a fancy name for a consortium. Or maybe it was vice versa. St. George and St. Patrick? The patrons of the two British Isles. Well, that wasn't fair to St. Andrew or St. David, who had been assigned Scotland and Wales respectively, was it now?

The patrons of England and Ireland. Did those two even talk to each other in heaven?

None of it made any sense. Nothing made any sense.

You're a fool I told myself.

Finally I slept, only to be awakened at nine o'clock with a handwritten note from Lord Longwood-Jones inviting me and Nuala to lunch the next day at his town house.

What were those two handsome folk up to now?

– 32 –

"You ought to be visiting your parents the weekend after next," I said to Nuala. "And themselves dying to see you, aren't they now?"

Her hair wet from swimming, she was working on the translation again. I was about to take my turn in the pool. We had disengaged, by implicit mutual consent or so it seemed to me, from swimming together.

"Would you be giving me the weekend off again?"

"I didn't say that, did I now?"

She turned away from the Compaq to look at me. My heart — and other crucial parts of me — surged with affection for her. She looked so pretty and so vulnerable in her light blue sweater and dark blue shirt.

At that minute I wanted her more than I had "Angela" when that woman was in my arms, leaning against my naked chest.

"You did not," she agreed. "What did you mean?"

"I meant that I want to meet your ma and da."

"No!" she said promptly and vigorously. "I'll not have that at all, at all."

"You're ashamed of me, are you now?"

"*No!*" She whirled around and began to pound furiously on the computer keys.

"You're ashamed of them?"

"I won't have you making fun of them."

That reaction, I argued mentally, was proof of the immaturity that justified my refusal to respond to her protestations of love.

I strode across the room, captured her face in both my hands, and forced her to look at me. "It really is time for that nonsense to stop, Nuala Anne McGrail. Have I ever said or done anything that would lead you to believe I would make fun of your parents?"

A thunder cloud of rage sped across her face and then went on, out into the Irish Sea.

"And themselves having such a bitch of a daughter," she said sadly.

"I thought we forbade self-hatred on this job."

A smile tugged at her lips. "Sure, you don't give the poor woman a chance, do you now?"

My hands seemed somehow to want to caress her. So I took them off her face. "We go to Galway next weekend."

"Yes, boss." She winked, struggling to hold back her tears. "And we'll make a booking for you at a hotel in Salt Hill, except you'll have to tell me how to make a hotel booking."

I sat down for a moment on the couch next to the desk. "Call the concierge and ask her to do it. And also make a booking, two rooms both with bath, at the Imperial Hotel in Cork. We'll leave Thursday morning and stay Thursday night in Cork. Then Friday, Saturday, and Sunday in Galway. I'm sure there's no harm in you missing a day or two of class."

"In Cork, is it?" Her hands paused above the keys. "We'll be driving through Bealnablath?"

"We will."

"What do you expect to find there? Mick Collins's ghost?"

"I want to see it."

"So it isn't just a weekend off?"

" 'Tis not."

"In Galway, you'll be wanting to see the places in the story?"

I stood up. Time for the swim. "And talk to your parents to see if there's any memories of those days."

She nodded agreement. "I want to know too."

Would she be more obsessed by her imaginings of Ma's presence out there in the site of the stories in the diary? I would have to keep a close eye on her.

It was, I quite agree in retrospect, a dumb resolution. No one kept a close eye on Nuala Anne, especially on her own turf.

"I especially want to climb Mamene."

"You don't think the gold is still up there, do you?" Her eyes were wide as she turned around to face me again.

"It might be. I can't find any reports of it ever being found in the books about Roger Casement."

"What will you do with it if you find it?"

"Twenty million pounds in bullion? Give it to Ireland. Who else does it belong to?"

"Grand." She nodded her approval and smiled affectionately. "I shouldn't have had to ask that, should I now?"

Get out of here, Coyne, before you do something that both of you will regret.

"And, Nuala, tell the concierge to book my usual car. . . . Do you have a driver's license?"

"Meself? Sure, I've never driven a car in all me life."

"You can work on the translation in the car."

"It'll be keeping me out of trouble."

I went out to the public phone and checked in with George and told him about my plans to journey to the West of Ireland. I didn't tell him it was Nuala's plan.

"With herself?" he asked.

"Who?"

"The person who answers the phone. She'll be with you on your pilgrimage to the West?"

"I want to meet her family. They may remember the old stories about Ma and Pa."

"Indeed they might."

"There's nothing in it, George."

"Send me her picture, will you?"

"I don't have her picture."

"Your camera broken?"

"No."

"Surely you'll take it with you to Carraroe?"

"I suppose so."

"So send me a picture."

"You're worse than Mom."

George chuckled. "We clergy have a vested interest in the continuation of the species . . . and in human love, which gives us a hint of God's love."

"Sure," I said, and hung up.

George was a nice man and a good priest, but he should mind his own focking business.

Yet he was correct, I should have a photo of Nuala to keep with me for the rest of my life.

She had left the suite before I returned, as I had hoped she would. As usual there was a printout of the translation. This time another note was attached.

Two for the price of one this time, Dermot Michael. I don't know whether you'll like the second entry. I did.

N.

– 33 –

July 24, 1921

We heard today that there is a truce between the British and the Irish government. The order to stand down from fighting hasn't reached Galway yet, but everyone says it will in a day or two. The IRA is worn out from fighting. So are the British. Mick Collins has won his war. They say Collins and Dev, the Big Fella and the Long Fella, and Arthur Griffith are going to London to negotiate a treaty that will make Ireland free.

So we've won.

There is little rejoicing at our house here in Carraroe. We buried Tim yesterday. He was shot in a skirmish with the Tans, probably after they had agreed in Dublin on the truce.

Peace and freedom and victory don't seem worth the loss of my only brother and himself just nineteen, the same age as Liam Tomas, who is beside himself with grief, the two of them being friends since they were both gossons.

Everyone is still weeping, especially Moire and herself due any day now, everyone but me. I can't cry yet. I will soon, maybe today, maybe tomorrow, but now I'm numb and cold and angry at God.

Why does he give us men like Tim and then take them away before they can even see their own children?

Why does he let the Brits rule our country for so long and themselves being Protestants at that? Why do our men have to die so that Ireland can be free?

It doesn't seem fair.

It was always Liam Tomas that I worried about. I took it for granted that Tim would be all right, though I prayed for him too, God knows — but kind of as an afterthought.

I woke up this morning convinced that he was still alive and that it was a terrible dream. Then I heard Ma weeping softly and I knew that the nightmare was true and me dream was false.

Will my Liam be next? Da says that there'll be skirmishes despite the truce and that not all the lads will accept any treaty the English might give us. Will the shooting continue? Will a stray bullet find Liam's back too?

We still love one another; but we have such a hard time talking. He knows I don't trust Daniel O'Kelly. He can't understand why. He tells me that I'm the only person in County Galway who doesn't worship the ground that his commandant or colonel or whatever he calls himself now walks on. And I tell him that if what he says is true, and I doubt it, then I'm the only one in Galway that's not an eejit.

In my heart I don't think it was a Tan bullet that killed Tim. I think he was shot in the back by Daniel O'Kelly about whom he'd found out something terrible.

The last time Tim was here at home, on the run at night as always, he said to me, "Little one, you might not be all wrong about the colonel."

He wouldn't tell me any more. Now he never will.

Eternal rest grant unto him, O Lord. May perpetual light shine upon him. And I promise You and him that there'll be justice. Daniel O'Kelly will not get away with murder.

I won't let him kill my Liam too.

Dear God in heaven, please help poor Moire. Not even twenty and she's already a widow and herself about to give birth to her first child.

She's pretty and good-natured and has some fine land, so she'll dry her tears and find herself another good husband eventually, not that I blame her for it. She'll always have the wee one to remind her of Tim. Still, she's desolate now and she needs strength and faith. So You'd better help her, do You hear me?

What if I should lose Liam too, and ourselves not even married, not even thinking of being married? Well, at least not saying a word to each other about it.

I won't have anything to remember except a couple of kisses stolen on the strand at night

— and a lot of harsh words when I was angry at him, poor dear man.

I don't want to lose him that way. If he is killed, if that terrible man shoots him in the back, I want more to remember.

I hope You aren't too angry at me for thinking such terrible things. I know the priests, even the young priest who is so kind and understanding, would say that I'm thinking about a terrible mortal sin.

Meself, I'm not so sure that for us it would be. I'm willing to trust in Your love for me.

You see, dear God of my heart, I love him like You love me. I will always love him. I will never stop loving him. I believe that You will always love me and never stop loving me.

So, whatever I do or try to do, You'll be there loving me and Liam. I know You'll take care of us always. Even as You take care of all of us all the time. I'm sorry I was angry at You about Tim. You understand so much more than I do.

I give You fair warning, O Lord. I'm not going to make it easy for You to take care of me, and it being Your own fault for making me so stubborn and contentious.

And Yourself, just like Liam Tomas, loving me the way I am.

– 34 –

June 1922

Them that says lovemaking is a terrible burden are liars!

'Tis the grandest thing in all the world, even if like my Liam and I you're novices at the game.

[Translator's note: I can't believe she did it, and myself knowing all along that she would! I don't think it was sin either, not with all that killing and dying all around them. I know the tale has a happy ending, but as I read her words, I feel that her Liam will die and she'll be all alone like Moire with a child and herself not being the kind that would ever find another husband. I can tell you one thing: The tone of her voice as I hear these words says that she's not ashamed or sorry at all. Mind you, she'd never approve of her daughters or grand-daughters doing the same thing!

[I'll erase this from the hard disk after I print it out. I know you're dying to hear about me daft reactions to this story!]

There are a group of Tans in the neighbor-hood. They're still angry about what happened in Oughterard and the regular army being ambushed on the way up to burn the town by the Clare and Galway flying squads. They're looking for a few innocent people to kill before the English government pulls them out and sends them to Palestine.

They'll not be finding any victims because people fade away when they hear that the Auxiliaries are coming. The lads keep track of them and shoot out their tires. The orders are not to kill them unless they are about to kill civilians.

The night before last Liam and two other lads blew up the Tans' motor car by shooting their Mausers at the gasoline tanks over in Salt Hill. It made a grand fire, I'm told.

The lads use the Mausers now even though they have only a few bullets for each one of them because they don't have any more bullets for their Lee-Enfields.

So yesterday morning even before the sun comes up, doesn't Liam Tomas sneak into our house? He's under orders, he says, to hide here until the lads are sure that the Tans have taken the train back to Dublin.

"Good riddance to them," says I.

"You'll be wondering why we didn't just shoot them?"

"I am not. Sure, didn't the Big Fella tell you not to violate the truce?"

" 'Tis yourself that should be in London, negotiating the treaty with Mick and Art and Eamon." He grins his big wonderful grin at me.

"I'd be doing a better job at it than a bunch

of stupid men, excepting me good friend the Mick of course."

Well, we both laugh and we're friends again. The rest of the day was very pleasant and meself biting off my tongue not to start another one of me fights. Moire brings over young Nell Tim, who is a little handful, let me tell you, almost as bad as her godmother, and my ma and da loving Liam almost as much as they loved poor Tim.

I miss him every day. I cry for him almost every day at Mass. The young priest says I'm a deep one.

[Translator's note: I called the store in Carraroe where I leave messages for my own ma and da. When they call me back I'll ask them to see if the parish priest has any records of marriage for Nell Tim Malone. We might be able to find where she lives. I wonder if your ma and pa kept in touch with her. And herself asking me whether I'm a terrible eejit altogether for thinking that they wouldn't keep their eye on her godchild, no matter where she lived.]

While Liam is napping in the afternoon, I take some sheets and blankets and some candles to the old ruined house over by our lough and make a little bed where a couple could sleep for a few hours if they wanted to.

After tea when it starts to get dark, me ma and da leave for a wake in Oughterard, taking the pony and the jaunting car. They say they'll be back by midnight at the latest, and I'm not

369

doubting that because they're uneasy about the way Liam and I are laughing.

I suppose if I were them I'd be uneasy too. There's no telling what wild kids will do when there's a war going on.

So Liam and I leave for a walk on the strand.

"I hope there's peace, Nell Pat," he says, so tired and weary. "This war will be the destruction of all of us if it goes on much longer."

" 'Tis a terrible thing, I agree," putting my arm around him.

"I thought I was a brave soldier." He hardly seems to notice me. "I'm not. I was not meant for fighting and killing."

"I'm thinking that's a true thing if there ever was one . . . but now there's a truce, isn't there?"

"The commandant is saying that Mick Collins is a traitor, himself and Art Griffith and Bill Cosgrave and Kevin O'Higgins, and that they've sold us out to the English. So maybe we won't observe the truce."

"And what will you not observe it with — make-believe bullets?"

"Aye, that's the truth, isn't it now? Ah, I'm thinking it doesn't make much difference anymore. Sure, we don't have the bullets to fight the National Army if we wanted to, and I'm not sure I want to, not with the Big Fella saying that we should accept the treaty."

"And I'm thinking that after it's all over and Ireland is free finally, you and I will have a lot of things to talk about."

"Ah, that is as it may be."

Then he begins to kiss me, so fierce as to take my breath away.

This time I don't even pretend not to want it. I kiss him back every bit as fierce.

Then he begins to caress me, something a man has never done before, except the poor man I killed in Oughterard. I know it's going to happen and I'm not sure that I'll like it. But when Liam does it to me, I think I'm going to die with joy.

So we walk along the strand and the moon is coming up, just like God arranged the light for us, and we're kissing a lot and Liam is playing with me and I love it and before we know it we're at the abandoned house.

I whisper an aspiration to the Our Lady that there be no rain tonight.

I take my man by the hand and lead him into the house and light the candles. He stands at the door, looking at the clean sheets and the flowers and the jug of poteen I've stolen from me father, and knowing what I intend and himself not sure and maybe a little frightened too.

It's up to me, as I knew it would be. So, petrified with fear, and also to tell the truth dying of curiosity, I take off me blouse and skirt, real quicklike, and stand there in me shift

371

for Liam to look at.

"Nell Pat," he says, still terrible hesitant. "We shouldn't!"

"We should too," says I, not even perfectly sure what we should do, though God knows I've seen the animals do it often enough and I'm not thinking we're all that different from them.

He doesn't move, though I can tell he likes what he sees and why shouldn't he?

I take a deep breath and slip off me shift so that I'm standing there in me drawers. I'm terrified with love and shame and doubt. But there's no turning back now, is there?

So I kick off my drawers and stand there with my arms outstretched, offering all that I am to my love. He's drinking me in with his eyes, like I'm a cool glass of water at the end of a long day.

Then I walk over to Liam, take his hands, and put them on my bosom where I know he wants them to be and undo the buttons on his shirt.

Well, I won't put anything more down on paper, except to say that it was a grand night and both of us had a grand time and we couldn't do it often enough before we had to go back to the house to beat me parents.

And didn't me man sneak into my room after Ma and Da were asleep and love me again?

That was the most fun of all.

Nell Pat, you wonderful woman!

Of course you want the story told. Why else would you have left the diaries? Why else would you have made him bring me here?

He'll never solve the mystery without my help, not at all, at all.

Sometimes I think he knows that, and other times I don't. I wish I could understand him better. Is he a mystery because he's a Yank, oops, Irish American or because he's a man or because he's this particular man?

Could I do what you did to win your man?

I don't think so. It was a time of war and death then and it isn't now. Women have more options than they did in your time. I have my career to think about, don't I?

I know that you're after telling me that the two of us are not supposed to imitate you and your man. I'm not even sure my man, if he's my man and I don't know that at all, at all, would succumb the way yours did. Probably he wouldn't.

So probably I won't.

But at some point I'm going to challenge him just the same.

There's lots of good reasons why I shouldn't, but I don't care. I'm not going to let him get away without telling him what I think.

I don't know whether my love is a lifelong love like yours, but I don't care about that either.

I'm going to have it out with your man and that's that.

The poor amadon has no idea what we're going to find out in Galway. I'd better keep a close eye on him. Otherwise he'll make some terrible mistake.

I love him, I love him so much.

When I'm through writing these notes to you I will erase them from the floppy disk I'm putting them on.

– 35 –

"You didn't tell me that we were to have lunch with the toffs."

"Even the perfect boss forgets now and then."

We were in His Lordship's Rolls inching our way through heavy traffic and heavy rain.

"Like you forgot to check in with George day before yesterday and himself calling me all filled with concern, poor dear man."

"You set his mind at ease, I gather."

"Wouldn't you'd forget your head if it wasn't fastened on?"

"That's probably true."

"So here I am in their fock — in their grand Rolls-Royce, looking like a shopgirl and meself planning a big batch of translation this afternoon."

Nuala's complaints were for the record only. She was pleased to be invited for lunch at the Longwood-Joneses', confident now that she was more than a match for the poshes.

She was wearing her gray outfit, with the light gray sweater and a silver Celtic cross around her neck, the latter a recent addition to her wardrobe.

She was not afraid to spend her money or to give it away to the travelers who begged on the streets.

Yet somewhere there was a computer file that budgeted every penny, of that I was sure.

She had not brought along her rain slicker. "Sure, won't your man Arthur be having an umbrella for me? You really don't understand how the poshes live, do you, Dermot Michael?"

"You might look like a hippie if you choose," I said to her in the Rolls after the chauffeur had shut the glass barrier between himself and us, "Nuala Anne, but never a shopgirl."

"You're just making excuses for humiliating me altogether." She was grinning broadly, enjoying herself immensely.

This one never lets up on you.

"I'll not humiliate you by staggering down the stairs after lunch."

"We'll have to wait and see, won't we now? And why are you calling home everyday?"

I glanced at her. As I expected, she had her shrewd, fishmonger expression. "My family worries about me."

"Shouldn't you be calling your ma?"

"She's busy with her patients. George is kind of a communication center."

She wasn't satisfied with my answer, but she decided to drop the matter for the moment. I would have to tell her the whole story before our trip in a few days to Cork and the West. What would she think of it all, especially given her weird identification with Ma?

"You haven't said whether you were shocked by what herself did in the abandoned house, have you now?"

Damn right I haven't.

"Each generation thinks it has invented sex, Nuala, and is shocked and not a little displeased to discover that its predecessors enjoyed it too."

"That sounds like a line from one of your stories."

"It isn't, but now that you mention it, it surely will be."

"And yourself never bothering to back up your hard disk either." She was launched on a new complaint. "Isn't it a good thing that I'm a responsible person?"

"That's why I hired you, Nuala."

She laughed. " 'Tis not, at all, at all. . . . And wasn't I asking the poor priest if he had made copies of your grandma's diary should there be the odd fire in your hotel?"

"Had he?"

That was something else I had planned to do. Memory was never my strong point.

"Brilliant, Dermot Michael, just brilliant. Sure, 'tis a surprise to me that you've managed to survive as long as you have without a minder taking care of you."

"Did George make copies?" I snapped at her.

"Is the Pope Catholic?" she sniggered back.

"You'll be the death of me, woman," I protested. "You'd try the patience of a saint."

"Would I now . . . but what do you think about herself in the cottage without a roof and herself without a stitch on?"

That subject was not to be avoided, even if we were at the bottom of FitzWilliam Street only a couple of blocks from the Longwood-Jones town house.

I was afraid that her identification with Ma was so strong now that she'd feel bound to try the same tactics on me. Would I be able to resist them?

If she was as blatant as Ma seems to have been, not a chance. If Nuala wanted me that badly I'd be a pushover.

She was not, however, Ma, not really. Rather she was, for all her shyness, better educated and hence more sophisticated and hence, I devoutly hoped, more inhibited.

"She wanted him, Nuala." I shrugged my shoulders. "And she was afraid he would be killed like her brother. There was a war on and danger and death lurked everywhere. In peacetime she would have pursued him just as effectively if somewhat less spectacularly. The poor man, if you ask me, never had a chance, maybe from his tenth birthday on."

"You're not really shocked?"

"No, not really. A little surprised at first maybe, but not shocked. Ma was a passionate woman till the end of her life."

Nuala's pretense was that she was objective, merely trying to explore my thinking — if I was to believe this particular mask, which of course I didn't.

"And you're not thinking they committed a terrible mortal sin, are you?"

"We all had better leave that to God, who, as your friend Prester George would say, is neither a catechist nor a moral theologian."

"Praise be to God." She sighed.

Ma and Pa were passionate people, not merely sexually hungry, but the kind of young folk who followed their strongest instincts through life and never looked back. A little bit of education drains that out of you. It makes you think twice, which is often a good idea but not always.

In Merrion Square Arthur dutifully opened his umbrella and conducted the Lady Nuala Anne up the door stoop, while I trailed behind. At the door, however, she linked her arm around mine. Today we would play the sweethearts' game for the toffs.

"So good of you to come." Martin dithered in the parlor after we had been conducted to it by the butler. "Liz and I had such a nice time talking with you the other night that we thought it would be most pleasant to have a more, ah, personal chat."

"I do so prefer informal lunches to formal dinner parties," Liz agreed.

Informality meant a three-piece dark gray suit for him and a long light gray dress for her. In my yuppie uniform — dark blue blazer and chino slacks — I was the only one out of sync in the gray symphony on this gray Dublin day.

"Some sherry?" Martin gestured towards a full bottle on the coffee table. "It's rather on the dry side, but I think you might like it."

"Yes, thank you," said Nuala. "Actually I rather like dry sherry."

The little fraud didn't know the difference between dry and sweet, of that I was sure. "Waste not, want not, as my ma — Grandma that is — always used to say."

"The woman from Galway?" Martin asked casually.

Was he involved in this business? Was he a member of the Consort of St. George and St. Patrick? Perhaps its head?

"Yes indeed, a fierce little woman named Nell Pat Malone, Pat for her father, I guess, to distinguish her from another Nell, Nell Mike or Nell Joe or whatever."

"Didn't you say that they had to leave during the Troubles?"

"Yes. As best as I can reckon, my grandfather

379

was on the far fringe of the IRA, as Collins's Irish Volunteers came to be known. He seems to have been on the antitreaty side during the Civil War, against Collins, that is. Then they left, rather suddenly, apparently under threat of death."

The sherry was excellent. I resolved that I would have two glasses of sherry and two glasses of wine and not another drop. Herself might just let me fall on my face in the rain today.

"There were a lot of hatreds left over when peace finally came." Martin sighed. "A lot of scores to be settled. A number of people left at the time, sick to death of all the fighting and hatred. There seems to have been some unspoken agreement that if you went into exile you were granted an immunity from execution."

"Did your grandparents," Liz asked, "have any communication with their families in Ireland after they left?"

"They never said much about Ireland or their families. I knew that Ma had a brother Tim to whom she was very close and that he died young, but I never was told how he died. Now I wonder if he was killed in the war."

"Poor boy." Liz refilled my glass.

"Occasionally they spoke of relatives somewhere else in the States. They might have even visited them. But my recollection is that once they came to America, they wiped the slate clean and began a new life."

"How difficult that must have been."

"Immigration is never easy," Nuala said grimly. "It's like a divorce from your own country and people."

"Very true, my dear." Martin had adopted a professorial tone. "You may be unjust to your grandfather, however, Dermot, in describing him as a radical. The lines were not clearly drawn in those days. Personal loyalties to commanding officers were much more important than principled positions on the treaty."

He spoke with the confidence of someone who had the conversation on the right track. But what track was it?

"So I gathered."

"Looking back on it" — the lecture was now flowing easily — "the miracle is that Ireland ever survived as a nation. Surely there were many who did not expect that it would, particularly after Collins was shot. You see, most of the ordinary folk were more than satisfied with the treaty — peace and freedom, if you know what I mean. Moreover, the IRA GHQ in Dublin knew that it did not have the munitions to continue a war. However, the political leaders were badly split, although I think none of them really wanted or expected a civil war. Both sides reckoned that the other side would collapse. Men like Brugha thought that their deaths would stir the people as the deaths of the 1916 martyrs had. They completely misread the popular reaction. People were tired of martyrs."

What the hell was he up to?

"Idiots," Nuala said crisply, nodding to Liz that, yes, of course she would have another wee sip of sherry.

With the toffs she didn't say eejits.

"You must not be too hard on them, my dear. Those were wild and uncertain times. Perhaps one should not have revolutions, but, you see, when one does, the revolutionaries will almost always fall out one with another over principle. That is exactly what happened. Poor Michael Collins was the one man in the leadership who tried to keep both sides happy. The remarkable thing is not that he failed but that he almost succeeded. Griffith was under no illusions about De Valera and his faction. He wanted to crush them completely. Dev made an error in judgment, one of the few in his life and one he would correct a few years later when he took the oath and joined the government. However, he was implacably against the treaty at the time. And he never quite forgave the Big Fella for being the man who made Ireland, as Tim Pat Coogan calls him in his book."

"Occasionally in error but never in doubt?" I murmured.

"Which is just what your man's brother the priest says about himself." Nuala chuckled lightly.

"In the spring and summer and autumn of 1922, the time your grandparents left I assume —"

"Yes. In the fall."

He knew too damn much about Ma and Pa. So he was worried about them too.

"At that time" — he hardly noticed my correction — "the country was in chaos. Perhaps half the IRA commands accepted the treaty out of loyalty to Collins, if nothing else. The other half rejected it. Many if not most of the latter had done little fighting during the Anglo-Irish War. The new National Army of the Free State that Collins had pulled together was an untried force. As you may remember, the dissidents in Dublin, Rory O'Connor and Cathal Brugha, the so-called defense minister of the republic, seized the Four Courts and the Gresham Hotel. Both men were friends of Collins, as was Harry Bolland, another one of the dissidents."

"And his rival for Kitty Kiernan," Nuala noted.

"Precisely. You know your history well, my dear."

"I've made a study of those times."

Fraud!

"So Collins hesitated and pleaded. His friends were convinced he was a traitor. It is said that Bolland's last words when he died in an attempt of the National Army to arrest him in Skerries was 'Have they got Mick Collins yet?'"

"Before he died on the operating table," Nuala corrected him.

It is the nature of Irish women to correct men when they are wrong, even on small details.

Especially on small details.

"Finally, Griffith, O'Higgins, and Cosgrave, the new hard-liners if you will, insisted on action. The Four Courts were demolished by gunfire and with them most of the archives of Irish history. Brugha was killed, O'Connor and Childers were executed later, and the Civil War began."

"A horrible time."

Right, and one that herself and I had already demonstrated we understood, she with more accuracy about the details than he. Why the history lesson?

"No one expected it to happen. They were all bluffing. Finally the bluffs were called and the country was plunged into chaos. Units of the IRA controlled most of the country, but it was a weak control. In the meantime, British troops were still under attack, the National Army was unproven, and the Provisional Government with Collins as chairman, minister of defense, and minister of finance — oh, yes, he was a financial genius too among other things — did not seem strong enough to restore order, although it had won an overwhelming victory in the Dáil election, which was supposed to be a plebiscite on the treaty."

"He had the people on his side then?" I asked, knowing damn well that he did but playing the game with him.

"Oh, yes, indeed. And the bishops and most of the clergy for that matter."

"He said once," Nuala observed primly, "that he half wished the bishops were not on his side."

The woman would not be silent. No way.

"He did indeed, my dear. You must have made quite a study of that era. Most young people your age are not interested. . . . Nonetheless, Westminster was most reluctant to provide the arms and munitions that the National Army needed. You must remember the violence of the previous years. Collins wiped out the English intelligence unit here in one raid. Then the Black and Tans sprayed Croke Park with weapon fire during a football game and killed forty people. They burned Cork City almost to the ground. The Irish destroyed several convoys of British troops and shot up the Tans whenever they found them. Then they assassinated Sir Henry Wilson, the former British chief of staff, on Collins's order. There was a general feeling in England, I very much fear, that the Irish were a savage people."

"Occupying as they were someone else's country?"

Martin smiled mirthlessly. "Precisely, Dermot. Moreover, many people here were tired of the violence and death. I daresay that if you were sitting in this house with my own grandfather and a group of his friends in 1922, drinking sherry as we are now and at this very table, you would have agreed that the Provisional Government would fail and the only way to stop the bloodbath would be to restore British rule, however temporarily."

"We would have been wrong."

"Only just. Churchill had ordered General McCready to storm the Four Courts and might have insisted if the Free State troops had not attacked first. Grandfather, I might remark, was an Irish patriot who believed in home rule and peace. He deplored the violence and naturally supported the treaty, however problematic its success seemed at the time. We have some splendid correspondence with his friend from the Boer War days, Winston Churchill, in which he tells poor old Winston how badly he understands Ireland."

"Winston always did misunderstand Ireland," Liz remarked as if she had known Churchill personally.

"An imperialist character to the bitter end," I added.

"Oh, yes," Nuala agreed, showing me that she had really been doing her homework. "He gave a speech in which he warned the Provisional Government that if they didn't wipe out the rebels in the Four Courts, Britain must consider the treaty void. That almost produced the opposite effect. Collins said that Churchill should come over to Ireland and do his own dirty work."

This from a young woman who two weeks ago wasn't quite sure who Michael Collins was and had barely heard of Winston Spencer Churchill.

"I hate to interrupt this discussion," Liz said as she stood up, "but I'm afraid luncheon is ready. It's a cold snack — I hope you don't mind, my dear?"

"I rather like cold lunches." Nuala rose gracefully, placing her sherry glass on the table with a hand that was steadier than mine, and herself drinking three glasses compared to my two. "Warm lunches make one so sleepy in the afternoon, especially after one has helped to demolish a bottle of sherry."

Her accent was so much Dublin now that you'd be willing to bet that she too was Anglo-Irish.

"Yes, we did rather finish it off." Martin seemed surprised. "Didn't we?"

"Destroyed it altogether." I pretended that I was from the West of Ireland, much to the general amusement of the group.

"Yank that he is" — Nuala sighed — "Dermot is not used to drinking sherry at lunch."

More laughter.

Bitch.

The "cold snack" was in fact a large meal, an assortment of pâtés, jellies, salads, and cuts of meat and smoked fish. Nuala's vast blue eyes glowed in delight.

There was, needless to say, white wine. Two bottles of it.

"The mistake we would have made had we been here in, let us say, the spring of 1922," Martin said returning to his lecture, "was to underestimate the importance of organization and administration, even in a guerrilla war. Genius that he was, Collins did not make that mistake. He controlled the apparatus. Once he had concluded, however reluctantly, that the conflict was inevitable, he went about fighting it with the skill and determination with which he did everything."

Would he ever get to the point? I glanced at herself. She frowned, perhaps warning me not to push.

"He was a most complex man," Liz observed.

"Oh, yes, indeed. Very much so," her husband continued. "In Britain he had the image of the gunman, the terrorist, albeit a romantic terrorist, and then, after he died, a great man, a genius whose death hurt both sides. In fact he was something much more — a fastidious administrator with a passion for detail, a careful financial officer who accounted for every penny spent. He saw reality much more clearly than did the romantic revolutionaries around him. He was a quite brilliant mathematician and as late as 1915 wanted to migrate to America and study to be an engineer. His last occupation in England before the Rising was as a bank clerk. In fact, when he told his chief that he was signing up, the chief thought he meant joining the British Army and paid him a bonus. Three years later this bank clerk, still in his middle twenties, was sitting across the conference table from David Lloyd George as the representative of Ireland."

"A bank clerk guerrilla?"

"It was the bank clerk mentality that enabled him to build the structure, if you take my meaning, that survived his tragic death. Looking back on it, there should never been a doubt about the outcome, despite all the doubts that existed then. Rather quickly the National Army cleared out Dublin and the other cities. Cork, for example, was supposed to be a stronghold of the IRA, but Emmet Dalton reduced it in a single day's skirmishing."

"It was a war of skirmishes."

"Quite. Like the Anglo-Irish War before it. We must not think of our more modern total war concepts. These men were not Marxist ideologues bent on destroying the entire social order. Rather they were fighting for control of a society whose basic premises they all accepted. Imagine, for example, this city just before the assault on the Four Courts. The horse show went on, naturally."

"Kitty Kiernan came down for it, and herself in poor health at that," Nuala remarked.

It was all right for her to push towards the point of the history lesson but not for me.

"As did the schools and the theater and the papers and the business corporations and the ships coming in and out of the docks. The battles at the Gresham and the Four Courts were brief fights that we could have heard from this dining room and noted that perhaps we would not have high tea at the Gresham for the next week or

389

two. Men continued to take their afternoon drinks in their pubs or their clubs. The Cork yacht race took place on schedule, even though Emmet Dalton was skirmishing with the Irregulars in the heart of the city. Most Irish businessmen in this city argued about the fighting, you see, though they didn't go near it. Life went on not much differently than it does in Belfast today."

"And the Free State won," Liz said, filling my wineglass again. "I'm glad you like our Galway smoked salmon, my dear."

"I like everything from Galway."

"Mind you," Martin went on, "the death of Collins was a severe blow to the Free State. We have a letter from Winston in our archives in which he says that he will absolutely oppose sending any more arms to the Free State for the National Army and that reassertion of British control is inevitable."

"He wouldn't have been sad about that," Liz said somewhat bitterly. "He believed all his life, as you know if you've read him, that the Irish are incapable of self-government."

"But Kevin O'Higgins and Richard Mulcahy proved at least as determined and more ruthless than Michael Collins," I concluded the story.

"Quite so. O'Higgins was later assassinated, perhaps in reprisal for the execution of Rory O'Connor, but by that time the Free State had won. Lieutenant General Mulcahy lived to ripe old age — he and Dev were the last of the leaders. They never did like one another. I knew Dick of course, listened to him tell stories at the club for hours on end."

"Did he ever say who he thought killed Michael Collins?"

"He never spoke about it, Dermot. I gather that for the record at least he believed that it was an accidental mistake made by a renegade band of Irregulars who had no idea whom they had killed. Why do you ask?"

"I think my grandfather might have pulled the trigger for the fatal shot."

– 36 –

"A lovely woman, isn't she now?" Nuala sprawled on the couch, by her own admission "destroyed altogether."

"She is."

"Pretty boobs. And every inch a lady, isn't she?"

"Every inch."

"Only a tiny bit of a hooker, isn't she?"

Nuala spoke in a flat, dispassionate tone of voice, simply stating an obvious fact. I judged it best to keep my mouth shut.

"And himself, a good and decent and honorable man, isn't he now?"

"He gives that impression."

"Of course, he's full of shite!"

"Ah?"

"He'd only order someone to try to cut us up for a good and holy cause, one that's identified with his own fundamental decency."

"You think he did?"

She paused. "Maybe. What do you think that lunch was all about?"

It was the first hint that this gorgeous young woman was also a detective. Foolishly I paid it little heed. "I'm not sure. I'll have to think about it."

"You have to think about everything, don't you now? Do you ever have a spontaneous reaction to anything or anyone?"

The drink taken had made her contentious. "Sure."

"And after you've thought about it, you always decide to the opposite?"

"Only sometimes."

"I should either take a nap or do my swim." She yawned. "Anyway, I can still walk a straight line."

"So can I."

"And yourself not having half the jars that I had."

"Two-thirds. . . . We're both short hitters, Nuala Anne."

"Isn't it the truth? Do you really think your granda shot Mick Collins?"

"I have a hunch that's what happened.

Why else would they have had to leave the country?"

"Do you think he knew who it was that he killed?"

"That I doubt. Apparently the Irregulars didn't know Collins was in the convoy. Though your man Tim Pat Coogan says they did, but they really didn't intend to kill him. Maybe Ma will tell us more in the diary."

"Sure, I should get to work on it, instead of indulging in me heathen pleasures in the pool."

"Swim first while I think."

She stood up. "Who was this Winston Churchill fella?"

"Who was Winston Churchill?" I repeated in disbelief.

"I know he had something to do with one of the wars, but I don't remember which one." She did not seem apologetic about her appalling ignorance. But she wasn't a history major, was she now?

"Both world wars, Nul. He was first lord of the Admiralty in number one and prime minister in number two. He resigned from the Admiralty after the disastrous attempt to invade Turkey in 1916 and went to the front in France. But he was minister of state for the colonies during the negotiation of the Anglo-Irish treaty. Then the Lloyd George government fell a few months later, partly because a lot of Brits thought that they had given too much to the Irish. He was out of power till 1940 when he became England's wartime prime minister. Remember his 'We will never surrender' speech?"

"Vaguely." She bit her lip. "Sure, I'd better look him up too."

"First you go swimming, you hear?"

She stretched leisurely, her elegant breasts pressing against her sweater, much more compelling boobs than those of Lady Liz. "If you say so, melord. But I'll tell you one thing: It's the gold a lot of them are worried about and not your ma and pa."

"Could be. I keep forgetting about the gold."

"Would you be the one to do that?"

She stretched again, driving me almost out of my mind. I yearned to touch and caress those breasts, to kiss them and nibble at them, to feel her nipples grow firm in my fingers, to fondle her for hours on end.

I should keep those images, I told myself, out of my fantasy life. It was like telling the tides to take a day off.

The phone rang; she instantly became the perfect secretary again. "Mr. Coyne's office. . . . Is that you, Ma? Glory be to God and yourself calling me!"

Her face lit up in an ecstatic smile and she began to speak in Irish, reaching for a notepad and jotting down what her mother was telling her.

"Himself?" She glanced at me and returned to Irish.

It was pretty easy to figure out what she was saying. Her amused smile and mother-with-a-little-boy tone gave it away and deliberately.

"Ah, sure, he's harmless enough. A rich Yank who writes stories and wants everyone to like him. No, he makes no passes, worse luck for me. Sure, he's probably deficient in hormones, if you take me meaning. Am I interested in him? In a manner of speaking, but it's probably a waste of me time. Should I be serious about him? Well, let's wait and see what you think on Saturday morning when we arrive in Carraroe. Ah, glory be to God, woman, no, we'll not put him up at the house. He belongs in one of them fancy hotels in Salt Hill."

Good enough for you, Dermot Michael Coyne.

"Sounds like character assassination," I muttered when she hung up.

"I won't translate a word I said," she insisted triumphantly. " 'Tis none of your fock . . . darn business."

"It is my business because it was all about me and you don't have to translate it because, as you very well know, I figured most of it out."

"Well, anyway, we found out some things about your family, not that they'll do us much good. Your granda was an orphan and there's no trace of him either at his parish or at ours, save for his marriage to one Mary Anne Malone in September of 1922. There's a baptism record for a second Mary Anne Malone born to Timothy Malone (deceased) and Marie or Moire Hurley and a record for the marriage of Moire Hurley Malone to James Flanigan in 1924. The second Mary Anne Malone was married to John Sheerin in San Francisco in May of 1942. So they did migrate because there's nothing more about Moire and her family. Nor is there any record of the burial of your gram's parents. They either migrated or moved from Carraroe to somewhere else in Ireland, and a lot of folk were doing that because, sure, you can't eat scenery, can you now? Me ma says there are few folks who remember the Troubles because there's been so much immigration, but she thinks old Mike Sean Cussack might remember though he's too old to be trusted completely. Satisfied?"

I had never seen my Nuala so animated or so beautiful as when she was talking to her ma. Was that the ur-Nul, the woman behind all the masks? If it was, then she was even more dangerous than I had thought.

"I'll have to think about that too."

"Well, think away." She kicked off her shoes. "I'm going to have me swim."

"Fine."

I sat on the couch trying not so much to figure out how all the pieces fit, but groping for the picture that kept flashing across my brain and then disappearing, like Irish sunlight, before I could grasp it.

It was someone's face, that I knew for sure.

But whose face and where had I seen it?

Nuala reemerged, robe open over her bikini. Ah, how soon modesty vanishes and — passing thought — how solid she is with the muscles of a well-disciplined athlete. Was there anything at which Nuala was not good?

Would she be good in bed, I wondered again, inexperienced at first but exciting like Ma must have been?

Foolish question. Nuala would put on the mask of an accomplished mistress and play that role to perfection too.

I was filled with longing for her — her breasts and her belly and her thighs and her heart and mind and soul. The yearning for was not as imperious as ordinary lust. Rather it was something far more subtle and far more dangerous. Nuala Anne McGrail could be an addiction from which one would never escape.

I thought of a wisecrack about fastening her robe before she went into the corridor and decided against it. "Have a nice swim, Nul."

"Won't I do just that?" She swished out of the room, a galleon under full sail — and with guns loaded and ready to fire.

I pictured her running naked through the woods, black hair flowing in the wind and rain.

Naked in the rain?

Well, if you were a goddess, you had to spend a good deal of time naked, didn't you? And that meant, if you were an Irish goddess, you'd

397

have to get used to running naked in the rain, didn't it?

Maybe I had too much of the drink taken in Merrion Square, too much altogether. I should get up out of my couch, desist from my lewd thoughts about my employee, and get on with the serious work of the day, if I could only remember what that was.

I remained in the parlor for perhaps a quarter of an hour, thinking about Nuala and about my life. She was too young and too talented for me to interfere in the possibilities of her own life. If I did so and cut short her career, in the years to come she would never forgive me.

I was attractive because I treated her with respect and because I represented a world she had never experienced. But once she had recovered from her adolescent crush on me, she'd discover that she was wasting her talents and her opportunities.

We'd never be happy under those circumstances.

Would we?

Thus reassured, I donned a raincoat and wandered out of Jury's for a walk along the Grand Canal. The rain was intermittent, interludes of fierce downpour alternating with periods of rapidly moving clouds and an occasional hint of sunlight: Dublin weather teasing us with the possibility that the rain was about to stop and then turning the bucket upside down on us.

Dublin was a tricky lover, promising loveliness and then dancing away when one reached out to grasp her.

Would Nuala dance away?

Had Nell Pat?

The Irish, used to living in an island that had been a sponge for thousands of years, seemed to be philosophical about the rain. I thought of the sonatina of colors in River Forest at this time of the year and was thoroughly homesick.

Would Nuala like River Forest?

Is the Pope Polish?

Would my family like her?

Is the Pope Catholic?

The sooner I left for home, the better it would be for both of us.

After we found the gold in Mamene, right?

I forced my thoughts away from home and Nuala — and the very dangerous subject of Nuala at home with me — and tried to concentrate on my mystery, if that was the proper label for it.

Again the explanation, the complete picture, the key to the puzzle, the face for which I was looking floated through my brain, hazy like the Cathal Brugha barracks in the distance, and disappearing sometimes in the rain, just out of reach like a woman who was attainable if not yet attained.

Damn, I don't want to think about Nuala. Why does she obsess my metaphors? Why does she disrupt my thought processes, like a virus in a computer program?

An image of her naked on a bed — pale, vulnerable, and eager for me — tore at my brain. I winced with the painful pleasure of it.

A sly thought warned me that I would never be able to think constructively about the Consort of St. George and St. Patrick until I possessed her. A wiser thought replied that if I possessed her, she would then possess me, and I wouldn't be able to think constructively about anything.

So back to Martin Longwood-Jones. Why the lunch? Why the lecture? Was he a member of the Consort? Was he the head of it perhaps? How did I even know that there was such a shadow group? Only from Angela Smythe who, however desirable, was by no means thoroughly trustworthy.

Patrick had hinted at the same group, had he not? I could trust Patrick, couldn't I?

I could trust no one if it came to that, but, as a working hypothesis, there was indeed, on both sides of the Irish Sea, a group that was waiting patiently for the chance to reunite the two British Isles into one nation, ruled in the final analysis from Westminster. That group might well have existed since the time of the treaty. Martin's father and grandfather might have been involved in it. Perhaps membership was passed on from father to son.

Yet Martin and Liz seemed to reject the notion

that the Irish couldn't govern themselves. They both seemed to accept and indeed approve of an independent Ireland. Then why the long lunch with the lecture about the uncertainties in the time of the Troubles?

Martin's occasion to begin the lecture was my remarks about Pa and the Galway Brigade opposing Collins. Maybe the purpose of the lunch was to determine how much I knew.

I had spilled it all when I said that Pa might have been the man who killed Mick Collins. Both Martin and Liz had seemed shocked, horrified. Were they Collins supporters? Of course they were, they were on the pro-treaty side, were they not? They knew how much longer and more ruthless the Civil War had been after his death.

"Surely there's no way to determine with any certainty whether he fired the gun after all these years," Martin had murmured.

There was a way: Ma's diaries. The diaries were still my wild card.

"And it doesn't matter anymore, does it?" Liz had said, her pretty face grim. "You really should let the dead bury their dead, shouldn't you, Dermot?"

Liz knew that I found her sexually appealing and was pleased with that knowledge. She didn't exactly flirt with me, much less tease me, yet there was a hint of invitation, the barest hint, in her manner towards me.

Just a tiny bit of a hooker, as Nuala had

shrewdly noted. A rainy afternoon in bed with me, she seemed to be insinuating by the amused look in her gray eyes, is not totally out of the question.

That was not fair, I told myself. You have no reason to think that she's not totally faithful to her husband.

True enough. Besides, you're not supposed to be thinking about her buxom charms. You're supposed to be thinking about the Consort of St. George and St. Patrick.

What if she phoned you and suggested a tête-à-tête, lunch or a drink, perhaps at her house? Would you accept?

In the interest of learning more about the mystery, sure.

Who are you trying to kid, Dermot Michael Coyne?

Nuala was responsible for these absurd fantasies. She was the one who had incited the flow of hormones into my bloodstream.

Nuala and the God who put the hormones there in the first place.

Maybe I should let the dead bury their dead. The only reason anyone had to fear me was my search for the gold. Maybe the Consort, or whatever it was, had used the gold to pay its expenses — Imperial German gold of the Second Reich, sent for the cause of Irish freedom, now picking up the tab for a long-term, and faintly batty, plot to subvert that freedom.

Batty . . . yes, that was the word. The whole

402

story was batty. The scheme described by Patrick was, as I had told him, a load of shite. The fear in the eyes of Martin and Liz was absurd. The shadowy organization at which Patrick had hinted sounded like a premise for a comic film.

Why all the bother?

The gold, as herself had said?

Well, if all of it was still up there in the cave, it would be worth approximately twenty million pounds. That was a lot of coin of the realm admittedly, but barely the cost of a wrench to repair a B-2 in a Pentagon budget.

I was missing something.

My trouble had started when I began to ask questions about the Galway Brigade of the Irish Volunteers, later renamed the Irish Republican Army. That seemed to suggest that they were fearful I would find a connection to the gold.

How did the death of Mick Collins fit in, or did it? Gold is more important than a long-dead patriot, even if the latter was a genius.

I was missing something.

For a moment I had it. I saw what the key question was and why its answer might be devastating. I saw the face I was looking for.

Then I lost it.

"Wasn't I wondering if you were ever coming by here again?"

I looked up in surprise. It was the old fella, the one who had claimed to know Ma and Pa, sitting on the same bench on the bank of the

Grand Canal, a rain slicker over his black suit, the thorn stick still firmly grasped in his hands.

"Have you been waiting every day?"

I had been so captivated by my heady brew of thought and fantasy I had not noticed that the late afternoon sun had definitely, if temporarily, appeared and that the streets of Dublin were glistening red and gold, as if someone had placed a color transparency over the city, and that the canal was a dusky rose band sprinkled with glittering rubies, Dublin's last alluring trick for the day.

Somehow I had turned around short of the barracks and walked back towards Pembroke Street.

"I have not," said the old fella, "but wasn't I thinking to meself that I'd wait here some afternoon in case you'd be after strolling by. Grand day, isn't?"

"Brilliant."

We had thus disposed of two crucial Dublin words.

I sat down next to him.

"So they haven't driven you out of Ireland, like they did Nell and Liam?"

"They have not."

"Good enough for you." He nodded his approbation.

"Did me granda kill Mick Collins?" I demanded bluntly.

The old fella laughed at that and his laugh turned into a cough. "Sure, you don't understand anything at all, at all, if you're thinking that."

"Who did?"

" 'Tis a mystery, now isn't it?" There was a sly gleam in his faded blue eyes.

"Were you there?"

"When they killed the Mick, God be good to him, and himself maybe a hero and maybe a traitor and who is to say?"

"Were you there?"

"Wasn't I saying I was not?"

"Did my granda kill Daniel O'Kelly?"

"Aren't you missing the point altogether?"

"Did he kill O'Kelly?" I leaned forward and stared in the old man's face and was overwhelmed by the smell of tobacco.

"Would it have mattered if he had, and I'm not saying he did?"

"O'Kelly was a traitor?"

"Sure, aren't you on the right track now?"

"Were you there when he died?"

"He deserved to die for what he did to all of us, didn't he?"

"I suppose so."

I wasn't going to get any direct answers from the man, though he'd confirmed some of my hunches. Once more the truth slipped out of the mists in the back rooms of my brain and leaped at me.

I missed it and then it disappeared into the now deep purple waters of the Grand Canal.

"Sure" — the old man sighed loudly —

405

"weren't the worse ones those for whom he was working?"

"Ah, isn't that the truth?"

"The politicians, you know?"

"Haven't I said so?"

"And didn't your gram find out all about them?"

"She didn't miss much, that one."

"Not at all, at all."

Another long pause.

"And wouldn't she want the truth to be told at last?" I tried again.

"As sure as the sun will rise tomorrow morning."

A declarative sentence from the man!

More silence.

"Sure, weren't they thinking on going to America anyway, but they saved Ireland, didn't they now, and wasn't exile a cruel thing for them?"

Saved Ireland! Ma and Pa?

What the hell!

"Weren't they" — I'd try to play his game to the end — "the real heroes of the Troubles in Galway?"

The old fella's eyes, normally dull and lifeless, glowed for a moment in memory of great events and great people.

"And aren't you a smart one for figuring that out? If it hadn't been for them, we never would have got the guns we needed, would we now?"

Guns?

"Not at all, at all!"

"Aye." The old fella struggled to his feet. "And myself worrying all these days that you really weren't herself's grandson and wouldn't sort it all out. Well, won't I enjoy a fine night's sleep, Liam? We'll sort it all out at last, won't we, you and Nell and I?"

The old man hugged me — almost suffocating me with the smell of tobacco — and tottered off, his thorn stick at a jaunty angle.

"Dermot, not Liam," I said under my breath.

As dusk rolled rapidly off the Irish Sea and pulled down the curtain on Dublin's late afternoon show, I hurried back to Jury's, somehow exhilarated. My grandparents had saved Ireland! Ma wanted the story to be told at last! Well, damn it all, the story would be told!

In that exhilaration I wanted a woman, any woman would do. No, that wasn't true. Only one would do, and herself asking for it all these days. Well, we'd see what she was like in bed, wouldn't we now? And after that we'd have to see whether she was able to drag me to the altar as Nell Pat had dragged Liam.

The first Liam.

Was I kidding myself? Would I really have made love with Nuala if she was still in my suite?

Or did I suspect that she would have already left and hence that my grand and brilliant ideas were nothing more than frustrated fantasy?

Does the Pope live in Rome?

407

Naturally, she wasn't in the room.

I was disappointed and, as I knew deep down, I was fully expecting to be disappointed.

Dermot Michael Coyne assault a teenage virgin, even a mostly willing virgin?

Is the Pope a Baptist?

There was, however, the usual note and printout, the latter perfectly typed by my perfect translator:

Dermot Michael,

There are bad things about to happen to them. She's figured it all out, though I'm not sure what it is. Or who it is. She's pleased with herself too, terrible strong woman that she is. I love her.

But I'm not Nell Pat. So you don't have to worry about me trying to seduce you the way she seduced your granda.

I don't have that much courage, not that the idea has not occurred to me the odd time.

Love,
Nuala Anne

– 37 –

August 17, 1922

Maybe 'tis true what the nuns say about me, that I am a terrible sensualist. Faith, don't I love being loved?

I'm thinking about it on this day when I'm filled with terrible worries. 'Tis the love that keeps me going and gives me hope, the thought of himself pulling off me clothes and playing with me something terrible and then inside me and meself screaming with delight.

Sure, I shouldn't be writing down these thoughts at all, at all.

'Tis a grand day altogether, only a week after Mary's Day in harvest and the fields already bare. The sky is blue and clear and the Aran Islands seem only a few yards offshore in Galway Bay, stark and rocky like ancient forts and wanting the worst way to join with the land so they won't be isolated all winter long.

Like I want to join with me Liam for winter and for the rest of me life.

The houses of Carraroe shine in the sunlight and most of them painted fresh so that they look like homes in a fairy tale, all blue and pink and white along the bay and the loughs.

'Tis a day for dreaming about me and me Liam and not worrying about gombeen men and traitors.

Ah, Liam, do you know how much I love you? I want to be in your arms this very minute!

Some women say that love soon stops being fun, if it ever was. Well, not for me and me man. He loves me something fierce and I love him the same way. Ah, there's so many wonderful things we do to one another and ourselves being beginners at that.

I've promised him that never in all my life will I ever stop giving him as much pleasure as he needs and wants. That's a big promise because so many women seem determined to give their men as little pleasure as they possibly can.

Eejits, says I.

Why be stingy to men and themselves enjoying it so much? What harm is done if you make your man as happy as you can?

Liam takes it for granted that we'll be married as soon as the Troubles are over, though the man has never asked me, and himself being shy though not when he's kissing and licking and nibbling at me all over and pumping up and down like steam tractor inside me.

He also says that, sure, ought not we be thinking of moving to America and there being no chance for an ambitious man here in Ireland?

I'd leave in a moment if he says, though I'd miss something terrible me ma and me da and me dear little pony and little Nell Tim. But as Ma says, you go where your love calls you.

They might come to America too because they see hard times ahead for Ireland when the war finally ends. Like Da says, you always have to pay a big price for winning anything.

Liam is terrible smart and ambitious; Da says he'd make a wonderful estate agent and himself knowing the value of land better than anyone in the whole of Connemara. No working the farm for that bucko, me da says.

Da is now all for me and Liam. He and Ma pretend not to know that there's anything between us and keep praising Liam, sort of hinting that I should take him seriously.

And I pretend that I can't be bothered by such nonsense. Sure, aren't there other men in Ireland, says I, besides Captain Liam Tomas O'Riada?

And all the time we having such wonderful love together over in the abandoned cottage!

Do me parents know about it?

I'm thinking that they won't let themselves think about that.

And meself still going to Mass every morning because I'm sure God don't mind, not with the war on and Liam in danger of death every day.

Oh, I love him so much! I want to cry and laugh and pray! I'll be saying the rosary for him now and then come back to me diary.

Well, I've said the rosary and dried my tears.

" 'Tis not that Liam and I are together all

that often. Sure, the treaty has been signed and ratified by the Dáil, but now the lads are fighting with one another, bloody eejits, says I.

They're saying terrible things about poor Mick Collins, that he's a traitor and a killer and that he let Lloyd George and Churchill trick him at the conferences in London because he was so busy whoring in the East End and seducing Hazel Lavery. I don't believe a word of it. I know from his own mouth that he loves Kit Kiernan and that he'd no more be unfaithful to her than my Liam would be to me.

The National Army, which Daniel O'Kelly says is no better than the Black and Tans and the RIC, is slowly taking over the country. Didn't General Dalton chase the Republicans out of Cork City just the other day? 'Tis said that they'll come up through Limerick and have some terrible fights in Clare — sure aren't those Clare men the worst amadons in all the world! Then they'll come to Galway, though there's them that says there's no reason to bother because there's nothing in Galway worth fighting about at all, at all.

Poor Liam keeps wondering whether Mick is a traitor.

"Is he the one man in the whole Irish Republican Brotherhood," says I, "who is not a total eejit? Is he the only one who knows you can't fight the British Empire without bullets?"

"Aye, that's true." Liam sighs. "We only have the odd few bullets left."

412

"And yourselves marching every night of the year up and down the County Galway pretending that there's someone left to fight here!"

"The colonel says we must be ready for when the Free Staters come to take away our country from us."

"Do you believe that? Do you think you'll be fighting the Free Staters? Will you shoot at other Irishmen?"

He's quiet for a long time. Then he says, "I'm not sure, Nell Pat. I hope to God I won't have to."

I almost tell him that he can forget about me if he does that, but, sure, it isn't true.

He's off today, just himself and O'Kelly on some secret mission that the gombeen man says will bring peace to Ireland, and Liam all puffed up with happiness because he thinks he will do something wonderful, though he doesn't know what it will be.

I'm terrible worried about him because I now know for sure that O'Kelly is a traitor. Haven't I seen it with me own eyes? I didn't have enough time to explain it all to Liam, but when he comes back I'll tell him the story and take him up to see the gold. (I've been there meself now and know exactly where it is, only thirty paces south of the old shrine, and no one would have the slightest idea that there's a neat little cave, save they know where to look.)

Then I'll tell him what I saw in Lettermullen just the other day and meself hardly able to believe me two eyes.

It was the day after Our Lady's day in harvest and a Saturday and wasn't everyone in the County Galway sleeping late in the morning as they do after harvesttime?

So I decide that I need to ride me bike for a bit of a trip, and it being a day like this and the roads dry, I'm thinking that I'll ride over to Golam Head and look out at the Atlantic Ocean and it being one of my favorite places to think and dream in all the world, and itself being a bit of land jutting into the ocean with a lake behind it, a narrow road right down to the strand, and some rhododendron bushes so you couldn't see the strand from the pub just beyond.

I sit there for a while and dream about America and how I'll be a grand lady and have a big family and cute little grandchildren with me Liam.

I decide it's time to be going home and it still being the heat of the day. Then I see how calm the ocean is in the little cove where I've been sitting and I'm thinking how hot I am and wondering what would be wrong with a little plunge into the cool water.

There's no one around but me, so, wicked thing that I am, I take off all me clothes and jump into the water.

Let me tell you, it cooled me off in a hurry!

I climb out of it pretty quick and lie there on the strand in the sun until I dry off and

414

me not ashamed of meself at all, at all.

You see what love does to you!

I dream about Liam and me lying in the sand together forever and ever. Amen. I must have fallen asleep, the saints protect me, because the next thing I know I hear a motor car up on the road. Quicklike I roll over and cover meself with me shift, but I don't have to do it because the people in the motor car can hardly see the strand at all.

What's a motor car doing on this little island with only a wooden bridge back to the mainland and the next parish west on Long Island?

It's none of my business, I tell myself. Yet, Mother of God preserve me, I'm a terrible curious eejit. So I put on me clothes, and feel hot in them — sure, wouldn't I like to be naked a lot of the time in the summer, so long as Liam is with me? I think about the motor car and I'm sure it's going to the pub down on the end of land about a half mile away, the place where me ma says English tourists used to come when she was a lass.

I'm calling myself an onchock for doing it, but I get on me bike and pedal down the road, and it being awful rough. There's a great clump of fuchsia bushes at the turn of the road before the pub and them in full bloom and the bees making a terrible din as if they know there won't be many days like this again. I stop and hide me bike in the hedge and peek around the corner.

415

The pub is a broken-down old place with a thatched roof and some dried flowers in pots on its windows and a few chairs and tables outside for the odd tourist that might come by on a hot day.

Well, there's this man all dressed up in a fancy suit and himself not twenty yards away from me sitting at one of the tables and drinking a jar of spirits. I know I've seen his face, but not in Carraroe or even in Galway town. He's too fancy a fella altogether for either place.

'Tis a face I've seen in the newspaper that Da has brought home now and again from market in Galway. I search for the name that goes with the face and finally remember it.

I almost die of fright because if he's here it means terrible troubles for the County Galway. Then I realize that he's taking a big risk coming out here by himself with only the driver in his huge black touring car.

Then again, I'm thinking, maybe not. Sure, he's probably got lots of friends all around Ireland.

Anyway, they never said he didn't have courage.

Then who comes out of the pub with two big jars in his hand but your man Daniel O'Kelly.

I've seen enough. No, I've seen too much altogether. I'm thinking now that it's a terrible dangerous place that me eejit curiosity has brought me. If either of them or the driver see me, I'm a dead woman, that's for certain.

I keep watching them, just the same, because of me eejit curiosity. They're talking and laughing but above the hum of the bees I can't hear what they're saying.

While I'm watching, the fella in the fancy suit takes out his wallet and passes money over to O'Kelly, a lot of money. Kelly counts it very careful, like he's just cashed a check at a bank, which in a manner of speaking he has.

Treason, I whispers to myself.

Then one of the bees decides I've trespassed in his country too long and stings me on the arm. The bite doesn't hurt that much, but I jump with surprise. They stop talking and stare at the hedge. I try not to move at all, at all.

O'Kelly waves his hand and begins talking again — there's nothing there, he says, just a bit of breeze in the bushes.

The other man is still suspicious. He continues to stare. I can feel his eyes penetrating through the fuchsia and into the hedge, hard, determined, deadly eyes. I'm sure he can see me own terrified green eyes staring back at him, and meself without me knife on this hot day in August.

Then he shrugs his shoulders and they return to counting the money.

As quiet as a mouse in the cheese house when he knows there's a cat around, I slip away from the fuchsia and into the ditch behind the hedge. I'm telling meself that I'll wait there as long as I have to even if it takes all afternoon and all night too.

But I don't have to wait for long because I hear the motor car starting up.

I pray to the Mother of God, whose octave it still is, that they not see my bike.

The car roars by, as loud as the surf is during a storm, and covers me with dust. I don't move until I can't hear it any more. Then I'm thinking that your man wouldn't have taken O'Kelly with him in the motor car. He's still at the pub, probably still drinking jars of spirits, if I know him.

How did he get there? Did he ride a horse? Did someone bring him there in another motor car who will come back for him later? Or did he walk in by himself, so as not to attract any attention?

I'm thinking that if I were a traitor, God help me, the last would be what I'd do. So probably he's waiting until the sun goes down and it's easier for him to slip out and not be seen by others who have wondered like the little red-headed eejit what a motor car is doing this far out in Connemara.

Like a total onchock, I creep up out of the ditch and peek around the bushes. Sure enough, your man is still drinking away and a whole bottle of spirits now in front of him.

If I had any sense at all, I would have waited there till dark. But I was scared and hot and eager to get away and maybe by then a little crazy too. So, real carefullike, I sneak around the hedge, pull out me bike, and drag it along the road, quiet as I can, till I'm maybe fifty or sixty yards away from the turn. Even at this distance, he could see me dust if he wasn't totally fluttered, which I'm thinking he is.

Besides, even if he did see me, I'm on me bike, and he can't catch up unless I fall.

As wet with sweat as if I'd been caught in a rainstorm and smelling worse than the cow barn in the morning, I climb on me bike and pedal madly away.

I glance over me shoulder once to see if he's following me. No one on the road!

I'm so happy that I don't even notice the rock till I hit it.

I'm thrown over the handlebars and land in the dust with a loud thud.

I'm destroyed altogether, I'm thinking. But somehow I'm still alive and me body hurting all over and me knees skinned and me face scratched and me skirt torn something awful.

I climb back on the bike and tell meself that it's like nothing happened and I must pedal as fast as I did before, no matter how much it hurts.

Finally, it seems like years later, I'm back at home and me ma bawling me out for being so clumsy.

I didn't have a chance to tell Liam when he came in the dark the next night what I had seen and O'Kelly with him every second.

I know he's in terrible danger now, but, sure, if I'd try to tell him with O'Kelly listening, we'd all be murdered on the spot.

Mother of God, bring him home safe, keep him from harm!

And don't let me be pregnant, not so soon anyway.

– 38 –

Major General Emmet Dalton's account of the death of General Michael Collins:

About three miles from Clonakilty, we found the road blocked with felled trees. We spent about half an hour clearing the road. General Collins, always ready for emergencies, great or small, directed the work and took a hand in carrying it out. Active and powerful in body as in mind, he handled ax and saw with the same vigor as he could exhibit in the direction of affairs of state, military or civil.

Having at last cleared a way, we went into the town of Clonakilty, which is the hometown of General Collins. Here he interviewed the garrison officer and had conversation with many of his friends. It was pleasant to see with what delight and affection they met him. We had lunch in a friend's house in the town before setting out for Roscarbery.

It may be mentioned here that, on his arrival in Clonakilty, the whole town turned out to welcome him. . . .

Just outside the town of Bandon, General Collins pointed out to me several farmhouses, which he told me were used by the lads in the old days of "the Terror." He mentioned to me the home of one particular friend of his own, remarking "It's too bad he's on the other side now, because he is a damn good soldier." Then he added pensively, "I don't suppose I will be ambushed in my own country."

It was now about a quarter past seven, and the light was failing. We were speeding along the open road on our way to Macroom. Our motorcyclist scout was about fifty yards in front of the Crossley tender, which we followed at the same interval in the touring car. Close behind us came the armored car.

We had just reached a part of the road that was commanded by hills on all sides. The road itself was flat and open. On the right we were flanked by steep hills; on the left there was a small two-foot bank of earth skirting the road. Beyond this there was a marshy field bounded by a small stream, with another steep hill beyond it.

About halfway up this hill there was a road running parallel to the one that we were on, but screened from view by a wall and a mass of trees and bushes. We had just turned a wide corner on the road when a sudden and heavy fusillade of machine-gun and rifle fire swept the road in front of us and behind us, shattering the windscreen of our car.

I shouted to the driver, "Drive like hell!" But the commander-in-chief, placing his hand on the man's shoulder, said, "Stop! Jump out and we'll fight them."

We leaped from the car and took what cover we could behind the little mudbank on the left-hand side of the road. It seemed that the greatest volume of fire was coming from the concealed roadway on our left-hand side. The armored car now backed up the road and opened a heavy machine-gun fire at the hidden ambushers.

It may be mentioned here that the machine gun in the armored car "jammed" after a short time. The machine-gunner, MacPeake, not long after this occurrence, deserted to the Irregulars, bringing an armored car with him.

It was the Crossley tender, which was in the charge of Commandant O'Connell, that received the first shot. The road had been barricaded by an old cart, which the occupants of the tender promptly removed out of the way. After a few minutes the firing at these ceased, and the ambushers concentrated their fire on Collins and the other men who had occupied the touring car. Sean O'Connell then ran down the road and joined them.

General Collins and I were lying within arm's length of each other. Captain Dolan, who had been on the back of the armored car, together with our two drivers, was several yards farther down the road to my right.

General Collins and I, with Captain Dolan who was near us, opened a rapid rifle fire on our seldom-visible enemies. About fifty or sixty yards farther down the road and round the bend, we could hear that our machine-gunners and riflemen were also heavily engaged.

We continued this firefight for about twenty minutes without suffering any casualties, when a lull in the enemy's attack became noticeable. General Collins now jumped up to his feet and walked over behind the armored car, obviously to obtain a better view of the enemy's position.

He remained there, firing occasional shots and using the car as cover. Suddenly I heard him shout, "Come on, boys! There they are, running up the road." I immediately opened fire upon two figures that came in view on the opposite road.

When I next turned round the commander-in-chief had left the car position and had run about fifteen yards back up the road. Here he dropped into the prone firing position and opened up on our retreating enemies.

Dolan and O'Connell and I took up positions on the road farther down. Presently the firing of Collins ceased. I heard, or fancied I heard, a faint cry of "Emmet!" Sean O'Connell and I rushed to the spot with a dreadful fear clutching our hearts. We found our beloved chief and friend lying motionless in a firing position, firmly gripping his rifle, across which his head was resting.

There was a fearful gaping wound at the base of the skull behind the right ear. We immediately saw that General Collins was almost beyond human aid. He could not speak to us.

The enemy must have seen that something had occurred to cause a sudden cessation of our fire, because they intensified their own.

O'Connell now knelt beside the dying but still conscious chief, whose eyes were wide open and normal, and he whispered into the ear of the fast-sinking man the words of the Act of Contrition. For this he was rewarded by a slight pressure of the hand.

Meanwhile I knelt beside them both, and kept up bursts of rapid fire, which I continued whilst O'Connell dragged the chief across the road and behind the armored car. Then, with my heart torn with sorrow and despair, I ran to the chief's side. Very gently I raised his head on my knee and tried to bandage his wound, but, owing to the awful size of it, this proved very difficult.

I had not completed my grievous task when the big eyes closed, and the cold pallor of death overspread the general's face. How can I describe the feelings that were mine at that bleak hour, kneeling in the mud of a country road not twelve miles from Clonakilty, with the still-bleeding head of the Idol of Ireland resting on my arm?

My heart was broken, my mind was numbed. I was all unconscious of the bullets that still whistled and ripped the ground beside me. I think that the weight of the blow must have caused the loss of my reason had I not abruptly observed the tear-stained face of O'Connell, now distorted with anguish, and calling also for my sympathy and support.

We paused for a moment in silent prayer, and then, noting that the fire of our enemies had greatly abated, and that they had practically all retreated, we two, with the assistance of Lieutenant Smith, the motorcyclist scout officer who had come on the scene, endeavored to lift the stalwart body of Michael Collins on to the back of the armored car.

It was then that we suffered our second casualty — Lieutenant Smith was shot in the neck. He remained on his feet, however, and helped us to carry our precious burden around a turn in the road and under cover of the armored car.

Having transferred the body of our chief to the touring car, where I sat with his head resting on my shoulder, our awestricken little party set out for Cork.

The darkness of the night closed over us like a shroud. We were silent, brooding with hearts heavy over the ghastly blow, known to us alone, that had fallen upon our hapless country and upon the Irish people throughout the world. We had all left Cork City that morning, confident and happy, intent on improving the machinery of the only possible government that could bring peace to a sorely afflicted, long-suffering people.

We had with us the man in whom the people of Ireland had entrusted their destiny: the man who had risked his life a hundred times in their interests; the man who was adored by his friends and respected by all his foes.

Our day had been a succession of triumphs. And now at its close, like a bolt from the summer sky, fight had been forced upon us. We had fought with success — but our victory was as nothing in the crushing immensity of our loss. Michael Collins was gone!

The much-loved and trusted "Big Fellow" — statesman and soldier too — now leaned against me in the darkness, rigid and dead, with the piteous stain on him — Ireland's stain — darkening my tunic as we jolted over the road. So long as I live the memory of that nightmare will haunt me.

– 39 –

They jumped us on Sunday night as I was bringing Nuala home from our date, the week before our planned trip out to the West.

A date with Nuala, you say? Whatever made me risk a date with Nuala?

She invited me for Sunday brunch after I encountered her after the nine-thirty Mass in Clarendon Street. (She had told me triumphantly that at the Trinity College chapel, the C. of I. had a "Eucharist" and the Catholics had a "Mass.") I couldn't refuse, could I? One thing led to another.

Well, I didn't refuse anyway.

Did I expect to meet her when I strolled into St. Teresa's for Sunday Mass?

How did I know which Mass she'd attend?

Was there a chance I would meet her? Was I taking that chance?

'Tis none of your business at all, at all!

Was she hoping I would show up at the same Mass? Was that why she was so quick with the brunch invitation when we walked out of church together?

Especially since she told me that she'd already made bookings?

What can I tell you?

I'll admit that I glanced around the crowd at the nine-thirty Mass when I entered the church, looking for a dark blue jacket with a hood.

Perhaps because the nine-thirty was an Irish-language Mass.

The jacket was easy to find, right on the edge of an aisle and spanking clean, another investment of the salary I'd paid her.

"Are you owning this whole pew, young woman? Or may a poor sinner sit in it with you?"

Nuala jumped, startled out of her prayers to a God about whose existence or concern she was uncertain.

Occupant.

"Eejit." She smiled up at me. "You should be quiet in church."

"In the focking church," I whispered in her ear.

"Shush." She slapped my hand in reproof. "I'm saying me prayers."

"Am I included?"

"God knows that you need prayers." She turned away with a sniff.

We weren't saying rosaries any more, I thought to myself, as Liam and Nell did for one another and Michael and Kit. Shy children all of them, and me and Nuala too.

Now we sang hymns and responded to the priest. The Mass, renamed the Eucharist save at Trinity College, was in her own language and said by a priest with his face turned in our direction instead of his back. Nuala probably had never known the Latin Mass. I could barely remember it.

I glanced at her again. I had been wrong in one respect: A rosary was wrapped around her long fingers, not so much to be said, if you take me meaning, but there just in case.

If I said anything to her about it, she would say that she certainly wanted the Mother of Jesus on her side.

Fair enough.

The Mass, oops, Eucharist, was in Irish, as I knew it would be, lovely lilting melodies in both song and word that I did not understand but that lulled me into a peaceful and quasi-religious repose. I looked around at the congregation. Most of them were young folks, like Nuala exiles from the Gaeltacht, seeking their fortune or at least their living in a faraway town and a distant culture.

Closer to home than Boston and better than illegal immigrant status. Not such good pay, however.

"You didn't tell me that the Mass was in Latin," I mumbled.

"Shush!" she ordered.

She took my arm firmly in hers as we walked out of church. "I'll be taking you to brunch," she announced with a determination that did not permit a refusal. "And there'll be no discussion about whose treat it is, do you understand, Dermot Michael Coyne?"

"And meself just coming out of the celebration of the Eucharist?"

"We'll have brunch at the Royal Hospital at Kilmanhaim, and you'll have to ride public transportation, which will be a terrible burden for you, won't it now?"

"Anything you say, ma'am." I permitted her to drag me along. "I must note, however, that I think brunch is a terrible Yank innovation."

"Shush," she instructed me as she shoved me towards a 78A bus. "I'm in no mood for ar-

429

guments and it being Sunday morning."

It was a clear, crisp day with bright sun and a fresh breeze on the air — weather for a Notre Dame football weekend and themselves playing USC yesterday and me not knowing the score.

"I wouldn't dream of arguing with you on Sunday morning, Nuala Anne . . . and yourself dragging me off to jail."

" 'Tis not a jail, amadon. That's across the road. 'Tis a hospital, like the Royal Hospital in Chelsea, and old soldiers' home if you take me meaning and a grand masterpiece of Georgian architecture. The brunch profits support its restoration."

"I'm edified."

"Sure, I've never been there meself." She giggled.

The Royal Hospital was indeed a masterpiece of Georgian architecture, though to tell the truth not one that I would want to live in if I were an old soldier — not an adequate substitute for a ranch house in Tucson or San Diego.

Brunch was served in the "ground floor," a low-ceilinged cryptlike place with heavy walls and low arches. It was not exactly a real Yank brunch because it did not have what I consider to be essential, raspberry coffee cake, preferably with lots of goo that sticks to your fingers. Like most Irish meals, as opposed to the Yank meals at Jury's, it was heavy and not particularly nutritious. The brown bread was good, however.

I had to pretend that I enjoyed every bit of

food. I ate because herself was watching me closely to make sure I did.

There was entertainment, naturally. There's always entertainment in Ireland. Today it was singing and dancing by primary grade students. They were not bad at all. At all.

The other brunchers were the real entertainment, however: families, young marrieds, courting couples, the inevitable noisy teens, and children — tons of children — as my adolescent nieces and nephews would say.

For some odd reason, I attract kids. Little girls flirt with me. Little boys stare at me and grin. Toddlers crash into me as they run away from their mothers. So I had a ball playing with the kids — while my hostess smiled approvingly.

Sure, isn't the big amadon wonderful with kids and himself being no more than an overgrown kid himself?

When I went to the buffet to replenish my supply of brown bread, a little Viking princess with the prettiest blue eyes in all Ireland careened into me in desperately giggling flight from her mother, a black-haired woman younger than me and with a babe in her arms.

I picked little Maeve up and swung her into the air — I knew her name was Maeve because I heard her ma calling after her.

"Ah, Maevie me love, haven't you the prettiest blue eyes in all of Ireland? Why don't we run away to the South Pacific together?"

She seemed delighted at the prospect.

431

"Sure, isn't she a terrible nuisance?" Her ma beamed at the wee lass. "I don't know why we bring her here at all."

"She has her father's hair, I see." I spun Maevie around again, producing paroxysms of delighted squeals.

"Aye, and his sense of responsibility too." Her ma laughed. "Maeve Anne, aren't you bothering the nice Yanks?"

I had put the winsome little lass back on the floor and she clung to my leg.

"Irish American," I corrected her, determined to have done with this Yank nonsense.

"Me sister lives in America, in Chicago with all the gangsters, you know?"

Nuala, who had been watching the whole show with vast amusement, thought that was pretty funny.

"Where in Chicago?"

"Ascension Parish," she replied promptly, understanding the proper Chicago response. "Glory be to God, are you from Chicago too?"

"Next parish over almost. Sure, Maevie, if you come to Chicago, will you be visiting me? I'll protect you from all the gangsters in town, meself and the mayor, whose family is from Dungarvin!"

So we compared notes and Maevie was persuaded to go back to their table where a proudly smiling father was tending yet another child, this one a boy maybe a year older than Maeve.

"You Irish have big families," I said to Nuala

when I rejoiced her with my new supply of brown bread.

"Not as big as we used to. We just have them young and are done with it. . . . Irish American, is it now?"

"Yanks are white Anglo-Saxon Protestants from New England and maybe New York."

She grinned. "Won't I be trying to remember that?"

"Have some more brown bread."

"You certainly charm the wee ones, Dermot Michael . . . and their mothers."

"How old would you say that girl was?"

"The mother? Sure, maybe five years older than I am."

"Three children already."

"I bet herself had three by that age."

"Ma?" I smeared a huge amount of clotted cream on my brown bread and added strawberry jam — not exactly gooey raspberry coffee cake but not bad either. "Let me see, four as a matter of fact, and the first conceived out of wedlock."

"Poor dear woman."

"I don't hold it against her." I propelled the bread towards my mouth. "And himself a bishop now at that."

"The first child is a focking bishop!" Nuala was shocked.

"Family secret we don't talk about too much." I savored the bread and jam, certainly better than peanut butter and jelly. "William T. Ready, by the grace of God and tolerant inattention of the Apostolic See, Bishop of Alton Illinois."

"A focking bishop," Nuala whispered. "Does he know that he was conceived in cottage without a roof on the shore of Lough Carraroe?"

"He does not! I don't think it would bother him much. He's not a bad man for a bishop."

"It's strange how things work out, isn't it?" Nuala suddenly was thoughtful, preoccupied.

"If you ask me, it was all those candles they were lighting and all the rosaries they were saying at the parish church. You should be careful with the rosary, Nuala Anne. You can't tell what will happen."

"The woman fancies you, you know."

Did she mean herself or the young mother who liked my charming smile?

"What woman?"

"Lady Elizabeth."

"Oh, her. . . . Yeah, I know."

"You do?" She was surprised.

"Are you thinking I'm a complete amadon?"

"Only partial. . . . So what happens when she calls you and asks you over for a drink?"

"You think she will?"

"I didn't say that, did I? What if she does?"

Nuala was careful not to seem jealous, only curious. The glint in her marvelous blue eyes suggested amusement rather than anger.

"I lied."

"You lied?"

"I did."

"To whom?" She frowned, warning me that

434

it had better not be her.

"To herself."

"To Lady Liz?"

"Am I a total eejit altogether, woman? Was I not talking about Maeve Anne? And didn't I lie when I told her that she had the prettiest blue eyes in all of Ireland? And isn't it yourself that has the prettiest blue eyes in all the British Isles, in fact in all Western Europe?"

"Go 'long with you." Nuala turned a lovely pink and patted my hand. "Sure, aren't you all talk?"

"As to Lady Liz, as much as I might fantasize about other responses, I'd be busy in the afternoon all week and most of next week, if you take me . . . my meaning."

She considered me like a judge would consider a clever witness. "You'd turn her down?"

"I don't approve of adultery, Nuala, no matter how delectable the woman might be. Do you?"

She tilted her head forward and rested her hand on her wonderful chin. "You're a strange and interesting man, Dermot Michael Coyne."

"Maybe only a proud man, Nuala Anne McGrail. If she's the kind that would make a pass at me, I wouldn't be the first and not the last either. Maybe I don't want to be on someone's list of conquests, especially in the middle."

She nodded again. "I have a terrible confession to make, Dermot."

Now what? Did she have a lover or a boyfriend somewhere? Well, if she did, so what?

"I grant absolution beforehand to my penitents."

"I'll get that from me priest. . . . Well, I'm terrible ashamed of myself and it's hard to admit it but I *did* read the rest of your story despite the confidential note you put on it and if you fire me, won't it be what I deserve?"

"Do you think I'll fire you?"

"Well, if you're interested in what I think, I'm thinking that you put that warning on just to torment me and you wanted me to read your imitation of your man Seamus and you're surprised that I haven't read it before."

I hugged her and kissed her cheek. "Marie Fionnuala Anne McGrail, you're wonderful."

She leaned against me. "So was your story and itself all about a woman and water and life and vitality and mystery and wonder. If it was about me, wouldn't I be awful flattered, but course 'tis not about me, is it now?"

I felt the fabric of her bra under her (blue and gold Notre Dame) sweatshirt. "And if it was about you?"

She sighed. "I'd be tempted to think I'm pretty important and that wouldn't be right, would it?"

I released her from my grip. "My word was not important, but wonderful."

"I can print out a copy for me ma?"

"Glory be to God and all the holy saints of Ireland, you wouldn't be showing that lascivious story to your ma?"

"It's not lascivious and Ma's not a prude."

"Would she even let me in her cottage next week if she knew I was thinking such dirty things about her daughter?"

"They're not dirty, Dermot. I'm not a prude either." Her eyes were glistening with tears. "They're beautiful."

Oh, boy, I'm in deep trouble right now. How do I get out of it?

"I'm glad you like my story, Nuala, and you can certainly show it your ma. I hope she likes it too. . . . Now, what about the tour of this Royal Hospital place that you said we had to take?"

"Sure, we'd better hurry or we'll miss it."

The young woman who conducted the tour was a couple years older than Nuala. She had all the facts down about the architects and the kings and the princes and the lord lieutenants and all the rest of the important people whose pictures hung above the "great hall" where the old soldiers ate their meals, a room that had as much warmth and intimacy as Holy Name Cathedral without the stained glass — not a place to eat your morning meal.

Nuala beside me was restless at the end of the tour. She waited till several other questions had been asked and then put up her hand, as if hesitant and modest.

"Ah, 'tis been a grand tour," she began, "and yourself giving a brilliant presentation about all them royalty and noble folk that paid for this

437

glorious place. But wasn't there now another culture going on at the same time in Ireland" — she gestured at the paintings of the kings high above us — "as them fellas, another tradition, a bit older as a matter of fact and a bit more Catholic, and isn't it a shame now that there's no sign of it in this marvelous room at all, at all?"

"Aren't you absolutely right?" The other young woman, recognizing one of her own kind, was smiling happily. "Absolutely right. But, sure, didn't the government of the Republic of Ireland want to restore this old building just the way that it was at the time of its glory? So isn't the only thing Irish in the whole place the St. Patrick's blue of the carpet?"

I guffawed, loudly I fear. Everyone else laughed, including Nuala, who realized she had met her match and, being a good sport, especially since the match was another woman, was not about to make a scene.

"Wonderful," she whispered to the young woman as we left. "Grand."

"Brilliant," I added, thus honoring the two essential Dublin adjectives.

Well, as I said, one thing led to another. We rode out to Howth on DART and wandered about and watched at the sea with its orderly ranks of whitecaps piling up on the shore like lines of parochial school students marching into school. Several more little kids, some Vikings and some Celts, caromed into me and thus required my attention.

I then proposed that we see *Remains of the Day*, which Nuala had admitted she had yet to see. "And meself hardly having the time to go to the films at all."

Time or money, I supposed.

She was delighted at my suggestion.

Nuala was a good date, a fun date. She did not complain or sulk or nag, as not a few of my previous dates had done. Rather she enjoyed herself with charming exuberance and entertained me with a steady flow of stories about her family, her friends, her teachers, and her fellow students.

Nuala lived in a world of delightful eejits.

We ate sandwiches at O'Neill's before the film and herself knowing everyone in the pub but escaping without a song because, as she explained, she didn't sing on Sundays unless she was paid for it.

After the film, which she thought was both "grand" and "brilliant," I insisted on tea at the Shelbourne, arguing that jeans and sweatshirt were not inappropriate there even on Sunday because people would think she was a Yank tourist, especially with the Notre Dame sweatshirt, and Yank tourists could get away with anything, couldn't they?

"Irish American, Dermot Michael . . . and wasn't I trying to find a Marquette sweatshirt, but sure they don't have any in all of Dublin's fair city."

I was permitted a "tiny sip of sherry," which in fact amounted to two glasses. I contended that the "jars" were so small that the two should only count for one.

Then she asked, "Would you ever take me out to the Abbey Tavern in Howth for the singing?"

"Woman, I would, though 'tis nothing but a tourist trap for Yanks, ah, Irish Americans."

"I've never been there."

"Then we'll go."

Despite her claim that she never sang on Sunday unless she was paid for it, Nuala sang loudly and charmingly at the tavern. In short order she was leading the songs. She began with "Molly Malone," accompanied by a saucy tilt of her head towards me.

The crowd applauded enthusiastically. Then my Nuala took over. They went wild when she sang "Danny Boy" in Irish — "Maidin i mBeara," I was later informed, as if every eejit knew *that*.

After that triumph there was no holding her back.

"You know every song that Percy French ever wrote," I told her.

"And some of his songs he didn't write too," she boasted.

The manager asked her whether she would like to sing there two nights a week. Nuala said she had a job already and was attending

Trinity College but when she was finished with the job . . .

The manager said that she should stay in touch with him. Please.

Had she expected that she might receive a job offer?

Certainly she did, and why not?

She's a shrewd one, isn't she? Just like Ma!

When we left the Abbey Tavern at eleven-thirty, we discovered that the clouds, which had rolled in while we were at Howth, were the forerunner of a fierce rain storm. Lightning cut jagged lines across the night sky and torrents of rain poured down on us.

We were both drenched by the time we finally found a cab that would take us back to Irishtown Road and around the corner to one of the side streets behind the pumping station and across the River Dodder from the electric works. By the time we pulled up to Nuala's flat, the rain had stopped but the sky was still dark and glowering.

"I hope you're not angry because I went job-hunting and meself not telling you."

"Not at all," I said. "And on that subject, your translations are excellent, pretty much publishable the way they are. I'll be flying home after our visit to the West next weekend. I'll lend you my Compaq and leave copies of the diaries with you. You can Federal Express them to me in Chicago every day. I may come over in the spring to finish it up. You can count

441

on employment till then. There isn't any rush, so if they want to hire you at the Abbey Tavern, don't let this job stand in the way. I'm sure you can find a way to do both."

A nice, romantic speech at the end of a pleasant date, right?

"You'll be going home next week, is it now?"

She seemed surprised because I hadn't told her I was. In fact, I had just made up my mind about it myself.

"I am."

She wanted an explanation.

So I thought of one. "I want to make some arrangements with the publishers about the book."

"Ah," she said, patently unconvinced.

I paid the taxi because it would be only a short walk to Lansdowne Road and back to Jury's.

"You'll catch your death of cold if it rains again," Nuala warned me for the record, as Mom and Ma had warned me about rain for all of my life.

"Yes, ma'am." I provided the same response that had satisfied them.

Perhaps, I thought, this relaxed and happy young woman is the real Nuala, the ur-Nuala who lurks beneath all the masks. A nice girl, fun on a date, hard not to like.

At the door of her flat, I bent over and kissed her.

I meant it to be a casual good-night kiss.

That's how it started out. I had forgotten that when a young man and a young woman spend a long and enjoyable day together, their hormones begin to get ideas. Our casual affection became passionate, violent, demanding. My hands found their way under her sweatshirt and up to her breasts for which I had longed since I had first seen her. She yielded herself to my caresses as eagerly as I caressed her.

"I love you, Dermot," she moaned.

That did it. I must either stop or respond that I loved her too. I forced myself to stop.

"I'm sorry." I gasped.

"Don't be," she replied.

That's when they hit us.

From that instant on it was like a surrealistic dream you have with a high fever, lightning and thunder and the great hulking monsters of the electric works looming against the blazing sky and big men pounding me into the ground.

Their initial hit felt like a truck had rolled over me, first the front wheels and then the back wheels. Nuala screamed. I was dazed by the impact of two solid bodies and confused by suddenness of the attack and the deep darkness.

As I hit the wet pavement the rain started again. A quick flash of lightning illumined the scene — two men on top of me, one holding Nuala, and a fourth standing near her with a knife.

"We're going to cut your girl up a little,

focker," the man with the knife said with a sneer as the darkness returned, "to teach you not to meddle in things that are none of your gobshite business."

In a mental flash as bright as the lightning I realized that while I had destroyed all the output from the diary translation, anyone could come into my suite and read the computer files.

We were in deep trouble this time, four of them and by the skill with which they had put me down, not amateurs.

Nonetheless, they had underestimated me, as people usually do when it comes to a fight.

That's what I had the fight with the Fenwick coach about.

Besides, I had to save Nuala.

I shoved with all my strength against one of my assailants. He grunted but hung on.

We were outnumbered and outfought.

I had to save Nuala.

Nuala was busy taking care of herself, as she promised she could.

The second scream I heard was not from her but from one of the other two men, "She's cut me, Paddy! I'm bleeding! She's got a focking knife!"

Then he screamed again.

A focking knife, is it?

The two men holding me down were distracted by their friend's screams. They released their pressure on me. I kicked and shoved and then chopped. Somewhere an arm broke and another man cried with pain. I clubbed down with my wrist in the direction of where I thought a neck might be, and there was a loud sigh as someone lost consciousness.

I stumbled to my feet as another bolt of lightning tore across the sky just behind the pumping station. I saw Nuala, her white down jacket covered with blood, swinging a trash can at the man with the knife. It hit his head with a loud thud the instant the lightning flash died.

Who said we were outnumbered?

I charged the man with the knife.

A roar of thunder, scarcely a second away, drowned the end of his yell. I hit him yet another second later, burying my head in his stomach. He collapsed with a loud "oof" as the breath rushed out of his gut.

I fumbled in the darkness and found his knife. I grabbed it and pressed it against his neck. "Call off your friends, focker, or I'll cut your throat wide open!"

There wasn't anyone left to call off. The man Nuala had stabbed was still screaming that he was bleeding to death. The other two sounded like they were trying to get on their feet and figure out what was happening.

Nonetheless, the knife wielder was most cooperative. "Clear out," he choked, "or the focker will murder me!"

Then I heard cars slamming to a halt, doors opening, and hammer of feet on the sidewalk.

"Seventh Cavalry, Dermot," Patrick called.

445

"In the nick of time."

"A trifle late." I gasped.

Yet another lightning explosion, right above us now with almost instantaneous thunder, revealed Nuala swinging the trash can again, this time at the dark figure who was certainly Patrick.

"Ouch," he shouted. "Dermot, call off Grace O'Malley here."

"That focker is on our side, Nuala," I yelled. "He's a Yank!"

"Irish American!"

Grace O'Malley indeed.

The entire incident did not consume more than a half minute, much less time in the event than in the telling.

Someone turned on a couple of flashlights.

"Good heavens, Dermot" — Patrick sounded dismayed — "you've made quite a mess here."

Blood, mixed with rain, had drenched the pavement. "Henry, tie up that man's wrist. He'll be much less trouble to us alive than dead. . . . Joseph, drive Dermot and Grace O'Malley back to his hotel and secure it. . . . Dermot, you can safely leave the rest to us. I don't think your friend with the knife at his jugular vein will want to argue with my Uzi."

"You were late." I struggled to my feet.

"Sorry about that. Bad weather, you know."

Another pair of arms took possession of me, but not another assailant. Nuala, alias Grace O'Malley, was clinging to me for dear life, her

446

heart pounding, her body shaking like that of a child in convulsions.

"She made me take the knife," she choked. "I didn't want to, but she made me."

"Who, Nuala, who?" I held her tightly and tried to soothe her with comforting hands.

"Your gram! She said I might need it!"

– 40 –

" 'Tis grand stuff, truly it is." Nuala gulped a large swallow of Bushmill's Single Malt (Green Label). "Faith, I haven't known what I've been missing."

She was wrapped in one of Jury's terry-cloth robes, over her minimal but functional white underwear. Her jeans were salvageable; her white jacket was slashed and covered with blood, as had been her Notre Dame sweatshirt, which I had promised to replace with one of my Marquette supply in the morning. The assault had dazed and numbed her, but it had not made her hysterical or caused her to weep.

Grace O'Malley indeed.

She asked several times if she had "murdered the poor man" whom she had sliced up with her knife and whose blood had ruined her jacket.

I told her that she had not. Patrick and his

friends would take care of him.

That satisfied her.

When Joseph had pulled up in front of the hotel, she had regained enough of her self-control to dispute with me.

"I'll not spend the night in your room."

"Don't argue with me, woman. You will too. I'll not have you in Irishtown tonight, after what has happened."

"I will *not!*" She had jumped out of the car, tumbled forward, and sagged against me. "Oh, Dermot, take care of me."

That settled that.

"Who were those men?" she asked me as she took her second gulp of the Green Label.

"The attackers? I don't know."

"No." She gasped as the whiskey hit her stomach. "Patrick and his bunch?"

"They work for the American government and don't try to name which agency."

"Do you work for them too, Dermot?"

"No. They're interested in protecting me, however."

"I won't ask why" — she sighed — "because after another jar of this" — she gestured with the glass at me — "sure, I won't hardly know me own name."

"I'll explain everything in the morning. I'm sorry about all this."

"I'm all right," she insisted. "I'll be grand after a good night's sleep." She peered at me over the glass. "Now I know what I'm like in a crisis, don't I?"

"Grace O'Malley!"

"A terrible fierce and dangerous woman." She sipped more of her drink. "I scare myself."

"I'm sorry it happened, Nuala. All my fault."

"You're a good man, Dermot Michael Coyne." She licked her lips, so as not to waste a single drop of the precious fluid. "And yourself telling me you have to think everything out!"

"I didn't mean to put you in danger. I thought they wouldn't know about the translation. I was an eejit not to realize they could sneak in here and look at the computer."

" 'Tis all right. Wasn't Patrick there with his friends?" She finished her jar and filled it again.

"I should have told you."

"Tomorrow morning, Dermot."

I was still angry — at myself for the chances I had taken, at Nuala for carrying a switchblade, at Patrick for being late, and most of all at the other side, which had put my woman in jeopardy. I'd take care of them in the morning.

"Where did you get the knife?"

"Hmm?" She swayed slightly in her easy chair. "Oh, I borrowed it from one of me flatmates." She giggled. "I told her I might use it on you."

"Why did you borrow it?"

"I told you that *before*, Dermot." She sighed impatiently at my stupid question. "Your gram whispered in my ear that there were all kinds of dangerous things in her diaries and, like her, I ought to take precautions."

449

"She did, did she?"

"She did. Now I'm going to bed and I'll wake up in the morning and find that this is all a silly dream, won't I?"

"It's not a dream, Nuala." I stood up to assist her to the door of the bedroom.

"Sure, isn't that what you'd be saying in a dream?"

"Good night, Nuala. God bless."

"God bless you too, Dermot." She kissed me quickly. "Sure. It must be a dream. I wouldn't be sleeping in your bed except in a dream, would I now?"

I flipped on the light, guided her to the bed, helped her off with her robe, eased her into the bed, and tucked the covers around her.

"Terrible soft mattress," she murmured. "Sinful."

I kissed her forehead. "Sleep well."

She nodded, almost asleep already.

I tiptoed to the door out of the bedroom, turned out the light, and closed the door.

Then I helped myself to a large glass of the second bottle of Green Label I had stored away, as I had told myself, for a rainy day — which could be almost any day in Dublin town.

A beautiful woman in scanty attire in my bed and I as devoid of desire as I had ever been in my adult life.

A great Sean Connery I was.

We might have routed them without Patrick's help. Nuala was a fearsome woman, a terror.

450

Never fight with that one.

Nonetheless, someone would have to pay for the attack on her. I'd start tomorrow morning first thing.

A light knock on the door.

"Yes."

"Patrick."

I peered through the peephole in the door. Sure enough, it was Patrick, clad in the approved trench coat and black turtleneck.

"Green Label." He smiled when he saw the bottle in my hand. "Is herself asleep?"

"She is, with the help of some of this. Want a drink yourself?"

"Wouldn't dream of taking it from you. . . . She's all right?"

"Pretty much."

"Yourself?"

"I'm Sean Connery, it happens to me every day."

"If you were 007, you'd be in there with her."

"At as much risk to my life as her friend with the knife."

"Which reminds me. We have recovered hers for her." He handed a wicked-looking switch-blade to me. "Better you have it than I have it."

"The Guards will be interested in what happened?"

"I hardly think so, not the regular Guards anyway."

"Conlon?"

"I think he'll be very interested, though not so much as to stir out of his secret office in Dublin Castle to visit his four friends in the hospital where they're being patched up after a fight with a rival gang over in the Liberties."

"Not Irishtown?"

"Certainly not." Patrick grinned thinly. "You're a pretty fierce twosome. I'm glad I'm on your side. We'll be keeping watch all night. Sleep well if you can."

"I can't. And I don't want to."

"Oh?"

"I'm planning an assault on Dublin Castle tomorrow. I'll not let them get away with this."

Patrick stared at me for a moment, weighing the costs of protecting an Irish-American madman. "I won't try to talk you out of it. Be discreet."

"Not a chance."

He told me where I could find Conlon's office at the back of the Dublin Castle complex.

– 41 –

"Breakfast, Nuala." I pounded on the door of her — my — bedroom.

I had ordered two enormous breakfasts sent up to the suite: juice, cereal, bacon, pancakes with maple syrup (which the Irish don't do exactly right), brown bread, scones, and lots of jam.

I listened at the door. The shower was running. I opened the door a crack and hooked on the inside doorknob a blue and gold Marquette sweatshirt and an Aran Island pullover with cap and scarf, which I had bought for my sister Linda and of which there were many more to be found in Dublin.

The shower stopped. I closed the door. "Breakfast, Nuala."

"I'll be right out."

I read the *Herald-Tribune.* Notre Dame and the Bears had both won, a grand weekend. Brilliant.

She was true to her word — no long morning preparations for herself.

"It smells good," she said.

I turned away from my paper. She seemed a little haggard, but much more attractive in a Marquette sweatshirt than a Notre Dame sweatshirt.

"You look grand in Marquette's blue and gold. . . . Can you eat?"

She walked slowly over to the table where I joined her and removed the covers from the food. "I can always eat, Dermot Michael. . . . That man didn't die, did he?"

"He did not."

She sat down and drank her orange juice in a single gulp. "Ah, that's good now." She sighed contentedly.

"How are you, Nul?"

"I'm all right, Dermot, not grand." She smiled wanly. "And certainly not brilliant, but I'm all right and I'll be better soon. . . . Who was ringing the chimes last night?"

"St. Bart's in Clyde Row. Prod noise pollution. After a while you get used to them."

Her eyes twinkled. "Will I now?"

"You're a strong woman, Nuala Anne McGrail."

She smiled again. "I told you I could take care of meself. . . . Are these your American pancakes? Am I supposed to be pouring this syrup stuff on them?"

"You are. After breakfast we'll go over to Dublin Castle and sort out a thing or two and then I'll tell you the whole story."

She nodded as she swallowed a substantial chunk of pancakes. "No rush about that. Ah, this is good now. You Yanks, I'm sorry, Irish Americans, make some nice things to eat."

"I'm sorry about what happened last night."

She waved my apology away. " 'Twas not your fault, I'm sure, and no permanent harm done."

Why won't she be angry at me?

"You were so good and kind to me," she continued, "taking off me bloody clothes and giving me that wonderful whiskey and putting me to bed so gentle and sweet. You're a grand man, Dermot Michael Coyne. I don't understand you a lot of the time, but you're a good man."

Instead of giving me hell, she was praising me.

"I'm not sure that I am, Nul, but thanks anyway."

"Did you like undressing me?" She did not look up from the bacon that she had begun to demolish.

No point in denying that.

"I loved it. To undress, however partially, a beautiful and vulnerable woman whom you are protecting is a very pleasant experience, though to tell the truth there wasn't much desire in me last night."

She looked up and grinned. "Not a bit?"

"Only a little." I felt my face turn hot. Hell, she was the one who was supposed to be embarrassed.

"And you liked me?"

"You already know how much I admire you. In white lingerie you're enough to make a man wonder why he's been a bachelor so long."

"Ah, well" — she went back to the bacon — "then the day wasn't a complete waste, was it now? . . . Eat your breakfast, Dermot, and stop staring at me. We have to go to the castle and then I must attend one of my classes so that they're not thinking that I've gone back to Galway."

"How will you explain where you were last night?"

" 'Tis no problem at all, at all." She stole some of my unconsumed pancakes.

"These are quite good actually. . . . Won't I be telling them that I spent the night in your bed?"

"Nuala!"

She laughed and kept on eating my bacon. "I won't say that I spent it in bed with you, if you take me meaning, will I?"

I ate my breakfast and tried to tell myself that I did not have an enormous desire to take her back into the bedroom and claim her as my own, even if that meant I'd have to take her back to America with me.

Nuala and I walked into Dublin Castle as if we owned it, not that the dilapidated courtyard is guarded at all. The only remnant of the old castle is the record tower, the gate, and some of the wall. The rest is a hodgepodge of eighteenth- and nineteenth-century buildings, all of them ugly, and modern construction even more ugly.

The Garda on the ground floor of the old building where Conlon hid himself was quite polite. I had dressed in my best suit and looked very much the part of the rich Yank, uh, Irish American. Nuala hesitated behind me, wanting to have as little to do with the police as possible.

"Chief Superintendent Conlon, is it, sir?"

"That's right. Mr. Dermot Michael Coyne to see him."

"I'll ring him, sir."

It was another lovely autumn morning, Dublin putting on all her charm to persuade me that

456

it could match the glory of a Notre Dame football weekend.

Would Conlon see me? Most likely, if only to see whether I had been properly frightened by last night's battle.

I was tense and exhilarated, ready for the snap when a blitz has been called. I was about to sack Chief Superintendent Conlon. They might try an unnecessary roughness penalty on me afterward, though that didn't seem likely.

"You may go in, sir." The Garda put down the phone and gave me directions to Conlon's office in one of the back rooms of the old fortress.

"I don't like this place at all, at all." Nuala grimaced. " 'Tis a bad place altogether."

"It will take centuries to exorcise all the evil things done to Ireland here."

When Mick Collins took possession of it from the Brits in the spring of 1922, just a couple of months before his death, it was the first time in the more than nine-hundred-year history of the city that it was not under control of an occupying power.

"You're seven minutes late, *General* Collins," the Brit said, sniffing supercilliously and glancing at his watch.

"No, General," Collins replied. "You're seven centuries late."

There were two women Guards in Conlon's outer office, both working away diligently. He must be a pretty big deal. I barged right by them, now a charging end tearing in for the sack of a quarterback.

"Here, sir!" one of them shouted. "You can't go into the chief's office!"

"He already has," my companion informed her.

I shoved open the door. Conlon's office was small and dusty and old. Light filtered through a tiny window, which may have been washed last in the time of King Billy. Behind his ancient desk with his coat off, he looked exactly like what he was — an overweight, paper-shuffling bureaucrat.

I reached across the desk, pulled him to his feet, and wrapped my arm around his neck.

"You've no right —" He gasped.

"The hell I don't!"

"Should I call security, Chief?" The woman Guard rushed in after me.

"I wouldn't if I were you," Nuala commented.

"Go ahead call them." I tightened my grip on his throat. "I'll have a grand story to tell them, won't I, now?"

"Please leave us alone," he begged her. "It will be all right."

"The hell it will be all right," I said when she had closed the door. "Listen to me, Conlon, and listen to me closely. One more caper like last night and I'll break your neck. It's real easy to break a cop's neck. You use the grip I've got now and just twist, like this, see?"

He screamed, "You're hurting me."

458

"So the big bully is a coward too? I figured as much."

"Please let go!"

"Get this, focking asshole: Not only will I kill you, I'll cut up your wife and daughters so that no man will ever look at them except with disgust. Understand?"

I didn't know he had any daughters but I didn't much care about that.

"Don't hurt them," he screeched. "They're innocent!"

"They're related to a traitor, that's enough guilt for me! You tried to hurt my woman, so your women are in danger, got it?"

I tightened my grip even more.

In truth, I had no idea how to break someone's neck, though I could probably choke him to death. I wasn't going to do that either. And of course I had no evil intentions about his wife and daughters — poor dear women to be stuck with an asshole like him.

"*No!*" he begged me. "Please, *no!*"

He was quaking in terror now, the way quarterbacks are supposed to quake when Richard Dent closes in on them.

I pulled Nuala's switchblade out of my suit pocket and held it at his throat. "Your thugs were going to cut her last night. Why don't I slice you up a wee bit so you won't forget my warning!"

"No!" he begged again. "It won't happen ever again!"

Aha, confession, just what I wanted.

"Yeah" — I held the blade against his ear — "maybe just cut off an ear, what do you think?"

"They were told not to disfigure her, just a little cut! Please!"

I touched his scalp with the point of the blade and he began to blubber. I threw him into the corner of his office where he collapsed like a garbage bag.

"This is just a hint of what I can do to you if I want to, Conlon. Don't ever, ever try to push me around again, understand!"

"I won't! I won't!" he sobbed. " 'Twas all a terrible mistake!"

"You'd better believe it was! Come on, Nul, let's get out of this shite house!"

Dutifully she trailed along after me.

The two women Guards were crying in the outer office.

"You can't get away with this!" one of them screamed at me.

"Ah, but we can," Nuala said, dismissing her.

Dear God, she really is Grace O'Malley returned from the dead, not Ma but a pirate queen.

Most women would have reproved me for my violence. Nuala didn't seemed to mind.

"Was that necessary?" she asked me as we reentered the courtyard.

"It was, Nuala. They have been trying to frighten me. Now that they know that the only result is I get meaner, I think they'll leave us alone."

That notion was a miscalculation if I ever made one.

"You're a good bluffer, Dermot Michael Coyne," she said as we stomped out of Dublin Castle. "You had those gobshites scared to death."

"Bluffing, was I?"

"Sure you were, but wasn't it a good act? I don't think we'll have any trouble with him again, not at all."

I didn't even have to explain why I had sacked Conlon.

Patrick was leaning against the outside wall, waiting for us.

"Good morning, Dermot," he said cheerfully. "Have a pleasant morning so far?"

"Reasonably pleasant all things considered."

"I'm glad to hear it." He smiled. "And I believe I met this young woman last night, at the wrong end of a trash can. I'm Patrick, Nuala Anne. Nice to meet you in the daylight."

"Dustbin," she murmured.

"Quite right, two peoples separated by a common language, as another Irishman said, and himself a Protestant, for which God forgive him."

"You're Mick Collins." Nuala shied away from him like a skittish filly.

Patrick's face froze. "Mick Collins died of a single bullet wound in the back of his neck on

461

August 22, 1922."

"You look just like him!" She pointed at him. "Just like him."

"Lots of Irish and Irish Americans do, Nuala. My name is Patrick."

"If you're not Mick Collins, you're a relative." We were all standing still near the entrance of the castle. Nuala was still pointing at him.

"I'm not even Irish." He managed to smile again. "I'm an Irish American, a Yank, as you would say."

"You've come back to take vengeance on those who killed you!" Nuala was positively terrified.

"Nuala!" I said. "You're letting yourself be carried away!"

She hardly noticed me. "I know what I know."

"In my line of work, my dear" — he grinned — "we don't have time for personal vendettas."

"I don't mind if you have your revenge," she said. "It's only that you scare me."

He took her arm to guide her down the sidewalk of Dame Street and away from the castle. "As your man Dermot would tell you, Nuala, the rules of our little game are that you and he don't ask me any questions unless I indicate I'm ready to answer them. Understand?"

She glanced at me, as if seeing me for the first time. "Yes, Patrick," she said slowly. "I guess I'm frazzled this morning. I'm sorry."

"Not at all, my dear." He relinquished her arm to me. "I'm sure last night was a very trying experience."

So we had survived that weird little interlude. Patrick *did* look like Michael Collins, astonishingly like him. Maybe he *was* a relative. I would never persuade Nuala that he was not. When she thought she smelled revenge in the air, she would not be talked out of it.

Maybe she was right.

"I think I can assure you" — Patrick was his usual bright self again — "that our opponents are properly terrified of you, Dermot. They now believe that you have a large group of very talented agents at your beck and call, which is not altogether false, is it? Their present intent is to have nothing more to do with you, an intent that I suspect you strongly reinforced in your little tête-à-tête with the super just now."

"Bent cop!"

"Quite, but not part of the conspiracy. Paid help, if you take my meaning. In any case, should there be any change in their plans, we will be made aware of it and will pass on our information to you. Naturally, we shall continue to be in, ah, *attendance* seems to be the right word, doesn't it?"

"We might be planning to go to Cork and Galway on the weekend."

"Are you now?" He smiled, a Mick Collins smile, I was sure. "I see no reason not to. Who knows who may bump into us out here, though not if we're careful enough? Leaving Friday?"

"Thursday morning."

"A long weekend, is it? Well, enjoy it. . . ."

Oh, incidentally, Dermot, here's an envelope whose contents you might want to peruse before the day is over. . . . And now, Nuala Anne, if you'll excuse me, I'll have to take my leave. And as a parting shot, you know well that the dead don't walk in the daylight, do they now?"

"They do *not*," she agreed. "I'm sorry, Patrick, that I misspoke."

"Not at all. If I don't see you, I'll see you."

As he disappeared into a side street and strode towards the Liffey, Nuala whispered, "They *usually* don't walk in the daylight."

"I'm not about to argue, Nul. However, he does work for the American government."

"What does that have to do with it?"

"At any rate he's on our side."

"He focking well ought to be!"

We walked silently for a few moments along Dame Street as I pondered the truth that Nuala was not only unpredictable but indecipherable. A member by her own half-ironic admission of Europe's last Stone Age race.

"Now we'll be stopping in at Bewley's for midmorning tea, won't we, Dermot Michael, and you'll be telling me the truth about all these strange doings, the *whole* truth?"

"Haven't I been promising to do just that?"

"And you'll do it *now*."

"Yes, ma'am, and yourself wanting another meal after that breakfast you destroyed."

"Only one scone." She took my hand and led me down Grafton Street.

She had two scones, actually, with the usual thick amounts of butter and jam. I had four. We argued about her use of marmalade, which I thought was a sin against nature and which she thought was "altogether grand."

Then she said crisply, "*Now,* Dermot Michael."

So I told her everything, except about my reaction to Angela Smythe and that person's late-night visit, which I converted into a phone call.

She listened impassively, absorbing it all.

"Focking eejits," she said when I was finished.

"Who, Nuala? Am I included?"

"Saints protect us and keep us, no!" She touched my hand. "Sure, despite yourself aren't you Sean Connery with wavy blond hair? I mean the eejits that think the Irish people would ever agree to become part of England again, no matter how fancy the Union might be. Most of us aren't revolutionaries, but I'm thinking a plot like that would turn us all into Sinn Feiners over night!"

"That's what I was thinking too."

"So what's in the envelope?"

"What envelope?"

"The one your man gave you on Dame Street, isn't it now?"

I had forgotten the envelope from Patrick.

I reached into my jacket pocket and pulled it out. Plain white envelope, inexpensive not to say cheap.

As I opened it, Nuala peered over my shoulder, a bit of scone still in her hand. 007 had an assistant now, who, given half a chance, would take charge — as the womenfolk never did to Sean Connery.

Even then, however, I was the assistant.

I took out the single sheet of paper and unfolded it. It was a Xerox of a handwritten document of the top of which was neatly printed in large block letters:

CONSORT OF ST. GEORGE AND ST. PATRICK

"Brigid, Patrick, and Columcille!" Nuala exploded.

"And all the other saints of Ireland."

I glanced down the list of perhaps fifty English and Irish names, many of them prominent — journalists, writers, artists, civic leaders, politicians — all in careful alphabetical order.

Brendan Keane was on the list with the letters "T.D." after his name — a member of the Dáil, the Irish parliament. There were five or six others with the same identification and maybe a dozen with "M.P." after the name, members of the British parliament; a couple of them were, I thought, from the Six Counties of Northern Ireland, one of them a member of Mr. Major's government. Keane was the only member of the present Irish government on the list, though one of the other T.D.'s was a prominent spokesman for the opposition.

"The Longwood-Joneses are on the list," I observed to Nuala.

"Sure, wouldn't they be?"

"I wonder why so many prominent people would be mixed up in such a daft idea."

"I'd be ready to wager that your man's father and grandfather were on it before him. And the others, well, wouldn't some of them be in it for the money?"

"What money, Nuala?"

"Roger Casement's gold. Wouldn't they be using that to finance the whole foolishness. Daniel O'Kelly had told the stranger where the gold was?"

"Or more likely the stranger's spies followed him just like Ma did."

"Daft and dangerous, Dermot. . . . Why did Patrick give it to you? Wouldn't it be better to have turned it over to the Irish government?"

Her mind worked too fast, too fast altogether. I was, after all, Sean Connery, wasn't I?

Not hardly.

And what was there about that list that bothered me? Damn, it was the face that almost floated in and out of my internal vision, a familiar face yet mysterious, lurking in the fogs just beyond the threshold of my consciousness. A dangerous face. Whatever was wrong with the list was perhaps not as important as that brooding face, but it still might be important.

"Maybe he doesn't want them to know that his crowd is watching them so closely."

467

"Or maybe he's not sure who else in the Irish government might be involved."

"Or maybe . . . maybe there's some other things we have to find out first. It wouldn't do at all, for example, if the C.I. — uh, the American government found the gold, would it?" I was trying to think furiously to keep up with Nuala's racing mind.

"Should we turn this over to someone?"

Note the "we."

"To whom, Nul? As you say, we don't know who in the Irish government we can trust."

"So it's off to Cork and Galway on the weekend, is it?"

"I'm not sure that —"

She cut me off. "If you don't go, sure, won't I be riding back on the train and climbing Mamene by meself?" She filled my teacup. "And don't I know pretty well from herself where it was — or where it used to be? We'll have no more talk of backing out of this one. I'm no focking patriot, but I won't let me children be part of focking England again."

"I thought you didn't want children?"

She turned purple with embarrassment. "In case I should change me mind!"

"Will the gold still be there?"

"Why else would they be so worried that you might find it in your searches for the truth about Nell Pat and Liam? Wouldn't it be hard now to ship it away? And the paper trail it might leave? The odd bar of gold now and then

468

would take care of the matter, wouldn't it? Maybe only one person knows where it is. That would fit this daft business, wouldn't it?"

It would indeed. I needed time to think. Or maybe with Nuala in charge I wouldn't need to think, just do what I was told. "You're sure you want —"

"Didn't I say that matter was closed altogether?" She stood up. "Now you finish your tea and them last scones and I'm off to class. There's a lot of translating to be done this week. I want to know what happened before they left for America and herself pregnant, poor woman. . . . Oh, by the way, Dermot Michael, may I have me knife back?"

"Your friend's knife, isn't it?"

"She gave me the use of it, didn't she?"

I handed it back to her without trying to warn her not to carry it again. Such a warning would be a waste of time.

Off she went, head up, back straight, rear end switching defiantly.

My heart sank, not because Nuala was now in charge. There was nothing wrong with that. Despite my chauvinist impulses, if she was quicker than I was, let her take charge.

I didn't really believe that, of course. But at that moment it was necessary for me to believe that I did.

If only she gave me a little time to think.

No, my heart sank because I realized how

much I would miss her when I flew back to Chicago.

An image of her in skimpy white lingerie returned, a picture that had not been erotic in last night's horrors but that was now deliciously appealing.

Could I really give her up? I asked myself as I prepared the last scone for consumption. Could I ever give her up?

– 42 –

I was talking with some other prisoners on the night of August 23, 1922 (in Kilmanhaim Jail) when the news came that Michael Collins had been shot dead in West Cork. There was heavy silence throughout the jail and ten minutes later from the corridor outside the top of the cells I looked down the extraordinary spectacle of about a thousand kneeling Republican prisoners spontaneously reciting the Rosary aloud for the repose of the soul of the dead Michael Collins. . . . I have yet to learn of a better tribute to the part played by any man in the struggle with the English for Irish independence.

— Tom Barry

Like the other Republican prisoners, Tom Barry was an enemy of Michael Collins in the Irish Civil War.

— 43 —

August 23, 1922

Mick Collins is dead.

I'm crying something terrible as I write these words. They killed him. I hope and pray that me Liam had nothing to do with it.

But, sure, where else would he be?

Liam would never shoot the general if he knew it was him. That divil incarnate Daniel O'Kelly wouldn't tell him. He'd trick him into it — and then maybe kill Liam and blame him for it.

If Liam actually fired the gun, he's a dead man. The Free Staters will kill him if O'Kelly doesn't. If he isn't killed, he'll hate himself for the rest of his life because he let himself be tricked into pulling the trigger. With my big mouth I've been warning him for trusting O'Kelly too much. That will make him feel more guilty.

What will happen to our love then?

And meself knowing I'm pregnant for certain now.

Glory be to God, what are we going to do!

The church was filled at Mass this morning and everyone weeping and sobbing for General Collins and this being Republican country.

I said two rosaries for him and one for poor Kit Kieran.

'Tis clear to me now that the fella in the fancy suit was after paying for the death of Michael Collins. I'll have to tell Liam that and take him up to the cave with the gold when he comes home.

If he comes home.

I'll be praying for him and for General Collins.

Mother of God, take care of us all.

Is it my fault for not telling Liam what I saw in front of the pub? Am I as guilty for the death of Michael Collins as the man who pulled the trigger and the man who paid him to pull the trigger?

I don't know! I don't know!

Maybe I should talk to the young priest about it and himself so kind and understanding.

But would he give me absolution?

If me poor Liam is already dead, won't it be my fault?

– 44 –

Liam came home last night.

I was in me bed, covers off and only in me shift because we're perishing with the heat these days and the moon being full.

There's a knock at the shutters and a whispered voice and I'm wondering if it's a dream.

So I open the shudder and it's Liam and himself with a great blond beard and I'm beside meself with joy. Mother of God, I thinks to meself, at least he's still alive and we have a chance of beginning again.

"Nell," he says gentlelike but with a terrible hunger in his eyes, "I've been longing for you all these days."

"Well," says I, "here I am so you can stop longing."

When your man needs you something desperate, you're a total eejit if you don't give yourself to him.

He pulls off me shift, violentlike, so I know he needs me real bad.

That makes me terrible happy and meself needing him almost as bad. I tell him not to make too much noise because it will wake me

473

ma and da, so he's very quiet.

Even though he wants me real bad, he kisses and caresses me and plays with me in the moonlight till I think I'll lose me mind altogether.

"The look of you, Nell Pat, is almost as good as the possessing of you."

"Possess me now, Liam me love," I say, "or you'll have a woman on your hands whose been driven out of her mind."

"Is that true now?" He grins. "Well, sure a little bit more of tormenting of you shouldn't do any harm at all, should it?"

It didn't do any harm, though I thought I'd die with pleasure before he was finished with me.

We lay there in bed, the sweat covering the two of us and breathing heavy and holding hands and meself knowing that I'd die without him.

So he begins to whisper the story of the strange mission he went on with O'Kelly and I understand that he doesn't know General Collins has been murdered.

Liam is carrying his Lee-Enfield and the commandant, as an officer, has a Mauser in his holster.

They had taken a long roundabout journey south, on foot for a time then in a motor car from Ennis, then on foot again through Limerick and by horse through Kerry, then on foot again into the mountains so that Liam didn't even know where he was.

In Cork, I tell myself, between Crookston and

Bandon, not all that far from Sam's Cross where the general was born.

It's late in the day and growing dark and his commandant leaves him in a hedge and goes away to meet someone. Then he comes back and they climb a high hill on the east side of the road and hide behind a barn. There's a lot of fellas drifting along the road and over the hill — the lads who have been driven out of Cork, O'Kelly tells me man, by the National Army.

'Tis the first Liam knows that the National Army is in Cork.

Daniel takes Liam's rifle and gives him the Mauser pistol. He empties the bullets out of it and puts in a set with a cross cut on the front — dum-dums that explode on contact.

They look down at the other road, which is running through a kind of gloomy valley, and Liam sees a group of troops on the west side of the valley waiting in an ambush in a laneway above the road.

"Eejits," says O'Kelly. "What are they doing here?"

As Liam and O'Kelly wait, most of the troops — they have no uniforms, so they're probably Irregulars — drift away. No discipline at all, says Liam. That's the curse of the Irregulars.

There's only four of them still in the laneway as the day comes to an end. A light mist is blowing in, like maybe it will rain at the end of a hot summer day.

Then, all of a sudden like, there's a convoy coming around the corner, first a motor-cycle, then a yellow motor car and a couple of tenders, then bringing up the rear an armored car. Brits, Liam thinks, wondering what's happening. He knows that the Irregulars are still fighting the Brits as well as the National Army. Surely the National Army doesn't have an armored car yet. Maybe this is a big ambush, though there's not enough men down there to stop an armored car.

There's a fierce lot of shooting, with no one hitting anyone else. It's so dark now that me man cannot even see the color of the uniforms in the convoy. He still reckons they're Brits.

Then the shooting stops and Liam can hear the Irregulars running away. No discipline at all, he thinks to himself.

Suddenly there's an explosion right next to him and Liam realizes that O'Kelly has fired a shot.

There's some answering fire but it doesn't come close. O'Kelly keeps firing and they fire back but in the opposite direction. Then down the hill on their side, some more people begin to shoot. The rest of the Irregulars, arriving after the battle is over. It's so dark now that Liam can barely make out anyone, but he thinks he sees someone faceup on the road, by the looks of him an officer. He thinks maybe they've killed General McCready of the British Army.

Finally they're out of ammunition and doesn't

O'Kelly say, "Let's get out of here, Liam, me lad. We've done a fine day's work."

They run up the road towards the top of the hill and the troops now firing after them but not hitting either of them.

Then Daniel throws the Lee-Enfield to Liam, takes the Mauser back, and says, "We'd better split now, me lad. See you back in Galway."

And off he goes in the night, leaving Liam with a rifle and no bullets except for the dumdums that are in it.

Me man knows they're on the run and while he doesn't want to lose the rifle, he knows it will make him a marked man if it's murdered an English general. So, smart fella that he is, he throws it down the side of the hill and takes off up the mountains.

I'm thinking to meself that he's a smarter man that Daniel O'Kelly thinks he is.

It's only days later when he stumbles into Mallow that he knows where he is and begins the long walk back to Galway.

"And you're the first one I've talked to since the ambush."

I'm glad because he's innocent of murder.

"I'll tell you who that gombeen man killed, Liam Tomas. It was General Michael Collins. And he left you there to be arrested and accused of the crime. And he was paid to do it."

– 45 –

In the morning a steamer set off from Dublin to bring the body back. It passed another steamer flying the new state's colors at half-mast. There was wild talk of a massacre of prisoners by way of reprisal. Mulcahy, rightly interpreting the dead man's thoughts, resumed the negotiations where his death had broken them off. But he did so unknown to his colleagues. The day of lofty ideals was over.

It seemed as if life could never be the same again. The greatest oak of the forest had crashed; it seemed as if it must destroy all life in its fall. It did destroy the Sinn Fein movement and all the high hopes that were set in it, and a whole generation of young men and women for whom it formed a spiritual center. It destroyed the prospect which, we are only just beginning to realize, Collins's life opened up; fifteen years — fifteen years — perhaps more, perhaps less — of hard work, experiment, enthusiasm, all that tumult and pride which comes of the leadership of a man of genius who embodies the best in a nation. . . . Collins had spoiled them for lesser men.

O'Higgins once said, "I have done nothing without asking what Michael Collins would have done under the circumstances — which is as though I were to say I have written nothing without asking myself what Shakespeare would have written."

— Frank O'Connor, *The Big Fellow* (1937)

Frank O'Connor, the great Irish short story writer, was on the other side in the Civil War. He wrote the book, as he himself admits, as an "act of reparation."

— 46 —

"I'd very much like to have a private chat with you, Dermot."

Lady Liz was on the phone, just as Nuala and I had anticipated. Her voice was low, discreet, breathy.

Oh, boy! "I would certainly like that too, Liz."

My fantasies exploded. A wild romp with an attractive older woman, a young man's delicious dream!

"Perhaps a drink in your suite or here at our town house."

"It would have to be there," I temporized.

"Grand. Martin is in London, as you know,

for the weekend."

"No, I didn't know."

"It is rather important that I have some very private words with you."

"I'd like that, Liz, but I'm afraid I'm leaving town this weekend. I'll be back Monday. Perhaps I can give you a ring then."

"I'm so disappointed."

"So am I, but I'm afraid I'm committed for the weekend."

"Irrevocably?"

"Irrevocably."

"Oh, dear."

"I'll call you first thing Monday morning."

"I'm afraid I'm going to be quite busy on Monday. I'll ring you up in the course of the day."

"I'll be looking forward to our tête-à-tête." I hung up the phone, sweating and exhausted.

Well, damn it, I had been virtuous.

I was sick of virtue.

Fock virtue, as Nuala would probably say.

That worthy Irish goddess came rushing into my suite in her robe.

"Sorry to be late," she said. "I did an extra quarter mile. Glory be to God. What's wrong with you?"

"Nothing."

"Liz called?"

"Damn you, mind your own focking business!"

She was not in the least offended. Quite the

contrary, she kissed my forehead before she went into the bathroom to change into her work clothes. "You're an astonishing person, Dermot Michael. The last of the gentlemen."

"Her bed is the enemy camp!"

The bathroom door had slammed shut. Nuala did not walk through life, she galloped.

Then I realized what seemed wrong about the list Patrick had given us.

I pulled it out of file and studied it carefully.

Yep, that's what had troubled me.

It was wild! So that's what's going on!

Well, Nuala hadn't figured that out.

Yet.

– 47 –

September 1, 1922

We saw the gold last night and now Liam believes me completely. We've got to protect ourselves from O'Kelly till we can prove he is a traitor.

Liam has a wonderful plan for doing it, though he's running a terrible risk.

We're betting that the traitor will take his time before he comes back to Galway. I'm thinking that he'll be leaving Ireland pretty soon and I'm thinking to meself that he probably reckons he has a score to settle with me.

I tell Liam the whole story about the gold and the man in the touring car and the meeting out at Lettermullen. He listens real careful and doesn't say anything for a moment.

Then he sighs and says, "Well, I've learned one thing anyway."

"And what would that be?"

He smiles sort of sadly. "To listen carefully always to what me woman says!" And he hugs me and kisses me and takes me breath away.

"Thank God for that," I says with a sigh of me own.

We're sitting on the strand watching the seals and the cloud banks that will move in with rain before the day is over. 'Tis truly the end of summer. In a few days we'll be longing for the time when we were perishing with the heat.

Liam is sad. I've argued that he didn't kill Mick Collins and that he was as much an innocent victim as Mick was. He half believes me and he'll mostly believe me in a couple of days, but for the moment he has to suffer. So I'm sympathetic and meself biting me eejit tongue every few minutes so I don't say something stupid.

"He'll be murdering you, Liam, just like he killed me poor Tim."

Me man scowls something fierce. "He did that too?"

"I'm sure of it."

He's thoughtful again. "Well, I'll tell you one

thing: He won't be killing me."

"What will you be doing?"

"I'll avoid him, till we go to America."

"That's definite then?"

" 'Tis. If you'll come with me."

"I'll go wherever you go."

"I'm thinking" — he scowls again, thinking real hard — "that the man who paid him off may come back. That fella wouldn't give him all his money before the murder, would he?"

"Not if he knew Daniel at all."

"Then I'll tell a couple of the lads — and the Brigade is down to a handful anyway — what happened and they'll be keeping a close eye on him. Then there's the garage in Galway that takes care of touring cars and fills them with petrol. One of our friends works there. He'll be watching for the car. That way we can capture your man and Daniel together and we'll have proof."

I'm thinking we already have enough proof.

"We could ask the young schoolteacher man who takes pictures with that big camera of his to take a picture of the two of them, couldn't we now?"

He smiles, pleased with me. "I hope you're always on my side, Nell Pat."

"What other side would I ever be on?" I wrap my arms around him and hold him close and the poor dear man weeps in my arms. I weep too — for all those poor men who have died during the Troubles. While I'm weeping I pray

483

for them. I include the Tans and the Brits and all our enemies.

And I'm thinking that it's terrible ironic that Mick Collins, who drove the Brits out of Ireland by ambushes, himself is killed in one. He who takes the sword, the young priest has said grimly, dies by the sword. That's not a law of God, Nell Pat, that's rather the way things seem to happen among us poor humans.

Ah, sure, he's right, isn't he now?

"We should go see the gold," I says to Liam.

He hesitates. "Why should we see it, Nell Pat? I believe you that it's up there."

"I want you to see it with your own eyes."

So we saddle up Dotty and Liam borrows a pony from the next farm over and we ride up to Maam Cross and tie the ponies down the road from the path to the shrine. I haven't told Liam but I have me knife again, in case Daniel appears, though I'm thinking he'll stay away for a while — at least until he finds out whether Liam is still alive.

I'm not as fast climbing up to the old shrine as I was the first time. The lad or lass inside of me is beginning to slow me down. I'm not unhappy about himself or herself, mind you. I love the little person almost as much as I love its father.

"You're not as quick as you were when you were a child," Liam says to me.

"Sure, I'm thinking I'd better climb slowlike so you can keep up with me and meself carrying this kit bag with the torches."

I have another use for the kit bag, but it's a secret and it'll be a secret till we get to America. I've thought about what I plan to do and I've decided that it's right and proper. Liam might not agree till I explain it to him, so the explanation will have to wait, won't it now?

I haven't told me man yet that I'm carrying his child. I better tell him soon, so that we'll be married, not that I have any doubt about *that*. At least I'm not sick in the morning and meself not telling me ma either.

I'm plumb exhausted by the time we get to the shrine so we sit for a while and say a rosary in honor of St. Patrick who will be our patron even when we go to Chicago, which is where me man says he thinks we ought to go.

"In America," he says, "you can still be Irish and be American too."

"Sure, how could we ever stop being Irish, Liam Tomas?"

Then we go up to the crevice in the rocks and I light the two torches and we slip into the cave.

"From what the young priest is telling me," I say, "they probably dug this little hole in the mountain to store poteen before the 'patterns' — themselves being festivals in honor of St. Patrick."

"Sure, there'd be less trouble from the poteen than the gold, wouldn't there?" He laughs as he squints at the crates that line the wall.

"A little less trouble," says I, though Liam drinks less than any of the other men his age.

"Glory be to God!" he says as his eyes adjust to the darkness. "There's a fortune in here!"

"A million pounds, Liam Tomas, less what your man has taken out of that open crate."

"How did they get it up here?"

"Brought it up one night, I suppose."

"It would have taken a dozen men at least and themselves working all night long."

I have to be careful because I don't want me man to think I'm a know-it-all — though God knows that's exactly what I am.

"The way I sees it," I say, "Sir Roger Casement, God be good to him, and himself being on the Supreme Council of the Irish Republican Brotherhood, actually wants to land gold at two spots, one in Kerry where the Germans will also be landing the guns and the munitions and one up here off Galway Bay. He trusts Daniel O'Kelly so he puts Daniel in charge of the landing here. Then Daniel, who is an informer even then, informs the Brits about the Kerry landing but neglects to tell them about the one here."

"Glory be to God! He betrayed Casement too, did he?"

"I'm not certain about that, Liam Tomas" — I touch his arm, gentlelike — "but it seems to fit, doesn't it? We know there was an informer and we know that there was more gold, like the rumors back then said there was, and we know that your man knows where the gold is and himself the only one, except us."

"He betrayed the men of 1916." Liam sobs. "If they had the guns. . . ."

"If they had the guns, the Brits would still have destroyed them altogether. They were eejits, Liam Tomas. 'Twas the younger ones, like Mick Collins, God be good to him, that knew how to fight the Brits."

"And neither the Free Staters nor the Republicans having enough guns now."

"You know what I'm thinking, Liam Tomas O'Riada?"

"What are you thinking, Nell Pat Malone?" He puts his arm around me and rests his head against me breasts, so naturally I snuggle closer to him.

"I'm thinking" — I sigh my best sigh, even though me poor body is already on fire for him — "that we ought to leave all the gold here."

"Do you now?"

"Liam, it won't do anyone any good in Ireland. If the Republicans find it out, they'll use it for guns; and if the Free Staters take it, they'll be buying more guns too. The Civil War will just drag on."

"You're right, woman," he says. "Let someone else find it in the future."

"I'm pregnant, Liam Tomas," I says, quite calmly.

"Glory be to God," he shouts, "and all the Holy Saints in heaven! I'm going to be a father!"

487

"You are that!"

"Sure, do you want to marry me as soon as we can announce the banns?"

"Sooner. The young priest says there are times when you don't have to announce them."

"I've been afraid to ask you all these months, Nell Pat, for fear you wouldn't want me."

"Why would I never not want you?" The poor eejit, I think to meself.

"I'm such an eejit."

"You are that, but it doesn't mean I don't love you something awful. . . . Sure, did you think the woman you made love to last night could live without you?"

"I know" — he holds me very close and caresses me — "that I can't live without you. And our child will be born in America, born free."

"He will indeed."

Liam is playing with me breasts and now I'm out of my mind with love. He starts to take off me blouse.

"Liam!" I says, on fire with love.

"Do you want me to stop?" the poor eejit asks. " 'Tis a strange place to make love, isn't it?"

"I'll make love with you, Liam Tomas," says I, "anywhere you want me, anytime you want me, till death do us part."

Well, it's not easy to make love in a rocky cave on top of a mountain and it being pitch black, but to tell the truth me and me husband, for sure, he's that now, don't mind at all, at all.

Did I mean what I said to him before we made love?

I surely did, as God and the Mother of Jesus be my witnesses. I'm Liam's, body and soul, for the rest of me life.

He falls asleep, poor dear man, when we're finished. So, with all me clothes off, I sneak over to the open crate of gold and take out a bar of gold and put it in me kit bag. We'll take it to America with us so that we won't starve to death and me man won't have to labor in the ditches.

The money, I tell meself, doesn't belong to anyone anymore. It won't be doing anyone any good sitting here by a broken-down shrine in the County Galway. It would be wrong, wouldn't it, not to use a little bit of it so we can begin well in America?

And haven't I asked the young priest about it?

Well, not about the gold, poor man.

What I did ask him went something like this: "Suppose I find a treasure, your Reverence, I mean like a twenty-pound note lying in the road, and I don't know to whom it belongs or how to return it: Do I have to give it to the church?"

He laughs as he usually does at me. "Sure, now, Nell Pat, aren't you the great casuist?"

"I don't know what a casuist is, your Reverence, but if you say so."

489

He laughs again. "It's someone who works out deep moral problems. Well, the answer is that of course you don't have to give it to the church unless you want to, and you probably need it more than the church, don't you?"

"I haven't found a twenty-pound note, your Reverence."

What I have found is a million pounds in gold, and I wouldn't be trusting the church with that, would I?

Like Mick Collins is supposed to have said when the Free Staters beat the Republicans in the election, "We seem to have won everything. I wish at least the bishops were against us."

"You can keep whatever you find under similar circumstances, Nell Pat."

"It wouldn't be mine, would it?"

"Ah, but it would. As we say in Latin, 'Res nullius fit primi occupantis.'"

"Do you now?" I pretend I know what he's talking about.

"It means" — he sees through me fakery — "that which belongs to no one becomes the property of the first one who finds it."

"Finders keepers?"

"In the circumstances you describe, yes."

I write down the Latin words so I can quote them to Liam later on.

Actually, I'm thinking that if the young priest is right (and why wouldn't he be?), the whole treasure belongs to me so I'm being very restrained by copping only one bar of gold.

And itself heavy in me kit bag as me man and I ride back to Carraroe to tell the young priest we're going to be married.

And what does that eejit with the pretty brown eyes do?

He laughs and says, "Well, isn't it after being time for that?"

– 48 –

"You wouldn't be focking in a cave filled with gold, Nuala Anne McGrail?"

She pounded my arm. "We don't use that language in me office, do we?"

Note whose office it had become.

"Yes, ma'am." I began to reread the latest chapter in Ma's astonishing diary.

"Promise me you won't talk that way in front of me mom?"

"She wouldn't be offended by my fantasies about you in my story but she would be offended by my language?"

"We don't talk that way at home, Dermot Michael. We may *think* that way but we don't *talk* that way."

"So you start to talk that way when you come to Dublin because that's the way a shy girl from Carraroe protects herself from being considered a greenhorn?"

She glared at me and then smiled. "And your-self taking off me psychological clothes. . . . Anyway, I'm trying to stop because you want me to act like a lady."

"I never said that!"

"You *think* that!" She jabbed her finger at me, still grinning.

"Anyway, has your friend Nell Pat finally shocked you?"

"She has not." She rose from the chair at her desk and picked up the phone. "Nora, would you mind sending tea for two to Mr. Coyne's room. That's right, Earl Grey, he's very par-ticular about that, poor man. . . . Ah, no, himself doesn't want any sherry. Well, he does, I sup-pose, but it wouldn't be good for him at this hour of the day, would it? And a double order of scones for him and a double order of clotted cream and raspberry preserves. . . . Ah, sure, Nora, he's not the worst of them."

That settled that. Sweets instead of the crea-ture.

"Mind you." Nuala pondered the question of Ma's behavior. "I wouldn't exclude the possi-bility of fock — uh, lovemaking in a cave filled with gold if I were pregnant and the man was going to marry me in a week or two. But I can't imagine such circumstances."

"The opportunities for that sort of behavior don't come very often, do they?"

I'd have to be very careful in that cave on Saturday morning.

"Your gram is . . . was a wild woman, wasn't she? I admire her, but I'm not all that much like her, as she keeps telling me."

"Does she now?"

"She does." Nuala nodded seriously. "She likes me and thinks I'm a nice wee lass, but she says I'm a quiet one compared to her and that's all right too."

"Ah."

"She doesn't have any regrets. Not at all, at all. She still doesn't think it was wrong to seduce her man or to take the gold."

"She wouldn't. We always wondered where they got the capital to buy a string of two flats their first year in America."

"You think I'm daft, don't you, Dermot Michael?"

"I think you're a very sensitive woman and a good actress and you have identified with the author of the diary so well that you can imagine her thoughts and actions."

"That's it, I suppose," she agreed. "Ah, here's your tea."

"Our tea."

"Wasn't I saying that?"

I put the manuscript into the Federal Express envelope. I had, at Nuala's suggestion, printed out all the previous translations and sent them to George, who knows some people in the publishing industry. Now we were sending each day's copy to him.

" 'Tis insurance," she said, "against losing the

493

original or a hard disk accident."

"Or against our friends who won't be able to suppress the story, once George has it?"

"I hadn't thought of that."

Naturally she had thought of it. Jane Bond. A know-it-all, just like Ma.

"Will she be ashamed of her love life being spread out in the open like that?" I asked herself.

She looked at me as if I were the worst eejit in all the world. "Is the Pope Buddhist?"

"Incredible!" George exploded on the phone after he'd read the early translations. "What a woman!"

Would no one be scandalized by this fierce redhead with the green eyes and a mind of her own?

"You're not planning to show them to Mom or the bishop?"

"Why not? Nell Pat was their mother, wasn't she? Hell, Punk, they won't be surprised. They knew what she was like better than we did."

"But the bishop?"

"Uncle Willy is likely to be pleased at the thought he was conceived in a passionate union out of wedlock. He's no prude."

I apparently was surrounded by people who were not prudes. Worse luck for me, I guess.

"Here's a wee sip of sherry." She poured half a tumbler of it for me. "Dry sherry at that. Sure, you need to recover from the shock of your gram's wanton behavior."

"Where did you get that, woman?"

"I bought it with the change from the flopping disks you were wanting. I figured we might need it."

"On a rainy day."

"Which is almost any day in Ireland, isn't it?"

"They call them floppy disks, Nuala."

"And they don't flop at all, do they now?"

You never won.

A storm from the northeast was battering Dublin like a drunken pooka. A deluge of rain was pelting our windows, and the windows themselves were rattling in the wind. It was dark enough to be the day of the end of the world.

Dear God, I wanted to go home.

Nuala poured a "wee sip" for herself and buttered a scone for me.

"It has shaken you, Dermot Michael, hasn't it?" She touched my hand. "Did you really think she wasn't a plotter and a schemer?"

"No. . . . I'm sorry I didn't know her better. I'm shaken by what a fierce wonderful woman she was — whom I never did appreciate."

"But who knew her better or who appreciated her more than you, except himself? You're the only who still carries her pictures, aren't you now?"

"I am."

"I understand, Dermot Michael." She pointed an accusing finger at me triumphantly. "You're thinking you'll never see Nell Pat again to tell her how much you love her and yourself believing in life after death and meself not being sure and yet knowing that she's still alive and taking care of the two of us, so that everything will work out well."

I did not want to pursue the last words. Would Nell Pat want me to bring Nuala home with me, if not on the plane a few days from now at least after she graduated from TCD?

Are the Jesuits a Catholic order?

"We may well need her help in the West this weekend."

"Go 'long with you." She handed me another scone, drenched in an outrageous layer of raspberry jam over clotted cream. "It'll be easy."

I doubted that. Quite the contrary, I dreaded our journey to Cork and Galway. Terrible things would surely happen.

– 49 –

September 8, 1922

Mrs. Liam Tomas O'Riada now, if you please.

The young schoolteacher man took a picture of us at the wedding and we already have some prints. I'll be after packing the plate in our bags when we leave from Cork.

We both look terrible young.

I don't care. I'll never have any regrets. Never.

We're living in the room in my own house that used to be mine. It's crowded and there's no privacy for us at all. Me ma and da are wonderful, but we need a house of our own — which most people in Ireland don't have for many long years after they're married.

I wonder if the gold is spoiling me. I wonder if Liam will be furious at me when I tell him about the gold. He's a good man and a hard worker and a smart man too. But he's a tad unpredictable, perhaps because I haven't had much of a chance to study him yet up close. He doesn't seem to mind a woman who is plotting and scheming all the time. He says I am twice as smart as any man he knows.

I don't want to have any secrets from him. I want to be able to tell him everything. But I don't how to do it yet.

Well, if he's angry at me, I'll tell him the truth — that I didn't know how to tell him all the truth.

That's the only problem which keeps me from being the happiest woman in the world.

Well, that and migrating to America. One moment I can hardly wait and the next moment I'm terrified to leave.

I know it will be all right when we do it,

but I'll miss poor old Carraroe something terrible.

Later.

I'm terrified. The schoolteacher man, the one
with the big bloody camera, came over to the
house a few minutes ago to say there was a
phone call at the post office from the garage
in Galway City. The black closed touring car
is back and is staying there for the night. The
driver told the garage man that they're driving
out to Connemara tomorrow.

Liam's plan is to get to the pub early and
seize the colonel, as he still calls him, when
he comes in. Then at gunpoint he'll force him
to meet with the man in the car. The pho-
tographer man will take a picture of him handing
over the money to the colonel. Then Liam will
arrest both of them and turn them over to the
Free Staters.

"It's a grand plan," says I, me knees shaking
with fear, "but I'm not sure about arresting
the man in the car."

"And why not?"

"I don't think the Free Staters would want
him. They wouldn't know what to do with him.
They certainly couldn't put him on trial."

"Aye," says me man, "true enough."

"The picture might be more use to them than
the man himself."

Liam looks at me narrowly. "You're a deep
one, Nell Pat Malone."

"I hope you're not angry at me, Liam Tomas,"

498

I says, and meself being close to tears.

He wraps me up in his arms. "Woman, I don't know what I'd do without you. I never would have thought it, but I'm thinking now that I find deep women terrible attractive."

So I blush and feel real good about meself.

Liam is making all his arrangements for tomorrow. Then he'll come back and I can tell by the look in his eye that he'll want me.

Well, he'll get no fight from me on that account, because I'm wanting him too.

Then when we're finished with our loving, I'll tell him that I intend to be with him tomorrow out on the end of Galway.

He may argue that it's not safe and that it's no place for a woman.

I'll say wasn't it a woman who found out about this traitor?

He'll agree to that and then he'll ask why I want to be there and I'll say that I want to make sure you amadons don't do some stupid thing like killing the man in the car.

But the truth will be that I'll be going out to that meeting to make sure that Daniel O'Kelly doesn't try to kill me husband like he killed me brother before him.

I'll kill the traitor meself before I let him harm my Liam Tomas.

I don't want revenge. I'll leave that to God. I just want to protect my Liam Tomas. I pray right now to the Sacred Heart of Jesus and to

Our Lady of Knock to help me protect me man.

I can hear him coming in the house and meself alone here and me blood as hot as a peat fire.

– 50 –

"Are you afraid of a third strike, Dermot Michael?"

"Where did you hear that phrase, from baseball?"

We were sitting in the restaurant in the Imperial Hotel in Cork City, on South Mall, just above the Lee River. It was here that Major General Emmet Dalton had set up his headquarters after he had outmaneuvered the Irregulars and captured Cork. Here too Michael Collins had spent his last night of life. I didn't want to know in which room he had slept. I continued to wonder whether he would approve of our quest.

We were behind schedule but content after a glorious day of touring the southeast of Ireland. In the old-fashioned brass and dark red atmosphere of the dining room, it was easy to imagine that time had rolled back and we were part of the Edwardian era, the optimistic time before the Great War. Perhaps we were an Anglo-Irish aristocrat and her wealthy American lover eating a large if rather unimaginative dinner and consuming enough drinks to make them forget tomorrow before they retired for a night of stolen love.

The light in the restaurant was soft and dim, we were both pleasantly tired, we had both a couple of jars of wine taken and a fine roast beef dinner eaten. There were only a few people in the room, and the woman who was playing the Irish harp sang with a gentle and restful voice. ("She's quite grand indeed," Nuala had commented. "Brilliant!")

A perfect setting for romantic fantasies, although there wouldn't be any stolen love tonight, that was for sure.

"Your brother said something about a third strike and he explained it to me."

"About me?"

"No. But I applied it to you." She was watching me intently, doubtless trying to figure me out the same way Ma tried to figure out her own man seventy years ago.

Except I was not Nuala's man.

"And what does it mean?"

"It means" — she put down her claret glass — "are you afraid that, having made a mistake with two women before me, that I'll be your third strike?"

That was precisely what I was afraid she meant. "What makes you think that, Nul?"

"You fancy me a lot, I can tell that."

"My story would make that clear even if my actions didn't."

"From the first moment you saw me in O'Neill's?"

"Just about."

"Yet you don't want me?" She seem baffled rather than annoyed.

I shifted uneasily in my chair. "Nul, you're the most remarkable woman I've ever met . . . attractive in every way that a woman can be attractive. Spending the rest of one's life with you would be delight."

"But?"

"But you're too young."

"I'm twenty at Christmastime."

I knew that I should have begun this conversation with her before we left Dublin. My reluctance to talk to her about our relationship was irresponsible and cowardly — just as had been my postponement of an explanation about the puzzle of the gold and the death of Michael Collins.

Now I must face a quarrel at the tag end of what had been a perfect day.

We had left Dublin early in the morning, in the bright red Mercedes that the rental agency had brought over.

"Would you look at it now!" Nuala had pointed at the car in delighted astonishment. "Isn't it a mistress car?"

"Just a Benz 250. Do you mean a car for a mistress or a car that substitutes for a mistress?"

"Isn't it both?"

She was dressed in her jeans again with the

502

new blue jacket I had purchased for her, my Marquette sweatshirt, and the Aran Isle scarf and cap I had given her the day after the attack in Irishtown. She looked very much like a college girl on a football weekend — at Notre Dame since, alas, Marquette doesn't have a team anymore. In fact, she looked like any one of a couple score of young women from the neighborhood, though taller than most of them and more beautiful than any of them.

"Put your bag in the trunk, woman, and don't give me a hard time."

"Here we call it the boot, and if I can't give you a hard time, sure, what's the point in the trip?"

"Into the car with you, woman." I had shoved her rump gently. "You'd try the patience of a saint."

"And yourself being the saint, is it now?"

She had put her suitcase — spanking new — into the boot and jumped into the car.

"Take me to Carraroe, please, Arthur. By way of Cork if you don't mind."

"Yes, miss." I had bowed politely.

Despite her pledge to give me a hard time, a pledge that she honored, Nuala was a fine traveling companion. She didn't complain or grumble or ask how much longer the trip was. On the contrary, the trip was a fun experience for her. "And meself never traveling anywhere except back and forth to Dublin on the train."

"Not even to Cork?"

503

"Not even to Kilarney."

The weather was perfect again, blue sky and rapidly moving ice-cream clouds, a brisk, sunny football weekend to match my brisk, sunny football weekend companion.

The southeast region of Ireland — Wicklow, Waterford, Wexford, East Cork — is soft and serene, a vast green checkerboard blanket in which, a person might imagine, it would be pleasant to relax with one's love for a night (or a day) of rest and love.

My plan had been to drive through Cork City and then on to Clonakilty and the vale where Michael Collins had died. However, it had become evident early on that we'd not be able to go beyond Cork. Nuala insisted on stopping often and scampering, once more the playful filly, over the hills and fields and strands of counties Wicklow and Wexford.

"Bring your camera, Dermot," she would shout. "I'll take the pictures of you and you can take pictures of me."

Scenery without people in it, you see, she had pronounced dull and therefore unacceptable.

I would have not one picture of her to send to George, but several rolls — an Irish model with a knit beret and scarf, perfectly acceptable if not for *Vogue* or *Bazaar* then surely for *Ireland of the Welcomes*.

Any man would come to Ireland to see such radiant, happy young beauty.

"I think I'll make a grand world traveler someday, Dermot," she cried after lunch in Rosslare (off the main road to Cork but a place " 'twould be a sin to miss): "Sure, isn't it a beautiful and exciting world and yourself a writer that knows that without me shooting off me big mouth."

We'd been watching the waves break at the harbor wall, great giants, glittering white foam in the sunlight with dark purple bases hurling the foam over the wall.

I kissed her then, quite chastely. She responded with equal chastity.

Wandering to the ends of the earth with this frolicsome young woman would indeed be a joy.

At the dinner table over our cake and tea when she confronted me about our relationship, I wondered if the exuberance of our ride from Dublin to Cork was a part of a carefully orchestrated plan of action to prepare for this dialogue.

Are the Jesuits an all-male order?

My only distraction from a pleasant and exhausting day was an occasional brief attempt to capture and hold the image of the face that I was sure would break open the puzzle that was bringing us to Cork and Galway. The face would float across my imagination, hazy and undeveloped save in its outline, torment me for a fraction of a section, and then lazily float away.

Who was it? The mystery man for whom Ma and Pa had lain in wait at Lettermullen? Someone I knew from modern Ireland or modern

505

America? Maybe Martin Longwood-Jones or Brendan Keane?

I couldn't quite place it, yet I was more than ever convinced that if my preconscious would let me look at that face a little longer, I would solve the mystery.

At the end of dinner, she had looked up from her port somewhat shyly. "You know what this weekend is, Dermot?"

It was a question Ma had asked me often. I tried to think. Someone's birthday? No. A feast in the church year?

"All Saints?"

"And All Hallows Eve."

"Trick-or-treat time in the States."

"And everywhere else; we invented it here in Ireland. 'Tis said that the dead walk at Sahmain."

She had pronounced the word as if it were spelled Saurain.

"An old Celtic festival not quite Christianized yet, but certainly made harmless."

"I'm thinking it's a scary time of the year even if you are a Christian. The world turns dark and dangerous, doesn't it now?"

"Do you believe the dead walk at Sahmaintide, Nuala?"

"Sure, in Dublin I don't. In Carraroe I half did."

"No self-respecting ghost would walk in Dublin anyway."

"We're different folk out here. The world

506

is a mysterious and sometimes threatening place. Good and evil lurk where you'd least expect them."

I had not wanted to argue with her West of Ireland mystical visions.

"Do you think the dead will be walking in Carraroe when we arrive there?"

She shook her head. "I'm thinking they're already there and themselves waiting for us."

I felt myself shiver. "Should we go back to Dublin?"

Her eyes widened. "We can't disappoint them, can we, Dermot Michael? And themselves expecting us?"

"Are you serious, Nuala?"

"What was it your gram used to say? Half fun and full earnest?"

"You're really superstitious?"

"If you're raised in the Gaeltacht, you might not be religious but you will certainly be superstitious."

Then she asked me about the third strike.

"You don't want me because I'm an uncultivated lass from the Gaeltacht who never took a shower once in her life till she came to your suite."

"Have I ever said or done anything that would make you think I'm that kind of a snob?"

She replied promptly to that question. "You have not, Dermot Michael, and me being ashamed of myself for even thinking that, but

507

I don't understand. You fancy me, maybe even love me a little, and yet you're going home to America . . ."

She didn't add the implied phrase, "without me."

"There's nothing wrong with you, Nuala." I shifted again in my chair in the restaurant. "You're a young woman of enormous talents and possibilities. You have the promise of a rich and productive and exciting life."

"As an accountant?" She frowned.

"As a singer, an actress, as almost anything you want to be."

"Well." She drank a deep draft of her red wine, finishing the glass. "I don't think I'm good enough or at least have enough training to be a brilliant success in either singing or acting."

"You could get the training."

"I suppose I could. There are lots of unemployed singers and actresses in Dublin, Dermot Michael. With the new Financial Services Center opening on the Liffey, isn't there likely to be a terrible shortage of accountants? Maybe I can act and sing in me spare time, but I'm not Hollywood material or the Hollywood type."

"I'll be blunt, Nul. You're too young to marry or even to be caught up in a serious relationship. You need time to develop, to find yourself, to permit your talents and abilities to grow and to flourish, to discover your full potential, to uncover the real Nuala."

She sighed nosily. "I'll not be denying the

truth of any of that, though some of it sounds like clichés to me. I don't understand how it matters."

"Let's be honest with each other, Nul. We're talking marriage, aren't we? People like you and me don't play around with our own emotions or other people's. Love means marriage."

She nodded. "The sooner the better."

No messing around with circumlocutions for Nuala Anne McGrail, not tonight.

"We'd be happy at first, of that I'm sure, mostly because you're such an adaptable woman. But it wouldn't last, Nul. You'd discover all that you really are and you'd realize that you are a young woman of great and many talents and that you could not develop them because of marriage and children — we are talking children, aren't we?"

She nodded vigorously. "Maybe not seven, but three or four."

"Then," I went on with my gloomy scenario, "you'd feel frustrated and unfulfilled and begin to resent the marriage in which you were trapped and then to hate me for trapping you."

"I'd never hate you, Dermot."

"Maybe not." I touched her hand. "But you'd be unhappy and I couldn't stand seeing you unhappy. . . . Believe me, I've seen so many women caught in that trap. And it's not just marriage that does it to them. A serious and prolonged relationship has the same effect."

"Suppose there's another scenario." She continued too, relaxed and casual as if we were two doctors discussing the case of an absent patient. "Suppose that I'd be needing a husband to love me and a brood of kids to contend with as a condition for developing me talents, which I'll concede for the sake of the discussion."

She did not give up easily, did she?

"I don't think that's very likely."

"All right. . . . Yes, we'll both have a wee sip of port, thank you very much. . . . Where was I? Ah, yes. If I were twenty-five, would that be old enough?"

"It would certainly cast matters in a different light."

"I'll wait till I'm twenty-five."

"Come on, Nuala, that would be as bad as being married, maybe worse."

The port was served. Nuala tasted it as if she were an expert on port. "Ah, 'tis grand!"

When the wine steward had departed, beaming happily at her compliment, she continued the argument. "I don't understand it. Shouldn't I have the right to say whether I want to be exploited or not? Don't I get a vote at all?"

"You could be exploited, Nuala Anne, without knowing you're being exploited, not at first. Then you'd find out and you'd become very bitter."

"Are you thinking I have a teenage crush on you that I'll get over as soon as you're on the plane back to Yank-land?"

"Have you ever been in love before, Nuala?"

510

"I have not. Sure, I've never met a man like you before."

"First love ought not to be trusted."

She nodded. "Maybe you're right. Still, I wish I had some say in it. You're treating me like an inexperienced child who needs someone to protect her from herself."

"You are still technically a teenager, Nul."

" 'Tis really good port, isn't it? I wouldn't be knowing" — she sipped it again — "but it does taste grand, doesn't it?"

"It does."

"You're a good and sweet and wonderful man, Dermot Michael Coyne." She sighed. "I'll never meet anyone like you again. I love you with all my heart. I think you love me too. Yet after you hired me to work on your gram's diary, you backed away from me."

"I didn't want to exploit a vulnerable woman."

"How many times must I tell you" — now she *was* annoyed at me — "that I can take care of myself? Didn't I prove that to you the night at Irishtown? I wouldn't even let you touch my hand like you just did, unless I wanted you to touch it. Don't you know me well enough to know that? Am I the kind of woman who would have gone off to your bedroom with you just to keep my job? Would I make love with you unless I wanted to? You know all about me talents, Dermot Michael Coyne, but you don't know me at all, at all."

"Nul —"

"You didn't have to make your eejit promise that there'd be no passes. Let me tell you one thing: There wouldn't have been a second one unless I wanted the first."

"What would have happened?" I couldn't help grin at my Spanish galleon in full sail again and with the guns firing.

"You saw what I did to your man Patrick in Irishtown!"

"You would have slept with me in the suite if I asked?"

"I'd do anything to keep you, Dermot, anything." Tears began to form in her eyes. "I'd even try to capture you like your gram captured her man, though I don't think that would work and anyway she says I oughtn't."

Would it work? Would a naked Nuala Anne in my room tonight make this discussion seem foolish?

It would indeed, but I wasn't about to tell her that.

"That's good advice."

"I suppose it is. . . . Still, I'm thinking that you're afraid of me. You have those two strikes on you and you don't want to be hurt again, for which, God knows, I don't blame you. But won't you feel that about any woman you begin to fancy? Tell me the honest truth, Dermot Michael Coyne, are you likely to be meeting another woman like me for the rest of your life?"

"I doubt it."

"I'm not Kelly Anne, I'm not Christina," she

shouted, causing the two couples still in the dining room to stare at us. "I'm Nuala. I'll never hurt you. I'll never betray you. If you think I would, you're a terrible eejit and an awful amadon too."

"It's you I'm worried about, not myself."

Was that true? Was she not being more honest than I was? Was I not afraid about being hurt again? Was Nuala Anne McGrail too good to be true, was that my fear?

Was I being a terrible eejit altogether?

And an amadon too?

I would have to think about it.

Now that I've had a long time to think about it, as I write these words, I conclude that maybe I was indeed an eejit and an amadon both.

In the dining room in Cork, however, with the soft light and the music of the harp, I was filled with the sense of virtue that comes from romantic sacrifice.

"I don't want to sound patronizing or chauvinist, Nuala. In a year, in six months even, you'll know I'm right."

"Maybe you are," she conceded, shrugging her shoulders. "Sure, am I not half convinced meself that you are right? Tell you what." She took on her shrewd fishmonger expression. "If I'm not totally convinced in a year that you're right, can we open up this conversation again?"

It was a nice compromise on which to end the argument.

"I'll always be happy to talk to you, Nuala."

So that was that. We finished our port and went to our rooms, Nuala announcing that she would translate the next entry in diary before she went to sleep.

"That's not necessary."

"I want to earn my keep. . . . Besides, am I not dying of curiosity to find out what happened out at Lettermullen that day?"

"We know that O'Kelly was shot and his body left at Maam Cross, not turned over to the Free Staters."

"Would not they have shot him too?"

"True enough. A trial would have made matters worse for the Free State because many of the Republicans would have thought him a hero."

We had left the elevator on our floor.

"Good night, Dermot."

"Good night, Nuala."

We did not kiss one another, mostly because I turned away before we could. I was so shaken by our argument — dialogue, whatever — that even a brief moment of tenderness would have turned me into a raging fury of passion.

In my room I took off my clothes except for my shorts and put on my robe. I had a lot to think about before I tried to sleep.

I didn't do a good job of thinking because I was too confused — and too aroused. If she came to the room tonight I would have no choice.

Was I truly afraid of sustained intimacy with

a woman? Had I been hurt twice and hence made incapable of risking a third swing and a miss?

On the other hand, as Nuala did not know, not being a baseball aficionado, you can with a three-and-two pitch be called out on strikes by just standing at the plate and watching the ball float over.

Was I not missing an opportunity of a lifetime? The last great opportunity? A bit of wondrous good fortune that made my triumph in the Standard and Poors pit look like a parish raffle prize?

Maybe I was. Yet, if for Nuala it was only a late-teen crush, an inadvisable first love, would she not be over it in a year? If she still wanted to discuss marriage then, could I not then enter into the discussion with confidence that I was not exploiting her?

Where does gentlemanly respect end and fear of the third strike, a swing and a miss, begin?

I didn't know. I needed more time to think.

Eejit?

I guess.

The face of the man in the touring car floated by me again. He moved more slowly this time and I saw the face more clearly.

Damn, I missed it again.

I'd have it before the weekend was over.

I returned to the subject of Nuala, always pleasant, always tormenting.

If she came to the room tonight I would let her in. We would make love and the matter would be settled. The early phases of our affair and marriage would be a grand success. Brilliant! Maybe the later years wouldn't be as bad as I feared. Maybe she would experience payoffs that would outweigh her frustrations.

Then I began to wish that she would come. To hell with all my fears. I'd never meet another woman like her, that was for sure.

My imagination filled up with images of what I would do with her when she came into my room. I had progressed in my reverie to a situation in which she was half naked; then weariness triumphed over conscious desire and I drifted away into a half sleep.

Could I have walked down the dim corridor to her room, only three doors away, and taken the initiative?

Would I be welcome?

Sure I would.

Wouldn't that be exploitation?

Is it exploitation when a woman wants you as much as you want her?

Not if she's old enough to know what the risks and the costs are.

Nuala was an innocent and shy child from the Gaeltacht. I was her first crush. She had no idea of the risks and the costs of intimacy. I had to protect her from herself.

If, however, she became aggressive and tried to seduce me, wasn't I dispensed from my duties to guard and protect?

Such eejit rationalizations show how confused

I was at the time.

Then someone knocked at the door. Startled and surprised, I jumped out of bed, wild with excitement and desire.

"Yes?"

"Nuala."

I tightened the belt on my robe and opened the door.

She was fully clothed. In her hand she held several sheets of lined paper and a Federal Express envelope. "This is the next entry. I think you should read it now. My handwriting is not so good. I'll stay with you while you read it. Then I'll take it down to the desk for Federal Express pickup tomorrow."

"It's that bad?"

"It solves most of the mystery, I think."

— NUALA'S VOICE —

Nell Pat, me heart is breaking. I suppose that's the way it is at the end of all adolescent crushes and I have only myself to blame. He turned me down. I didn't throw myself at him, the way you threw yourself at your man. I simply couldn't do it. But, despite what you tell me, I would have done it if I had the courage.

What if it's not just a crush? What if he's the great love of me life?

Well, even if he is, I've lost him and I feel like crying myself to sleep. But I'll never let him know that he's broken me poor heart. I'll show him that he's not the only man in the world and that I can do just fine without him!

I'm not even sure he's wrong. Maybe I shouldn't fall in love, I mean real love, till I'm twenty-five. He'll still be an Irish bachelor then and probably useless. But he's useless now and I still love him with all my heart and soul.

I'm furious at him and I love him more than ever. He really does care about me and me career, even if that's an excuse. We could work it out. Maybe we should and maybe we shouldn't.

He still doesn't understand who the real murderer is. Sometimes he's pretty close to it and then he loses the truth of the story — which is as plain on the nose on me face.

The focking bastard is an eejit.

And I'll always love him!

– 51 –

September 15, 1922

Well, it's all over now. I'll never forget it. I don't want to write about it, but I'd must while the memories are still fresh and ourselves getting ready to leave for America.

The Brigade, that's me and Liam and three of the lads, whose names and I'll not put down even in this private book, and the teacher man with his camera, took over the pub early this morning. The publican and his brother and their wives were terrible scared, though we assured them that they would not be hurt if they co-operated.

Poor folk, they weren't sure which side was which and I'm thinking they didn't know they'd done anything wrong by cooperating with Daniel O'Kelly.

I found meself a poker, just in case I needed it.

The sky was cloudy, but it wasn't raining and when the wind stopped, it didn't seem all that cold for this time of the year.

Our plan is to capture Daniel when he comes into the pub and tell him there would be a gun pointed at his head when the man came with the touring car. We wouldn't let him see the cameraman hidden behind the bar. When the man in car came in the pub and gave Daniel the money, the cameraman would, on a signal from meself, stand up and take his picture with his artificial light thing.

In the meantime one of the lads would sneak out and disarm the driver of the car.

I thought it was a pretty thin scheme, but we'd have at least captured O'Kelly and we'd have proof that he was meeting with the man in the car which we could turn over to the Free Staters and let them take care of O'Kelly while the Brigade disbanded altogether and Liam and I left for America.

Finally the sun came out, kind of shy and bashfullike at first but then, in all her glory, and chased the clouds from the sky.

About the middle of the day, who comes along the road, whistling "The Bold Fenian Men," but the traitor himself?

He fools us by sitting down outside and yelling for his jar. But I'm thinking that maybe that's good for us. We send the woman of the house out to serve him and warn her that she'll be in grave danger if she lets on the slightest hint to the man who murdered Michael Collins. We move the teacher man over to the window behind the curtain and give him a chance to set up the camera.

The woman of the house, once she knows that we're after the killer of the general, is on our side, God bless her, and she laughs and jokes with the gombeen man.

He's three jars taken and still there's no car and we wonder if the meeting is off.

Then we hear it thumping down the road and we all get ready, the teacher man fixes his camera, the lad who is to take on the driver sneaks out the back door, I stand by at the curtains, me poker in me hand, and Liam and the other two lads are prepared to burst out the door and arrest the criminals.

It's all going well, I'm thinking to meself. Too well. Something will go wrong.

Which God knows it did. O'Kelly was a

quicker gombeen man than we had expected.

The car pulls up and the man in it, wearing a brown tweed suit with a cloak, gets out and walks over to O'Kelly at the table. He's not smiling because he probably figures O'Kelly is worse than cow manure, but he has to pay him off if he wants to use him again to betray poor old Ireland.

They shake hands briefly and the man sits down. O'Kelly shouts for service and the woman of the house brings him out a jar and another one for himself.

She and her man and the other two hide behind the bar because they know there's going to be trouble.

The two of them drink for a while and chat about politics. 'Tis clear they think the Free State is finished because they're not getting enough guns from England to gain control of the countryside.

Then the man from the car takes out his wallet and counts out the bills. O'Kelly picks them up, counts them, and smiles.

"Now!" I says to the teacher as I pull the curtains back.

His light thing explodes. Both O'Kelly and the other fella jump out of their seats.

Liam and the two lads burst out the door.

"We arrest the both of you," Liam shouts at them, his Mauser (with only two bullets in it) pointed at O'Kelly, "for the murder of General Michael Collins."

Now here's where that traitor proves how quick he is. He leaps at me man, pushes the pistol out of his way, and points his pistol right at Liam's head, jammed behind his ear.

Liam didn't fire, I'm thinking, because a bit of him still respects the man he thought his colonel was. He wasn't planning to kill O'Kelly himself.

"If any of you move," the traitor says, "I'll kill your friend here. I'm going to retreat nice and slow to the car. You're going to tell the man over there whose got his gun on the chauffeur to back off and my colleague and I are going to leave real peacefullike."

Not at all, I'm thinking. He'll kill Liam and maybe shoot the other lads too if he can.

"Careful, O'Kelly," says the other fella, as cold as the ice at the North Pole. Or in the depths of hell.

Well, there's nothing left to be done. I'm standing inside the door, where Liam ordered me to stay. O'Kelly doesn't know I'm there at all.

"You fools don't understand!" Daniel yelled at us. "I did it for Ireland! I don't need the focking money! The fools in Dublin are not fit to run the country! I am! And I will! I'll help make Ireland a great country! I only regret that you won't be alive to see how much better a man I am than Mick Collins! Up the republic!"

He lifted the gun, about to shoot.

Without thinking about it much, I step out the door and bring me poker down on the back of his head as hard as I can.

I bashed his brains out.

Lord have mercy on the poor man's soul. What right do I have to think I'm any better than he was?

Lord have mercy on all of us.

I can't write any more.

– 52 –

[Not dated]

"You're not a killer, Nell Pat," said the young priest.

"Haven't I been telling you that, woman?" says Liam, holding me hand real tight.

"I know, but —"

"You killed the first man, if you really did, to protect yourself and your aunt from sexual attack. You killed Daniel to protect your husband from certain death."

"But —"

"You didn't start the war, Nell Pat." His pretty brown eyes were hard and angry. "You were caught up in it through no fault of your own, like so many other people have been in the last ten years. Instead of tormenting yourself, you should thank God that you and Liam are still alive."

There was no arguing with him and himself right, I suppose. He and Liam are also right when they say I'll get over it. I'll never be glad I killed either the Tan or Daniel O'Kelly, Lord have mercy on them both. Yet I'll always be glad I saved me man.

I hated Daniel O'Kelly because he killed me brother and tried to kill me husband down there in Cork by blaming him for the death of General Collins. I didn't want him dead. I didn't want to have to kill him.

I had to kill him and that's that. Maybe someday in heaven we can straighten it all out.

I dropped the poker after I smashed his head and vomited all over the table where the jars were.

"He's dead," Liam said. "The colonel is dead."

"Lord have mercy on the dirty bastard," says one of the lads.

The chauffeur tried to make a break for it, but the lad watching him tripped him and he fell flat on his face.

The fella that paid O'Kelly stood there staring at us with a contemptuous smile. We were Irish savages, not even real human beings.

"Let's kill these two bastards," one of the lads says. "They're murderers too."

"If we do," says Liam, "we're no better than they are."

"We can't turn them over to the Free Staters, Liam."

"It would be the ruination of Ireland if we did that or if we killed them."

"The picture we have is enough," says I. "In the hands of the right people it'll mean freedom for Ireland."

"Which people, Nell Pat?" says the lad who wants to kill them.

"General Richard Mulcahy and Kevin O'Higgins."

"Aye, that's true," he agrees.

The fella has been looking at me with even more contempt, a dirty, savage, stupid woman, too uncouth and crude even to clean out the chamber pots in his castle. Then he smiles faintly. "You are a very perceptive politician, young woman."

"I'm not a murdering bastard," says I. "We'll leave you to heaven, if you don't mind me quoting a poet."

"I do not deny" — his voice was rich and deep — "that I have killed for my cause. Collins killed for his cause too. If I am a murdering bastard, then so was he. I'd rather think that he was and I am soldiers — each fighting for a cause in which we believed."

He said a few more things that I will not write down here, though I will never forget them.

"Now get the hell out of here," says Liam finally. "And if you ever come back, you'll be as dead as O'Kelly."

The man stomps towards the car.

I whisper in Liam's ear.

"Just a minute," he says. "You should be after helping us dispose of the body of your informer. Lads, load the poor colonel's body in the boot and escort our friends here to Maam Cross, then let them go."

"Aye," they say.

That was that. Liam says they emptied their guns into his body so the constables will think it was an IRA internal fight.

They met last night and formally voted to disband the Brigade. So the Troubles are over here in Galway.

The young teacher man brought us the pictures and the plate this morning. They're perfect. They show the tables in front of the pub, the big car, Galway Bay, and the man paying off O'Kelly. Liam brought one of the pictures to a man in Galway who can get it to Dick Mulcahy with the message that the two of them are the murderers of Michael Collins and if he wants to know more there are those who can explain all of it to him.

The teacher man, who could not lie even if he wanted to, has given us the plate and all the pictures and says there are no more of them.

Everyone else — the three lads, the two couples at the pub, the teacher man — is sworn to secrecy. There'll be rumors as the years go on. Eventually when it doesn't matter any more people will figure out the truth. Maybe someone will even read me diary.

It's all over.

I hope Mick Collins is at peace. I hope Ireland always realizes how heavy a price the young people of our time have paid for freedom — Mick, Kit Kiernan, Tim, Moire, even meself and Liam, and all those like us. No matter what happens in the years to come and no matter how happy those of us who survived may become, we can never forget these awful times — and those who did not live through them. God have mercy on them and God help us.

I'm tired and sick and I want to escape from this terrible land and start me life again in America where you don't have to kill others to be free. That's where Liam and I want to raise our child, and those who come after.

– 53 –

The sun greeted us the next morning in Cork and the sky was sparkling blue, a hint of spring rather than autumn — a deceptive beginning in Ireland, I had learned. We drove through Bandon to Clonakilty, where Collins had attended secondary school. I could not find Sam's Cross on my ordnance map, though I had read somewhere that it was seven miles outside of Clonakilty.

" 'Tis easy to find out." Herself bounded out of the Benz. "You always ask at the post office."

She was back in a moment, two bouquets of flowers in her hand. "The woman says that not many people ask. We drive straight ahead towards Skibbereen. Four miles down the road there is a village called Lisavaird. We turn right there and it's the fourth crossroad. She says it's marked, but in Ireland it means only one sign — except for the shrine at Mamene. Aren't the signs there everywhere?"

"Lisavaird is where he went to primary school."

"No Jesuits or Christian brothers for your man, is it?"

"National schools all the way. That makes his achievements all the more remarkable. He was the youngest of nine children. His father was already over seventy when he was born — married an orphan girl of twenty-three when he was sixty."

"He *never* did."

"He did so. And they were very happy too, according to the books."

"You can love at any age in life, can't you, Dermot Michael?"

"I hope so."

A single sign announced "Collins Shrine." Then suddenly we were at the fourth crossroad — on the left a whitewashed pub with a white sign with the name "O'Cullean." I stopped the car.

"It must be that place on the right," Nuala said. "There's a flagpole."

Beyond it was a small shrine — a pillar with a Celtic cross carved on it and his name and dates. The house with the flagpole was an old stone cottage, elegant for the time Collins was born. Later his mother would build a much better house only to have it burned down by the Black and Tans.

Spontaneously Nuala and I knelt on the stone base of the shrine and said a quiet prayer. Well, a quiet decade of the rosary because I wasn't about to stop praying till she was finished. She laid one of her bouquets in front of the shrine.

"He deserves better of Ireland," I whispered.

"Doesn't he now?"

"The pub is where he met with his brother and some of his friends the morning he died and reportedly a 'neutral officer' in his quest for peace."

"Poor brave eejit," Nuala commented.

"That's right. Poor brave, great-souled eejit."

We went back to Clonakilty and then to Bandon where, I informed herself, there was once a law forbidding Catholics after sunset — West Cork being one of the places that Elizabeth and Cromwell had "planted" Protestant settlers but with less success than in Ulster. The West Cork Prods became as Irish as the natives if not more so — the "Black" Protestants of the

529

Somerville and Ross stories, totally daft by the time the two women recorded the doings of the Knox clan in Skibbereen — the "Skibawn" of their stories.

"Isn't it meself that's attending a graduate seminar in Irish history and literature on this trip?" She spoke tentatively, hoping not to offend me again since we had declared an implicit truce in our struggle.

I laughed, louder than was necessary. "The back of me hand to you, woman."

"You wouldn't dare." She laughed too.

She was right: I wouldn't dare.

Well, we weren't snapping at one another anymore.

We took the wrong road out of Bandon towards Bealnablath (the Valley of the Blossoms) and found ourselves bumping down a paved but narrow country road in the middle of a forest with an occasional house. Still wild country. It must have been wilder seventy years ago. No wonder the IRA could hide so easily out here.

Nuala, more convinced than I that we had taken the wrong road or maybe a back road, insisted I stop while she asked some kids who were apparently waiting for a school bus where we were.

Being Irish, all four of them answered at once. Nuala tried her Irish on them and they fired back. One of the gossons seemed to take charge and give her detailed instructions. She handed them a pound note to divide among themselves and could have easily been elected to the Dáil from that district.

We drove back to Bandon and tried again. The weather had changed while we were in the woods. Clouds had raced in from the Gulf Stream and brought with them mists and rain. That suited my mood perfectly.

I drove carefully down the new road, noting that it was the same one that was in the TV film. And that it certainly hadn't been paved in 1922.

"They could hardly tear it up just for the film, could they?"

Then it started to rain.

We were almost to Crookston when we turned and suddenly came upon another shrine, larger than the one at Sam's Cross — low brick wall, supporting a concrete platform with large stone crucifix, this time with an inscription in Irish.

At first I could hardly believe that this was the place of the ambush. It seemed like just another bend in the road. Then I looked around and saw that it was the site of the RTE reenactment and that it was a perfect place for an ambush.

"They have some kind of memorial service here every year," I said solemnly.

"Which my generation ignores, even after the RTE film."

"I can understand that," I said.

"A few weeks ago I would have said that they were a bunch of eejits. I guess I did say that, didn't I now, Dermot Michael? The letters changed me mind."

"Pa and O'Kelly must have been up there." I gestured towards the side of the high hill. "Up on that road. The National Army convoy was right here where we are now, and the Irregular ambush was on the other side, maybe two hundred yards in that direction. The laneway must be behind those hedges up there."

Nuala huddled under our one umbrella. "I don't like this place." She shuddered. "There's evil here."

"A great man died here, Nuala."

"Even before that." She shuddered again and rested her head on my shoulder. "It's been evil for centuries. It's not evil because he died here. He died here because of evil. It's a place of death."

I had read her handwritten translation of the two entries the night before in stunned silence. (Her penmanship was excellent, by the way. What else?) Ma's account of the final ambush was plain and harsh, yet agonized. She had lived her life with those bitter and ugly memories and had managed somehow to overcome them. Neither her faith in God nor her love for her man had been tarnished.

It wasn't fair that two such innocent young people, two shy children if there were ever any such, should have been forced to go into exile and to carry such heavy burdens with them.

All right, they were an indomitable twosome

and they had made it. All right, they had survived and Mick Collins had not. All right, Ma still had her man and Kit Kiernan did not. Still, the whole agonizing story should never have happened. What a mess the human condition was.

Were there worse events in the twentieth century? Hell, yes. Auschwitz made the Troubles look mild. But . . .

I wished I could weep for that young couple and what they had suffered. Had anyone ever wept for them? Her parents possibly and Moire. Maybe even the young priest with the pretty brown eyes.

Probably they didn't even weep much for themselves. They were survivors and survivors don't cry. The faraway look I had seen on rare occasions in Ma's sparkling green eyes must have brought her back to Carraroe and that youth which was cut short so quickly by war and death.

"Are you all right, Dermot Michael?"

"Fine." I had handed Nuala the translation to put in the Federal Express envelope.

She had slipped it into the envelope and sealed it.

"Does that have to go out before we retype it?"

"I'll finish the first book on the road tomorrow. Shouldn't we get the translations off to himself as soon as possible?"

"In case anything happens to us?"

"It's insurance, Dermot." She was watching me intently. "Your brother will have the whole story. They won't be able to do anything to us then."

"You're right, as usual."

"Do you want to talk about it?" Her soft, gentle voice was like a caress. Yes, I wanted to talk about it.

"I'm all right, Nuala. I'd better get some sleep."

I knew I'd not be able to sleep.

"Are you sure?"

"Yes, damn it," I had snarled. "Leave me alone!"

I had startled her.

"I'm sorry if —"

"I have a mother in Chicago should I need mothering. Now get the hell out of here!"

She had left quietly and without protest.

A man is entitled to be alone when he wants to, isn't he?

Even if she had been my wife, shouldn't she have had enough sense to get out of that room instead of hassling me?

A wife would not have put up with what I had said. I had known that even then.

I had not slept a wink. Nuala apparently fell asleep only towards morning. She overslept. I had waited impatiently in the dining room, munching on the hotel's brown bread, which was only fair, until nine.

Then I had rung her room.

"It's nine o'clock. We're already an hour behind schedule."

"I'm sorry."

"If it wouldn't be too much trouble, perhaps you could get up now."

She had hung up on me — which I suppose I had richly deserved.

I had complained all the way to Clonakilty about the lorries (trucks, as I called them), about Irish roads, and about our late start.

Nuala had snapped and snarled back at me, sniffling occasionally, whether with a cold or suppressed tears I could not tell and did not care.

"Don't try to pass here, you eejit. What if there's another lorry coming at us from the opposite direction?"

"This car has only one driver and it's me."

"And you're acting like a focking amadon."

"Do you want to walk from here to Galway?"

"It would be better than being carried in a casket."

So it went until we reached Clonakilty where by unspoken agreement we became civil to one another again.

Then we had come to the gloomy vale (as one of the books had called it) of Blath — Beal na mBlath in Irish. It was now a dismal day in the pounding rain, with clouds obscuring the tops of the hills on either side of the vale. I turned off the ignition. Now there was no traffic left on the road.

"I don't like this place, Dermot," my companion said again. "Not at all, at all. What do you expect to find here?"

"I want to see it and get the feel of it."

"Do we have to?"

"I do. You can suit yourself."

I climbed out of the car and, oblivious to the rain, tried to drink in the taste and the smell of the place. Nuala stood next to me, holding the umbrella over my head, the second bouquet in her other hand.

" 'Tis a bad place to be at Sahmain time, Dermot," she said after she had told me that the place was evil. "The dead are everywhere."

"You can see why Pa didn't know what was happening." I unfolded my ordnance map of West Cork. "The convoy was heading back to Cork through Crookston. He had lost all sense of direction. If they were that far away and dark was falling and the sun behind him, the convoy would have been in deep shadows. There was a mist and a touch of rain too. You wouldn't be able to tell whether the uniforms were khaki or dark green. He didn't think the National Army had an armored car. It was a long shot from way up there, that's why there was no exit wound. O'Kelly must have been a crack shot or very lucky."

"Your granda didn't kill Michael Collins."

"The enemy, whoever the enemy was, must have kept O'Kelly informed day by day about the progress of Collins's tour. Maybe they even

536

tipped off the band of Irregulars who slowed down the convoy. Still, it could have easily gone the other way."

"Poor Kit Kiernan."

"Poor everyone."

Once again the mysterious face seemed to float by, today in the mists around the vale. De Valera? Had he engineered the death of the man who had arranged his escape from prison?

Many had said through the years that the blood of Michael Collins was on Dev's hands. Maybe he used the gold too for the campaigns that eventually won him at the polls the political power he could not take by force. Maybe the government of Ireland, administered now by his political heirs, was terrified of the truth being revealed to a nation where Michael Collins was a folk hero even if youngsters like Nuala Anne McGrail were not sure what he had done.

Had not Dev lamented on occasion that he would never be as popular with the Irish people as Mick Collins had been?

How then did the Consort fit in? Wouldn't their goal be the opposite of Dev and his successors?

Politics made strange bedfellows, did it not?

"We should leave the dead in peace," Nuala whimpered besides me.

"Ma?"

"She's not dead."

"She's as dead as Michael Collins and Daniel O'Kelly."

537

"No, she's not."

"You get in the car, I want to walk up the road a bit."

I turned and walked towards the spot where the ambushers had laid the mine, to the very spot where, best as I could estimate, Michael Collins had died, perhaps whispering "Emmet" as he died.

Not "Kit."

Well, maybe. The two words would have sounded pretty much the same.

"They're watching us." Nuala had followed me, holding the umbrella over my bare head — herself wearing a rain slicker.

"The dead?" I asked incredulously.

"No."

"Patrick and his bunch?"

"No."

"The people who attacked us in front of your apartment?"

"Maybe."

I shivered, more because of Nuala's fey sensibility than because of any fear of the Consort. It was not unreasonable to assume that they were following us, but I was confident that Patrick would be following them.

I did trust Patrick, didn't I?

I found that I wasn't so sure anymore.

I peered into the mists up to where Pa had waited. Was there someone up there with a gun aiming at me?

It was my turn to shudder.

"They were pissed," Nuala said thoughtfully, sniffing the air, "pissed blind. The whole lot of them."

"Huh?"

She continued to sniff, as if she could smell the alcohol in the air. I should have realized then that I was dealing with a detective of extraordinary, almost scary, talent.

"They were young men, a lot of them younger than yourself, riding around the country on a hot summer day and stopping at pubs to meet the Big Fella's friends and neighbors. Sure, they wouldn't be Irish if they didn't take the occasional drop now and then, would they? A whole day of occasional drops adds up, doesn't it now? And the young eejits up there" — she nodded towards the laneway — "wasn't their headquarters in Long's pub? Would not they have taken a bit of refreshment more than once in the course of a long summer day? By the time it was twilight and they were shooting at each other, weren't they all focking fluttered? Wasn't that why no one else was killed?"

I was tempted to ask her if she could really smell the booze, but I really didn't want to know.

"That seems reasonable, Nuala," I agreed.

She nodded solemnly and continued to sniff the air.

I shivered again.

We found the entrance to the laneway and

walked along the lane up on the left side of the road. It was an ideal spot for an ambush, with plenty of shelter behind hedges as the lane ran parallel to and above the road and the drainage ditch.

The road was far enough away so the four men, firing as they moved along the lane, could not see whom they might hit.

Nor could they see anyone who might be hiding across the way on the higher hill, even though there was less cover over there.

I stopped at the point above the shrine that marked the place of Mick Collins's death. On the other side, far up on the hill, there was a group of trees and bushes — the place where Pa and O'Kelly had hidden.

"Come on, Nul, let's get out of here!"

I strode back to the car, now as eager as she was to flee Beal na mBlath. She trotted alongside me, still struggling to keep the umbrella over my head.

"Just a minute, Dermot." She shoved the umbrella in my hand, dashed up to the raised platform of the shrine, and placed her waterlogged bouquet at the foot of the crucifix. She made a quick sign of the cross and ran back to the shelter of the umbrella.

I opened the car door, took the umbrella from her, and pushed her gently inside. Then I hurried around to the other side and jumped in. I started the car immediately and drove cautiously down the road towards the end of the vale and the town of Clonakilty — the town near Collins's birthplace at Sam's Cross.

Nuala grabbed my arm. She was trembling.

"Are we in danger now?" I asked her, now fully prepared to believe that the vale was swarming with evil spirits living and dead.

"Not at the moment," she replied, "but they don't like us."

"Is Mick Collins here?"

"He is not. He's one of those waiting for us in Carraroe."

She clung to my arm till we came to the first string of farmhouses on the edge of Crookston. Then she sighed, released me, and relaxed.

I stopped the car. We must end our quarrel.

"Thanks for the umbrella out there, Nuala. I think the place sort of got to me."

She leaned her head against my chest, her black hair right beneath my chin. "I'm sorry that I've been fighting with you, Dermot Michael. I have a terrible nasty streak in me when I become angry. Me ma says I'm the worst of all her children for sulking."

"It was my fault, Nuala. I was shaken by those two translations last night."

"Me ma says the only good thing about me sulks is that they don't last more than a day."

"I'm sorry." I put my arm around her.

"So am I."

"Friends again, Nuala Anne?"

"Haven't I said so, Dermot Michael?" She straightened up and grinned at me. "Now, why

541

don't we have a cup of tea in Crookston to tide us over to till we get to Killarney and a proper lunch?"

"That was a terrible place," I said as we ate our first scones of the day.

"You shouldn't pay attention to me when I get in one of my spooky moods," she replied. "I act a little daft. Was your gram that way?"

"Not that I can remember."

"But I do think we're being watched. I felt that ever since we left Dublin."

"I suppose we should expect that."

"Aye. I hope your man Patrick is good at what he does."

"He should be if he's some sort of relative of Mick Collins."

"Oh, he's that all right. Isn't his name Patrick Michael?"

"He never said that it was."

"But it is just the same, and now would you mind if I ordered another plate of scones?"

Would a Jesuit mind teaching at the high school he attended?

Patrick *Michael*, was it?

And my Uncle Micky, the second of Pa and Ma's kids, the one that was the psychiatrist in the family (and the one who introduced my mother to my father), was he named after Michael Collins? It was Michael C. Ready, wasn't it?

How did a sane, sensible, sometime commodity trader distinguish between the real and the

542

phantasmagoric in the West of Ireland at Sahmaintide, especially when his guide and umbrella carrier seems to cross the lines (which at this time of the year were supposed to be thin) between the two with considerable ease?

Did Uncle Mike know the meaning of his name? Probably Ma had told him something about the Troubles; not much I'd bet.

And my second name was owed to him.

So in a manner of speaking I was named after the man who carried her laundry basket back to the house in Carraroe.

The man who, according to Nuala's spooky mood, would be waiting for us at Carraroe when we got there.

The area around Skibbereen in West Cork and from there up to Bantry Bay and Kenmare and the Ring of Kerry is, by all travel book accounts, the most beautiful in Ireland. We didn't see much of the beauty because the rain continued to pelt us and the wind to rock the Benz as we followed the winding roads. We did, however, take pictures and imagine what the region must look like on a sunny day.

Nuala scribbled away at the translation of the last entry in Ma's first notebook and we talked about the puzzle.

I told her my theory about De Valera.

She considered it for a moment. "The government wouldn't have to be so sneaky, would it? Couldn't they just expel you from Ireland on some trumped-up grounds?"

"I feel like I've left Ian Fleming's world and entered John le Carré's."

"His is much more realistic, isn't it? The world in which a lot of amadons make eejit mistakes?"

"I think we can rule out the modern IRA. I don't see why they would care about the death of Michael Collins or anything else in which we're engaged."

"They're daft, so there's no telling what they'd do. But right now they seem more interested in blowing up British barracks and killing women and children."

"Attacking British soldiers in their barracks is the strategy Michael Collins invented."

"And himself having enough sense to stop it when the time came."

"The IRA might want the gold."

" 'Tis true." She stirred uneasily beside me. "All we need is to have them eejits after us."

"How much do we know about the puzzle?" I slowed down to avoid a motorcyclist who was passing a lorry on a hill.

"Eejit!" exclaimed my companion, who watched every move on the highway. "Well, we know who killed Michael Collins. We know who killed the man who killed Michael Collins. We half know why your granda and gram couldn't come back to Ireland, and we'll know all of that when we finish this section I'm after translating. She's on the boat and she's talking about Dick Mulcahy."

"We know where the gold is or at least where

it was. We know pretty much how it got there and who stole it."

"We're not absolutely sure who the man in the car was. Or are you?"

"I see his face often, Nuala, but it fades away on me."

She did not comment so I went on. "I don't know what there's left to figure out, except to make sure the gold is still up at the shrine in . . ."

"Mamene."

"Now, how much do we know that they don't know we know?"

"That really sounds like John le Carré."

We both laughed again, our friendship cautiously restored.

How long could I resist the woman's charm?

"We have to assume that they come into my suite when I'm not there and read your translation on hard disk."

"No, we don't."

"Why not, Nul?"

"Because being only a partial eejit and not a total one, don't I back up each translation on two of them cute little three-inch floppies that don't flop and erase the text from the hard disk?"

"And what do you do with the floppies?"

"Don't I send one to his Reverence with the translation and deposit the other in the vault at the hotel?"

"How long have you been doing that?"

"Since the night in Irishtown."

"Why didn't you tell me?" I demanded stiffly.

"Wasn't it a small detail of me work that was not worth bothering you about?"

And wasn't I a total eejit altogether for not realizing then that Grace O'Malley was light-years ahead of James Bond?

"They could have come into the suite and read Gram's diary if they brought an Irish speaker along with them."

"Sure, they could have, couldn't they? So unless I was round the bend completely wouldn't I have put the book in the vault too each day when I went back to me flat?"

"Did you now?"

"Haven't I said that I did?"

I ground to a halt as a dog herded a band of cattle across the road. He seemed bored by his work and uninterested. Then when he heard us he began to bark, as if to convince us that he was competent.

The cattle didn't move any more quickly.

"That mutt is the typical Irishman," I said.

"Faith, isn't he more energetic than most of us?"

The cattle finally crossed the road and we started up. The mutt barked a friendly greeting at us.

"Friendly too."

"We can't help ourselves, I'm afraid."

"I suppose you had no problem explaining

546

to that nice manager what you were putting into the vault?"

"Wasn't I telling the God's honest truth? Wasn't I even showing him some of the darling passages herself wrote about the countryside?"

"He could have read it, couldn't he?"

"Not without disturbing the tiny piece of wax I had glued to the envelope before I put it in the box and himself giving me the key."

Nuala could probably get a job working for Patrick and his bunch of eejits.

"So they don't know that we know the secret of Collins's death."

"Probably not."

"And they have no idea whether we know about the visits to Lettermullen. They may not even know that such visits ever occurred."

"Wouldn't you think" — Nuala waved to a countryman who had waved his pitchfork at us — "they'd be knowing that the man, whoever he was, ordered the murder of Collins? They'd not be wanting us to find out."

"Why not, Nuala? Why ever not? It was so long ago. The man is certainly dead by now."

"If you ask me" — she laughed — "and I know you are, wouldn't I be thinking that these people aren't killers or they would have killed you at the start? They don't want you to find out either who killed Michael Collins or where the gold is. They knew enough about what happened in those days to know that your gram and granda were involved. When you began to search for the reason why they had to leave Ireland and never came back, they were afraid you'd find out the other things. When you do, if you do, won't they be trying to persuade you to keep it all a secret for the good of both the countries?"

"So I can expect a conversation after we search for the gold."

"If they don't know where it is or if they've hidden it somewhere else, then it doesn't matter. But if we find it and discover they've been using it, they'll be terrible upset."

"They will indeed. How would they know about Ma and Pa's involvement or about the gold?"

"They'd know about Nell Pat and Liam from the man in the car. I reckon he was a friend of your man Martin's granda. Maybe the man in the car found out about the gold and left it to them for their work."

It was a very plausible scenario.

"They don't know that I have the list of their members."

"Not unless your man Patrick *Michael* told them, which I don't think likely since he wants revenge."

I wasn't about to argue that with her.

I did not, however, tell her my little secret about the list. That seemed irrelevant.

"They may not be a tightly organized group at all, Nul. It would be hard to maintain a communications link among all those people. Perhaps only a few people know who the members are. So it may be that some of them are working independently of the others."

"And aren't they not really professional spies like your man?"

"So all we have to find out is whether the gold is at Mamene and who the man in the car was."

"Then our job is finished."

"Maybe I'd better let you have some peace so you can finish the translation."

"I do want to see the lakes of Killarney when we get there."

"We can't miss them, we go right by Lady's View."

That was true enough, but the rain clouds were so thick at that observation point that the lakes were invisible.

We drove into Killarney and pulled up at the parking lot of the Great Southern Railway Hotel, built across the street from the train station.

"I'm starved," said Nuala. "And spoiled from living like a *fockingrichyank*."

We both laughed heartily, our friendship completely restored again.

"I thought we weren't going to use that language once we left South County Dublin?"

" 'Tis the only exception."

We strolled into the dining room of the Great Southern, which was damp from the moisture that cloaked the hotel, but no more damp than we were. Before the maître d' could show us to a table, we were greeted by a hearty voice.

"Dermot! Nuala! Haven't you picked a terrible day to visit the West? You must be my guests at lunch. And you, young woman, haven't you been deceiving me and the rest of Lord Martin's guests?"

Brendan Keane.

— 54 —

"Me deceiving you, Mr. Minister?" Nuala had turned on all her charm. "Sure, would I be deceiving a member of the government of Ireland?"

We were seated at his table, waiting for our sherry, only one glass for me because I was driving. The minister had come for the opening of an art exhibition in Tralee and was taking the late train back to Dublin.

"Sure, it's a slow ride but I wouldn't want to be on the highway today, would I now?"

He was so disarming that it was easy to forget that he was on the handwritten list of the Consort, between Peter B. Joyce and John H. Mc-Mahon.

In the back of my head I wondered again

550

how Patrick had come into possession of the list and why he had given it to me.

Moreover, a cabinet member of the republic would certainly have a limousine at his disposal for official business. Hence the train story was unlikely. What then was he doing in Killarney? Waiting for us? Why not then in Galway? How did he know we would stop at the Great Southern for lunch when we didn't know it ourselves until a mere half hour before? Or was he waiting for someone else?

Nuala was fending him off while I watched him closely.

"Well," the minister went on, smiling benignly, "you told us that it was a pleasure to watch the lass who played Pegeen Mike, and how does a person watch herself?"

"Sure, don't you watch yourself with the internal eye" — the little fraud smiled her most appealing smile — "with which every artist watches his own work?"

"Martin and I were both astonished when the American attaché called us and said his wife told him on the way home that our young guest was Pegeen Mike and she herself had seen the play, but she didn't want to embarrass you at the dinner."

Martin had not mentioned that at our lunch. It would probably have interfered with his principal agenda.

"Sure, wouldn't it have been a terrible thing if I admitted it was me after all the nice words had been said?"

"I grant that, young woman. And I tip my hat to your modesty. Moreover, we would have discovered the truth eventually as your career on the stage develops. I'm only sorry I missed the performance. By the time I read the reviews it was already too late."

"That's very kind of you, Mr. Minister. But I'm studying to be an accountant."

"My dear, what a terrible waste of talent!" He raised his sherry in a toast to both of us. "Can't you persuade her to change her mind, Dermot?"

"The woman has a mind of her own," I said. "I wouldn't dream of trying to change it."

Brendan Keane was sleek and smooth in his morning suit — Irish pols wore them as often as they could find a pretext to do so — a hardworking and ambitious politician on the make. However, today in the dim dining room in this old hotel in the Kingdom of Kerry, I noticed a touch of sleaze that I had not seen in romantic Georgian atmosphere of the town house on Merrion Square.

The lines at the ends of his lips, the darting eyes, the forced high spirits, the too-rapid flow of his words, the nervous motions of his fingers — all these quirks made him appear tricky.

Like a politician trying to explain away a mistake on a Sunday TV program back in the States, he was clever, but not clever enough.

Or too clever by half.

Or was I reading my knowledge about the Consort into his behavior?

No, I was not. He was indeed a bit of a gombeen man — too much perhaps ever to rise quite to the top of the Irish government. It was permitted, indeed expected, that Irish politicians be tricky. But they ought not to *seem* to be *too* tricky.

He was under pressure at the moment. He knew that we were on the trail of mysteries, the explanation of which might be a powerful embarrassment to his career. Was he trying to talk us out of our search by flattery? Was he trying to persuade us that he was a nice fellow so we would not put him in jeopardy? Or was he talking away a mile a minute with his occasional Richard Nixon smile merely because it was in his nature to do so?

As Daniel P. Moynihan once remarked of Henry Kissinger, "He deceives not because it is in his interest to do so but because it is in his nature to do so."

It seemed to be in the nature of Brendan Keane to talk.

"There are scads of young actresses and singers in Dublin," Nuala was explaining her career choice, "and most of them working as shopgirls or, if they are lucky enough to do word processing, as secretaries. I have no reason to think I'm any better."

"The review in the *Times* suggests that you

553

have more talent than most."

"I'm probably good enough" — she weighed her skills judiciously as she nodded for another glass of sherry and shot a warning glance at me — "for amateur theatricals, and that's grand for me. I can earn a better living as an accountant over at the Financial Services Center, and if they want me in the theater I can do that too."

Need I say that I declined the second glass of sherry?

I had been planning to do it anyway. Well, I think I was.

"You're not migrating to America, are you now?"

After ever so slight a pause, Nuala responded, "I have no plans for doing so at the present moment."

I remained silent.

I was also tormented by another thought. Suppose Nuala should come to the United States in pursuit of me. She would make common cause with my mother, my sisters, my sisters-in-law, my brother the priest, and indeed everyone else in my family. I'd be finished, like it or not.

Was she capable of such strategy?

Was the Pope bishop of Rome?

Did St. Ignatius found the Jesuits?

Brigid, Patrick, and Columcille!

And Fintan, Finbarr, and Finian too, thrown in for good measure.

"I could, of course," Keane babbled on, "say a word or two in the proper places for you

554

and would be happy to do so."

"Wouldn't I be terribly grateful for that, Mr. Minister, and yourself not even seeing me act."

He waved his hand airily. "All I would have to do is show people the review in the *Times.*"

"After I graduate in the spring, they can find me at the Financial Services Center."

"You already have a position there?"

"Not exactly." She smiled at the waitress who placed the Galway smoked salmon in front of her. "But haven't a number of companies shown interest in me?"

"Such as?"

"Such as Saatchi and Saatchi and Arthur Andersen."

Arthur Andersen was a Chicago-based company of enormous size and influence. They would have no need to import talent from Ireland, would they?

The minister babbled on as we turned to our meat course (overcooked but tasty roast beef) about dramatic and vocal opportunities in the republic. Nuala calmly repeated her rock-bottom position: She would be delighted if she could perform on the stage, but she was going to be an accountant.

At the Financial Services Center being built on the banks of the Liffey? Hadn't she told me that she planned to work in Galway City to be close to her parents?

Maybe she merely planned to pick up some experience there for a couple of years before returning to Galway.

In the frantic world of international business, an intelligent and beautiful and naive young woman would be an easy target for phonies.

What, me jealous?

Besides, hadn't she demonstrated the truth of her assertion that she could take care of herself?

Then, as I was finishing the roast beef, the minister turned to me. "What are your plans, Dermot Coyne? Are they quite as firm as Nuala's?"

"Just the opposite, I'm afraid." I tried to make my laugh sound casual as I groped for a response and settled on truth, most of the truth anyway.

"Oh?"

"I plan to fly home to Chicago sometime in the middle of next week. I've absorbed as much as I can on this visit. I suppose I'll settle down and try to write some stories this winter."

Did I note palpable relief in his darting eyes?

"Surely you'll return to Ireland?"

"I would think so. However, I've been away from home for almost two years. I've wandered enough for the present."

"So this is a first and last look at the West of Ireland? Pity the weather is so bad."

"It could improve tomorrow. My mother's family came from Galway, your district, in fact. I hope to visit the places where they grew up, which happen to be where Nuala's family lives, so we're combining two projects this weekend."

"Soak up atmosphere there, eh?" He drummed his fingers on the table as the waitress removed our plates.

"And take some pictures. My grandparents never returned, as I think I mentioned the other night. While my parents and all of my siblings have been in Ireland at one time or another, none of them ever went to Connemara, as far as I know. So we need a few photos for the family archives."

"Commendable, commendable." He rubbed his hands together. I noted that he wore too many rings. "I certainly hope you have good weather tomorrow and Sunday."

"I do too."

"I would like to ask you a very great personal favor." He continued to rub his hands. "Do you expect to publish any stories as a result of your visit here?"

"I hope to."

"Would you send me offprints of them when they are published? I think it is important to circulate them in this country. Irish Americans, I note, are quite relaxed about the Irish influence on their cultural works. Here there is a tendency to resent that influence, as if the Irish Americans have no right to be Irish, if you take me meaning. I consider that most unfortunate. We are indeed planning a prize of some sort to be given by Ireland to Irish-American artists and writers.

Nothing very large financially, yet the spirit would be there. I hope you wouldn't find it offensive if we submitted your work?"

"Not at all."

He insisted on picking up the tab for lunch. "Ministerial budget. You can pay when I visit you in Chicago."

I didn't fight it.

In the car Nuala spat out, "Gobshite! I know I'm breaking my rule and I won't ever do it again till we return to Dublin, but the man is a gobshite."

"Did I fool him?"

"You were wonderful, Dermot, and you saying *I'm* the great actress. I'm thinking you reassured him, but he's so anxious that no one could completely reassure him. . . . Now give me a few more minutes and I'll be finishing this translation of herself's entry on the boat. We'll see if she tells us who the man in the car is."

– 55 –

October 4, 1922

I'm as sick as I've ever been in all me life.

The boat is rolling something terrible and the tiny cabin in which Liam and I are staying smells of coal and vomit (mine and his) and all kinds of other smells I'd not like to think about.

I'm sick from the ocean and I'm sick from me poor baby and I'm sick with loneliness for Ireland.

I've told Liam about the gold bar. He was surprised but not angry at me at all, at all. He laughed as I raved on about what the young priest said and he took me in his arms and whispered, "Don't ever be afraid, Nell Pat, to do what you think you should do. I'll never disapprove of it or resent that you're so much smarter than I am."

Wasn't that wonderful!

"I'm not, Liam Tomas, not at all, at all. Wasn't my poor da saying that you were the smartest young man in the County Galway?"

"That's as may be, Nell Pat, but I'm still not as smart as you are; and that makes me happy and grateful to God and Himself sending me such a fine wife and herself a beauty too."

"I'm already starting to get fat," I moan.

"You'll always be beautiful," he says, kissing me.

I'm almost in tears at the mention of me da whom I'll probably never see again. And me ma and Moire and me cute little godchild, who may never meet her cousin.

And ourselves knowing now that we have no choice but to leave Ireland and that we'd be putting our lives in danger if we ever come back.

" 'Tis just as well," says me man, "after everything that's happened, Nell Pat. I don't think I'd ever want to come back. We'll have to close the door on that part of our lives."

"Aye." I agree with him because I know it's true, especially after our talk with General Mulcahy.

He's not at all like Mick Collins. He's slim and kind of short and wears his hair slicked back and has sort of an altar-boy face. At first you think he's a little brat pretending to be a general in his dark green uniform with big black boots and a thick Sam Browne belt and his big pistol and the red tabs on the collar and a riding crop just like a British officer. Or a toy soldier come to life. He's also sort of stiff and formal, not casual like our Mick was.

However, you change your mind after you've talked to him for a few minutes. He's smart and determined, and he believes in Ireland and peace just the way General Collins did.

"None of us will ever get over what happened last August." He sighs, slapping the fancy black boot of his uniform with his fancy riding crop. "But we'd be false to Mick if we let his dream die with him. The men who have caused this civil war are desperately misguided, but they're Irishmen and our former comrades. We must make peace with them as soon as we can."

We're sitting in a hotel room in Galway. The Free Staters occupy the city now, and there's not much conflict to the north, though the eejits

560

in Clare are still making trouble and that Dev's own district.

"And poor Kit Kiernan?"

"Mick told you about Kit?" He shook his head. "Poor woman! She's bright and pretty and great fun. But her health is poor, something that seems to run in her family. Mick worried a lot about her. When she feels poorly she's a bit unstable, though Mick loved her with all his heart. She's still inconsolable, but I think, poor health and all, she'll recover. General Felix Cronin is looking after her and himself a very able man. Eventually she'll be all right. She'll never forget Mick, however, not as long as she lives."

"Poor dear woman."

"We'll make his dream come true, Mrs. O'Riada, never fear. It won't be as bright as he would have made it. It won't be as joyous, but, please God and the Blessed Mother, it will be his dream. He did not die in vain."

"I'm glad to hear that," says me man.

"I wonder if you two comprehend how enormously important your contribution has been to the realization of Mick Collins's dream?"

Me and Liam look at one another. "We do not," says he.

"Not at all, at all," says I.

"This picture" — he taps it with his riding crop — "and the story you've told me will bring the Civil War to an end soon. I've been afraid it would drag on for years. You see, the National

Army is poorly armed and equipped and trained. We can occupy the cities and those parts of the countryside that support the treaty. We don't have the guns and the bullets to bring our rule to the whole country. The Republican Irregulars have relatively little in the way of equipment, but they know we're not much better off. Therefore, they can continue with their occasional ambushes and thereby control much of Ireland. We simply cannot expect to assume our place in the family of nations without internal peace. Moreover, there are elements in England that are still hoping for an excuse to reoccupy Ireland. Those elements ordered Mick's death because they believed he was the only person standing between Ireland and permanent chaos."

"They were wrong," says me man.

"I fervently hope so, Captain." He sighs and swats his boot again with his riding crop. "They have been wrong about the Irish many times in our mutual history. But they've always won. Some of them are not convinced that they won't win again."

I'm thinking to meself that I hope Ireland is finally free but that I want to live somewhere else where there isn't so much killing in the name of freedom.

"You have to control the countryside then?" Liam says, a soldier for a moment again.

"That we do, not all of the countryside but enough to persuade the more moderate of the

Republicans, Dev for example — we'll never persuade poor Liam Lynch — that the sentiment of the country is in favor of the treaty and that they can't win ever. Mick's skirmish strategy, you see, works only in a very limited set of circumstances, and he himself telling everyone that and they not listening."

"You need more guns and bullets?" I says.

"Precisely, Mrs. O'Riada, and while we have the American money to pay for them — though not as much as we used to have — we can get them only from across the Irish Sea. Until now they have not been forthcoming. I think that will change shortly. . . . Curiously enough, the very fact that we will have the guns will preclude the need to use them."

"And why would you think that you'll get the guns now, General?" Liam asks.

"Because of this picture" — he taps it with his riding crop — "and the story you've been telling me."

"They'd be afraid to have it ever come out!" I exclaims.

Dick Mulcahy smiles, the only time he smiled during our conversation. "I rather think so, Mrs. O'Riada. It would be an enormous embarrassment to them. And while they're often not perceptive when the question is Ireland, they will understand this document very clearly."

I feel very proud and meself expecting that the Free Staters would know what to do with the picture.

"So you see that it's no exaggeration to say that you've played an important and critical part in winning Ireland its freedom."

"We'll always be proud of that," says me man.

"Won't we indeed?" I add.

"That's why I am so sorry that I can't urge you to stay. You deserve a rich reward for your ingenuity and courage. You deserve, in fact, to be honored as hero and heroine in the country we're trying to build here. Eventually perhaps, long years from now, we may be able to acknowledge your bravery. Now. . . ." He shrugs his little shoulders and taps his boot again with his riding crop. "As you will understand, I'm sure the value of this photo and the story I've written down as you've told it to me depends entirely on our willingness to keep it secret for many years, at least till the man in question is dead."

"I see," says Liam.

I don't see, not that it matters and meself not wanting to be a heroine of Ireland.

"Your decision to emigrate then is most fortunate as well as most wise. There is an informal agreement among all parties that no action will be taken against those who leave the country. Should you remain, there are several different groups on various sides who would like to see you dead, Captain, and perhaps you too, Mrs. O'Riada. Many people on this island have long memories."

"Well, we're leaving anyhow," says me man.

"I understand that and I lament it and I praise it. I wish it could be otherwise."

"Someday we'll come back when it's all over," says I.

The general looks at me with those soft little blue eyes of his. "I wouldn't recommend it, Mrs. O'Riada, not for a long time anyway. It will be years, perhaps decades, before you could return safely to this land you've helped to free. In all candor, and it pains me deeply to say this, it might be wise never to come back."

And so that's that. We shake hands and he thanks us again for all we've done and he leaves for his car and we get on the third-class coach for Cork, never to return again to Ireland.

" 'Tis just as well," says Liam. "I'm not sure that I would ever want to come back."

He knows that's not true and so do I, but we have to pretend and we'll have to pretend long enough so that we actually believe it.

"We have ourselves" — I take his hand — "and our future life together."

"Aye." And he pats me belly. "And our young one."

— 56 —

Nuala was sobbing next to me in the car. She had begun to cry part of the way through her reading of the last entry in Ma's notebook. Having finished the story, she gave way to tears of pain, grief, rage.

I let her cry.

"I'm sorry for breaking down, Dermot." She sniffled finally. "I'm nothing but a hysterical woman."

"A woman you are, Nuala Anne McGrail. Hysterical you're not. Those pages demand tears. Mine will come eventually."

"When you've had time to think about it." She sniggered through her sniffles.

"You got it."

We both laughed.

"Still, it was horrible sending those two children off into permanent exile. Ireland isn't worth it."

"It doesn't take away the agony of that entry, but, as I have said, they got over it. They were very comfortable indeed till the Great Depression, and they survived that. Mom told me that they never expelled any of their tenants because they couldn't pay their rent and that they lowered everyone's rent. Pa bought a lot of land during those years, and they raised their kids and sent them off to college and became wealthy during the boom after the war."

"That doesn't lessen the suffering of those days."

"Nor the memories. Even at the worst they were happy and far more affluent than they would have imagined possible. Carraroe must have seemed a dream of their youth when they were busy with their own children and their company."

We were struggling through the ancient city of Limerick on the Shannon River, back in main flow of Friday afternoon traffic. Great sheets of rain, thick and dark and monotonous, continued to float across the land. It would be late at night before we arrived in Galway at this rate.

Beyond the rain, the city itself, which Nuala had insisted was "grand" even though she'd never seen it, seemed like a set for a futuristic movie of the world after a nuclear war — drab, ugly, broken, sick.

"You don't know whether they saw any of their family ever again." She was wiping her face with a tissue, having come prepared for a good cry as she translated the final entry.

"If the family migrated to America, I'm sure they did. I'll have to search the others out if the baptismal records from Carraroe give me any hints."

"Maybe they didn't have much in common

with them as the years went on. That's the way it is with Ma and Da and me brothers and sisters: They still love one another but they don't have much to talk about."

"She didn't tell us the name of the man in the car, did she, Nul?"

"She did not. I didn't think she would. Do you have any ideas?"

"I don't trust Mulcahy. Obviously he wasn't the man in the car himself. But he seems a little too slick for my taste — a small man with a big gun. He had a lot to gain from Collins's death. He could take over the war and fight it his way — and he was reputed to be closer to the Republicans than Collins was. Eventually Kevin O'Higgins, who was the backbone of the Free State until he was shot, dumped Mulcahy because he thought he was too soft. If he was behind the plot, getting rid of Liam and Nell was a smart move."

"I hadn't thought of that," she admitted. "I didn't like him much either."

"It was all a little too smooth to suit me," I went on. "I can't see that two kids, both barely old enough to go to university, would have been in all that much danger, particularly in the years ahead. So maybe the story about using the picture to force the British to sell them arms was concocted to be sure you were rid of them and make them feel that, even in exile, they had helped Ireland."

"You're a deep one, Dermot Coyne."

"That's my line!"

"It could all be the truth. I don't know that we'll ever be able to prove it if it is."

"I'm not sure that we'll ever know the full story." I stopped for a red light, a blur in the swirling, spinning, dancing sheets of rain.

"You don't think it was the Brits?" Nuala asked.

"General McCready of the British army was furious because of the assassination of his friend Field Marshal Wilson and suspected Collins of ordering the execution. He might have wanted revenge. He had advocated withdrawal from Ireland, however, because he knew the war no longer could be won. If they attempted to re-impose English rule, the spigots of Irish-American money would have opened again, the Republicans would have been able to buy more weapons, and the situation would have reverted to the way it was before the truce."

"And Westminster?" she asked, as if she hadn't already thought these questions through herself and more quickly than I could.

"The civilian government, Lloyd George and Churchill, didn't want to give up Ireland, but they didn't want the costs of a continued war of skirmishes. Historians agree that Churchill was not speaking seriously when he threatened a reoccupation. He would have liked to retake the country, bloody imperialist that he was, but he knew that the costs would be too high. It doesn't follow, however, that he didn't

give cautious moral support to those who had
retained the dream of one kingdom for the two
islands."

"Your friends in the Consortium? Maybe your
man's granda?"

"That's a distinct possibility, Nul, one that
would explain why Martin Longwood-Jones is
on the list, even though, when you stop to think
about it, it doesn't sound like his cup of tea.
He might be stuck with a duty of honor that
has been passed on to him."

"They're odd people, but" — she was prepared to defend the descendants of the founders
of Trinity College — "they're as Irish as we
are."

"And maybe more Irish than we are."

"That's your favorite theory?"

"I don't know. As I say, I don't trust General
Mulcahy at all. I can't believe permanent exile
was necessary."

"Some of us Irish have long memories."

"Tell me about it."

"Is there a link between Casement's gold and
Collins's death" — Nuala had put on her thinking cap and was in no rush to take it off —
"besides the fact that Nell and Liam knew the
truth of both events?"

Or maybe she merely wanted to see how I
worked when I had my thinking cap on.

"The link, unless I totally misunderstand it,
is what they don't want me to learn. I won't
necessarily find it out here. Daniel O'Kelly, as

we know, was involved in both projects, but he's long dead and gone and I doubt that anyone would want to protect his reputation."

"So maybe it all comes to the identity of the man in the car?"

"I've thought that for a long time, Nuala. We may never find out who he was. Or if we do find out, it may not make any difference after almost seven decades. Or we may never have even heard of him. He might have been someone who was well known in the Galway of 1922 but who means nothing to us. Or, if he were a cousin of Longwood-Jones's twice removed, someone who doesn't matter anymore."

"Maybe." She wasn't convinced.

"What do you think, Nul?"

"I think that we're dealing with eejits who don't know the risks they take when they call back the dead, particularly at Sahmaintide."

We had our tea — with wonderful homemade scones — in the lobby of the Old Ground Hotel in Ennis, a quaint and charming place where, it was alleged, the Clare Brigade of the lads used to meet in bygone days. ("Them Clare eejits." Nuala dismissed the whole county and its citizens.) It was already dark, night coming early in these late-autumn months in northern Europe.

"The traffic should improve now that the working day is over." I tried to sound cheerful.

"Sure, isn't it still a long drive to Galway

City and Carraroe beyond?"

"You can stay at the St. Catherine Hotel overnight."

No kidding, that was the name of the "fancy hotel in Salt Hill" where Nuala proposed to put me. I suspected that her notions of "fancy" and mine might be different.

"I can *not*. If I'm that near me da and ma I'll stay the night with them. I can take the bus from Salt Hill to Carraroe."

"Not while you're working for me."

"I'll not have you driving a Connemara road at night in a storm like this," she insisted, "and yourself at the wheel all day with that wiper thing swishing back and forth and lulling you to sleep."

The solution, I thought to myself as I gave up the argument, was that she would stay in Salt Hill, a resort suburb of Galway City on the road out to Connemara. I'd insist and argue and she'd agree finally that I was right.

With Nuala there'd always be arguments and herself giving up only when she was obviously wrong, which wouldn't be too often.

As we chugged along the road through County Clare, we passed The Burren, the rocky land rushing down the Atlantic about which the poet laureate John Betjeman wrote when he spoke of the rocky land, "Where a Stone Age people breeds the last of Europe's Stone Age race" — an imperialist metaphor if there ever was one.

Except that being a people with a direct line

to their own archaic roots made the Irish more important to the world instead of less. No British imperialist could possibly understand that.

I was able to see only the Clare highway and that dimly as the wipers labored futilely to sweep the windshield clear of rain. Beside me Nuala was sleeping, her face looking incredibly young when I glanced at it quickly. A shy child for all her verve and intelligence.

I must stress that while I was sleepy, I did not fall asleep. I can sleep almost anywhere and under almost any circumstances and for any length of time, from a couple of minutes to a couple of hours.

I do not, however, fall asleep at the wheel of a car. Never.

Mind you, I was close to it a number of times during that long, dark, and somber day.

I was awake, if not wide awake, when the accident occurred.

We were on the road from Dramore into Galway City, almost on the fringes of the city. Traffic had thinned out so that only an occasional pair of headlights assaulted my eyes as I peered through the rain searching for the proper side of the road.

I was thinking to myself that I should have decreed that we spend the night at the Old Ground in Ennis. It would have been sensible and reasonable. Nuala, however, wanted to sleep in her own bed.

Stubborn, contentious woman.

What happened next happened very quickly — in time shorter than it required for me to write the first part of this sentence.

Afterward I've tried to reconstruct it many times. Each time I'm sure there were two sharp retorts, both of them before I lost control of the car.

Tires don't blow gaping holes in themselves in the rain on the road from Dramore to Galway, do they?

If there were two explosions, it was not an accident caused perhaps by a sharp rock on the road, but attempted murder.

Anyway, I heard, as best I can remember, a sharp sound and then another. Almost at once, the car began to grind and skid. I struggled with the wheel but it did not respond.

"Blowout! Blowout!" I yelled.

"Dermot!" Nuala awoke and threw her arms around me.

The Benz careened in one direction, hit something, and then caromed back across the road and plunged nosedown into a ditch. The last thing I can remember is that it heeled over on its side like a sailboat in a high wind.

Then the world went out.

– 57 –

"Are you all right, lad?"

The most Irish face I had ever seen peered anxiously at me — a round, mobile, intense face of a man in his early sixties, ready to smile or grieve, to laugh or console, to pray or to denounce in a fraction of a second.

I blinked at the face. I hadn't been out long, but where was I and who was this man with the Irish face and the black raincoat and beret?

A blowout! The front tire had blown out!

"*Nuala!*" I shouted.

"Still alive." She sighed. "Next to you and grateful I was saying me rosary."

"You were sleeping, woman!"

"I was *not!*"

"I think we're all right, sir," I said to the man in the beret.

"Call me Ed, call me Ed! Now, there's nothing to worry about at all, at all. We'll get this door open first thing," he announced. "Make sure you can move all your limbs. We don't want to hurt you worse if you're injured. I'll be calling the ambulance if we need one. Now don't worry. Everything will be all right. Bejesus, your guardian angels were working overtime, weren't they now?"

The car had heeled over on the side of the ditch, smashing one door and binding the other against the ditch. The crash had smashed the windows and the sunroof. The rain had swept in, drenching us.

I ached in every part of my body. However, my arms and legs seemed to be all right and I had no difficulty breathing.

"I guess I can navigate all right. What about you, Nuala?"

"I'm destroyed altogether" — she sighed — "but nothing is broken."

"You have a nasty cut on your head, lad, but don't think anything about it." He pulled fiercely on the door. "Don't give it another moment's worry. We'll take care of everything in a jiffy. Sure, the hospital is just down the road a bit. Now push hard against the door, if you don't mind. Again. Aha, there it is now. Let's see if we can get you out of there."

He helped me out and we both gave a hand to Nuala, whose only complaint was that her brand-new jacket had been destroyed altogether.

"Have you the drink taken, lad?" Ed asked as I tried to walk and found that I still could.

"I have not," I said, "except for a glass of sherry at lunch in Killarney."

"I know." Nuala backed me up. "Wasn't I watching him real careful?"

He laughed a big, raucous, infectious laugh. "Well, I don't know about you Yanks, but here in Ireland that's not what we call the drink taken.

I was wondering, and please pardon me for asking, because it's none of me business and I'm not a Guard at all, at all. I saw you veer off the road suddenlike, and sure, didn't I say a prayer as quick as I could and I'm wondering if the driver has the drink taken."

"We had a blowout, Ed. It's a good thing you prayed because it must have woke up the angels who are supposed to be patrolling this road on stormy nights."

He shook with laughter. "Sure, aren't they the most overworked angels in the world! Now take a few more steps just to make sure you are in good shape. Don't worry about a thing. We'll have a truck tow for your car first thing in the morning, and I'll ring to the rental agency and we'll have another one for you first thing. Are you all right, lass?"

"Me angel did a better job than the one who works for himself. I don't even have a cut."

"Well, then, good enough. We'll just take you down to the hospital and have them take a wee look at you and then worry about where you'll be staying for the night. Don't give it another worry. We'll take care of everything."

"I don't think we need a hospital, Ed."

"Sure, it will do no harm at all, at all to be sure. And I'll be calling the Guards and giving them an account of the accident and that's a terrible big hole in your tire, isn't it now? Your Michelins aren't supposed to do that, are they? But they weren't designed to deal with our Galway rocks, were they, lass? Now we'll put you in my car and yourselves soaking wet and drive over to the hospital, won't we?"

"You Galway good Samaritans are certainly efficient," I said.

He roared again, the biggest, most energetic laugh yet. "Ah, sure, you have great wit for a Yank."

"Irish American," Nuala corrected our new friend.

"Wasn't I knowing that from the first time I saw his face with the rain pouring down on it? Now, where were you driving at this hour of the night and in the worst rainstorm to hit the West of Ireland in five years at least?"

"Carraroe," I said. We were limping towards his car, a big black Lancia, which stood at the side of the road, lights on and door open — a welcome port in the storm.

"Isn't that one of the most beautiful places in all the world? Sure, you can travel a long way before you find a nicer place or finer people. 'Tis one of the grandest towns in all of Ireland."

"Herself is from there, as were my grandparents."

"Well, now, then we must take special care of both of you. We can't let folk from Carraroe be neglected, can we? Not at all, at all."

I suspected that he had found an excuse for generosity that would have been lavished on us anyhow.

Who the hell was this fast-talking Samaritan with the thick West of Ireland brogue?

"We should get our bags and the things in the car," Nuala said.

"Haven't I thought of it already? Don't worry another second about it. We'll get you in out of the chill and then we'll take care of your things."

We were ushered into the car and Ed trotted back to our car, oblivious to the rain.

In a moment he came rushing back with our bags, Nuala's purse, my camera, and the papers and maps from the front seat.

"I think I have everything. If there's something else, won't the Guards collect it tomorrow morning? Don't give it another second's worry. We'll take care of everything."

He climbed in the car and shut the door. I was in the front seat, Nuala in the back. She still seemed a little dazed.

"If you weren't wearing your seat belts, you'd both might be dead now."

"Himself made me," Nuala announced.

I had not. I had merely fastened mine and she had followed suit.

Ed made the sign of the cross. "Praise be to God, sure there'd be a lot less traffic deaths in this country if everyone was that prudent, let me tell you."

He turned over the ignition.

Nuala spoke to him in Irish.

He turned off the ignition, surprised apparently, and spoke back to her in the same language. Their exchange was rapid and half humorous with a nod from each of them in my direction, a shrug from Nuala, and a laugh from Ed.

"Wouldn't I have the Irish," Nuala returned to English, "and meself from Carraroe?"

"The finest town in all the County Galway, bar none," Ed insisted. "Mind you, don't quote me or I'll be in terrible trouble."

"I won't. . . . Milord, may I introduce Dermot Michael Coyne from Chicago, Illinois, and himself not a bad man even if he is a writer. He has a brother a priest and his Uncle Bill is the bishop of Alton, Illinois."

"Pleased to meet you, Dermot." He crushed my hand with his large paw.

"Dermot, this is Dr. Edward Patrick Hayes, Bishop of Galway and Kilmacduff and Apostolic Administrator of Kilfenora."

"I'm knowing your Uncle Billy, a grand man altogether, and himself from a Galway family and concerned about justice for the poor and the oppressed. A brilliant man, great theologian, and terrible proud of the young priest in the family."

"I'm happy to meet you, Bishop," I said when I could find a pause in his torrent of words.

"Since your uncle is a friend of mine and a bishop too, you'd better keep on calling me Ed. The lass, being from Carraroe, couldn't possibly do that — wouldn't the bishop's first name stick in her throat?"

A burst of loud laughter. " 'Twould, milord," Nuala said dutifully, my first hint that she was, beneath it all, a clericalist.

"Sure, wasn't the Mother of God good to have me coming home from a confirmation down on the Shannon right behind you when your tire blew up on you? There's nothing to worry about at all, at all. We'll take care of everything and you'll be on the road to Carraroe first thing in the morning. Wouldn't I have to insist that Billy Ready's nephew stays the night at me house and himself barely surviving an accident?"

"We really can't —" I began.

"Not another word! Not another word! We'll just stop a few moments at the hospital and then we'll find you some dry clothes, a place to sleep, and a drop or two to warm you up."

A bishop. An Irish bishop. As Nuala might have said under other circumstances, a focking Irish bishop!

— 58 —

"What did you tell him about me when you were talking that heathen language?" I demanded of Nuala Anne McGrail when the bishop left his parlor to make more Irish coffee.

The bishop's house was a big Victorian pile with a large yard and garden and Galway Bay in the distance, "though you won't be seeing it in the rain."

Nuala, wrapped in robe, towels, and blankets, had been singing songs in Irish and English for an hour and was very content with herself.

"Sure, didn't he ask me if you were my fiancé or my lover and didn't I have to say that you were a good man and a gentleman and that you were neither yet and worse luck for me."

My face, already hot from the huge fire blazing in the bishop's fireplace, became hotter.

"And he said?"

"He said that you seemed a fine young lad and that I was lucky to have met someone as good as you and yourself being a Yank. And I said your man wants to be called an Irish American. And he said that you looked like your uncle only bigger and I said that, sure, you were a great big amadon, weren't you now, and —"

"Enough. Enough. . . . Does anyone ever sleep in this house?"

" 'Tis said that His Lordship often stays up all night singing and arguing with his guests and is at work the next morning bright and early, none the worse for wear."

"And his guests?"

"Aren't they destroyed altogether?"

"I wouldn't be the least surprised."

"Here's the Irish coffee." Bishop Hayes, wearing a black turtleneck sweater with his black

582

trousers, burst into the room. "Sure, it's my own special concoction. Wasn't it invented in San Francisco by a Limerick man and myself being from Limerick? Now, drink it down while it's hot. Sure, won't it help you to sleep when you go to bed in another quarter hour?"

I wasn't sure of that because coffee doesn't help you to sleep and bed had been scheduled for another quarter hour for the last hour and a half.

'Twas the singing of songs that was keeping us awake. The bishop and my Nuala were determined, I thought as I sipped the coffee (with thick cream and, it seemed, thicker whiskey), to sing every song either of them knew. She was having the time of her life, the simple peasant girl from Carraroe matching song for song His Lordship the bishop of Galway (and let us not forget Kilmacduff and Kilfenora, wherever the hell those places might be). I ached all over, despite the Irish coffee, and could barely keep my eyes open.

In the back of my head an idea was forming. Bishop Ed Hayes was a man we could trust. If I turned the whole puzzle over to him, he'd probably know exactly what to do and what men in the government of Ireland to call for help.

"Sure, don't give the matter another second's thought. Won't I call a couple of lads and take care of the whole thing? It's all settled, we'll not have another word about it."

Not a bad idea actually. He was a lot less mysterious and spooky than Patrick, Patrick *Michael* as may be, and certainly knew this country a lot better. Monday morning, after we had poked around during the weekend, I'd come back here and lay it all out for him.

He had swept through the friendly, sleepy hospital like a benign tornado.

"Ah, 'tis his grace, the bishop of Galway," the young nurse in the emergency room had announced at the top of her voice, "with two Yanks that were almost destroyed in an accident. Sure, we'll take care of them right away."

"One Irish, one Irish American," Nuala had mumbled, still shaken and dizzy.

Almost at once a swarm of doctors and nurses and technicians descended on us. I had the impression that they were competent but under normal circumstances in no rush to do anything. However, with his gracious Lordship the bishop of Galway and whatever and whatever on the premises, the staff swung into high gear — ah, and they'd be telling the tales about his visit for the whole week.

"And wasn't the Yank a great big blond amadon from Chicago, a football player would you believe, but as gentle and sweet as you could ask?"

"And herself being from Carraroe and as pretty as a picture and a student at TCD as friendly as you could imagine and herself having Irish and making fun of your man and of the

584

bishop himself too and His Lordship loving it?"

"Were they lovers? Well, now, that's hard to say, but, sure, I don't think in the technical sense of the word, if you take me meaning, but, mark me words, she's set her cap for him and I wouldn't blame her for it at all, at all."

"Aren't there some lovely women from the Gaeltacht? The boobs on her were something special, let me tell you."

"No, there was nothing wrong with them at all, at all. His Lordship was just being careful. You know what he's like. Wasn't your man calling him the good Samaritan of Galway, and that's true enough, isn't it? We kept them there while we took some pictures and made some tests and put a butterfly bandage on his cut and sent them on their way."

"Sure, the ass on her was pretty neat too, wasn't it?"

"Isn't that a terrible thing to say and the poor girl lucky to be alive? Well, I didn't say it wasn't true."

They didn't know that your man was a writer and that he was imagining a story with that kind of dialogue as they shone lights in his eyes and tapped his knees with little metal hammers.

It would be a grand story. Brilliant.

Except would anyone believe that such a dazzling man as Bishop Edward Patrick Hayes existed anywhere in the world?

Well, fock 'em if they don't, says I.

After the hospital was finished with us, and

several of the nurses and the women doctors asking for the bishop's autograph, there was no question about Salt Hill or Carraroe, no question at all.

"Sure, isn't it too late? The hotels would be closed and it's too dark and wet to try to drive to Carraroe even if you had a car. And would Billy Ready ever forgive me if I turned his nephew and his translator out into a furious night like this? No, the matter is settled completely. You can sleep in me guest bedroom and herself can have the maid's room next to the housekeeper who's a little deaf so she won't be hearing the noise when we come in. 'Tis all settled."

Naturally it was all settled.

And we sang, well, Nuala and the bishop sang, till three o'clock in the morning.

And I listened to the bishop's stories of his days in London as a young priest when he decided that his people needed housing so "Bejesus, I built housing for them."

"The largest private housing scheme in London," Nuala, who apparently was well informed about the Ed Hayes legend, added.

The party went on. We argued about El Salvador and Nicaragua and Ronald Reagan and the Irish-American contribution to the IRA in the North. I tried in vain to convince the bishop that I was a Democrat and could not stand Reagan and had voted against the former president.

"Your man is about to collapse on us alto-gether, milord." She finally took pity on me. "Maybe we ought to let him go to bed."

"Bejesus, is it sleep you want, Dermot Michael Coyne?" He grinned broadly. "Ah, you'd never succeed as a bishop, not at all, at all. Well, to hell with you, says I. Go to bed and spoil the party and see if I care."

"It's been a grand evening." I hoped I could remember it all for my story.

"Not another word about it. 'Twas my priv-ilege to entertain you. Now, sleep as late as you want. It's been a hard day for the two of you. First thing in the morning I'll be ringing the store in Carraroe so they can speak to your parents, Nuala." He pronounced her name so that is sounded like pure melody. "I've already rung the Guards and I'll talk to the leasing com-pany first thing in the morning. They'll have a car here even before you wake up."

We were ushered to our rooms at opposite ends of the building, me carrying Nuala's bag and himself carrying mine. The bishop then charged back down the stairs to "clean up some of my work and finish my breviary before I take my sleep."

As I was trying to organize my bemused mind to unpack and undress, Nuala knocked at my door.

She leaned against the door jamb, wrapped cozily in the thickest robe, I thought, in all the world, a grinning womanly leprechaun, though

587

not in her bedraggled state a particularly seductive leprechaun.

"Don't worry, your man is downstairs pounding away on his word processor. I only came to kiss you good night and to ask you whether you're going to fantasize about making love in a bishop's palace."

"If I wasn't so tired, woman, and so shook by the accident and so befuddled by Irish coffee and by your man the bishop and by the whole day and if the right woman was here, yes, I'd have such a fantasy."

"I was thinking you'd say something like that, worse luck for me. Otherwise, to tell the truth, I wouldn't have knocked on your door. So a good-night kiss will have to do."

Our kiss started out fervent and became passionate. I wanted to hold her in my arms for all eternity and beyond.

"I'm glad I didn't lose you out there on the road to Dramore," she said when we stopped.

"I'm glad I didn't lose you, Nuala."

I tell myself today that if I wasn't utterly exhausted I would have indulged in acting out the fantasy she had proposed. But I know that I would not.

"I love you." She broke away and slipped out of my room. "And, Dermot Michael Coyne, welcome to the County Galway!"

The Nuala of Carraroe was the real Nuala, the Nuala I had presented to Chicago's mayor in Dublin: a shy child not only in Bergman's sense of the word as a vulnerable lover but in the literal sense — a young girl who was as quiet and as skittish as her charming and handsome parents. This Nuala was the sort who meekly said, "Yes, Ma," when her mother gently rebuked her: "Ah, love, you shouldn't be talking Irish with your young man here and himself not having the language."

Then she would apologize to me without a hint of irony. "I'm sorry, Dermot, I forgot me manners."

Later she would whisper, "Sure, we're all quiet people out here in Carraroe."

"I like the Carraroe Nuala best of all."

"Do you really?" She seemed surprised. "Why ever would you do that?"

"Because she's so much like her wonderful parents."

She shook her head, unable to understand. Then she blushed and said, "Maybe I should have been like her more often."

Her Carraroe mode made her even more appealing. It also made me more fearful of violating her youthful innocence.

Did I exaggerate that innocence?

Asking myself that question from the distance of many months and many thousand miles and a lot of that prolonged activity of mine called thinking, I must say no. She was as innocent as she appeared. The Dublin mode was a mask, though not completely unauthentic — none of the masks were. My mistake that fateful weekend was to imagine that innocence was incompatible with elaborate scheming.

After reading the translations of Ma's diary, I should never have made that mistake.

It was my turn to sleep till nine o'clock. I awoke to sounds of the traffic in the road by the bishop's house and the blue of Galway Bay in the distance glowing under a triumphant sun. I wanted to roll over and return to my pleasant dreams, whose erotic contents I could not remember. Then I realized where I was and what the day was. I jumped out of bed, raced through the shower (frigid), and hurried down straight towards the smell of breakfast.

Ed Hayes, in clerical shirt without the collar, and Nuala were sitting over the table, babbling away in Irish — with herself doing most of the babble. A bit embarrassed when I came into the room, they returned to English and, I was quite sure, changed the subject.

"I was explaining to herself," the bishop began, "me plan for modifying the adult education program in me diocese." He patted a folder on the table. "Haven't I been working on it since half six this morning?"

"You didn't wait breakfast for us then?"

"I say my rosary and my Mass and eat my breakfast every morning so that I can be at my desk at half six and get the work cleared away before the phone starts ringing. But, now, not another word, eat your own breakfast. Herself has left something for you?"

"Not all that much." I surveyed the table. "No brown bread at all, at all."

"Me cook will be delighted." Ed Hayes stormed out to the kitchen.

"More like it." I sat down and smiled at Nuala. "Good morning, Ms. McGrail."

"Good morning, Mr. Coyne."

"Did you sleep well?"

"Well enough." She smirked. "Not as well as I might have."

I attempted no response to that.

She seemed inordinately pleased with herself, as if the bishop had given her advice that she liked.

Bishop Hayes stormed back in with a vast plate of fresh brown bread. "Fionna is delighted. Eat up, you have all the time in the world. . . . Now." He rubbed his hands enthusiastically. "There's nothing more to be concerned about. The Guards have made their record of the accident. The rental agency has turned over the report to their insurance company. The car will be repaired here in Galway, though it

591

will take at least a week and you shouldn't give it another thought."

"Thank you very much," says I.

"They have a Renault outside already. It's not as big as your Benz, but it's a good sound car and the biggest they have here. You can drive it back to Dublin after your weekend is over or leave it here and take the train — it's only a three-hour ride. I talked to the St. Catherine Hotel in Salt Hill and they're holding your booking. I rang herself's mother and she didn't quite believe I was the bishop of Galway, but they'll be expecting you out there for lunch. Now, is there anything else I can do for you?"

"A winning ticket to the Irish sweepstakes?"

He roared. Even the fair Nuala smiled tolerantly.

"I'll call himself all the way in Alton, Illinois, this afternoon and tell him he has a brilliant nephew, that's what I'll do. And yourself a great teller of tales at that."

I couldn't remember any tales. "Thank you."

"Now, if you'll both excuse me, I have a call or two to make and a meeting with twenty of me priests that will take four hours. Be sure you stop on your way back to Dublin."

And the wind blew out of the room.

"Saints preserve us." I lathered strawberry jam on my brown bread, a tolerable substitute for raspberry. "What a dynamo!"

"And worshiped in the whole County Galway,

let me tell you. If all the priests in the world were like him, we'd have a grand church, wouldn't we now?"

"We would indeed. . . . How are you feeling?"

"Sore, but all right. You?"

"The same."

"I'll hurry up so we can be on our way to Carraroe."

"Don't rush, we Stone Age people have a different sense of time. So long as me ma an' da know I'm coming, they'll be grand."

The air was cold when we lugged our bags out to the Renault, but the sky was as clear as crystal, weather as different as it could possibly be from the day before. Galway Bay glowed like the Bay of Naples.

"It's just like Naples," I said to herself as I put our bags in the boot.

"I've only seen pictures, but, ah, 'tis lovely today, isn't it? Sure, I hardly need tell you that we don't always have Neapolitan weather, do I?"

Nuala was smiling contentedly, proud that her home county was putting on a show. Then I understood why she was in such a good mood — she was going home. I also understood why she had wept so bitterly over Ma's final entry in her first volume.

Nuala knew how hard it would be to leave this beauty, even if the sun didn't go down over Galway Bay, as the song says, every day.

"Sure, doesn't it rain in Naples too?"

"Ah, we're corrupting you, Dermot Michael, you're beginning to talk like a native."

"That'll be the day," I said as I started the car.

I was scared stiff at the wheel and drove very slowly and carefully, jumping at every car that came my way — once again trying to figure out which side of the road I should be on.

I worried, however, about more than other cars as I drove carefully along the shore of Galway Bay.

I was convinced that a bullet had ripped the tire to shreds, not a sharp rock. Thus far no one had attempted to kill us. A shot at a tire wasn't necessarily murder. It could be merely another warning. If murder was what they had in mind, they would have shot at the driver, not the tire. On the other hand, the blowout could have killed both of us. The other side was raising the stakes. They were now saying "We don't want to kill you, but if we cause an accident in which you die, that's your problem."

If I had been driving faster or we hadn't hit the ditch at the lucky angle we did, the Guards could have written off our deaths as an unfortunate accident, a Yank driving on a road he did not know and in bad weather.

Was it a message from Brendan Keane? Could he have passed us on the road and lain in wait for us?

Or, more likely, had he phoned ahead? Or was it part of the plan from the beginning, a more brutal and dangerous warning in the series that began with Superintendent Conlon in the lobby of Jury's?

I hadn't told Nuala about this speculation. Probably she'd thought of it too.

The St. Catherine Hotel was comfortable enough, though Jury's it was not. The people in the hotel were friendly, they all knew Nuala, so I pronounced it "grand" and we went on along the shore of the bay out highway L100.

Nuala continued her commentary on the countryside, which had begun with a description of the old fishing village called the Claddagh across the river from Galway, whose wedding bands had become popular all over the world.

"Sure, wasn't it a victim of urban renewal and itself another one of your alien subcultures?"

I heard a lot about St. Nicholas Cathedral (Church of Ireland), the Kennedy Park across from the railway hotel, the Spanish Arch, the merchant families of Galway and their castles — including the O'Kellys.

"Daniel O'Kelly must have been a descendant of one of those families, eager perhaps to recapture some of their lost wealth," I said.

" 'Twas lost long ago."

As we drove along the beach at Salt Hill, she pointed out the golf course to me. " 'Tis said to be one of the best in Ireland. I suppose that a big amadon like you wouldn't be playing golf, would you now?"

"Woman, I would."

595

"And yourself with a high handicap, I'm thinking?"

"Four."

"Four?" She seemed impressed.

How long was it since I had swung a club at Butterfield, the family country club?

"Wasn't I saying that?"

"Well" — she drew a deep breath — "you should play more so you can lower it down to zero." We both howled.

"It took you awhile to come up with that response."

"Would your gram have said that?"

"And my mom and my sisters and my sisters-in-law and the nuns who taught me in school!"

She told me about the fairs and festivals that are the big events in the life of Connemara. "Maybe your gram bought her pony at the festival when she was a lass."

"Did you have a pony, Nuala?"

"Ah, no. Weren't we too poor to own a pony? Sure, I had a bicycle after a while, and wasn't that enough?"

We drove beyond Spiddal (site, I was informed by my tour guide, of an Irish-language athletic meet — in which she had won a prize for sprinting) towards the far fringe of the Connemara peninsula where land and water and hill and valley mix in dramatic juxtaposition. The region was deforested long ago and is not mountainous enough for a comparison with the fjords of Norway, yet the combination of ocean, lake, white-

(or blue- or red-) washed homes on the side of lakes (loughs, as the natives called them), and steep paths lined with whitewashed rock fences was unique and dazzling.

"It's marvelous, Nuala. Incredible."

" 'Tis all of that," she said, radiant with anticipation of home, "but, Dermot, 'tis poor land and we're poor people, terrible poor."

"And I'm supposed to be shocked at that?"

"No."

"And my grandparents didn't come from here?"

"They did."

"Must I tell you again that I'm not a snob."

"Only a prude." She laughed happily. "Ah, Dermot me love, I'll not fight with you today. I'm too happy to be home again, home where I belong."

Indeed where she belonged, yet she was perfectly ready to give it up for me.

As Ma was ready to give it up for Pa.

I was coming home too in a certain sense. Ma had occasionally told me what beautiful country it was, adding almost in Nuala's words "and terrible poor at that."

Carraroe itself was like a crown of jewels in the bright autumn sunlight, the strips of green and brown land, farm and bog, being the structure of the crown and the loughs the large, glittering stones.

The town was not a concentration of buildings but several strings of cottages on the shores of

the loughs, minor jewels around the large di-
amonds.

"It's like Venice." I had stopped the car and
Nuala and I had stepped out to admire the area.
Somehow my arm found its way around her
waist.

"I've never seen it meself" — she leaned
against me — "but I'm sure Venice isn't as
cold in the winter."

"And Carraroe isn't going to sink under the
ocean."

"It only seems that way when the rains and
the winds sweep in from North America."

I led her back to the car. "Ma didn't paint
this picture in her diary, did she?"

"The poor thing had nothing to compare it
with and meself knowing what that's like. You
know your village is beautiful, but you don't
know how to describe it."

I started the car.

"Now, Dermot Michael" — she clutched my
arm — "they'll be having a grand lunch for
you. It's more than they can afford, but there'll
be no stopping them, so don't make a scene
about it or try to pay for it."

"I understand. . . . I brought a bottle of Green
Label for them. Will it be all right to give it
to them?"

"They'll nurse it all winter long and, sure,
into the spring too."

Nuala's people were very poor. Their cottage
was small and the roof thatched. There was a

single cow in the yard and a few sheep and a couple of small outbuildings that served as barns. However, the thatch was neatly trimmed, the whitewash of the cottage fresh and bright, the red and black trim carefully painted, and the sign "Teas given" clear and attractive in green and orange on white.

Her parents were waiting for us in front, sitting on one of the benches at the tables where they "gave tea" to tourist buses, arms around one another, himself in the gray suit that seems required of the Irish countryman and herself in a blouse and skirt not unlike that which Nell Pat might have worn.

"Welcome home to Carraroe!" Sean McGrail extended a big, callused hand.

" 'Tis good to have you home." Meg smiled at me.

"Och," says I. "With such a warm welcome, I'm thinking I never left!"

That's how you deal with Irish exaggerations — top them!

Whatever other Irish families might do to hide affection, that didn't seem to be a custom with Meg and Sean McGrail. They both hugged their youngest child fiercely. For much of the visit the two older people kept their arms around one another.

They were both tall, slender, and handsome. Nuala inherited her beauty from both sides of her family. Her father's hair was gray but his face glowed red with energy. Her mother's hair was mostly black still and her face radiant with joy. I suspected that she and Nuala could wear the same clothes.

A man married to such a woman as she for forty years and more would have no difficulty thinking erotic thoughts about her. Not at all, at all.

"God and Mary be with all who live in this house," I said as I was conducted inside.

"God and Mary and Patrick be with those who visit it," they replied together, pleased that I knew the right words.

"I don't suppose you take a drop now and then." I extended the box that contained the bottle of Bushmill's Single Malt. "But maybe some of your guests will need protection from the cold."

Meg accepted the gift. "Ah, well, Dermot Michael, sure we might sneak a wee taste of it ourselves at the odd time, might we not, man of the house?"

She handed him the bottle.

" 'Tis the truth you speak, woman of the house, even it embarrasses our youngest daughter to hear us saying it."

I liked them instantly, which was a foregone conclusion. However, they liked me, a phenomenon about which I was not so sure when we drove up. I was a Yank, a rich man from the big world, and moreover, I might carry away their youngest daughter, for all they knew. Would they not be shy and formal with me and perhaps servile?

Such reactions could occur in other cottages in Ireland and perhaps even in other cottages in Carraroe. But not among the McGrails. Their own dignity made it easy for them to welcome the stranger no matter who he was.

Better and better did I understand their daughter.

The lunch that was spread out before me could have done honor to any home in Ireland, even if it were served in a cottage with a stone floor and a peat fire burning in the fireplace. (Next to which, perhaps inevitably, there stood a small television, Carraroe's window to the big world.)

"Glory be to God, woman of the house," I exclaimed, "you've made brown bread!"

"Wasn't herself saying you were addicted to it, in a manner of speaking?"

"Me ma," Nuala said proudly, "makes the best brown bread in the whole County Galway."

I was asked to say the grace, as herself had warned I would be. So I recited the Irish grace I had dutifully memorized.

"Beal na gcuig ara agus an iase
A roinn Dia ar an gcuig mhile duine,
Rath on Ri a rinne an roinn
Go dtie ar ar gcuid is ar ar gcomhroninn."

Everyone was greatly pleased with my efforts

and did their best to hide their amusement at my terrible Chicago accent.

The prayer says:

> *The blessing of the five loaves and*
> *two fishes*
> *That God shared among the five thousand,*
> *The bounty of the King who made*
> *the sharing*
> *Come upon our food and all who share it.*

Meg and Sean were, for all their warmth, quiet folk. They spoke softly and gently and in allusive and indirect sentences. The room where we ate was charged with affection, but it was gentle and delicate affection, communicated by a flash of an eye or a touch of a hand.

Yet there was always a promise of a smile at their lips, and every second remark displayed quick wit that you would miss unless you were attending to each word they said.

If this were the last Stone Age race, give me the Stone Age.

They spoke proudly of their children and grandchildren and showed me pictures while we ate. Nuala helped her mother and watched and listened, her eyes beaming with pride over them and, God help us all, over me.

"It's a shame that they are all so far away, isn't it?" I said.

" 'Tis." Sean sighed.

"But then if they were near, wouldn't we

602

likely fight with them? As it is when they come home, isn't it a time for celebration? Sometimes" — Meg smiled quickly — "a bit of a celebration when they leave too, isn't it, Sean?"

" 'Tis good when they come." He wiped his lips with a linen napkin. "And not always bad when they leave us in peace."

The two of them sang the praises of their Nuala Anne.

"She's a grand child, so kind and loving."

"And a mind of her own too."

"Of course," I said with a wink, "she does have her sulks, doesn't she now?"

"She does that, heaven knows."

"But then they never last overnight, do they?"

"Not so far."

Nuala did not seem at all embarrassed.

"And weren't we proud of her when she won all those prizes?"

"And herself studying all the time when she wasn't singing?"

"Or acting?"

"Or dancing with the boys?"

"Or playing football with them too?"

"And hurley too, until the lads thought she was too good for them?"

"Ah, wasn't she a wicked woman with a stick!"

"A grand student, wasn't she?"

"Da!" Nuala was scarlet now. "Dermot Michael knows about me sulks, but now he will be thinking I was a terrible tomboy, won't he?"

"The thought would never enter my head."

We all laughed and Nuala got up to clear the table, firmly constraining with a hand on a shoulder her ma to stay with the menfolk.

In Dublin Nuala would not tolerate that, but this wasn't Dublin.

"Will you take a drop?" Sean asked me.

"I will, but only a drop because we have work to do this afternoon."

He brought out a plain bottle filled with clear liquid.

" 'Tis the poteen," he said reverently. "Only a little bit illegal."

"Just a mite," his wife agreed.

The clear liquid was poured into ordinary water glasses.

I lifted it to my lips. Nuala was watching me with an enormous grin.

I sipped it carefully.

Liquid electricity!

"It has a bite to it." I gasped. "A very nice bite."

They all laughed at me, soft, gentle laughter.

The Yank was a good sport.

He did manage to finish the poteen, although his head whirled for a couple of hours afterward.

Then we settled down to business.

They had collected from the PP (parish priest) brand-new baptismal and marriage and death

604

certificates. The "young priest" with the pretty brown eyes had become rector of the Pro-Cathedral in Galway and a canon. He still had a great reputation as a wise and holy man, if "a bit of a nationalist."

The only record that seemed important was the remark on the baptismal certification of Mary Anne Malone, Tim and Moire's daughter and Ma's godchild, that she had been married to a man named John Sheerin in San Francisco at the Mission Dolores in 1942.

"I'll try to check up on that. He could have been a sailor stationed there during the war. It'll be hard to track them down."

"There's almost no recollection of the Troubles," Meg said. "And no wonder, it being such a terrible time. Some of the old folks remember hearing about the Malones, once very important folks in Carraroe and themselves owning the best farm in the district. You'll see the house this afternoon, Dermot Michael. There's not much left to the old farmhouse, and it having been modernized."

"What do they say about the Malones?"

"They say that they sold their farm and went away together before 1930. Probably to America, but no one remembers where."

"Maybe we'll find that in the diary later on, Dermot. She'll certainly say something about them."

"Aren't you lucky, Dermot Michael" — her father winked at me — "to be having such an expert translator?"

"Her translations sound just like my grandmother. Almost as if she were speaking to us."

"Ah." Meg winked at me. "Isn't our little Nuala the deep one?"

You'd better believe it.

Over enormous protests from all concerned, I helped wash the dishes — with soap and water pumped from a well and heated on the peat fire.

"Isn't it nice, Nuala, that you've been meeting one of these nice feminist men?"

A number of winks that time.

" 'Tis. And me da helping you with the dishes every time the tourists come for tea."

"Wouldn't I be in terrible trouble, Dermot Michael" — a wink at me — "if I didn't?"

"Go 'long with you!"

The tourists were scheduled to come almost immediately. I was strictly forbidden to help with the service. "We'd have to teach you how to be polite to the Germans, wouldn't we now?"

I was, however, permitted to help them set the tables.

The bus arrived, the Germans were disgorged, brash and noisy by my Chicago Irish standards, and conducted to the tables. Tea and hot scones were served. The visitors consumed them with loud delight.

A couple of the men attempted to be fresh with Nuala and were stared into silence.

Leaning against the cottage, like a lord of the

manor, I tightened my fists. If those damn . . .

Nuala glared at me. Don't you dare, I can take care of meself.

That was for sure.

The tourists left.

"Them poor Germans, aren't they the relaxed ones now?" Sean McGrail sighed.

"And they don't work at all at traveling, do they, Dermot?"

"They travel the way they won the war," I said, and occasioned more laughter.

The remains of tea were cleared away. Again I insisted on helping.

"Sure, didn't your mother bring you up to be a grand young gentleman?"

"Write her and tell her that! She never believes me when I tell her the same thing."

More soft laughter.

Then Nuala and I left to visit what had been the Malone house and see Mike Sean Cussack.

We walked arm in arm — it seemed the natural and the only way to do it — down the lanes, lined with stone fences, to a big stucco house close to a lough. The home was painted yellow and the windows were trimmed with red and blue. Two TV antennas loomed above the slate roof.

" 'Tis owned by a merchant from Galway City. They're nice folk. I'm sure they'd let you in."

"There's not much of Ma's house left, is there?"

"Hardly anything."

"Let's not bother then."

The only trace of the ruined cottage where Uncle Billy had been conceived was a stone foundation near one of the loughs, barely visible in the grass.

I kicked at the stones with my foot.

"Disappointed, Dermot?"

"This is a beautiful place, Nuala, as I've already told you. I love your parents. . . ."

"They love you too."

"But I can't see Ma or Pa or their family and friends. It doesn't seem the locale for so much passion and energy and enthusiasm."

"She read her passion into the environment, Dermot."

"I'm sure she did that."

"There's passion here, God knows." Nuala sighed. "Like everywhere else in the world."

"Wasn't I noticing that in your cottage? . . . I guess I feel so empty because I can find no trace of the woman who wrote that diary."

"She left for America, Dermot, and the world she left behind changed."

"I guess so."

"A woman like Nell Pat, however, leaves her mark, even if you don't see it."

"She tell you that?"

"She didn't have to. . . . Now let's visit Mike Sean Cussack. He's always claimed to have belonged to the Irregulars."

The old man, smoking his pipe in front of

a rundown cottage, was not much help. He remembered that Daniel O'Kelly had been shot as a traitor, over at Maam Cross by the order of General Collins himself."

He also claimed to remember Liam O'Riada, "and wasn't it a shame himself being shot in the back and his wife expecting a child?"

Nell Pat Malone was a wonderful lass with blond hair that later tended bar in a public house in Galway.

I slipped a ten-punt note into the old man's hands and thanked him and even praised him for his memory.

"Not much help, was he, Dermot?"

"We didn't expect him to be, did we? The old fella on the bench at the Grand Canal seemed to remember more accurately."

I thought about the man and who he almost certainly was and almost told Nuala. Then I decided that there was no reason to do so.

"I'm sorry, Dermot."

"It's not your fault."

We started walking back down the lane to her house. The sun was already sinking in the west, casting magic shadows over the stark, lovely land.

"It's All Hallows Eve, isn't it, Nuala?"

" 'Tis." She sighed.

"No dead walking yet, are there?"

She glanced at me curiously. "They're all around us."

I didn't pursue the matter.

"I suppose we should put off the visit to Mamene" — I glanced at the mountains in the distance — "till tomorrow morning."

"May I make a suggestion?" she asked timidly.

"Have I ever said no?"

"The shrine will be filled with people tomorrow and it being the Feast of All Saints. . . . You'll be coming out here for Mass?"

"I will and to take your Ma and Da to lunch at a good restaurant."

"Grand! They'll love it! I'll make the bookings!"

"Then we go up to the mountain after lunch."

"No. When it's about this time tomorrow, you drive back to Salt Hill. I'll see that another car company parks a wee Ford for you down the street from St. Catherine's and leaves a key in it. When it's dark, you sneak out the back door and down the street to it and drive out here. Then we'll go over to Maam Cross at night. If anyone is watching the hotel, they'll be after thinking your car has never left and yourself asleep in the hotel."

"Brilliant!"

Siobhan Connery!

"You'll be thinking I'm a know-it-all," she said dubiously.

"I'm thinking I'm glad you're with me."

I did, however, think she was a know-it-all. Just like Ma.

— 60 —

There was no moon, as I would have known if I had bothered to look in the papers. Moreover, the road up to the Little Cell of Patrick was rocky and steep.

Mamene (or Maumean), the Pass of the Birds — so called because of the clouds that fly through it — is a windy passage through the Maamturk Mountains. It's about three miles west of Maam Cross on T71 and connects the County Galway, where the path begins, with the County Mayo, which starts halfway up the mountain. As you climb the path up to the shrine, you have Galway Bay behind you. At the top in the distance you can see Lough Corrib. In pictures it's a wild and fierce place. At night it is even more scary.

Cautiously I kept the beam of my flashlight on the path immediately ahead of me. My guide leaped up the trail like a mountain goat.

"Just think, Dermot Michael," she enthused. "Pilgrims were walking up this path to pray to God in the time of Abraham."

"On dark nights?"

"If it was the time of the year for a pilgrimage,

they'd climb to the shrine regardless of the moon. On their bare feet. Can't you see the thousands of torches and hear them chanting their heathen hymns!"

"Not really."

She slapped my arm. " 'Tis because you don't want to. Should I insist that you take off your shoes like a good pilgrim?"

"I will if you will."

"I don't want to embarrass you."

We had attended Mass, in Irish, at the same parish church where Ma and Pa had been married, as Ma's parents before her. Then we drove up to Costelloe for lunch at the hotel there. It did not look very promising, but the food was wonderful.

"Not as good as your lunch, Meg," I assured Nuala's mother.

"Did your young man kiss the stone while you were driving through Cork?"

"Faith, Ma, he doesn't need it. He was born that way."

I wasn't her young man and never would be, but her parents did not seem opposed to the prospect, not at all, at all.

That night it was a long, hard climb up the mountain. I was glad I was wearing shoes.

"Is this it?" I asked as we picked our way with flashlights to a level place.

"Sure, don't you sound like a young one? Och, we're not even halfway up to the shrine, are we?"

612

"I don't think I was cut out to be a pilgrim, Nuala Anne."

" 'Tis night after all."

"Is it now?"

She laughed and on we went.

Finally, it seemed years later, we arrived at another level spot.

"Almost there," she said. "Dermot, would you ever look back at the bay?"

The view was spectacular. Every star in the sky seemed to be caught in the net of Galway Bay.

"No wonder they thought this was a sacred place."

"Be real careful now. Aren't there lots of loose rocks?"

"What if I sprain my ankle?"

"It won't be as bad as breaking your leg, will it?"

We stumbled to the very summit of the mountain. On the top, looking as if he owned the whole world, was himself, St. Patrick, carved out of solid granite by a modern sculptor who believed that a saint should be strong and broad and imposing — like a good shepherd guarding his sheep.

There was a path cut out of the rocks for Stations of the Cross, each of the fourteen stations marked by a Celtic cross.

"Nice statue."

"Isn't it now? Me cousin Mihail, and himself a Jesuit, is the man responsible for restoring the shrine. . . . There's the ledge where St. Patrick was supposed to have slept. We'll have to measure out thirty paces and poke around."

"I don't think I'd want to sleep on that bed."

"And yourself alone in it just like you were a monk." An unnecessary comment, I thought.

Just beyond the pass was a little lake that looked very cold and foreboding. Nuala pointed out the pagan "station," a holy well that was supposed to have great power.

"A well at this altitude?"

"Sure, 'tis only a cistern. . . . Now we must walk around it seven times, throwing seven pebbles in during each circle. Pick up some pebbles, Dermot Michael."

"Pagan superstition."

"It doesn't have to be, not if you say seven hail Marys for each turn."

"In the dark?"

"In the dark . . . so the Mother of Jesus will take care of us."

"I thought you didn't believe in her."

"Up here I do."

We spent more than an hour "poking around" at various thirty-pace distances from the Little Cell.

I was tired enough by then to settle for Patrick's bed.

"Nuala, it isn't here," I said wearily.

"Sure, herself wouldn't be making it up, would she?"

"Maybe it was filled in long ago."

"Why would they do that? No one ever came up here until the shrine was restored and when that happened, wouldn't they be afraid that they'd be seen if they tried to carry the gold away? I know it's here, Dermot, I absolutely know it."

"Well, we won't find it at night." I leaned against the rocks. "Even if we did, what difference would it make . . . hey!"

The rock on which my hand was resting slipped away and fell to the ground.

"Here it is, Nuala! They piled up stones to hide the entrance!"

Hurriedly we pulled the stones away and directed the beams of our flashlights into the tiny crevice.

"It's there! Dermot, look at it glittering!"

"Gold!"

"Irish gold, Dermot, not futures contracts!"

We giggled hysterically and hugged one another.

"Five crates," I said, "and part of a sixth. Half the gold is still here! Ten million pounds sterling!"

"Sure, 'tis crowded for making love, isn't it?"

"Not if you're almost married."

That was all we said on that subject.

We replaced the stones.

"What next, Dermot?"

"I don't know. I'll have to think about it."

We hiked down the side of the mountain. I

drove her back to Carraroe and then, utterly exhausted, I returned to Salt Hill.

I fell asleep, knowing that I would have to make some important decisions the next day — after giving long thought to the problems.

My last thought as I slipped into sleep was "We found the gold, Ma! We found it! Just as you said we would!"

– 61 –

When I woke up Monday morning, I knew the name of the man in the touring car. Of course. Who else could it have been? And about whom else would everyone be so worried? I had been an eejit not to have seen his face before.

Damn. I pounded the bed. Why has it taken me so long? Well, I'd beaten Nuala to it.

Outside rain was falling again and a wind was roaring in off the beach — nothing between it and North America, as the locals say.

I lay back and thought about it carefully. I couldn't prove my conclusion, not yet. Maybe I wouldn't have to. Somewhere later on the diaries, perhaps after the second war, Ma would have given a name to the face.

Even if she didn't, I had enough proof to seek Bishop Hayes's help. I reached for the phone to call him and then thought better of it. There was no point in trusting the phone. I'd get in my Renault and drive over to his house in Galway City.

I glanced at my watch. Time for a quick breakfast before I left. It was all over now. We'd take the train back to Dublin this afternoon. I'd pack tomorrow, make the final arrangements with Nuala for finishing the translation, and then leave on the Wednesday plane for Chicago.

I'd be home in time for the Notre Dame–Southern Cal and Bear-Packer games.

I showered, went down to the dining room, devoured all the brown bread in sight, and returned to my room to pack my things so that after my meeting with the bishop I could collect Nuala and board the early-afternoon train.

Someone knocked at the door. I opened it.

Chief Superintendent Conlon forced his way in and stuffed a nine-millimeter Beretta in my stomach. Two other men rushed in behind him. One of them snapped cuffs on my hands.

"Come along, me fine lad. We have a score or two to settle. I don't like being humiliated in my own office, if you take my meaning."

One of the others tapped me lightly on the head and I lost consciousness.

I woke up in an abandoned farmhouse.

"He's awake now." Conlon grinned. "Time to get to work."

He produced a massive billy club and beat me till I lost consciousness.

Someone threw a bucket of cold water on my

face. Conlon, his face red with effort, his eyes wide with pleasure, sweat pouring down his face, beat me again and again. He enjoyed his revenge.

Finally they dragged me out of the house and threw me in the backseat of a car.

"We're going to church." Conlon giggled. "Sure, won't your girlfriend be waiting there for you?"

— 62 —

"So, my dear, as I promised, we've brought your lover for you. He seems a bit the worse for wear, doesn't he? Take the handcuffs off him, Chief Superintendent, we're going to have a pleasant little chat."

Brendan Keane's eyes shone with the frantic glow of the madman.

"He might still be dangerous," Conlon warned.

"Do as I say!" Keane shouted hysterically. "I am the minister. I give the orders! Moreover, he's not likely to do anything with our automatic weapon pointed at his young woman's pretty tits, is he?"

Grudgingly and with a little twist at my aching arms, he removed the cuffs.

Mistake, I thought.

We were inside what had once been a monastery chapel, a room perhaps forty-five feet long and twenty feet wide with low arches, a roof that had half fallen in, empty windows, and the remnants of a stone altar at the front in a small sanctuary. So many such bins littered the fields of Ireland that you hardly noticed them as you drove by.

God damn Oliver Cromwell.

The chapel provided some shelter against the rain, though it still swept down the nave from the broken rose window in back. It did not, however, keep out either the cold or the biting wind. The cold made the pain in the various parts of my anatomy feel worse.

Conlon was an expert at torture. He had hurt me badly enough, but I could still walk, still think, still talk, still suffer more when he wanted me to, and still anticipate that suffering.

I recalled again what the Japanese master who had taught me martial arts said about controlling pain and concentrated on his exercises.

I was more awake than Conlon realized and more capable of fighting back if I had a chance.

"Dermot, I'd like you to meet my colleagues, Professor Nolan and Dr. Hughes. I believe you spoke with Professor Nolan about certain issues of Irish history before I had my first conversation with you. They are rather interested in the outcome of your search for the origins of our little group. First of all, we have a small ritual to perform."

There was another man in the room, a blond

giant in a black jacket. He held an AK-47, by the looks of it, and it was pointed right at Nuala.

"You two, outside," Conlon snapped at his men. "Take care of any of his friends that might show up."

Keane piled Ma's diaries in front of the altar. "I rather think," Keane mused, "that this would be a good place to offer our little sacrifice. Safe from the wind and the rain, don't you know? Sorry we had to choose such a drafty spot, Dermot, but we were forced to act quickly, if you take me meaning."

Again they had underestimated me, or rather the capacity of a defensive end to absorb pain when he learned from his Japanese martial arts master how to concentrate it temporarily out of existence. There were five men in the old chapel. Conlon still held his billy club and the giant guard seemed firmly in charge of his AK-47. Nolan and Hughes were apparently un-armed and looked scared. Keane carried no visible weapon.

I could probably take care of them, battered ribs and aching gut and all, if the Russian weapon wasn't pointed at Nuala.

She seemed tense but composed. What did she have up her sleeve now?

Don't rush the gun, woman.

"You recognize these documents, don't you, Dermot? Your grandmother's diaries, are they not? We had to remove them, illegally, I fear, from the safe at the hotel. A robbery by the

620

IRA is our explanation. Clever, ah? We are going to offer them as a small sacrifice to whatever deities may occupy this place of worship. That should end any question of a search for buried treasure, shouldn't it?"

Only if there were no copies in Chicago.

"Answer the minister." Conlon jammed his club into my stomach.

"I guess it will."

He lighted his cigarette lighter and touched one of the notebooks. The old paper burned quickly.

"You see how rapidly they burn." Keane's face lit up in a demonic grin. "The past is finished now, isn't it?"

It would take more than that to burn Ma's fierce spirit.

"I guess so."

Nuala's eyes were warning me: Don't tell him about the copies.

Grand.

A statue of some long-forgotten saint stood just above the head of the man with the gun. On the edge of the pedestal, half on, half off, a rock rested, a hunk of the stone from which the monastery had been built. It had probably broken away from the roof long ago. If it moved a fraction of an inch, it would topple on the head of the gunman.

Not much hope there. The rock probably had been in the same position for half a thousand years.

Just the same, I tried to will that it would fall.

"Isn't a pretty fire, my dear?"

"You're a focking eejit," she said calmly.

"We'll have to teach you better manners before this little interlude is over."

"You promised there'd be none of that," Dr. Hughes pleaded.

He spoke with a clipped Oxford accent. A distinguished-looking gray-haired man in a trench coat, his pale face was tight with anxiety. Maybe he could be of some use.

"That's right, Brendan," Professor Nolan, the man who had betrayed me in the first place, begged. "Only the minimum necessary violence."

He was short and round and rubicund, a genial Irish academic caught up in a game that was too cute for him by half.

"Absolutely. Only the minimum *necessary*. But then who is to say what is *necessary*, if you take me meaning."

Where was Patrick? They couldn't have abandoned us, could they?

In the last desperate moment I would have to rush the man with the automatic weapon. I must wait till something distracted him — if something ever did.

"Now then," Keane continued leisurely. "Suppose you tell us exactly what ancient history you have gleaned from this foolish search of yours? Come, Dermot, I'm sure you don't want

622

your young friend to suffer the same, ah, annoyances you've suffered."

We must not let them know what we had discovered. Maybe they would release us and forget the whole matter. That's what Nuala was trying to signal me.

"We know who killed Michael Collins," I began tentatively. "And who stole Casement's gold."

Nuala nodded slightly.

"And we know that the killer and the thief were the same man and how he died. We don't know who paid him off and where the gold is hidden."

"Wasn't I telling you the same thing?" Nuala spoke contemptuously. "And yourself reading the translations on the hard disk of the computer."

What translations? Hadn't she said she'd erased them?

Later on, when I tried to figure everything out, I realized that she had left on the disk sanitized translations to deceive anyone who might try to read them.

Dear God, what a woman!

"I understand, my dear. However, can I be certain that those are accurate translations?"

"And yourself just burning the diary like an eejit?"

He slapped her. "Mind your manners, slut!"

"Here, now," Hughes protested. "There's no cause for that."

"There's cause for whatever I want there to be cause," Keane yelled at his colleague. "I'll do what I want to do."

"Settle down, Brendan," fat little Professor Nolan begged. "The diaries are gone. Even if the translations have been edited, and these two little fools are not smart enough to think of that, they can't prove anything. Let's drop it all and get out of here."

They had not burned the first notebook of the diary. That was in my room at Salt Hill.

"Slowly, slowly, Seamus, me good friend. Am I not thinking that there might be more of the translations in Miss McGrail's pretty little head? Ought we not, ah, clear that hard disk too?"

"No!" the other two pleaded.

"No choice," Conlon agreed with his patron. "After we're having a little fun with her. Sure, it would be a shame to waste all them good looks, wouldn't it now?"

I continued to act as if I were dazed and disoriented, which wasn't very difficult given my condition. The rock above the gunman's head seemed to move a fraction of an inch. Probably my imagination.

Nuala stood up slowly; the gunman moved the muzzle of the gun to stay with her.

Outside the wind was howling more loudly and the rain beating down more fiercely.

"All right, Mr. Minister," she said calmly. "I'll tell you the whole truth. Copies of those diaries are safe in another country. Those were edited translations you read on the computer. But the real translations and the floppy disks that contain them are in the hands of the bishop of Galway."

She'd made three backup disks, had she?

"Very clever, my dear." Keane sneered. "But you don't expect me to believe that, do you?"

"As you please, Mr. Minister. Of course, we know where the gold is and who gave the order of the death of Michael Collins. So does His Lordship, Bishop Hayes. At this very moment he is in the cave with your very good friends, the minister of justice and the commissioner of the Civic Guards."

"Brilliantly acted, Nuala, grand altogether. But, alas for you and your battered hero, quite untrue."

"His Lordship will give the minister and the commissioner the translations and you and your friends will be finished."

Keane cackled gleefully. "I ask you, Seamus, LeMont, isn't she wonderful?"

"What if she's telling the truth?" Hughes sputtered.

The man with the AK-47 was confused by the argument. He lowered the muzzle of the weapon a fraction of an inch. The play was blitz and the object was a sack.

"Oh, she's not telling the truth at all. Come, Nuala, admit to these nice gentlemen that you're acting and make the end easier on yourself."

"Look in me purse there on the floor." She

gestured at the large shoulder bag. "You'll find a bar of gold in it."

Frantically Keane lunged at the purse and tore it open. Sure enough, he pulled out a bar of gold.

"Bitch!" he screamed insanely. "Cunt!"

"We're finished." Nolan moaned. "And the minister of justice hating your guts!"

The muzzle of the gun dropped lower. I tensed for my blitz.

Keane swung around, bar in hand, as if to hit Nuala with it.

She stepped back.

"Among the documents the bishop has given to the minister and the commissioner is one that you didn't know we had — a list of the members of the Consort of St. George and St. Patrick. Your names are all on it. So is Longwood-Jones's. You'll recognize the other names: MacCarthy, Waldron, Rollins, Harcourt, Crawford, McMahon, Clifford, Jackson, Smithers, Clinton, O'Meara, Nicholson, Joyce, Tierney, Clancy, Roberts. . . . Your name isn't on it, Chief Superintendent, so I guess you're just a mercenary. But they know about you too."

Keane stepped away from her as if from a witch or a demon, gold bar in one hand, her purse in the other. "You're lying! None of it's true!"

The muzzle of the automatic weapon was almost in a position where I could blitz the gunman with a fifty-fifty chance of survival.

"Oh, it's true, Mr. Minister. It's all true," Nuala went on implacably. "Incidentally, if you'll take out the photo that's also in me purse, you'll find that it is very interesting. It's only a Xerox copy His Lordship made of the original, but it's clear enough."

Keane dropped the gold bar and frantically tore out of the purse a piece of paper.

"Oh, my God!" he shouted, clasping his hand to his forehead.

The two other members of the Consort rushed to look over his shoulders.

One more second and I rush the gunman.

"That's right!" Nuala was triumphant. "The man who ordered the death of Michael Collins. Your great focking British superhero, Winston Spencer Churchill!"

– 63 –

[Translator's Note: This entry, made in January of 1950, was attached to the final page of the first notebook, glued to the back of it in fact, and written on thin paper, so that you wouldn't even know it was there unless you decided to look for it. It is written in English, not Irish like the first book of the diary, and in American script, not the old Irish style she used in the early years. I'm not sure when she changed to English. But

the answer to that question is in the copies Father George Coyne has in America.]

It's time now that I record the rest of the conversation I had with your man that day at the pub near Lettermullen, with *Time* making him the "Man of the Half Century," which I suppose he is, though I think FDR might have been a better choice. I'll never forget a word of that conversation.

"He was ready to die for Ireland," he says. "I am ready to die for England. I suppose you Irish feel that no one else in the world is capable of patriotism. I assure you that, as in so many other matters, you are quite in error."

"What does patriotism have to do with murder?"

"He ordered the murder of my friend Sir Henry Wilson just as I ordered his murder. . . . You Irish are quite incapable of governing yourselves for long. This foolish civil war demonstrates that. We gave you the best agreement we could possibly permit. As it is, our government will probably fall before long because of it. Collins was the one man who could hold the country together for a while, but he too would have failed. Then there would be anarchy and eventually some military dictatorship that would be hostile to England."

He had a fine speaking voice, which everyone in the world knows now, and a grand flair with words.

"So?" I'm still gripping my poker and wondering about whether I ought to use it on him too.

"Do not think we came to Ireland because there was much wealth to be had here. Oh, a few men made a lot of money at various times, and others led a comfortable life. But England did not need Ireland for that. Our purposes from King John on were always defensive."

"Defensive?" I snort.

"You are not well educated, child, so you cannot understand. England cannot be safe if there is a hostile government in Ireland. Were not your rebels allied with the Hun during the war? And Bonaparte a hundred years ago? We must control Ireland, we must maintain peace here by force if necessary for our own protection, indeed for our own survival."

"Indeed!"

"Yes, indeed! There will come another war with the Hun, probably in my lifetime. If we do not control Ireland, then the Hun will make common cause with whatever demagogue happens to be in power here and England will be vulnerable. I cannot permit that to happen!"

"How do you know that we'll be on the side of the Germans?"

"Because they will take advantage of your weaknesses, which everyone in the world knows. Even if through some miracle they do not occupy all of Ireland, your government, such as it may be, will deny us the use of the ports which the treaty promised. I saw that as soon as I read the accounts of the absurd debate in your Dáil. The *unterseeboots* will prowl like wolves again, devouring all that they can. The lives of thousands of English and American, and, yes, Irish men will be lost because of Irish stubbornness. I cannot permit that to happen."

You can imagine the drama in his voice as he said those words. Blood, sweat, toil, and tears indeed.

"So why did Collins have to die?"

"Because when your young fools tear the country apart, as they will now that he's gone, the whole world and most of the Irish people will know that this land cannot govern itself, and there will be little resistance to our restoring order."

Well, he was wrong or mostly wrong, wasn't he now?

But almost thirty years later and meself a grandma several times over, I've maybe learned a few things. God knows he's an English patriot and there's nothing wrong with that. And he was right about the Germans. And about the treaty ports. He even claims to have thought about seizing them during the war, but he wouldn't have done that because we Americans would not have tolerated it. Yet I can see his point. The Mick was a killer and so is your man, though the Mick never ordered the death and destruction of a hundred thousand people in the bombing of Dresden at the end of the

630

war, just to keep Stalin happy. They're all idiots, I say now, just as I did then.

But I suppose that many poor boys did die because De Valera wouldn't turn over the treaty ports — though in most other ways the Irish government, my husband tells me, cooperated closely with the British and us.

So I don't know any more who's right and who's wrong. I guess we all do what we think we have to do and maybe deceive ourselves into thinking that we're completely right and they (whoever they are) are completely wrong.

But the worst irony of all is that if the Big Fella had been alive and in charge in Dublin instead of the Long Fella, he would have honored the treaty and opened the treaty ports to the British and us. Your man himself was responsible for all the sailors who died.

I wonder if he ever realized that.

— 64 —

"I'll strangle you, bitch." Keane jumped across the room and dug his fingers into Nuala's throat. "You've ruined everything!"

The man with the AK-47 snapped back to awareness and pointed the gun at me. It would not be quite so easy to sack him. I would almost certainly be killed.

Where was Patrick?

The rock above the gunman seemed to be tilting. It must be my pain-crazed imagination.

Nuala was screaming and fighting back furiously. She kicked and punched and tried to knee him, but Keane, now thoroughly demented, continued to squeeze at her windpipe.

"Stop, Keane," Nolan begged. "I say, stop. We'll be accused of murder!"

"Die, bitch!"

I'd have to try to sack the gunman anyhow.

The rock on the ledge above his head tilted dangerously.

I took a deep breath. Nuala was turning purple and her screams were gagging. Here goes!

The rock tumbled and banged the giant's head. He dropped the gun and collapsed.

Ignoring the ten thousand needles of pain that raced through my body, I rushed for the gun. Conlon came at me with his billy club.

I turned and charged him. I didn't have a helmet on, but spearing a man in his gut is pretty effective with a hard Irish head.

Conlon fell back and the breath rushed out of his body. I grabbed for the club and wrestled it out of his hands. He reached inside his jacket for his gun. I brought the club down on his shoulder. He screamed with pain and doubled up.

Broken.

Well, too bad for him. I hardly noticed my own spasms of pain.

I slugged Conlon in the stomach to make sure he'd be out of action for the next few moments.

Behind me, Nuala was weakening. In a few moments she would be on the edge of death.

No way!

I slammed the club viciously down on Keane's shoulder. He shrieked with pain and released her. He tried to grab for something in his jacket, so I broke his other shoulder.

Mess with my woman, will you?

Hughes and Nolan were cowering in a corner. One of the two guards from outside appeared in the doorway, drawn by the screams of the two agonized men.

Before he could grasp what had happened and lift his gun, I hit him in the face with my club. He dropped his gun and fell to his knees, hands over his face, yelling with pain as blood poured from his nose.

I looked around for the other two members of the Consortium.

Nuala was pointing the AK-47 at them. "One move and I'll send the lot of you to hell where you belong!"

Nothing wrong with Grace O'Malley's voice, it seemed. A little hoarse maybe.

I advanced on them, vaguely thinking of bashing them with my club. Just for the hell of it.

Then I remembered the other guard. I had a bit to settle with him.

It was too late for that final revenge.

Feet pattered outside. Four men, in black and

wearing ski masks, suddenly were in the room. They waved Uzis like they knew how to use them.

"Good afternoon, Dermot. The Seventh Cavalry again. My, you've made your usual mess, I see. The odd lot of people screaming."

"The man outside!"

"Not to fear. We neutralized him . . . and, ah, Nuala, my dear, if you'd be so good to give that weapon to one of my colleagues. You could hurt someone with it."

"Yes, Patrick *Michael* . . . and don't be angry with me, Dermot! Herself told me to tell the bishop!"

– 65 –

[*Not dated*]

I think this will be my last entry. I looked at the first one over seventy years ago. What a passionate little eejit that child was. Still, I have a soft spot in my heart for her. She wanted happiness and she seized it when she could and never looked back.

I sometimes think we could have taken the chance and gone home at least for a visit. Still, what would the point have been? Seven-eighths of my life has been here. I'm a Yank now and from Chicago, not Carraroe.

Dick Coyne and I both know that I'll be dying soon and himself a doctor. I think me Monica knows too and herself a nurse, but she won't admit it, poor dear woman. She's the nicest of all my children, the most gentle, even more than poor Billy the bishop and himself conceived out of wedlock in the cottage in Connemara. Well, I never told him that, but maybe he's guessed. He doesn't miss much, that one.

Monica is more like my Liam than she is like me. Sometimes she's so nice I want to scream at her, but that would hurt her feelings, so I try to keep me big mouth shut, which has never been easy.

Dick wants to call Dermot Michael home so he can be with me at the end. He knows what no one else will admit out loud: that Dermot is my favorite of all the children. And grand-children. But I don't want to disturb the poor lad while he's wandering around Europe. He's a good boy and he'll be a great man if he gives himself a chance to dream and to think like he wants to.

I don't know why I love him so much. He's the spitting image of my Liam when he was a gosson — and Liam being the father of four children by the time he was Dermot's age.

He's not at all like Liam. Or like me. A lot of his mother in him. And some of Dick too. Not at all like that smooth-talking George who reminds me so much of the young priest back

635

home. I mean in Carraroe. I'll be calling George after I finish, to go to confession. I know that God loves me and that when I die I'll be with Liam as soon as I do a bit of purgatory. Still, like I always says, there's no reason to take unnecessary chances and meself living a pretty wild life in my day and with me terrible tongue too.

Anyway, Dermot Michael is a special young man and I knew it the first day Monica brought him home from the hospital. I'm glad they called him Michael for his middle name because he reminds me of Mick Collins whom I met so long ago on the lane in Carraroe. He doesn't look like him at all. And, poor boy, he couldn't lead a pack of guerrilla vampires to a blood bank. And he's not an organizer or administrator at all at all. Himself as secretary of the treasury like the Mick was finance minister would be a terrible disaster.

But he has the same glint in his green eyes, the same hint of divilment and charm and understanding of people and, well, I'll use the word, genius.

Do I exaggerate because I love the poor little tyke so much?

I don't know. Maybe it's only an old woman's fantasies. Yet I haven't met anyone like Mick except him in all me life.

Poor Mick, dead and gone these seventy years. I wonder if I could have saved his life if I had warned Liam about O'Kelly. Probably not. He'd done his work and God wanted him home.

Anyway, after I find me Liam up in heaven, I'm going to look up Mick and Kitty and have a long talk with them.

And we'll all be young again.

Or is it all a trick? Sometimes I think it may be. Not often and I believe the opposite, but I say to myself even if there's nothing more I'm grateful for what I have.

So should I burn all the little books in this diary? Sometimes I think I should. Let the dead bury the dead, as the scripture says. Well, I think it's the scripture anyway.

What does any of it matter anymore? They're all dead now except me and I'll be dead soon enough.

Or should I leave them? Maybe someday someone will find them and the truth will matter. Maybe Dermot Michael will find them and write a story about all of us and what it was like in Carraroe back in the time of the Troubles. Maybe he can decide whether it's time to tell the truth.

Dermot Michael will be a great man, but only if he meets the right woman. The good Lord knows how much I've prayed for that, and himself pursuing little chits that are not nearly good enough for him. Well, when I get up there, I'll talk to Himself personally about the subject.

I'll have to make up my mind about the diaries pretty soon now, won't I?

And what about the man that gave the orders

and paid the bills to O'Kelly? Will I see him in heaven?

Sure, that's up to God, now isn't it?

At first I didn't put his name down because I was terrible scared of what would happen to me and my family if anyone ever found these little books. Then after he was dead I saw no point in it.

He didn't change much through the years — loving the dramatic and the sensational. And his only morality was whether something was good or bad for England. If it was good, then he'd do it no matter how much it hurt other people. I guess now, after reading all his books, he was telling the truth that hot day so long ago. He felt that England had to have a secure base in Ireland and that if the Free State survived, it would take those bases away.

The Mick killed people too — for our side, but then killing is killing, isn't it?

Well, let God judge him, as I say. 'Tis not up to me.

I wonder about the gold.

Somehow I think your man knew about it. I suppose it's all gone now. Yet what if it isn't? Has it been used to make trouble all these years, or is it still up there near the shrine in the Pass of the Birds?

I wonder.

I suppose it belongs to Ireland now if it belongs to anyone. I don't figure I owe Ireland much. If there's any debt it's the other way around.

Still, there's all those poor kids with their college degrees and no work. Maybe the money would help some of them.

Well, if I don't burn these little books and if Dermot Michael finds them and if he thinks it's worth the effort to search for the gold and if some of it's still there, I'll leave it to him what to do with it.

Not a very good way to end an account of a wild life, is it now?

What more can I say?

I don't mind dying. I miss Liam too much.

I love them all.

Bill, I know you're near. I can almost hear you coming as I did at my window in Carraroe so long ago!

Come quickly!

— 66 —

"Raspberry preserves, is it?" said the president of Ireland as she offered me a plate of scones.

" 'Tis, Ms. President," I agreed.

I wasn't sure whether that was the proper title. However, if it would do for the chief executive of our battered but durable republic beyond the sea, should we ever manage to have a woman president, it would surely suffice here in Phoenix Park for the *an'tUachtairan ne h'Eireann.*

Here in her official residence, aras an'tUachtairan, the Uachtairan (chief cattleherd) had just
placed around our necks two medals suspended
from green, white, and, orange ribbons. Then
she poured the tea for us.

I felt terrible, even worse than when I was
in the hospital. My head ached. I had wild
dreams at night. I was drifting around in a fog
as if I were in a prolonged hangover. When I
finally got home I'd ask my father to check
me out. I was not about to trust my health to
an Irish doctor.

"The statue of O'Kelly has already been removed" — the president sighed — "and work
on the statue of your grandparents has begun.
It should be in place by spring."

"I would be happy to defray some of the expenses, Ms. President."

"Not at all, Dermot, not at all. It's little
enough this nation can do for two brave people,
or should I say four."

"Maybe three."

"And, if I may say so" — she ignored my
self-deprecation — "it was a stroke of genius
to reveal the story of the treasure at the
same time as the story of the murder of Michael Collins by a traitor. Ten million pounds
for education today is more important in this
country just now than a killing long ago. We
wish to do all we can to protect our Anglo-
Irish peace initiative."

"It may have been a stroke of genius, Ms. President, but it was Ms. McGrail's stroke, not mine."

"Speaking of which" — the Uachtairan turned to her — "Bishop Hayes has promised us that you would sing a song or two. I would be so happy if you would. . . ." She gestured towards the Celtic harp in the corner of the drawing room.

I had noted that (a) the president of Ireland and Nuala had exchanged a few sentences in Irish at the beginning of our visit (I was sure they were talking about me) and (b) the former's West of Ireland accent (and herself a Mayo woman) became progressively thicker as she spoke with us.

Naturally Nuala would sing for us. Still playing the shy Gaeltacht lass that had been her persona through the publicity, Nuala tuned the harp and then, with Ed Hayes proudly humming, she sang the Gaelic lullaby I had first heard in O'Neill's pub at the beginning of our story.

We all applauded, discreetly and politely — raucous noise was inappropriate in the official home of the president in Phoenix Park.

Then with the barest hint of a glance at me she began again.

"In Dublin's fair city,
Where the girls are so pretty
I first set my eyes

On sweet Molly Malone.
She wheeled her wheelbarrow
Through streets broad and narrow,
Crying cockles and mussels
Alive, alive oh!

"Alive, alive oh!
Alive, alive oh!
Crying cockles and mussels
Alive, alive oh!

"She was a fishmonger,
But sure 'twas no wonder,
For so was her father and mother before.
And they both wheeled their barrow
Through streets broad and narrow
Crying cockles and mussels
Alive, alive oh!

"Alive, alive oh!
Alive, alive oh!
Crying cockles and mussels
Alive, alive oh!

"She died of a fever
And no one could relieve her,
And that was the end of sweet Molly
*   Malone.*
But her ghost wheels her barrow
Through streets broad and narrow,
Crying cockles and mussels
Alive, alive oh!

"Alive, alive oh!
Alive, alive oh!
Crying cockles and mussels
Alive, alive oh!"

I am not proud of my behavior towards Nuala during the days between our escape and my return to America. In my defense I plead that I had a headache most of the time, that I was a physical wreck, that my body was sore from the lumps I had taken, and that I frequently saw double — not one Nuala but two. Two scheming connivers instead of one. Moreover, as I can see now, my male ego had been injured because she had solved the mystery before I had. But, as valid as these excuses are (especially the headaches), the simple truth is that I was now terrified of the woman.

"Why didn't you tell me?" I had asked her two nights after the fight in the monastery. I had been released from the hospital and ensconced in Ashford Castle for a few days' recuperation away from the Irish media — though I felt sicker when I left Ashford than when I left the hospital. Bishop Ed's doctors wanted to keep an eye on me to make sure that my ribs were properly taped and that I was not suffering from serious internal injuries.

Ashford is one of the great hotels in all the world (built around a real medieval castle) and only five miles away from the ancestral home of the Coynes (all of whom had long since left).

It had intimidated Nuala when she came to visit me for the first time since I was carted off to the Galway Hospital.

" 'Tis truly a fancy hotel," she acknowledged with reverential awe. "A fine place for a honeymoon, wouldn't it be? When I marry, ten years or so from now, maybe I'll come here."

"I *said*, why didn't you tell me?"

"I knew you were thinking of asking Bishop Hayes for help." Her eyes were wide with concern for me. "And yourself being so tired from the long ride and so hurt from the accident that you might put it off for a day or two. I wasn't sure you heard the shots that destroyed our tire. When you didn't tell him that night at the house, I thought I'd better do it for you that morning at breakfast before you came down. Then I rang him from the store in Carraroe when we were sure where the gold was. Sure, I just anticipated you by a day or two."

"If I knew he knew" — my head hurt terribly — "we wouldn't have climbed up the cave and they wouldn't have come after us."

"But they didn't know we were in the cave, remember, Dermot Michael? They would have come after us just the same. Sure, your man Patrick would have saved us anyway, but

644

wasn't it a good thing we scared them at the end?"

We, huh?

"You could have been killed."

"Aren't you hurt worse than I?"

"Where did you find the picture of Churchill?"

"Sure, wasn't it in one of those crates? And wasn't I searching them to make sure we had all the diary books when I found it?"

"Ransacking them, you mean?"

"Well." She paused, determined not to lie. "I thought there might be the odd bit of clue that you'd missed."

"You should have told me, Nuala, you should have told me everything."

"I wanted to, Dermot" — she lifted her folded hands in a woebegone gesture — "but like herself with your granda, I didn't know how to do it."

"Did I ever complain when you told me anything about this mystery? Did I seem to resent that you were quicker and smarter than I was?"

"I didn't want to spoil the puzzle for you and yourself so close to the solution."

"I don't need to solve puzzles, Nuala," I snapped irritably.

"You're a grand man, Dermot Michael Coyne, the most wonderful man in the world. I never expect to meet another man as kind or as good or as gentle. But, sure, you're such a mystery."

"I'm no mystery, you are."

"Maybe it's because I'm just a lass from the West of Ireland and you're from the big world, but you have so many different moods that I never could figure out how to talk to you, and meself trying as hard as I could. I'd say to meself, Which Dermot will he be today and how should I act with him?"

"Don't be ridiculous, Nuala." I was annoyed with her now. "You're the one who wears the thousand masks."

She hesitated. "I don't want to argue with you, Dermot, and yourself just out of hospital, but, sure, I'm being transparent compared to yourself."

"I'm tired, Nuala, and my head hurts and I ache all over. Would you mind leaving me alone?"

She nodded silently and stood up. Her heart was breaking, I knew, but good enough for her. Besides, it would be easier for her to forget me.

"You saw the rock fall?" She turned at the door, her face a mask of sadness.

"I did. How did it happen? Did you make it fall?"

"I did not."

"Who did?"

"Wasn't it himself, coming back for his final victory?"

"Wasn't it who?"

"Sure, the Big Fella, who else?"

My headache grew worse. "Please, Nuala, I can't take any more tonight."

She left.

That was that.

Happy Feast of the Holy Souls, Dermot Michael Coyne.

"Angela Smythe here, Dermot, calling from Washington."

"Good afternoon, Angela."

I was in my suite at Jury's beginning to pack for my return to America and still feeling like a truck had run over my chest.

"I just wanted to congratulate you on the award and on how cleverly you protected Winston from publicity. It has to come out eventually that he was behind Collins's death, but if you had revealed it now, it would have been a savage blow to the agreement."

"Thank you, Angela. To tell the truth, it was Ms. McGrail's idea, not mine."

"I'm sure it was both your idea. Do give me a ring when you are in Washington."

She told me her real name.

After I had hung up, I pondered the new puzzle. Nuala had solved the mystery and saved the day. She was the one who had appeared with calm dignity on RTE that night to tell the carefully sanitized story of what had happened. Yet I was getting all the credit.

She had been asked, after her calm recitation of the facts (but not all the facts), whether she and the injured hero were lovers.

"Ah, no," she said with a modest smile. "I'm only the translator of his gram's diaries."

She did not, thank God, add, "Worse luck for me."

"A strange story for you, Mr. Coyne." The bright young man from the Foreign Office looked out at St. Stephen's Green as he paused in his attempt to explain the Irish Civil War to me. "The children of Kevin O'Higgins and the grandchildren of the man who killed him go to the same Mass once a year that is offered for both men."

It was another gray, drizzly day. I wanted to go home. My chest hurt now more than my head. Yet I had to listen to a few more Irish stories before my hosts would feel they had done their duty by me.

"That's nice."

"You see, they weren't sure they killed your man. So they walked over to where he was lying and prepared to shoot him again. They saw he was dying. He opens his eyes, recognizes them and smiles. 'Sure, 'tis all right,' he says. 'I understand why you had to do it. Don't worry about it. I forgive you.' Then he dies."

"Like Gandhi."

The young man glanced at me in surprise. "You'd expect it of your man, wouldn't you now? But not of O'Higgins."

"Why not? He was Irish, wasn't he?"

And so was the story and the rain and the green and my headache and my sore chest. The Irish were too much for me. Too much altogether.

"I had no idea that there had been any violence," Lord Longwood-Jones murmured. "I begged Brendan not to tolerate it. I'm afraid that he was more unstable than I realized."

Martin and I were sipping port in his club on FitzWilliam Street and watching the implacable rain pound away at Dublin's fair city.

"Ambitious." My breathing somehow seemed to have become more labored rather than less.

"Surely that. And well aware that he would rise no higher in government in the present scheme of things. That's why he embraced so vigorously the notion of the Consort, a daft scheme, if I may say so. Surely as a united Europe progresses, there will be a partnership between these two islands — if we can first settle the Ulster mess. But I should hope that it will be the genius of the two countries to keep the arrangement informal. The chance for anything else ended when Home Rule was not granted in 1912."

"Indeed."

"You will have noticed that there have been certain discreet withdrawals from public life in both countries in the past several days, including poor Brendan?"

"Yes."

"I will take steps to see that his wife and children do not suffer."

"Very generous of you."

"You must understand, my dear Dermot" — he closed his eyes, like a man unspeakably weary of life — "that for most of the last seventy years the Consort has been, how shall I say it, more of a debating club or study group than an active organization. Only the head of it — my ancestors and myself — and the treasurer, in this case the unfortunate Mr. Keane, knew where the gold was stored. We were most reluctant to remove it. We could have been caught so easily. Moreover, it would have been difficult to explain if a rather large supply of gold was dumped on the Irish market whence it came."

"No way to launder it?"

"Precisely. Moreover, my forefathers and I felt that the money was better kept for the day that it was actually needed. At times, especially during the war, it was used for charitable purposes."

"How did your grandfather find out about it?"

"I very much fear that he was Winston's link with O'Kelly. I can't prove that, of course, but I suspect it. He may have tricked O'Kelly into revealing what had happened to Casement's gold. Or he may have had him followed, as I take it your grandmother did. Grandfather had the reputation of being a very sly and clever man, traits that, unfortunately or not, my father and I did not inherit."

"So you sustained this little group of people who believed in reunion down through the years?"

"Yes. Precisely. I'm glad you used that word 'reunion.' I pride myself Dermot, on the fact that I am an Irish patriot, whatever my grandfather or father might have been. I believe in a voluntary union of the free states, if you will permit me that term, of the British Isles. It is not necessary, as far as I'm concerned, that the federal parliament be in Westminster or that the union be presided over by the house of Windsor or any British monarch. In this era of new unions all over the world, it seems to me to be an ideal that is not at all incompatible with Irish freedom."

"Perhaps not."

"Neither my father or I" — he shook his head slowly as if trying to banish an image from his brain" — "approve of what Winston did. He was not, I fear, a very moral man. Yet in his own way he believed in Irish independence."

"Come on, Martin."

"No, I really mean that. He was always a strong supporter of home rule and gave up the vision of a united Ireland most reluctantly. However, he believed that the Irish were incapable of governing themselves. The fighting between Protestant and Catholic in Ulster and between the Free State and the Irregulars in the South merely confirmed his prejudices. He feared Collins would prolong the strife and that with him out of the way, the various factions would deteriorate into such violence that the Irish people would demand the return of English rule. Then he would set up a new parliament which would, under his guidance, establish a constitution that would unite the two Irelands in a federal arrangement which London could guide and direct."

"So he had Collins killed to increase the violence in Ireland?"

"My grandfather told my father that Winston was convinced that the chaos would come eventually, in six more months perhaps. If Collins was alive it would have, he thought, been more violent, more destructive of Irish life, and perhaps impossible for England to control, save at enormous costs."

"However, in fact, he prevented the end of the Civil War and caused the death of thousands more Irish."

"With good intentions. . . . I'm not trying to defend Winston, only to explain what went on in his mind."

"He must have been astonished that the Free State finally put down the Irregulars."

"Winston never admitted to anyone that he made a mistake about anything. But I don't think he ever forgave Ireland for proving him wrong. . . . You must also realize that the Lloyd George government fell shortly thereafter. Bonar Law replaced Lloyd George, who never held a ministry again. A major reason for his defeat was that the more conservative of the Tories blamed him for the loss of Ireland. He and Winston had little more room to maneuver than did Collins and Griffith and Cosgrave."

I had heard enough about the troubles of Lloyd George and Churchill. "The Consort agreed with Churchill?"

"Definitely not." He colored slightly. "As I've tried to tell you, we are Irish patriots. We deplored the death of Michael Collins, who was our hero too. We believe that if he had lived, he would have seen the sense in our scheme for a federal union."

"You really believe that?"

"Certainly. He would have come to see the Consort as a logical successor to the Irish Republican Brotherhood."

Martin's eyes glittered for a moment with the enthusiasm of true belief. Then the light went out. He was a little mad, I decided. But so were they all. So, I told myself as I grew more lightheaded, were all the Irish.

"In the event our dream, which was possible perhaps in 1921, was no longer possible in 1923. Grandfather realized that it would be a long haul and that Winston was no longer part of the picture. So he assembled through the years a group of men and women who were quietly and discreetly committed to that goal without necessarily putting any time limit on it. My father and I continued the work. We did spend some of the money, removed one bar at a time, to facilitate quiet study and research on the subject."

"The revitalization of the shrine must have caused you concern?"

"At first. Then Mr. Keane pointed out that the pilgrimages would facilitate the quiet removal of the gold to an even safer place."

"Where he would control all of it."

"Yes. Precisely. I made a terrible mistake in trusting him. Unforgivable, really. As I said, I am not as shrewd as my grandfather. Brendan is a man of great ability and charm. Unfortunately, he has not been able to resist his proclivities towards overreaching. As you seemed to have surmised, his political career was finished. He was a bit too cute, as we say here, even for an Irish politician, and our standards in this matter are not very high. He saw a hasty move towards union as a means for reestablishing his power. You know or at least surmise the rest."

"When do you think this reunion for which you hope will be possible?"

"I joke with my wife that it will be U-Day plus twenty years — U-Day being the day when an Ulster solution is found that is acceptable to Catholics and to the republic. Until the problem of the six counties is removed, reunion is unthinkable. Mr. Keane failed to perceive this obvious truth."

"Greed made him blind."

"I fear that our best hope in this century died at Bealnablath."

"Really?"

"If Collins had lived, I am convinced rapprochement between the two islands would have been achieved long since. He may have been a cold-blooded killer in time of war, my dear Dermot, but he was not a hater."

"I think it died in 1800 when the Act of Union ended even the fiction of an independent and united Ireland."

"Perhaps you are right." He shook his head dejectedly. "I admit that the dream is utopian at the present moment. Pity."

"Pity the world is the place it is."

"Yes, really. I can only hope that my folly in trusting Brendan Keane has not made the dream even more distant."

Well, maybe it was not such an impossible dream. Only the future would say.

"I hope you realize, Dermot" — he sighed — "that I inherited the chairmanship of the Consortium. You can imagine, given my political orientation, how horrified I was when my father told me about it on his deathbed. I tried to limit it to nothing more than a discussion group. Unfortunately, I did not control how the money was spent. That was the task Brendan inherited. Liz repeatedly begged me to abandon it. That's why we're grateful, more grateful than I will ever be able to tell you, that you removed my name from the list before you turned it over to Bishop Hayes and the government."

We'd done that too, had we? What else had the woman done?

"It was Nuala's idea."

"Liz and I are most grateful to both of you."

Nope, she wasn't going to receive credit for this act of graciousness either.

"I'm glad it has all worked out."

"You have no idea how I have wrestled with my conscience over this foolish matter."

"That's why you gave the list of names to the CIA?"

He looked at me in astonishment. "How did you know that?"

"I received a Xeroxed copy. I recognized your handwriting and compared it with the luncheon invitation."

"Extraordinary," he murmured. "You understand that I considered it a matter of honor to include my own name?"

"Oh, yes."

"You won't reveal that I was in league with the CIA?"

"Certainly not."

Had herself recognized the handwriting too?

Does the Pope live in the Vatican?

"I shall be forever grateful for all that you have done for us."

"No big deal."

We had protected the peace initiative, we had protected Churchill, we had protected the Longwood-Joneses. How clever of us!

656

Ah, sure, Dermot, hadn't you thought of all those things yourself? Wasn't I only doing what you wanted me to do?

Shite.

I still did not understand a lot of things, especially the purpose of the phone call from his wife, the relationship between Angela Smythe and Longwood-Jones, and the origins and goals of Patrick.

In real life, I guess, there are always loose ends that are never tidied up.

Her Ladyship, I reflected sadly, was a very appealing loose end.

To guess about the three of them, Her Ladyship might have liked to drag me into bed, but probably she would do so only if she could tell herself that the reason was to protect her husband. Angela didn't know about the Consortium, but one of its members, possibly my friend Martin, had used her to try to influence me. Patrick was perhaps a relative of Collins combining business with family heritage as he snuffed out an operation about which his superiors were restless for reasons of their own.

Ma's relatives in America, if any? Maybe the rest of the diaries would reveal that.

So, Sean Connery as 007, you had three beautiful women pursuing you, each perhaps for her own reasons — need for one, fear for another.

For the third?

Love?

What was love?

Would I recognize it if I bumped into it on the street?

"Sure, Liam," said the old fella on the bench by the Grand Canal. "You did for them, didn't you? Wasn't I saying you would?"

"We did all of that."

"And they'll be putting up a statue for them in Oughterard?"

"They will."

"Glory be to God!"

"You were the young teacher man with the camera, weren't you?"

That was one secret that Nuala had not figured out — well, not as far as I knew.

"I was." Tears formed in his eyes.

"I thought you might want one of these pictures. You took it, after all." I gave him a copy of the photograph of Ma and Pa on their wedding day. "Wasn't she saying that you were the most honest man she ever knew?"

A bit of an exaggeration but legitimate in Ireland.

He held the picture against his chest and wept. "I never married, you see. I loved her all me life."

"Who wouldn't?" I agreed with a sigh.

As I stumbled back to Jury's, dizzy and disoriented, for the final packing before my departure later in the day, I realized, in what I now see was my frightened folly, that there were three trivial secrets that I had tried to hide from

658

Nuala: the shots at the car, the source of the list of the Consort, the identity of the old man on the bench.

She had figured two of them out anyway. Maybe the third.

She wasn't the only one who tried to hide secrets. I dismissed that scruple as irrelevant.

As we climbed out of the cab at Dublin Airport, I remarked, "I gave my copy of the wedding picture to the man on the bench at the Grand Canal. We have several more copies in Chicago."

"Ah, that was generous of you, Dermot, but sure, hadn't he taken the picture and himself probably loving her all his life?"

Out on strikes, Dermot Michael Coyne.

We talked about the arrangements for translating the rest of the diary and its possible publication. The new Compaq I had purchased for the project was working fine. I told her that a major New York company had already sent George a contract for the book with a generous advance. I insisted that there was no great rush about finishing the translation, so long as we could send it to the publisher by late spring. She could surely sing at the Abbey Tavern.

Head pounding and chest throbbing, I checked in and turned over most of my luggage to Aer Lingus. I would carry on only a hand bag and my Compaq. Nuala was carrying both of them because my ribs were still a little sore — not nearly as sore, I told myself, as the shoulders of certain other people.

I wanted nothing more than to go to bed and sleep for a month.

My headache began again, someone beating on my brain with huge drumsticks. The headaches would linger, the doctor has said, for a month or two.

"I'll carry these out to the plane for you, if you don't mind, Dermot."

She was dressed again in her student uniform of jeans and jacket — and my blue and gold Marquette sweatshirt.

"I'd appreciate that."

She sighed loudly and took a deep breath. "Well, maybe I'll be seeing you in Chicago, Dermot Michael."

"What?"

"Well, wasn't I winning the lottery for an American visa" — she wouldn't look at me — "and hasn't Arthur Andersen offered me a nice position in Chicago when I graduate?"

"When did this happen?"

"Ah . . . didn't it happen right after I started to work for you?"

"And you didn't tell me?"

"Wasn't I afraid you'd be angry if I told you? And now that I have told you, are you angry at me?"

"You've got it all figured out, haven't you, Nuala? I'll meet you at the airport, I'll take you home for a supper at my parents' house, you'll stay there till you find an apartment of your own, and you'll make common cause with all the women in my family against me. Isn't that what you're up to?"

"No, Dermot." She was on the verge of tears. "I haven't thought of that at all. . . . Well, not unless you wanted it."

The hell she hadn't thought of it. The little schemer thought of everything. Including, no doubt, a couple of honeymoon nights at Ashford Castle.

"There's no truth in you, woman," I shouted at her. "No truth at all."

"I'm sorry, Dermot, truly I am."

We were at the security checkpoint.

"Give me those bags. There's no need to walk out to the plane. . . . Now listen to me, Nuala, and listen carefully. We will finish this translation project because I am committed to it."

"Yes, Dermot."

"And as for seeing me in Chicago, you will only see me if I don't see you first, is that clear?"

The bags that I had pulled out of her hands hurt my ribs. No matter. I would have to carry them in Chicago anyway.

"Yes, Dermot. . . . I'm sorry, Dermot."

"You're an incorrigible conniver and schemer!"

I slammed the Compaq and the hand bag on the security machine belt and, headache pounding at my brain, strode through the barrier.

"No worse than your gram!" she shouted after

661

me. "And yourself loving her!"

Just like Ma, she had the last word.

On the plane I curled up in my seat and slept until Shannon, where they awakened me to clear American immigration. The agent told me that he had been on duty in Ireland for two months and that, even though it was a beautiful country when the sun was out, he was looking forward to returning home.

"Tell me about it," I agreed.

I collapsed again in my first-class seat on the 747. Dear God, I feel terrible. What's wrong with me? She had been right, naturally. Ma was a terrible schemer and an incorrigible conniver. When I had told her that once long ago, she had replied, her nose in the air, that that was the kind of woman Irish men, myself included, liked.

I realized that the game was not over, that I would have at some point to admit I was wrong and that my fear of Nuala was irrelevant. She would not betray me as my first love had. I told myself that it would all work out if only my headaches would go away.

I slept most of the way to Chicago, tormented by wild, drunken dreams though I had not touched a drop of the creature for several days. In the dreams three women kept changing, one into another — Ma, Kel, and Nuala.

I don't remember getting off at Kennedy or clearing customs or boarding the plane for Chicago. Mom and Dad met me at O'Hare. Dad took one look at me, bundled me in a car, and drove at high speed to the Loyola Medical Center.

Viral double pneumonia, he said as they put the oxygen tent over me.

"Why didn't you see an Irish doctor?" he demanded. "They are the best diagnosticians in the world. It was damn foolishness to fly home as sick as you are."

"Unless someone," George, the know-it-all priest, observed, "was running away from someone else."

"Focking gobshite," I murmured as I lapsed into unconsciousness.

I became rational again after two weeks. It was almost another month before I realized what a fool I'd been. My father warned me that I would be depressed from the pneumonia for a couple of months.

And depressed I was. Too late, I kept telling myself. I'd missed an opportunity of a lifetime. I'd lost the one great love of my life.

Then one day I was working on the disks she had sent me with further translations from Ma's incredible diaries. By mistake, I erased a chapter on one of the disks. I used my Xtree Gold unerase utility and discovered there were four other unerased files on the disk. I restored them too and discovered Nuala's conversations with Nell Pat.

Spooky nonsense!

I found myself weeping for my loss and her

pain. I felt sorry for myself for about a week — one of the great Irish indoor sports.

Then one bright, sunny March day I woke up with a big smile on my face.

<h1 style="text-align:center">– 67 –</h1>

As I have said before, I need time to think before making a decision. I've had a lot of time for thinking in the last few months.

I have discovered that there are worse emotions than guilt. Such as regret. And loss. And the sense that one has been a total eejit and a terrible amadon altogether.

Today I will mail the completed first draft of *Nell Pat*, translated by Nuala McGrail, edited by Dermot Coyne, to my publisher. I have checked the account in gold futures into which I put our advance. My trader, the most skilled in the precious metals pit, tells me that it has already doubled in size. A nice bar of gold for someone coming to America.

Marie Fionnuala Anne McGrail will arrive at O'Hare International Airport at five twenty-five this lovely spring afternoon on an American Airlines flight (information courtesy His Gracious Lordship, Bishop of Galway and Kilmacduff and Apostolic Administrator of Kilfenora). A half hour or so later she will clear immigration and stroll into the arrivals lounge. She will be dressed smartly and will carry two impressive bags and will walk with the self-confidence of the experienced world traveler. Even the guitar case slung over one shoulder will not diminish her image as a sophisticated woman of the world. No greenhorn this beautiful woman, the observer would say.

Chicago will, nonetheless, not be ready for her. It won't know what hit it. No way. Soon she'd be solving crimes for the Chicago cops. I could sign on as her Dr. Watson if I wanted to.

There will be not the slightest hint that she's scanning the waiting crowd in the remote hope that someone might be there to welcome her to Chicago, perhaps even to take her home to his mother's house. Yet her shrewd, fishmonger eyes will be taking in everything, a shy child, hinting at a God who is also a shy child.

And she'd be wondering whether there would be mysteries to solve in Chicago, with or without me as her spear carrier.

Then she'll see me.

She'll drop her bags and rush, like a Connemara hoyden, into my voracious, waiting arms.

I'll beg for forgiveness. I will be told that I'm an eejit for thinking that's necessary and meself perishing with pneumonia. How would she know about my pneumonia? George, of course. Then I'd tell her that I loved her and

would always love her. And she would hold me
very close and say, sure, hadn't she known that
from the first night at O'Neill's? Then I would
take her home to Mom.

Alive, alive oh!

Alive, alive oh!

NOTE

This story is an exercise in historical speculation. In all probability Michael Collins died as the result of a tragic accident of which so many happen in war. I have no evidence that Winston S. Churchill was directly involved in Collins's death. However, Tim Pat Coogan reports in his biography of Collins that it was widely believed in Ireland at the time that Churchill was somehow responsible. My fantasy, I believe, is justified by the attitude of British leaders past and present towards the Irish people. Churchill may not have been the worst of them, but his anti-Irish sentiments were nonetheless vile. To protect British power, he was quite capable of doing anything to the Irish.

In a larger sense, the British government and especially Churchill and David Lloyd George were responsible not only for the death of Michael Collins but for the deaths of all those who perished in the Irish Civil War and of those who have died in terrorist violence since then even up to this day. Their adamant refusal to grant Ireland the full independence to which it had a right in 1922 (and for centuries before) and their stubborn clinging to the six counties of the truncated Province of Ulster, the last remnant of English imperialism in Europe, set the stage for all subsequent violence in Ireland.

Their grudging concession of limited independence to the Free State guaranteed that Ireland would continue to suffer the effects of centuries of imperialistic English colonialism for years that are yet to come.

But to be fair as Nell Pat was in her later years, Lloyd George and Churchill probably had conceded all they could. When their government fell shortly after the treaty, their "concessions" to the Irish were one of the reasons. Thus the guilt for all the killings in Ireland from those times to this goes beyond the Lloyd George government.

Like his father, Lord Randolph Churchill, Winston Churchill supported "home rule" for Ireland, but it was a home rule in which Ireland was still very much subject to Westminster. In a speech in *support* of home rule in 1912, he made almost the same case as Patrick — tongue in cheek, no doubt — makes in this story: "What of all this vain and foolish chatter about separation? The separation of Ireland from Great Britain is absolutely impossible. The interests of the two islands are eternally interwoven. . . . The whole tendency of things, the whole irresistible drift of things, is towards a more intimate association. The economic dependence of Ireland on England is absolute. And quite apart from naval, military and constitutional arguments and quite apart from all considerations of the Imperial Parliament, of the flag, and of the Crown, none of which ties will be in any respect impaired, the two nations are bound together till the end of time by the natural force of circumstances" (*Speeches of Winston Churchill: The Young Tribune*, p. 235).

Alas for such an imperialist vision of "home rule," the Irish wanted more and still do.

Churchill was charmed by Michael Collins, as were most people who met him, and repeatedly offered him patronizing advice. Collins for his part did not think much of Churchill but kept his opinion to himself. ("Will sacrifice all for political gain. Inclined to be bombastic. Full of ex-officer jingo or similar outlook. Don't actually trust him.")

Churchill's savage contempt for the Irish is evident in his personal writing. See, for example, his letter to his wife in April of 1920: "What a diabolical sneak they have in their character! I expect it is that treacherous, assassinating, conspiring trait which has done them in the bygone ages of history and prevented them from being a great responsible nation with stability and prosperity" (Martin Gilbert, *Winston S. Churchill*, vol. 4, p. 449).

A half millennium of exploitation by a foreign nation was apparently not at all to blame for the problems of Ireland!

Tim Pat Coogan's recent biography, *The Man Who Made Ireland*, is the best book yet on Collins. While Coogan leans to the Sonny Neill theory, he quotes someone who was there as saying that Neill had already left the combat scene and hints at possible revelations still to come. He also doubts the charge of screenwriter Eoghan Harris that Collins had an affair with the Chicago-born Hazel Lavery during the treaty negotiations in London. That it was any more than a flirtation, Coogan suggests (in agreement here with Nell Pat and Nuala), is highly improbable. Coogan also flatly rejects Harris's assertion that Collins was a homosexual, a position, one hears, that is to be central to the possibly forthcoming Kevin Costner film.

The opening in 1993 of the files of documents of the British government from 1923 apparently confirms the rumor that there were elements in the British government which seriously discussed plans for reimposing British rule during that year.

Nuala's cousin, Father Michael McGriel, insists that I tell readers that in fact there is no gold anywhere near the shrine at Mamene. But he adds that you're always welcome to climb up there and say a prayer.

The visit to Ireland of the mayor of Chicago occurred several years before the time of the present story.

As for Nuala and Dermot, God willing, they will appear in subsequent stories to be titled *Irish Lace*, *Irish Linen*, *Irish Stew*, and maybe even *Irish Whiskey*. Will Dermot accept his Dr. Watson role as Nuala figures out solutions for

American puzzles? Will they sort out their relationship and perhaps even marry one another (as they surely should and in my priestly judgment as soon as possible)? Does the title *Irish Lace* suggest wedding garments?

Ah, that would be telling now, wouldn't it?

Chicago — Grand Beach — Dublin — Tucson
1989–1994

CHRONOLOGY OF THE
TROUBLES

April 21, 1916 (Good Friday) — Betrayed by informers, Sir Roger Casement is arrested in Kerry after coming ashore from a German U-boat. An arms shipment from Germany is seized as is a shipment of gold. Casement is executed in August.

April 24, 1916 (Easter Monday) — Despite certain failure (because of the loss of the German weapons) the Irish Volunteers seize the General Post Office and other strong points in Dublin. The British easily put down the Rising and execute the leaders. "A terrible beauty is born!" (Yeats)

December 14, 1918 — Sinn Fein ("We Ourselves") wins the first postwar election. Its members refuse to attend meetings of the British parliament and form their own republican parliament in Dublin, the Dáil Éireann. De Valera becomes president.

1919–1921 — Anglo-Irish War. Hit-and-run tactics keep the British army at bay. Michael Collins becomes de facto head of the Irish guerrilla war.

1921 — General McCready, the British commander, advises London that the war cannot be won. Collins realizes that he is running low on arms and that popular support for the bloody war is ebbing. Truce is proclaimed in June. Negotiations begin in July.

December 6, 1921 — Collins — maneuvered into being a delegate to the peace conference by De Valera, who does not want to be responsible for compromise — signs the treaty establishing the Irish Free State (and by his own admission his own death warrant) as the best deal Ireland can get under the circumstances. De Valera and a diehard minority of the Dáil reject the treaty.

June 16, 1922 — Pro-treaty forces win a majority in elections to the Dáil. Antitreaty forces seize strong points in Dublin and other cities.

June 28, 1922 — Under pressure from Britain, Collins's new National Army shells the Four Courts building, on the Liffey, where the leadership of the anti-treaty forces (now called the Irish Republican Army by themselves and the Irregulars by the Free State) have been holed up. Civil War begins.

July 28, 1922 — Fall of Limerick and Waterford to Free State armies.

August 12, 1922 — Arthur Griffith, nominal chief of state, dies and is replaced by Collins, who is now both head of the Free State and commander of the army. Emmet Dalton captures Cork in a single day's battle.

August 22, 1922 — Collins, perhaps on a peace mission to Cork, is killed at Bealnablath, near his home in Cork. Civil War rages for another year.

May 13, 1923 — "Cease fire" and end of Civil War.